RIDE WITH ME

MOTORCYCLE CLUB
COLLECTION

Ashley Zakrzewski

ASHLEY ZAKRZEWSKI

Contents

Jaxon

Chapter 1	5
Chapter 2	11
Chapter 3	17
Chapter 4	21
Chapter 5	27
Chapter 6	33
Chapter 7	43
Chapter 8	49
Chapter 9	57
Chapter 10	63
Chapter 11	69
Chapter 12	75
Chapter 13	81
Chapter 14	85
Chapter 15	89
Chapter 16	97
Chapter 17	103
Chapter 18	109
Chapter 19	115
Chapter 20	119
Chapter 21	123
Chapter 22	127
Chapter 23	131
Chapter 24	137
Chapter 25	143
Chapter 26	147
Epilogue	151

Brooks

Chapter 1	161
Chapter 2	167
Chapter 3	173
Chapter 4	181
Chapter 5	185
Chapter 6	191
Chapter 7	199
Chapter 8	205
Chapter 9	213
Chapter 10	219
Chapter 11	225
Chapter 12	231

Twisted Redemption

Chapter 1	239
Chapter 2	251
Chapter 3	261
Chapter 4	269
Chapter 5	277
Chapter 6	285
Chapter 7	291
Chapter 8	297
Chapter 9	305
Chapter 10	309
Chapter 11	315
Chapter 12	321
Chapter 13	329
Chapter 14	337
Chapter 15	345
Chapter 16	351
Chapter 17	361
Chapter 18	365
Chapter 19	371

Chapter 20   375
Chapter 21   381
Chapter 22   387
Chapter 23   395
Chapter 24   405
Chapter 25   409
Chapter 26   415
Chapter 27   421
Chapter 28   427

About the Author   431

Jaxon

JAXON

USA TODAY BESTSELLING AUTHOR
ASHLEY ZAKRZEWSKI

1

The shrill ring of her alarm shattered Rachel's restless sleep. She groaned, slapping a hand on the nightstand until she found the alarm clock and silenced it.

Another day, another dollar. The familiar mantra ran through her head as she dragged herself out of bed and into the shower.

Rachel let the hot water cascade over her body, wishing for a moment she could melt into the tiles. Eight years had passed since the car crash that took her mother's life, but the scars remained. Not on her body—those had long since faded. But in her mind, the memories were carved into her psyche as permanently as letters chiseled into stone.

She shook off the thoughts and finished washing up. As a nurse, she took her responsibilities seriously. Lives depended on her ability to compartmentalize.

But in the lonely hours of the night, the walls came tumbling down. She longed for connection, for intimacy—but that required trust. And trust led to pain.

Rachel sighed, fastening her watch and grabbing her bag.

Time to put on her mask again. If she focused on her routine, on the predictability of each day, maybe the ache inside would fade.

Maybe, but she doubted it. Some wounds ran too deep to heal. Her relationship with her father was proof of that. The survivor's guilt had torn them apart, and the chasm between them now seemed unbridgeable.

So she clung to order and control whenever she could, her defense against the chaos of the world. It was the only way she knew to keep the demons at bay. Rachel steeled her shoulders and walked out the front door of her apartment into the morning sun.

Another day. She'd get through it like all the rest. But she couldn't escape the truth: she was lonely, and it was a loneliness born of tragedy she couldn't seem to move past.

The sterile scent of antiseptic wafted through the air as Rachel Lewis walked into Baytown Medical Center for her shift. She breathed in the familiar, comforting smell and her muscles relaxed. Here, in the controlled chaos of the emergency room, she knew what to expect. There were procedures for almost every situation, a routine that gave her life order and purpose.

Rachel smiled at the charge nurse and grabbed a chart to review the incoming patients. "We've got a suspected heart attack in bed 3 and a bad MVA in bed 7," the nurse said.

Rachel nodded, her hands already snapping on a pair of gloves. She strode into bed 3, her eyes quickly taking in the details. A middle-aged man clutching his chest, pale skin, rapid pulse.

"I'm Nurse Lewis," she said in a calm, reassuring tone. "What's your name, sir?"

She listened to his heart, noting the irregular rhythm,

and barked out orders to the interns scurrying around the room.

A crash cart was wheeled in, EKG leads were attached, IVs were started. Rachel's hands moved swiftly and confidently, following the familiar motions she had done a thousand times before.

Another life saved.

As the man was wheeled off to surgery, Rachel let out a breath and wiped the sweat off her brow.

Why did she feel so unfulfilled? She loved being a nurse, loved helping people, but lately, an emptiness started growing inside her. A longing for something more.

"Rachel, the MVA victim in Bed 7 needs you," the charge nurse said, jolting her out of her thoughts.

Rachel shook off her doubts and misgivings, squaring her shoulders to face the controlled chaos of the emergency room once more. This was her life, these walls, this routine. She had chosen safety and security over the unknown, and she couldn't complain.

Or could she?

Rachel trudged up the stairs to her second-floor apartment, exhaustion seeping into her bones. She fumbled with the keys before unlocking the door and stepping inside the familiar space.

Everything was in its proper place, meticulously cleaned and organized. The living room held a plush couch, a TV, and a bookshelf filled with medical journals and mystery novels. The kitchen gleamed, empty counters bare of clutter or knickknacks.

She microwaved a frozen dinner and curled up on the couch, flipping through the TV channels until she found an old episode of Law & Order to watch.

As the familiar theme song played, Rachel's mind drifted to that day so many years ago. The gun pointed at her head, rough hands grabbing at her arms, the raspy voice of the robber demanding money. She had given him everything in the cash register, hands shaking in terror.

Afterward, she had vowed to never be vulnerable and out of control like that again. To surround herself with safety and predictability. But was it enough?

She looked around the spotless room, a pristine cage of her own making, and felt the first stirrings of discontent. When had this life of rigid routine become a prison?

Rachel turned up the TV volume, trying to drown out the unwelcome thoughts swirling in her head. But they persisted, whispering of adventure and risk, of life on the edge.

A life she had sworn off long ago, yet now found herself craving.

She didn't know which was more frightening—facing her trauma, or confronting the realization that she wanted more.

The next day at work, Rachel scrubbed into a surgery with Tess, her closest friend and colleague. As they prepped the patient, Tess said, "So, any fun plans this weekend? Or just the usual?"

Rachel felt her cheeks heat. Tess knew her routine all too well. "Just relaxing at home. Catching up on reading."

"Come on, live a little! We're only young once. When's the last time you went on a date or took a vacation?" Tess asked.

"I don't need that kind of excitement," Rachel said, adjusting her mask. "My life is predictable and safe. Just the way I like it."

Tess gave her a knowing look. "Is it really? Or are you

just afraid to step out of your comfort zone because of what happened when you were a kid?"

Rachel froze. How did Tess know about that? She never told anyone at work about the robbery.

"I'm your friend, Rachel. I can tell you're not really happy. You deserve to live life to the fullest, not hide away in your little bubble. What happened to you was awful, but you can't let fear rule you forever."

Tess's words struck a chord deep within Rachel. She wanted to deny them, cling to the familiarity of her restricted life. But the longing for something more was growing, refusing to be silenced.

Maybe Tess was right. It was time to start facing her fears instead of running from them. To step outside the comfort zone that had become its own kind of trap.

That evening, Rachel meticulously cleaned her apartment, as was her nightly routine, even though it didn't need it. She scrubbed every surface, arranged her few knickknacks at precise angles, then sat on her couch and watched a documentary about World War II for the third time.

Her gaze drifted to the window. What was it like to go outside at dusk, feel the warmth of the setting sun on your face? When was the last time she'd done something spontaneous, just for the joy of it?

A restless discontent stirred within Rachel as she thought of her colleagues' lives outside of work. Tess was always jetting off on some new adventure, while Jolene loved riding through the countryside on the back of her husband's motorcycle. Even shy, Maya had found love and started a family.

Meanwhile, Rachel clung to the safety of familiar routines. Her life was small and colorless, passing day after day in a blur of sameness. She longed to break free, but fear held her back with chains of doubt and what-if's. What if stepping out of her comfort zone led her straight back into danger? She shouldn't risk it.

With a sigh, Rachel turned up the volume on the TV and tried to lose herself in the black and white footage. But tonight, even the familiar voices of the narrator couldn't quiet the questions swirling in her mind.

Was this really living? Or just existing, trapped by the ghosts of her past?

She looked around at the room that had become more prison than haven. The walls seemed to close in around her, suffocating in their bleak emptiness.

Tonight, Rachel realized with sudden clarity, she was tired of playing it safe. She wanted to start living again, really living—before it was too late.

2

Rachel struggled to focus as her revelation running on repeat through her mind. During her break, she retreated to the empty staff lounge for a moment of peace. But as soon as she sat down, panic welled up inside her and threatened to drag her under. Her chest tightened, breaths came fast and shallow.

Rachel gripped the edge of the table, willing the attack to pass. But she couldn't stop the flood of worries crashing over her. What if she couldn't handle the changes she longed for? What if she failed and ended up right back where she started —or worse?

She was still trapped in the spiral of doubt when a gentle hand rested on her shoulder. Rachel flinched, glancing up with wide eyes to find Tess gazing at her.

"Easy, it's just me." Tess slid into the seat beside her, keeping her voice low and calm. "Breathe with me, okay?"

Rachel nodded, following Tess's exaggerated inhales and exhales until the vice around her chest loosened its grip. "I'm sorry," she said, swiping at her eyes with the back of her hand. "I don't know what came over me."

"Don't apologize." Tess gave her shoulder a squeeze. "It seems you've reached your breaking point. The question is, what are you going to do now?"

Rachel took a shaky breath, steeling herself against the fears that lingered at the edges of her mind. "I'm going to start living again."

Tess smiled, eyes crinkling at the corners. "That's my girl. It won't be easy, but I know you can do this."

Rachel managed a wry grin. "You have more faith in me than I do."

"Someone has to while you're busy doubting yourself." Tess bumped her shoulder playfully. "Seriously though, you're stronger than you realize. You survived a trauma most people can't even imagine. You can survive this too—no, you can thrive."

A warmth blossomed in Rachel's chest, chasing away the last dregs of panic. How had she gotten so lucky to have a friend like Tess?

She took a deep breath and stood, shoulders back and head high. "You're right. It's time I started living the life I want instead of hiding from the world."

Tess jumped up and threw her arms around Rachel. "That's the spirit!

She was ready to start taking risks again. Ready to live.

Rachel drove to the grocery store after her shift, lost in her thoughts. The road was busy, filled with people going about their day. She envied them their normalcy, their ability to live life unfettered by the shadows of the past.

A loud horn blared, and she slammed on the brakes, tires

squealing as a pickup truck rammed into her from behind. Her head snapped and everything went dark.

When she opened her eyes, she was slumped over the steering wheel, her car accordioned by the force of the impact. Panic rose in her chest as she struggled with the door, but it was jammed shut.

She pounded on the window, screaming for help as she flashed back to the night her mother died. The twisted metal, the rushing paramedics, her mother's lifeless body—

Rachel squeezed her eyes shut, hyperventilating. No one was coming. She was going to die here, alone and afraid, just like her mother had.

The familiar mantra cycled through her mind: order and control. But it was impossible to control this. No routine or predictable outcome could save her now.

As darkness crowded the edges of her vision, a single thought surfaced: If she died here, would anyone miss her? Would anyone remember the woman she might have become if tragedy hadn't stolen her joy?

A sob caught in her throat. She didn't want to die this way. Not when she'd never really lived. There was still so much of the world she hadn't seen, so much life she hadn't experienced. She wasn't ready for it to end—not like this.

A loud rumble shattered the eerie silence. Rachel's heart nearly leapt out of her chest as a motorcycle emerged from the inky blackness, rolling to a stop beside her crumpled sedan.

She squinted at the rider through the fractured wind-shield, panic and confusion warring within her. He was dressed all in black leather, a cut proclaiming his allegiance to the Green Devils MC. Tattoos snaked up his thick, muscular arms in a tangled web.

As he dismounted the bike and strode toward her, Rachel's breath caught in her throat. He was enormous, nearly a foot taller than her own five and a half feet, with a rugged, bearded face and icy blue eyes that seemed to glow in the darkness.

He tapped on her window with a gloved hand, his gaze raking over her small form huddled in the driver's seat. "You alright in there, sweetheart?" His voice was a low rumble, sending a shiver down Rachel's spine.

She hesitated, torn between desperation and wariness. What was a member of the Green Devils doing here, and could she trust him? But she was trapped, and this might be her only way out of this nightmare.

A ragged breath escaped her lips as the stranger had concern etched on his rugged features. Maybe—just maybe—her life wasn't over yet.

Rachel blinked at the man, stunned into silence.

"Can you move?" he asked. "We need to get you out of there."

She shook her head, panic threatening to overtake her again. "The door won't open."

Rachel swallowed hard, realizing with dawning horror that she had landed herself in a situation with no easy way out. But she was stuck, and this stranger seemed to be her only hope of escaping this alley alive. She had no choice but to put her faith in the hands of the Green Devil's MC.

"It's okay. I'm going to help you out through the window." He reached in and grasped her waist, lifting her up and out as if she weighed nothing at all. "Easy now."

Her heart raced at the intimacy of his touch and the sheer strength in his arms. No one had held her like that in years. She felt small and safe, cocooned in the warmth of his embrace as he set her down on the pavement.

"Are you hurt?" His gaze searched her face.

"Just shaken up." She wrapped her arms around herself, suddenly cold without his touch. She didn't even know this man, yet being near him filled her with a peace she'd rarely experienced. It was both thrilling and terrifying.

Who was he? All she knew was that he'd saved her life today—and that she wanted to know more. To see that look of care in his eyes again.

"The paramedics are on their way," he said. "But it looks like you'll live to see another day." A half-smile tugged at his lips, and her heart skipped a beat. "I'm Jaxon, by the way."

"Rachel." She took a deep, steadying breath and met his gaze. "Thank you for saving me."

She didn't know this man or his motivations, and her work as a nurse had exposed her to the depths of human depravity. Rachel bit her lip, leaning into him as he guided her toward a massive black motorcycle.

3

The wail of sirens in the distance caused Rachel to start pacing. He had found something he never thought he'd have again: hope.

And he'd be damned if he let her slip through his fingers.

"You're safe now," he whispered, giving her hand a gentle squeeze. "I won't leave you, sweetheart. I promise."

Her lips curved into the faintest of smiles. "You saved my life."

The words were barely audible, but they echoed in his heart like a vow. She was his to cherish and protect, always. Fate had brought them together for a reason, and he wasn't about to question destiny.

The chaos of the crash scene started to fade as emergency responders arrived. Flashing red and blue lights illuminated the dark road. Jaxon held Rachel's hand tightly as paramedics checked her for injuries.

"Can you tell me your name, miss?" one paramedic asked.

"Rachel," she replied. "Rachel Lewis."

"Okay, Rachel. Do you know what day it is?"

She blinked, gaze drifting to Jaxon for reassurance. He gave her hand a comforting squeeze. "It's Friday," she said.

The paramedic nodded, shining a light in her eyes. "Pupils look normal. Can you move your arms and legs, okay?"

Rachel winced as she slowly flexed her fingers and toes. "Nothing seems broken. Just some bruises and cuts."

Jaxon's chest tightened at the sight of her in pain. If he ever found the bastard who ran her off the road, he'd rip the bastard apart limb from limb.

"We'll get you to the hospital to be safe," the paramedic said. "Do you have any allergies or medical conditions we should know about?"

Rachel shook her head. Her eyes met Jaxon's again, a silent question in their depths. He knew what she was asking, and there was only one answer.

"I'll meet you," he said.

She blinked in surprise, a blush creeping into her pale cheeks. "Oh, but you don't have to—"

"I'm not leaving you alone." His tone brooked no argument. Rachel's safety and well-being were his top priority now, and he'd be damned if he handed her over to strangers.

She stared at him for a long moment before relenting with a sigh. "Okay."

Satisfaction hummed in his veins. He'd already claimed her, whether she realized it or not. And he wasn't letting go.

The ambulance doors slammed shut, sirens blaring as it sped off into the night.

Jaxon strode over to his motorcycle, helmet in hand, his mind racing.

A glimpse of movement caught his eye. Rachel's nurse ID badge lay discarded on the ground, the lanyard tangled in the wreckage of her car. He picked it up, the plastic card warm in his palm.

His bike rumbled to life beneath him as he secured the ID in his pocket like a promise. She would need that for work, and he aimed to return it to her in person.

The hospital lobby was chaos when he walked in, smelling of antiseptic and anxiety. A nurse at the front desk looked up as he approached. "Can I help you?"

"I'm looking for Rachel Lewis. She was just brought in by ambulance."

The nurse's fingers flew over a keyboard. "I'm sorry, but I can't give out information about patients."

Jaxon leaned over the counter, lowering his voice. "I was with her at the scene of the accident. I'm not leaving until I see her."

Her eyes widened, but she stood firm. "Only family members are allowed in to visit."

Family. The word reverberated through him as he gazed unseeing at the wall.

Jaxon looked back at the nurse, a wolfish grin slowly curving his mouth. "Then you can tell her that her husband is here."

4

Rachel came around the bend and locked eyes with Jaxon, surprised he actually came to check on her. She wasn't used to having people around her that cared.

"What are you doing here?" she asked.

"I told you I was coming. Found this on the ground. Important for work, I believe."

She took the ID badge from him and put it in her pocket. "Thanks."

"What do you say we stop and get you something to eat and then take you home?"

Rachel hesitated because she didn't know much about this man, but without a car, her only other option was a taxi. "Sure."

She followed him outside to his motorcycle.

A flicker of relief crossed Jaxon's face as he helped her onto the bike. "You're in good hands now," he said, and as the engine roared to life, Rachel found herself hoping with all her heart that he was telling the truth.

The powerful rumble of Jaxon's motorcycle vibrated

through Rachel's entire body as they sped down the dark, twisting road. Her heart pounded in time with the beat of the motor, a chaotic staccato rhythm fueled by equal parts pain, fear and adrenaline.

She didn't know this man or where he was taking her. For all she knew, she was being kidnapped. But her knee throbbed mercilessly with every bump in the road, a stark reminder that she was in no condition to escape. She had no choice but to put her faith in a stranger.

Rachel gritted her teeth against the agony, clinging to Jaxon as he whipped around a corner. The motion sent a spike of pain shooting up her leg and she couldn't stifle a gasp.

"You okay back there?" Jaxon's voice was gruff.

"Hurts," she managed through clenched teeth.

The motorcycle slowed. "Hang in there. We're almost at the diner."

They rolled to a stop outside a weathered building with neon signs flickering in the windows. A handful of motorcycles were parked outside, and through the glass Rachel could make out a few men in leather cuts drinking coffee at a counter.

Her heart stuttered. *A biker diner.* She was in a sea of strangers, vulnerable and injured, surrounded by the roar of engines and aura of danger.

Rachel swallowed hard, steeling herself as Jaxon killed the engine and turned to face her. "Still with me?"

She managed a jerky nod, breath coming fast. Jaxon seemed to understand her fear, giving her arm a gentle squeeze.

"You're safe here, darlin'," he said. "I won't let anything happen to you."

His steady blue eyes anchored her, a lifeline in the chaos, and Rachel slowly felt her panic recede. She didn't know why she believed him, but she did.

Nodding shakily, she let Jaxon help her off the bike and into the warmth of the diner, where a woman with kind eyes and a no-nonsense demeanor bustled over to fuss over Rachel's injury.

Jaxon guided Rachel to a booth, settling her in with a menu and strict orders to choose whatever she wanted. It was clear he was a regular here, on friendly terms with the staff. Rachel looked around at the worn wood and chrome decor, bikers lounging at the counter and in booths. It felt like a world apart from her own.

When their food was ready, Jaxon took the bags, helping Rachel back onto his bike for the ride to her place. The rumble of the engine and the solid warmth of his back against hers was oddly soothing.

Jaxon turned his head to murmur over his shoulder. "Doing okay back there?"

The timbre of his voice reverberated through her, as dangerously potent as the rumble of the motorcycle between her legs. Rachel swallowed hard, glad for the concealing visor of her helmet.

"I'm fine," she said, hoping he couldn't hear the breathlessness in her tone.

"Good." His hand squeezed hers where it rested on his abdomen, then returned to the handlebar. "Not much farther to go."

Too soon, the familiar apartment complex came into view. Rachel was disappointed, not yet ready for this ride to end.

Jaxon brought the motorcycle to a stop in front, the

engine sputtering and dying into silence. He swung off and turned to help her dismount, hands clasping her waist to lift her down.

Rachel found herself reluctant to meet his eyes, afraid of what he might read in her own. But his fingers remained curled around her arm, compelling her gaze upwards.

"Thank you," she said while grabbing her food, "for bringing me home."

Jaxon walked her to the door, hesitating on the threshold. "You gonna be alright now?"

Rachel nodded. "Thank you for everything. I don't know what I would've done without you."

A smile tugged at his lips. "My pleasure, darlin'." He ran a hand through his hair, suddenly looking uncharacteristically nervous. "I was wondering if you'd like to get dinner again. Without the car crash this time."

Her heart skipped a beat at the invitation. She should say no, knew he was dangerous in a way she couldn't quite define. But those blue eyes were hard to resist, and the memory of his strength and kindness stayed with her.

Rachel took a deep breath, throwing caution to the wind. "I'd like that."

Jaxon's smile lit up his face, making her pulse jump. He squeezed her hand, a spark of heat and promise in his gaze. "It's a date then. I'll pick you up tomorrow at 7."

With a wave he was gone, the engine rumbling into the night. Rachel leaned against the door, wondering what she'd gotten herself into—and why she was already looking forward to it.

It wasn't even two hours later, when she was curled up on the couch watching TV, when her phone buzzed with a text.

Unknown number: Hey, it's Jaxon. Just wanted to check in and see how you're doing.

Rachel's heart skipped, and she quickly added his number to her contacts before replying.

Rachel: I'm doing okay. Thanks to you. It was very kind of you to check on me.

Jaxon: My pleasure. I meant what I said earlier—if there's anything you need, just let me know.

Rachel smiled, warmth flooding her veins. He seemed genuine in his concern for her well-being, and she found herself regretting her initial distrust of him. Maybe he wasn't like the men from her past, after all.

Rachel: I appreciate that.

Jaxon: I should let you rest. Sweet dreams.

Rachel: Goodnight, Jaxon. Thank you again.

She set down her phone, a giddy feeling bubbling up inside. Her orderly world had been upended by this leather-clad stranger, and for once, she didn't mind the disruption. There was something about Jaxon that made her want to throw caution to the wind and see where this unexpected connection might lead.

Rachel went to bed that night with a smile on her face, already anticipating his next message.

The next morning, Rachel woke to a text from Jaxon.

Jaxon: Morning sunshine ☀ *Hope you're feeling better today.*

Rachel: Good morning! I'm doing great, thanks to you. How are you?

Jaxon: Can't complain. Had an early meeting at the clubhouse. Ready for our date tonight?

Rachel: Just working a shift at the hospital. Nothing too exciting. And yes, I am =)

Jaxon: A woman who saves lives for a living... very sexy.

Rachel: I work in the emergency room so never know if I will be saving a life or dealing with an overdose.

Jaxon: Bet you've seen it all in an ER.

Rachel: Unfortunately, yes, but it's rewarding to help people during what is often the worst day of their lives.

Jaxon: I can understand that. We may run in very different circles, but helping others in need is something we have in common.

Rachel: I have to admit, you've surprised me. I made some unfair assumptions about you based on your appearance and affiliations. I see now that there's more to you.

Jaxon: Likewise. You're not what I expected either, and in the best possible way. I'm glad we were able to move past first impressions.

Rachel: As am I.

Jaxon: See you at 7.

5

The rumble of Jaxon's motorcycle echoed down her street. She peered through the curtains, watching as he swung off the bike in a graceful arc of denim and leather. Her hands trembled as she checked her appearance in the mirror one last time. The little black dress was a mistake. It revealed too much, drew too much attention. She was exposed, vulnerable.

With a surge of panic, Rachel grabbed her phone and typed a quick message to Jaxon.

Rachel: *Sorry, not feeling well. Rain check?*

Before she could hit send, a sharp knock rattled the front door. "Rachel? You ready?" Jaxon's voice was muffled.

Rachel froze, her thumb hovering over the send button. She took a deep, steadying breath and caught her reflection in the mirror. When had she become so afraid to take a chance? So desperate for safety that she would hide from life behind these four walls?

The phone trembled in her grip before she set her jaw. It was time to face her fears. Rachel deleted the message, changed into a pair of jeans and a black top, and strode to the front door.

With a bright smile, she swung open the door. Jaxon looked devastatingly handsome in worn jeans and a leather cutover, all rugged masculinity and barely restrained power.

Rachel moistened her lips, acutely aware of the hunger in his gaze. "Shall we?"

Jaxon's answering grin was slow and predatory. "We shall." He offered his arm, and Rachel took it, allowing him to escort her into the night. Into the unknown. Rachel gripped her hands around Jaxon's waist, the roar of the engine vibrating through her body as the bike surged forward.

A thrill rushed through her veins. The wind whipped her hair. In that moment, nothing else mattered but the road stretching endlessly before her and the sweet song of freedom in her blood.

She had spent too long living a half-life, bound by rules and expectations. No more. Her brush with death shocked her awake, reminding her how fragile and fleeting life truly was.

Rachel tilted her head back and let out a shout of exuberance, the notes lost to the wind. When she glanced at Jaxon, a grin split his ruggedly handsome face. He revved his engine in response, the deep throb of his bike echoing her own.

"Time to really live, isn't it?" she called out to him, her heart swelling with possibility.

Jaxon's gaze burned into hers, a silent promise in those fathomless eyes. "Every damn day, babe. That's my motto now—live like there's no tomorrow!"

A delicious shiver ran down Rachel's spine at his words.

She had spent so long in the shadows, but now she was ready to step into the light—and into something far more dangerous with the man riding beside her. Adventure, passion, consequence be damned.

Today, she would start living.

They rode for over an hour, winding through back roads blanketed in gold under the setting sun. By the time Jaxon slowed and turned onto a narrow dirt path, Rachel's muscles ached pleasantly from the exertion.

At the end of the path stood a weathered diner with a sprawling terrace overlooking the valley below. "Best burgers in the county," Jaxon said with a grin. "Thought you might be hungry after that ride."

Rachel's stomach rumbled in response and she laughed. "Starving, actually."

The terrace was deserted, the other patrons having already headed indoors as dusk approached. They chose a table at the edge, with sweeping views of the dusky landscape.

After ordering their food, a comfortable silence fell over them, broken only by the chirping of crickets and the rustle of leaves in the breeze. It felt so easy being here with Jaxon, as if they had known each other for years rather than days.

"Do you come here often?" Rachel asked, curiosity getting the better of her. She wanted to know everything about this man who had burst into her life and shaken up her world.

"Used to," Jaxon said. "Haven't been back in a while. Kind of reminder of better days." A shadow crossed his face before he shook it off. "How about you? Got any favorite places from your childhood or something?"

Rachel hesitated, old grief and shame rising in her chest.

She looked away, tracing a groove in the wooden table with her fingernail. Did she dare share the truth of her past with Jaxon, as broken and messy as it was? She sensed that he had known great pain as well beneath the devil-may-care attitude.

"Not really. My mother died and my father...well he isn't the best."

She risked a glance at Jaxon, expecting pity or judgment, but found only understanding in his gaze. His hand covered hers, rough and warm, squeezing gently. "I'm sorry," he said. "That must have been hard."

Rachel swallowed against the lump in her throat, over-whelmed by the simple kindness. When was the last time anyone had offered her compassion without wanting some-thing in return?

"Yeah," she whispered. "But I survived. Made me who I am today, for better or worse."

"Who you are is amazing," Jaxon said, his voice low and intense. His thumb stroked the inside of her wrist, sending shivers up her arm. "A strong woman, from what I've seen. Despite everything you've endured, you still have so much heart. That's rare in this world."

His praise made her cheeks flush with warmth. No one had ever seen her the way Jaxon did, recognizing her intrinsic worth behind the scars. She found herself leaning closer to him, drawn like a moth to a flame. His cologne smelled of leather and spice.

"Jaxon," she breathed, nerves and desire warring within her. His gaze dropped to her mouth, eyes darkening with unspoken longing. Her heart stuttered at the realization that he wanted this as much as she did.

"Tell me to stop," he rasped, "and I will. But if you want this as much as I do...?"

"I don't want you to stop."

The words were barely out of her mouth when Jaxon closed the distance between them in a kiss that seared her to the bone.

The kiss deepened, a tangle of lips and tongues that stole Rachel's breath. Jaxon's hand slid into her hair, tilting her head to take the kiss deeper. She clung to his shoulders, drowning in the sensations flooding her body.

Every nerve ending was alive and tingling. Her skin felt too tight, heart pounding so hard she thought it might burst from her chest. But beneath the frenzied passion was a bone-deep tenderness in the way Jaxon held her. Like she was something precious, worthy of care.

When the kiss ended, Rachel blinked up at him in a daze. His chest rose and fell in ragged breaths, pupils blown wide with desire. But there was a question in his eyes, silently asking if this was okay. If he'd gone too far.

She smiled and stroked his jaw, rough with stubble. "You can kiss me like that anytime."

Relief and heat flashed across his face. "I'll hold you to that." His gaze dropped to her mouth again. "Because I really want to do it again."

"So what's stopping you?" she teased.

Jaxon's eyes gleamed with challenge and mischief. "Not a damn thing."

He claimed her mouth again in a kiss that melted her bones. Her fingers curled into his shirt, clinging for dear life as she was swept away in a riptide of passion with no desire to break free.

Rachel lost track of time as they kissed, the world

narrowing to just her and Jaxon. His hands roamed over her back in a slow caress, leaving trails of fire in their wake.

When he finally lifted his head, they were both breathless. "We should head back." His voice was rough with restraint. "Before I do something, we'll both regret."

She knew he was right, but disappointment flooded her. She wasn't ready for this day to end. For the magic of this perfect moment to fade.

"When will I see you again?" The question tumbled out before she could stop it. Needy, clinging in a way that went against her usually guarded nature.

Jaxon cupped her face in his hands, thumbs tracing her cheekbones. "Soon, angel. Count on it."

6

The next day at work, Rachel found herself distracted and jittery. Her date with Jaxon had been thrilling and intense, igniting a passion she'd never known. But in the harsh light of day, doubt crept in. What was she getting herself into?

During their lunch break, Rachel pulled Tess aside. "I have something to confess. I went on a date last night."

Tess's eyes lit up. "With who? Tell me everything!"

Rachel bit her lip. "It's Jaxon Jones. President of the Green Devils MC."

All traces of excitement fled from Tess's face, replaced by concern. "Rachel, those guys are dangerous. What are you thinking?"

"I know, I know." Rachel twisted her hands together. "But there's something about him. A woundedness I recognize." She thought of the shadows she'd glimpsed beneath Jaxon's bravado. "And the way I feel with him—alive, and free."

Tess grasped her shoulders. "You're playing with fire. I don't want to see you get hurt."

Rachel held her friend's gaze. "What if it's worth the risk? Don't I deserve a chance at happiness after everything I've been through?"

Tess searched her face for a long moment. Finally, she sighed. "You're right. You do deserve to find love in whatever form it takes." A wry smile curved her mouth. "Just promise me you'll be careful. And call me if you need anything."

Relief flooded Rachel. "I will. Thank you, Tess. For always understanding."

Tess pulled her into a fierce hug. "That's what friends are for. Now go get your man—and try not to get into too much trouble!"

Rachel laughed, the sound light and free. She had Tess's blessing, and her own fears were fading into the background. Tonight, she had another date with Jaxon, and this time she would dive in headfirst. Danger be damned. Her heart knew this was a risk worth taking.

Rachel stood before her mirror, scrutinizing her reflection. She'd chosen a flirty red dress that showed a hint of cleavage, paired with strappy heels. Her makeup was subtle but smoky, her lips stained cherry red. She hardly recognized herself. When had she become this woman, daring enough to court danger for the promise of passion?

Her thoughts drifted to Jaxon, conjuring the intensity of his gaze, the roughness of his hands. A delicious shiver ran down her spine. But along with the attraction came the familiar ache of anxiety in her stomach, a warning she couldn't ignore.

Rachel sank onto her bed, suddenly breathless. What was she doing? This man lived a life of violence and lawlessness. If she let him in, she'd be stepping into a world where nothing was safe or certain. Where she could be hurt in ways, she didn't dare imagine.

The old fears rose up to choke her, shadows of the past threatening to eclipse this newfound daring. Her fingers curled into the bedspread as she fought for control, torn between yearning and terror.

She had a choice to make, and no easy answers. Did she dare expose her fragile heart to a man who might break it? Or should she cut her losses now and cling to the security she knew?

Rachel closed her eyes, searching for the truth amid the chaos.

No, she wasn't going to back out of this. Jaxon and her had a connection, deeper than just attraction. Their souls were both wounded.

So, she got dressed and headed to meet him.

Jaxon pulled up on his custom chopper, black from handlebars to tailpipes. His piercing blue eyes gazed at her from beneath the black leather cut he wore, the words "President" and "Green Devils MC" stitched across the back in lurid green thread.

Rachel swallowed hard, clutching her purse. She had lived a sheltered life as a nurse, craving order and routine. Now she was plunging into a world of danger and unpredictability. But one look at Jaxon's ruggedly handsome face filled her with a thrill she had never known.

Jaxon killed the engine and swung off his bike, striding toward her with a predatory grace. "You came." His voice was a low rumble, like the bass growl of a big cat.

"I said I would." Rachel tilted her chin up, trying to seem braver than she felt.

Jaxon stopped in front of her, close enough for her to feel

the heat radiating off his massive frame. "A lot of people make promises they can't keep." His eyes darkened with old pain and bitterness.

Rachel sensed the shadows lurking in his past. She wanted to soothe away the hurt, to show him she was different. Reaching out, she laid a hand on his leather cut, feeling his heart pounding beneath.

"I don't make promises I can't keep," she said.

Jaxon's eyes widened. He grasped her hand, turning it over and pressing a kiss to her palm that sent shivers down her spine.

"Maybe you're not like the others after all," he said, a note of wonder in his voice.

Rachel smiled, her own cynicism fading in the warmth of his touch. "Why don't you show me your world...and I'll show you mine?"

Jaxon's lips curved into a smile that lit up his face, erasing the darkness that had lingered there. "It's a deal, angel. Hop on." He jerked his head toward the chopper.

Heart racing, Rachel climbed on behind Jaxon and wrapped her arms around his waist. Together, they roared off into the night, toward a future of thrilling possibilities.

The clubhouse came into view, a dilapidated warehouse with several motorcycles parked outside and the unmistakable roar of rock music blasting from within.

Rachel's heart skipped a beat. What was she getting into? She tightened her grip around Jaxon's waist, her palms slick with sweat.

Jaxon glanced over his shoulder. "You okay back there?"

She swallowed and forced a smile. "Just enjoying the ride."

Jaxon's laughter rumbled beneath her hands. "Atta girl.

You'll get used to this."

Used to this? Rachel didn't know if she wanted to get used to this world of lawlessness and danger. But she couldn't deny her fascination with Jaxon and the tantalizing glimpse into a life of reckless freedom she never knew existed.

The chopper rolled to a stop outside the clubhouse. Jaxon killed the engine and helped Rachel off, steadying her when her knees wobbled.

"Still with me?" His voice was gentle, his hand warm on her lower back.

She nodded. "Just a little shaky."

"Nothing to worry about, angel." His smile did little to reassure her. "The guys can look tough, but they won't hurt you. You're with me."

With that, he guided her toward the clubhouse. The heavy metal music grew louder, the bass thumping in time with her erratic pulse.

Rachel took a deep breath and walked through the doors into a haze of smoke and noise. A dozen bikers and scantily clad women populated the dimly lit room with its concrete floors and pool table.

All eyes turned to the entrance. A dozen pairs of assessing eyes settled on Rachel, more than a few unfriendly. Her steps faltered as a lump formed in her throat. What had she gotten herself into?

Jaxon's arm tightened around her waist, pulling her close against his side. "Relax, angel. I told you, you're with me."

His show of possessiveness did little to reassure the watching crowd, but no one challenged him. Rachel forced herself to keep walking as Jaxon guided her to the bar.

"Beer?" He raised his voice to be heard over the music.

She shook her head, clutching his leather cut. Jaxon ordered himself a beer and two shots of whiskey, passing one to her.

"Drink up, angel. It'll steady your nerves."

The liquid fire scorched her throat, but warmth blossomed in her belly, easing her anxiety. She managed a tremulous smile. "Thanks."

Jaxon leaned down, his lips brushing her ear. "See? Nothing to worry about." He nodded to a group of women shooting pool. "The old ladies can smell fear, but they won't give you trouble if you don't give them any."

Rachel surveyed the women, her gaze settling on a curvy blonde in a tight tank top, eyeing her with suspicion. She tipped her shot glass toward the woman in challenge and threw back her shot.

The blonde's eyes widened, but she gave Rachel an appraising look and a slow smile. Rachel straightened her shoulders, emboldened by the whiskey and Jaxon's solid presence at her side. Maybe she could get used to this after all.

"Atta girl," Jaxon said with a grin. "What do you say we get out of here? I've got a party to show you."

Rachel smiled up at him, pulse racing. "Let's go."

She was ready to see what else this biker world had in store. Tonight, she would dance with the devil and see if she survived the flames.

Jaxon's lips curled into a smirk, accentuating the scar that bisected his cheek. "You look beautiful." His voice was a low rumble, filled with unspoken promises.

Rachel flushed under his gaze, acutely aware of how little her sundress concealed. She cleared her throat and met his stare. "Shall we go?"

He chuckled, a sound that did dangerous things to her equilibrium. "Impatient, are we?"

Before she could respond, he grasped her hand and led her to his bike. "Climb on."

Her heart stuttered at the prospect of sliding onto the back of his motorcycle, of wrapping her arms around his solid torso. But she had made her choice, and there was no turning back now.

Rachel hitched up her dress and swung her leg over the seat, scooting forward until her chest pressed against Jaxon's back. His skin was hot, even through the barrier of their clothes, and she breathed in the scent of leather and spice.

"Hold on tight." He kicked the stand back, and the engine roared to life beneath her, vibrating in her bones.

She looped her arms around his waist, clinging to him as the bike surged forward. The wind whipped her hair, but she didn't look away from Jaxon. Not for a second.

The bike handled as smoothly as Jaxon himself, eating up the road in a blur of motion that set her blood racing. Rachel smiled against his back, laughing in delight.

She had taken a chance, and it was turning out to be the thrill ride of her life.

Rachel's curiosity deepened. What was it really like to live this life on the edge of society's rules? And what about Jaxon himself, with his air of danger and a hint of darkness in his past?

She glanced up at his profile, sharp jaw and full mouth, and heat pooled low in her belly. How had this happened, her sudden fascination with a man who was all rough edges and mystery?

Jaxon slanted her a knowing smile. "Thinking deep thoughts, angel?"

Rachel shrugged, a flush creeping into her cheeks. "Just wondering what I've gotten myself into."

"Don't worry," he said, tucking a strand of hair behind her ear. "I'll take good care of you."

The tenderness in his touch made her breath catch. Maybe she was in over her head, but she couldn't deny she wanted to dive in deeper.

Jaxon guided her inside.

Rachel approached the woman's shooting pool, pulse fluttering with nerves. The curvy blonde gave her an appraising look, but nodded in greeting.

Summoning her courage, Rachel said, "I'm Rachel. Jaxon invited me to the party tonight."

The blonde snorted. "We know who you are, sweetheart. You're with the prez, ain't you?"

Rachel ducked her head, a blush staining her cheeks. "That obvious, huh?"

A brunette with tattoos snaking up her arms laughed. "Jax has been waiting for a woman like you. You're not the usual crow-eatin' slut he drags around."

"We were taking bets on how long you'd last," the blonde said. "But maybe you're different."

Rachel leaned against the pool table, crossing her arms. "What's it like, being an old lady in the club?"

The women exchanged a look, a wealth of meaning in their silence.

"Ain't no life like it," the brunette finally said. "Wild and free, but it ain't ever easy. Life in the MC is raw and real— the good, the bad, and the ugly, all out in the open."

"But we stand by our men," the blonde added. "Through hell or high water. That's what an old lady does."

Rachel nodded, a surge of longing and fear twisting in

her gut. Did she have what it took to stand by Jaxon's side in this world? She had a feeling she was about to find out.

Jaxon emerged from the crowd, wrapping an arm around Rachel's waist. "Ready to head out?"

She glanced up at him, at the intensity in his eyes and the warmth of his touch. Her heart kicked into overdrive as she nodded.

They said their goodbyes and headed out into the cool night air. The rumble of bikes and raucous music faded behind them as they walked to Jaxon's Harley.

He handed her a helmet. "You still want to go to somewhere else tonight?"

Rachel stared at the helmet, hesitation flickering through her. She thought of the wild, raw world the women had described—and of Jaxon, a pillar of strength beside her.

She lifted her gaze to his. "If you're there with me...then yes."

A slow, sexy smile spread across Jaxon's face. He pulled her close and kissed her, a possessive, searing kiss that left her breathless.

"Count on it, baby," he rasped. "I'm not letting you out of my sight."

Rachel's heart kicked into a sprint, but for the first time, the fear was eclipsed by a thrill of excitement. She put on the helmet with trembling fingers, anticipation for the night ahead building inside her.

Whatever happened at this party, she had a feeling her old life was slipping further away with each passing second. A new world was opening up before her, dangerous yet seductive, and she was ready to ride into it with Jaxon at her side.

7

The neon glow of the Lila's Diner sign cast a pink haze over the parking lot as Rachel pulled up outside. She breathed in the aroma of fresh coffee and bacon grease as she walked through the entrance, the familiar scent evoking memories of Sunday brunches with her grandmother.

A jukebox in the corner played an old Elvis song, the melancholy tune at odds with the cozy atmosphere. Red vinyl booths lined the walls and a long counter ran along the back, where Lila stood chatting with a couple of truckers.

Rachel slid into a booth near the door, her gaze drawn to a table in the center of the room. Jaxon sat with one leg slung over the back of the opposite bench, deep in conversation with a massive man named Slick.

She studied Slick from beneath her lashes, taking in his shaved head and the snake tattoo coiling around his neck. His shoulders strained against a worn leather vest as he leaned forward, speaking in a low rumble she couldn't quite make out.

Jaxon threw back his head and laughed. Her heart

skipped at the unrestrained joy in his expression, a glimpse of the man beneath the aloof facade.

Rachel's hands curled into fists in her lap as she acknowledged the truth she'd been denying. She was falling for the man and there wasn't a damn thing she could do to stop it.

Slick slid into the seat across from her, resting his forearms on the table. "You've got him all wrong, you know."

Rachel stiffened. "I don't know what you mean."

"Jax. He's not the monster you think he is." Slick sighed. "He's been through hell and back, but he came out the other side a better man. The club, his brothers, we're what saved him. Gave him a purpose."

She furrowed her brow, curiosity warring with the urge to shut Slick down. As much as she wanted to cling to her preconceptions, she couldn't deny her growing fascination with the glimpses of vulnerability she'd seen in Jaxon.

Slick leaned forward, his voice dropping to a low rumble. "Jax was hooked on heroin for years. Nearly died from an overdose once, before I found him. But he got clean, went through rehab and came back fighting. Built the Green Devils from nothing, gave us all a family and a place to belong."

Rachel sucked in a sharp breath, stunned by the revelation. The Jaxon she knew was strong, formidable—she never could've imagined he'd struggled with addiction.

Slick gave her a knowing look. "There's more to him than you think. He's got a good heart, always looking out for people who ain't got nothin' else." He stood, towering over the table. "Just thought you should know."

Rachel stared down at her hands, a tumult of emotions swirling inside her. She couldn't reconcile the image of Jaxon as a ruthless outlaw biker with the man Slick described—a survivor, who'd fought his way back from the depths of addiction to build a family and a home for people who had nothing else.

Someone nudged her shoulder, jerking her from her thoughts. She looked up to find Jaxon sliding into the booth beside her, his thigh pressed against hers as he slung an arm along the back of the seat.

"Everything alright?" His gaze searched hers, a crease forming between his brows. She glimpsed the caring, protective side of him that Slick revealed. Her cheeks heated as she wondered what else there was to uncover beneath the surface.

She wanted to ask him about his past, to hear the story from his own lips, but she sensed these were wounds that had only just begun to heal. Instead, she mustered a smile and said, "Slick was just keeping me company. Telling stories about the club."

Jaxon's eyes narrowed, a muscle in his jaw twitching. For a moment she feared Slick betrayed his confidence, but then Jaxon huffed out a breath and the tension eased from his face.

"Yeah, he's always got plenty of those. Hope he didn't bore you too much."

"Not at all," she said,. "I enjoyed hearing about how the Green Devils came to be."

Understanding dawned in Jaxon's gaze. He gave her a slow, sexy smile that made her pulse skip. "So he told you about that, did he?"

"He might have mentioned something about how you built this family from nothing." She arched a brow, unable to resist teasing him. "How you gave everyone a place to belong."

"Is that so?" He chuckled. "Well, maybe I'll have to tell you the whole story myself one of these days."

His fingers curled around her chin, tilting her face up to his. The intensity in his eyes stole her breath as he said in a rough whisper, "If you're really interested, that is."

She swallowed hard, heat flooding her cheeks. "I think I'd like that."

The smile he gave her then was different from any she'd seen before—less guarded, almost shy in a way that made her heart squeeze. She found herself captivated by the glimpse of vulnerability, wanting nothing more than to see that smile again.

He leaned in slowly, giving her time to pull away if she wanted to. But she didn't want to. She wanted this, wanted him, with an ache that shocked her.

When his lips brushed hers, a spark ignited low in her belly, spreading warmth through her veins. She sighed into the kiss, parting her lips in invitation.

Jaxon made a sound deep in his throat and took it, sliding his tongue against hers in a dance as old as time. His hand cupped the back of her neck, holding her in place as he plundered her mouth in a kiss that left her dizzy and breathless.

She fisted her hands in the front of his cut, pulling him closer until she was half in his lap. The feel of his hard body against hers sent another wave of heat through her core, and she moaned.

This was dangerous. Reckless. She barely knew this man, and yet she couldn't get enough of his touch, his taste. It went against everything she believed in, but in that moment, she didn't care.

All that mattered was the feel of Jaxon's hands on her body, branding her with the memory of his touch. The broken, wanting sounds he made as the kiss deepened. The way her heart raced with a mix of fear and exhilaration, alive and awake in a way she'd never felt before.

She knew she should stop this before things went too far, but she didn't want to. She wanted to get lost in the moment and forget about the world outside these walls. To escape into something wild and forbidden, if only for a little while.

Rachel sank into Jaxon's embrace, abandoning her doubts as she gave herself over to the passion burning between them. Tonight, she would follow her heart instead of her head, and deal with the consequences later.

"So what's the deal with your club?" Rachel asked, curiosity getting the better of her. "I mean, it seems like more than just a bunch of guys who like to ride together."

Jaxon studied her for a long moment, as if deciding how much to reveal. "The Green Devils are my family," he said. "We've been through hell and back together. When the world turns its back on you, they're the ones who have your back."

His words resonated with her in a way she hadn't expected. She knew all too well what it was like to face life's challenges alone, without love or support. The thought of having that kind of closeness with others stirred an ache inside her she'd long forgotten.

"It's more than the bikes or the parties or any of that shit people see on TV," Jaxon continued. "We live hard and play hard, but we also stand by each other no matter what. There's a bond there that's hard to explain to outsiders."

Rachel nodded, a new understanding dawning. The Green Devils weren't just a gang of bikers raising hell. They were a family in the truest sense of the word, and Jaxon was the heart of it all.

And in that moment, she found herself wanting to understand it better. Wanting to understand Jaxon better, and the life he led. Her old fears and doubts still lingered, but curiosity and something deeper—an unnamable longing —were awakening inside her.

A longing for the kind of connection and belonging Jaxon had found with the Green Devils. And maybe, just maybe, she could find it there too. If she was brave enough to take the risk.

Rachel shifted, acutely aware of Jaxon's leg pressed against hers. The neon Budweiser sign in the window bathed them in a rosy glow, and she could smell the lingering aroma of his cologne mixed with the scent of well-worn leather from his cut.

It was intoxicating in a way she couldn't quite explain.

"You're staring," Jaxon said with a slow, dangerous smile.

Heat rose in her cheeks, but she didn't look away. "Just thinking."

"About what?" His fingers brushed a loose strand of hair behind her ear, sending a shiver down her spine.

"About how I might have been wrong about you. And the Green Devils."

His eyes darkened. "Yeah? How's that?"

She leaned in closer, emboldened by the look in his eyes and the warmth flooding her veins. "Maybe there's more to you than meets the eye. And maybe I want to find out just how deep that rabbit hole goes."

A low growl rumbled in his chest as his hand curled around the back of her neck, pulling her in. Her heart slammed against her ribs, drowning out the clamor of voices and classic rock in the background.

Nothing else mattered but the taste of Jaxon on her lips.

8

Rachel gripped the handle of her new little red hatchback. The Green Devils' compound loomed before her, with flickering neon signs and heavy metal music thumping from within.

Her heart raced as she walked up to the entrance. What was she doing here? She didn't belong in a place like this. But curiosity had gotten the better of her, and she had to see Jaxon again.

When she entered, the assault on her senses was immediate. The reek of alcohol, sweat, and cigarettes filled her nostrils. Strobe lights flashed across the crowded room, silhouetting dozens of leather-clad bikers. Their raucous laughter and shouts nearly drowned out the pounding music.

Rachel stood frozen in place, clutching her purse to her chest like a shield. Jaxon was in there somewhere, she was sure of it. She wanted to run, to escape back to the safety and order of her normal life. But she couldn't make herself turn away. Not yet.

She took a deep breath, steadying her nerves. *You're stronger than this.* She wasn't going to let a little apprehension scare her off. Rachel squared her shoulders and made her way into the fray, searching the crowd for a glimpse of Jaxon's tattooed arms and blue eyes.

She didn't know what she was getting herself into here, but after the perfect night with Jaxon, she had to find out. Rachel was tired of playing it safe. For once in her life, she was going to throw caution to the wind and see where the road might lead. Straight to hell, most likely, but if Jaxon was waiting for her there, she would gladly walk through the fire.

Rachel's heart thudded. What was she doing here? These were dangerous people. But a small, insistent voice in her mind whispered that she was tired of playing it safe.

She edged further into the party, watching and listening.

Two men stood nearby, smoking cigarettes and talking in low, gruff voices. "Did ya hear we're expanding our territory again?" the taller man said. "Gonna be more work for us, keeping those bastards out."

The other man grunted. "More work means more money. And if we don't do it, they'll move in on our customers."

Rachel's stomach twisted as she realized they were talking about protecting drug dealing and other illegal territory. She glanced around again, noticing the openly carried guns and knives for the first time.

Panic rose in her chest. What had she gotten herself into? She turned to leave—but a loud burst of laughter made her jump. A heavily tattooed man had appeared out of nowhere, grasping her arm. "Well hey there, darlin'. You look a little lost." His gaze raked over her in a way that made her skin crawl. "How 'bout I show you around?"

Rachel's heart pounded. She was in over her head—and now she was trapped.

Rachel forced a smile, trying to stay calm. "That's very kind of you, but I was just leaving."

He leaned closer, squeezing her arm. "The party's just getting started. Stay awhile." His breath smelled of alcohol and something sharper.

Rachel tried to pull away, but his grip tightened painfully. Panic rose in her chest like bile. She opened her mouth to scream —

"Hey." A deep, gravelly voice interrupted. "She said she's leaving."

Rachel turned to see Jaxon standing there, arms crossed over his massive chest. His gaze was hard as stone, but when he looked at her, his expression softened.

"She's not going anywhere," the tattooed man said. But he released her arm, eying Jaxon warily.

Jaxon stepped forward until he towered over the other man. "Yeah, she is."

The man glared, but backed away, disappearing into the crowd.

Jaxon turned to her, concern etched into his face. "You okay?"

Rachel let out a shaky breath, her heart still pounding. "Yeah. Thank you." She rubbed her arm where the man had grabbed her; she could already feel a bruise forming.

"Looks like this isn't your scene after all," Jaxon said. "C'mon, let's get out of here."

Rachel didn't need any convincing. She let Jaxon guide her away from the party, back into the quiet night.

Jaxon led her out of the garage and across the compound,

his strides purposeful. No one paid them any heed, too caught up in their revelry.

He brought her to a small cabin at the edge of the property, isolated from the rest. Rachel's heart raced as Jaxon opened the door. The interior was spartan but cozy, lit by a few lamps that cast a warm glow over the space.

Jaxon closed the door behind them with a soft click. He turned to Rachel, his eyes smoldering. She stood frozen in place, her breaths coming fast and shallow.

With slow, measured steps, Jaxon approached her. He stopped mere inches away, his body radiating heat. Rachel lifted her gaze to his, transfixed by the raw desire she saw reflected in his eyes.

"Tell me you want this," Jaxon said, his voice a low rumble. He brought one hand up to cup her cheek, his touch searing her skin. "Tell me, and I'm yours."

Rachel trembled, torn between longing and fear. But under the intensity of Jaxon's gaze, her resistance crumbled into dust.

"I want this," she whispered. "I want you."

A growl escaped Jaxon as he closed the distance between them, claiming her mouth in a searing kiss. Rachel melted against him with a soft moan, all thoughts fleeing her mind except for Jaxon.

Jaxon's hands roamed her body, stroking the curves of her hips and waist. He tugged at her, breaking the kiss long enough to pull it over her head before devouring her mouth once more.

Rachel fumbled with the buttons of his vest, desire clouding her senses. She pushed the leather off his shoulders, her fingertips exploring the solid muscle underneath. Jaxon made a low sound of approval, kicking off his boots and shrugging out of his jeans.

Then they were tumbling onto the bed, a tangle of bare limbs and racing hearts. Jaxon hovered above her, his eyes dark with lust. "Last chance to back out," he said, his voice rough.

Rachel gazed up at him, seeing the vulnerability beneath the passion. She lifted her hand to his cheek, her touch gentle. "I'm here because I want to be. I choose you."

Something flickered in Jaxon's eyes. He turned his head to press a kiss to her palm. "And I choose you," he said.

Then he was kissing her again, deep and slow and thorough. Rachel wrapped her arms around him, pulling him closer as a bone-deep ache built within her.

Tonight, she would find solace in Jaxon's embrace. Tomorrow could wait.

A loud bang suddenly echoed through the night, followed by shouts in the distance.

Jaxon tensed, pulling back from the kiss. His eyes narrowed as he peered into the shadows.

"What was that?" Rachel asked, breathless. Her heart pounded for an entirely different reason now.

"Trouble." Jaxon grabbed her hand, pulling her along as he strode toward the source of the commotion. "Come on."

Rachel hurried after him, nerves twisting in her stomach.

As they rounded the corner, Rachel caught sight of several bikers confronting a man she didn't recognize. He was outnumbered, but held a gun in a white-knuckled grip, shouting threats.

Jaxon stepped forward, hands raised. "Easy now," he said, voice hard with authority. "No need for this to get ugly."

The man whipped toward him, gun swinging in Jaxon's direction. "Stay back!" he shouted. His eyes were wild, pupils dilated. Rachel's heart leaped into her throat, cold fear gripping her. This was not going to end well.

Jaxon froze, gaze locked on the gunman. His hand tightened around Rachel's, a subtle warning.

The man's finger twitched on the trigger. Rachel sucked in a sharp breath, bracing herself for the crack of gunfire.

But a second later, the gunman crumpled to the ground. A trickle of blood ran from his temple - he'd been knocked unconscious and the property was in a blaze.

Rachel stared at the scene in shock, heart pounding. Before she could ask what had happened, Jaxon pulled her into his arms.

"It's alright," he murmured, one hand cradling the back of her head. "You're safe now."

She clutched at his shirt, the adrenaline rush leaving her trembling. "What was that about?" she whispered.

"Just troublemakers looking to cause trouble." His embrace tightened. "Doesn't matter. You're with me now."

With me now. The words echoed in Rachel's mind as her racing pulse began to slow. She breathed in the scent of leather and spice, felt the solid warmth of Jaxon's body against hers.

"Rachel," he said. "There's no going back from this. If you're gonna be mine, it means being part of this life. The danger, the violence...it's all part of the package."

His words resonated inside her, sparking a mix of fear and thrill. She knew, in that moment, she couldn't walk away from him. From any of this.

Rachel lifted her chin, heart pounding as she whispered, "I'm yours."

A slow, dangerous smile curved Jaxon's mouth. He dipped his head, lips brushing hers, and sealed her fate with a searing kiss.

9

Smoke lingered in the air as Jaxon strode through the ashes of what was once their clubhouse. His boots crunched over shards of glass and charred debris, fury simmering in his gut at the sight of the devastation.

This was the Wolverines' doing. Again.

"Bastards are pushing into our territory more each day," Slick said, joining Jaxon's side. "Something's gotta give before this feud tears us apart."

Jaxon sighed, running a hand over the scruff on his jaw. They'd been at each other's throats for as long as he could remember, warring over land, power, reputation. Every few months, a new flare of violence would erupt, a vicious cycle that left them with little more than bitterness and bloodshed.

He thought of the young prospect who'd died in the last shootout, the light fading from his eyes even as Jaxon tried to staunch the flow of blood. They couldn't go on like this.

"We need to end this," he said. "Once and for all."

Memories flashed in his mind of past confrontations,

each more violent than the last. The raid on their warehouse five years ago. The brutal attack at the strip club that had nearly killed one of their own. And now this—the charred remains of the place they called home.

Slick's eyes glinted. "You want to hit them hard? Hit them where it really hurts."

"It's the only way they'll listen." Jaxon curled his hands into fists, rage and grief tangling into steely resolve. The Wolverines would pay for this. He'd make sure of it.

"Just say the word," Slick said.

Jaxon stared at the ruins of the clubhouse, seeing the ghosts of better times. They couldn't go back, but they sure as hell could go forward. "Do it," he said, jaw clenched. "Let's end this damn war once and for all."

This was a declaration of war. The Wolverines had crossed a line this time, and there would be no going back.

He thought of the young prospect who'd been inside, the kid they'd taken under their wing and treated as one of their own. His hands curled into fists at the memory of the boy's laughter, the light in his eyes as he'd talked about his dreams for the future. Gone, all of it gone, reduced to ashes and bone.

Jaxon's knuckles ached with the force of his anger. They would pay for this. He would personally see to it that the Wolverines paid in blood. If that was the only currency they understood, he'd give it to them in spades.

Jaxon stared at the ruins of the clubhouse, grief and purpose twining together into a cold, hard resolve. "Gather the others," he said. "We end this tonight."

The Wolverines had started this war, but he would be the one to finish it. They could burn his clubhouse, but they would never break his spirit. He would fight to his last dying breath to protect his own.

Tonight, the Wolverines would learn the meaning of vengeance.

Rachel stepped forward, her brow furrowed. "You can't seriously be thinking of retaliation. This has gone too far already, and more violence will only lead to greater destruction."

Jaxon's gaze hardened. "They came after us on our own ground. We can't let that stand."

"You could be killed," she said. "All of you. Hasn't there been enough death already?"

His lieutenants exchanged uneasy glances, the memory of the Molotov cocktail fresh in their minds. They'd already lost one of their own tonight. None of them wanted to lose their president, too.

Jaxon's hand curled around Rachel's arm, his touch gentler than his tone. "I won't ask you to come with us, but I can't back down from this. My men are counting on me."

"Your men need you alive," she said. "I need you alive, Jaxon. Please don't do this. We'll find another way to handle the Wolverines, a smarter way."

For a long moment he was silent, torn between his duty as president and his feelings for the woman in front of him. In the end, there was only one choice he could make.

"This is bigger than us, Rachel. My club needs to see that we stand up for our own."

She jerked away from him, eyes bright with anger and fear. "If you do this, you'll be starting a war."

His chest tightened, but he kept his face impassive. "You do what you have to do."

As she strode away without another word, he turned to his lieutenants. "Mount up."

The coming battle might cost him the woman he loved, but some things were more important than one man's happiness. The Green Devils came before everything else. Tonight he would remind the Wolverines of that fact, even if it was the last thing he did.

The rumble of engines shattered the peace of dusk as Jaxon led his lieutenants and a dozen patched members down the winding mountain roads toward the Wolverines' compound. Rachel's parting words echoed in his mind with every twist of the throttle, a grim refrain he couldn't escape.

You'll be starting a war you can't possibly win.

He pushed the thought aside, focusing on the route ahead. They'd taken these back roads enough times to know every blind curve and hidden turn, but tonight he was on high alert. The Wolverines were expecting retaliation for the Molotov cocktail they'd lobbed at the clubhouse, and there was no telling what traps they might have set along the way.

His gaze scanned the thick forest crowding in on either side of the road, alert for any sign of movement in the deepening shadows. But the trees stood silent and still, cloaking secrets behind their gnarled branches. The only sound that broke the quiet was the roar of the bikes and the occasional call of a night bird in the distance.

After twenty minutes of hard riding, they emerged onto the outskirts of town, where a handful of businesses still boasted Green Devils stickers on their windows. Jaxon's chest swelled with pride at the show of loyalty from Lenny's Garage, Big Joe's Biker Bar, and Luigi's Pizza—the lifeblood of their territory. They'd stood by the club through good times and bad, and tonight he would make sure no harm came to them.

The Wolverines had made a bold move attacking the clubhouse, but they were about to learn that the Green Devils weren't going down without a fight. The feud between them might just have escalated into all-out war—but if that was what it took to protect what was theirs, so be it.

Jaxon gunned his bike forward into the night, rage and determination steeling his resolve. The Wolverines wanted a battle? They were about to get one.

Jaxon pulled up outside Lenny's Garage, the familiar smell of oil and grease sharp in the chilly air. His gaze swept the length of the building, but everything appeared untouched. No signs of disturbance or damage. Still, he wouldn't take any chances.

He killed the engine and dismounted, the rest of the group following suit behind him. "Fan out and check the perimeter. Look for any signs they've been here."

His men fanned out without question, disappearing into the darkness to scout the area. Jaxon approached the garage entrance, one hand resting on the gun at his hip as he peered through the window into the dimly lit interior.

"All clear," Ranger called, emerging from the shadows. The others echoed his confirmation, gathering once more in the pool of light spilling from the streetlamp overhead.

Jaxon nodded, a muscle in his jaw twitching. It seemed they hadn't made it this far into Green Devil's territory yet—but that was only a matter of time. He knew the Wolverines and their bloodthirsty leader, Dom, wouldn't stop until they'd left a trail of destruction in their wake.

"We need to shore up security at the clubhouse and

here." He looked to each of his lieutenants in turn. "I want round-the-clock patrols and eyes on the road leading out of town. If they so much as poke their heads into our territory, I want to know about it."

"You got it, brother," Ranger said. The others voiced their agreement and Jaxon felt a flash of pride in his men. They might be outgunned, but they weren't outmatched— not when they had this level of loyalty and dedication.

The Wolverines had started a war, but the Green Devils would damn well finish it.

10

The rusty diner bell jangled as Rachel stepped through the weathered door into of Joe's Roadside Cafe. Though it was barely noon, it was nearly empty, only a few truckers hunched over steaming cups of coffee at the counter.

Rachel walked to a booth in the back, sliding onto the cracked red vinyl seat. Her stomach churned with nerves and she rubbed her clammy palms on her skirt. What was she doing here?

A waitress in a stained apron ambled over, eyebrow cocked. "What'll ya have, hon?"

Rachel's mouth felt dry as sand. "Just coffee. Black."

The waitress grunted and shuffled off. Rachel glanced around the diner again, her heart pounding. The bell jangled again, and a woman strode in, scanning the room. Her eyes landed on Rachel and she walked over, sliding into the seat across from her. Officer Sarah Mitchell was tall and athletic, her brown hair pulled back in a neat ponytail. Rachel's stomach twisted into knots at the sight of her police badge and service weapon clipped to her belt.

"You must be Rachel," Officer Mitchell said, her voice brisk and businesslike. Rachel nodded.

"Thanks for meeting with me. I have some questions about the Wolverines and the Green Devils. I understand this may be difficult for you, but any information you can provide would be helpful in my investigation."

Rachel's fingers tightened around her coffee cup. She didn't want to get tangled up in this and end up in jail, but could she really refuse to help a police officer? She swallowed hard, staring into the depths of the bitter black coffee. What was she going to do?

Rachel looked up from her coffee cup and met Officer Mitchell's steady gaze. She opened her mouth, but no words came out.

Before she could figure out a response, the bell on the diner door jangled again. Rachel glanced over and her heart froze in her chest.

Dominic "Dom" Ramirez swaggered through the entrance, his predatory eyes scanning the room. He was of average height, but powerfully built, with a beard and slicked-back hair. Dark tattoos peeked out from under the collar of his leather cut. The President patch on his cut left no doubt about who he was. Rachel's pulse raced as Dom's gaze settled on their table. A cruel smirk curled his lips as he strode over to them.

"Well, isn't this cozy?" His voice was mocking. Rachel shrank back in her seat, panic flooding her senses.

Officer Mitchell's hand dropped to rest on the handle of her gun, her eyes wary. "Mr. Ramirez, I suggest you leave us in peace."

Dom ignored her, focusing his attention on Rachel. "Been a long time, sweetheart. Did you miss me?"

It was obvious he knew about my relationship with Jaxon and that made me vulnerable. Rachel's stomach churned and her breath came in short, sharp bursts.

She gripped the edge of the table, struggling to stay afloat. How had her carefully constructed new life collapsed so quickly? All she wanted was to escape this world that threatened to engulf her once more.

Rachel swallowed hard, forcing herself to meet Dom's gaze. "Leave me alone."

Dom leaned in closer, bracing his hands on the table. His cologne invaded her senses, the familiar scent churning in her stomach. "You're not getting away from me that easily this time."

Jaxon was never far away from Rachel, and this time she was glad.

Jaxon walked into the diner and walked straight up to Dom. "She asked you to leave." His voice was deceptively calm, but Rachel could see the tension in his shoulders and the steely glint in his eyes.

Dom didn't back down, sizing up Jaxon. The air seemed to vibrate with the animosity between them. A part of Rachel was screaming at her to run, to escape this world of violent men and the codes they lived by. But she was frozen in place, trapped by the threads of her past and the inescapable present.

The rules of the biker world were clear: loyalty to your club above all else. Dom would never stop coming after the Green Devils, and now she was tangled up in this web, causing Jaxon to step in and defend her. The conflict between the clubs would only escalate, fueled by a history of bad blood and a thirst for power.

Rachel closed her eyes, a sob catching in her throat. She

was drowning with no way out, the darkness closing in around her once more.

"Get out," Jaxon growled, his hand dropping to rest on the handle of his knife. "Before this gets ugly."

Dom held his gaze for a long moment before giving a sharp nod. But as he turned away, he looked back at Rachel, his eyes glinting with menace. "This isn't over."

Rachel slumped back into her seat as Dom strode out of the diner. She was trapped, caught between the two men and the rival clubs they represented. The rules that governed their world would dictate the outcome, rules written in blood and violence.

Jaxon slid into the booth beside Rachel, wrapping an arm around her shoulders. "It's okay," he murmured. "I won't let him hurt you."

Rachel looked up at him, tears shimmering in her eyes. "I never should have gotten involved with you."

"Don't say that." Jaxon cupped her cheek, his touch gentle. "I'm not letting you go that easily."

She closed her eyes, leaning into his warmth. He made her feel safe, as if the darkness couldn't reach her when he was near. But it was an illusion. As long as Dom and the Wolverines were out there, danger would follow.

Rachel looked around for Sarah, but she had left during the debacle between the two men and she doubted she'd see her again.

Jaxon paid for her meal and guided Rachel outside to his bike. Night had fallen, shadows clinging to every corner. Rachel climbed on behind him, wrapping her arms around his waist. The rumble of the engine vibrated through her as they rode off into the night.

When they arrived at the clubhouse, Rachel followed

Jaxon inside. Most of the other members were already there, the air thick. All eyes turned to Rachel as she entered, judging and assessing. She wanted to shrink away, to disappear, but she forced herself to lift her chin. She wouldn't show them her fear.

"The Wolverines won't back down," JT said, his face grim. "Dom's gonna come after her to get to you. We're gonna have a full-on war on our hands."

Jaxon's jaw tightened, rage simmering in his eyes. "I couldn't go after him in that diner. They were too many bystanders. We need to catch them away from the public. No one threatens what's mine."

Rachel's heart twisted at his words. She didn't want to be the reason blood was shed, the catalyst that plunged them into violence. But it was too late to turn back now. She had chosen this path, and she would walk it to the end.

11

The living room was dim, the only light filtering in through dusty blinds. Jaxon sat with his elbows on his knees, staring at the floorboards as if they held answers to questions he didn't dare ask.

Rachel watched him from the armchair, a knot of worry forming in her stomach. His broad shoulders were tense under his faded t-shirt, his hands clasped so tightly his knuckles had turned white. Something was wrong.

She leaned forward and placed her hand on his arm. He flinched at her touch before relaxing into it, but his gaze remained fixed on the floor. "Talk to me," she said.

For a long moment, there was only silence. Then he shook his head and ran a hand over his beard, scraping against the rough bristles. "Nothin' you need to worry about." His voice was gruff, but she could hear the strain beneath it.

"That's not good enough." She gave his arm a gentle squeeze. "We're in this together now. You can tell me anything."

He sighed and raised his head to look at her at last. His blue eyes were troubled, shadows lurking in their depths. "Somethin's brewing. Marcus got word they're plannin' to make another move into our territory."

Her heart quickened. She knew how much blood had already been spilled over turf wars and how much more would be shed if outright war broke out.

"We'll handle it," Jaxon continued, reaching up to cup her cheek. The warmth of his calloused palm was strangely comforting. "Ain't nothin' for you to worry about. I won't let nothin' happen to you."

She leaned into his touch, covering his hand with her own. His words were meant to reassure her, but they only amplified her concern. The Wolverines were dangerous, and if they were encroaching on the Green Devils' territory, violence was inevitable. She couldn't lose Jaxon, not now when they had only just found each other. She would do whatever it took to keep him safe, even if it meant stepping into a world she had tried her whole life to avoid.

"Rachel, I can't have you gettin' hurt. I won't allow it."

"I don't need your permission." Rachel lifted her chin, meeting his gaze unflinchingly. "I'm here because I choose to be, not because you allow me to be. We're partners, Jaxon, and that means facing difficulties together, not shutting each other out."

"Bein' together puts you in danger," Jaxon growled. "If somethin' happened to you because of me..."

"Life comes with risks." Rachel placed her hands on either side of his face, forcing him to look at her. "You're worth those risks to me. I love you, and we'll get through this like we have everything else. Together."

Jaxon stared at her for a long moment, the fight slowly

draining from his eyes. He leaned down and kissed her, a kiss full of unspoken emotion that made her heart ache with love for this complicated, vulnerable man.

"I don't deserve you," he said roughly. "But I ain't givin' you up without a fight."

Rachel smiled, brushing her thumb over his lower lip. "Good. I'd expect nothing less."

As she walked down the front steps of Jaxon's house, Rachel noticed a woman with kind blue eyes sitting in one of the rocking chairs lining the wraparound porch.

"Afternoon," the woman said. "I'm Daphne."

"Rachel." She walked over and held out her hand. "It's nice to meet you, Daphne. I'm actually Jaxon's...girlfriend."

"Well, aren't you a pretty little thing?" Daphne shook Rachel's hand with a firm grip. "Jaxon's a good boy. Bit rough around the edges, but he's got a heart of gold under all those tattoos." She chuckled, the sound warm and throaty. "How'd a nice girl like you end up with the president of the Green Devils?"

Rachel smiled, already charmed by the older woman's playful candor. "It's a long story. Jaxon saved my life, and I saved his soul, I think."

"Is that so?" Daphne's eyes gleamed with interest. "Well, sit down then, honey. I've got time for a good story, and something tells me yours will be worth hearing."

Rachel laughed and settled into the rocking chair beside Daphne's. "All right, if you're sure you want to hear it."

"I'm sure." Daphne patted Rachel's hand. "Now start from the beginning, sugar."

Rachel began to speak, finding it easy to open up to Daphne. There was a warmth and wisdom to the woman that instantly put her at ease, and Rachel got the sense that she'd found a friend.

As Rachel shared the story of how she and Jaxon first met, Daphne listened with rapt attention, her foot tapping in time to the creak of her rocking chair. A sense of peace settled over Rachel, easing the tension that had been coiled inside her ever since Jaxon revealed the threat brewing in the club. For the first time, she felt like everything would be all right.

Rachel glanced at her watch and was surprised to see several hours had passed. "Oh my, I should get going. Jaxon will wonder where I've gotten to."

"Nonsense," Daphne said. "That man can wait. We're not done visiting yet. Besides, it'll do him good to stew in his own worry for a bit."

Rachel laughed. "You're probably right about that. He does tend to fret."

"All men do, honey. It's in their nature." Daphne patted Rachel's hand again.

The sun dipped lower in the sky, shadows lengthening across the porch, but still Rachel remained. She and Daphne had moved on to lighter topics, swapping stories and bonding over shared interests.

By the time Rachel finally stood to leave, she felt happier and lighter than she had in weeks. "Thank you, Daphne," she said, squeezing the woman's hand. "I really needed this."

"Any time, sugar." Daphne patted her cheek. "You come find me whenever you're feeling low. I'm always here."

"I will," Rachel promised. She headed for her car with a smile.

The cheerful ringtone cut through the quiet. She dug the

phone from her purse, expecting to see Jaxon's name on the display.

Instead, it was Marcus. Heart skipping a beat, Rachel answered. "Marcus? What's wrong?" His tense tone set her nerves on edge.

"Rach, I need your help," Marcus said, his words tumbling out in a rush. "There's been an accident at a warehouse on Ridge Road. Can you bring your medical kit?"

"Oh god, of course!" Fear and adrenaline spiked Rachel's pulse as she hurried to her car. "I'm on my way."

Marcus hissed. "Hurry, Rach."

"I'm coming right now." Rachel slammed her car door shut and cranked the engine, peeling out of the lot. Her hands shook around the steering wheel as she navigated toward Ridge Road.

Rachel's mind raced as fast as her car, thoughts tumbling over each other in a frenzied rush. She needed to stay calm and focused.

12

Rachel pulled up outside the warehouse, her knuckles white as her hands gripped the steering wheel. Her heart pounded, torn between the desire to help and her deep-seated need for safety. The danger of this world Jaxon lived in went against everything she knew, yet here she was, walking into the lion's den once more.

The thick metal door creaked open and the scent of blood hit her like a wave. Her stomach churned, but she steeled her nerves.

Inside, a young man lay motionless on a table, a dark red stain seeping across his abdomen. The room swam before her eyes and she took a sharp breath, forcing the nausea back down.

Two Prospects hovered nearby, panic etched into the lines on their faces.

"He's still bleeding," one of them said, his voice trembling. "We tried to stop it, but..."

Rachel moved to the table and ripped open her medical bag. "Get me gauze, tape and alcohol. Now!"

The Prospects scrambled to obey as Rachel's hands moved swiftly and surely. The familiar motions calmed her, and soon she staunched the bleeding.

She looked up at the two young men watching her with something close to awe. "He'll live, but he needs a hospital."

They exchanged a worried glance, the unspoken fear of police involvement hanging in the air. Rachel sighed, knowing she had a battle ahead of her to convince them to do the right thing.

Her thoughts flickered to Jaxon, wishing he was here. She had a feeling he was the only one who could make them see reason. The danger of this life they led was spiraling out of control, and she feared what might happen if someone didn't put a stop to this endless war.

She took a breath and faced the Prospects, hands on her hips. "I know you're afraid of the police. But this boy will die without medical care. As his brothers, you have to do what's right for him."

They shuffled their feet, avoiding her gaze. "It's not that simple," one of them mumbled.

Rachel moved closer, lowering her voice. "I understand, believe me. But he's just a kid. You're supposed to protect each other, not let each other die for the sake of code."

One of the Prospects raked a hand through his hair. "Shit. You're right. But if we take him in, it'll start a whole new war."

"And if you don't, his death will be on your conscience forever." Rachel placed a hand on his arm. "Have faith in me. I'll make sure he's safe. You have my word."

He searched her face, as if looking for the truth in her eyes. Finally, he nodded.

Just then, a soft groan escaped Dirk's lips, his eyelids fluttering open. Rachel leaned over him, hands braced on either side of the bed.

"Easy now," she murmured. "You're safe."

He blinked up at her, gaze cloudy with pain and confusion. "What...what happened?"

"There was an attack," she said. "You were shot, but I've patched you up. You're going to be alright."

Dirk's eyes widened, a spark of panic igniting in their depths. "They came back? Son of a—" He started to push himself up, then gasped, collapsing.

"Stay still," Rachel ordered, placing a firm hand on his uninjured shoulder. "You've lost a lot of blood. Any sudden movements could tear the wound open again."

He gritted his teeth, chest heaving with harsh, uneven breaths. "We have to...have to warn the others. Before it's too late."

"Marcus has already increased security," she assured him. "But you need to rest. Getting worked up will only slow your recovery."

"I can't just lie here!" Dirk protested. "What if they attack again?"

Rachel met his gaze steadily. "Then we'll handle it. But right now, you're in no shape to fight. So do as I say and save your strength. Doctor's orders."

Dirk scowled but remained still, jaw clenched. Rachel could see the tension in every line of his body, could feel the coiled energy radiating from him, even in his weakened state. She didn't envy trying to keep him confined to bed rest.

Sighing, she straightened and turned to Marcus, who was hovering in the doorway. "We need to call Jaxon. He'll know how best to increase security and watch for another attack."

Marcus shifted his weight, shoving his hands into the pockets of his cut. "I don't know, Doc. Things are complicated enough without dragging Jaxon into this mess."

"Complicated or not, people's lives are at stake here," she said sharply. "We need all the help we can get."

He hesitated, then jerked his chin in a stiff nod. "Yeah, alright. But don't say I didn't warn you."

Exhaling in relief, Rachel retrieved the phone from her bag and held it out to him. "Here. Call him."

After a long moment, Marcus took the phone. He stared down at it for a few seconds, jaw tight, then lifted it to his ear and dialed.

The call seemed to drag on forever. Rachel busied herself checking Dirk's bandages.

They needed Jaxon. They needed his guidance, his resources, his men. If anyone could keep them safe from another attack, it was him.

Finally, Marcus passed her back the phone. "He's sending reinforcements to guard the perimeter. And he wants to talk to you."

Rachel took a deep breath and lifted the phone to her ear. "Jaxon?"

"Doc." His voice was gravelly and tense. "Tell me what the hell is going on."

She relayed the events of the past hour in a rush of words, sparing no details about Dirk's condition or the threats of violence from the Wolverines. Jaxon listened without interrupting, the occasional grunt or sharp exhale the only indication he was still on the line.

When she finished, he was silent for a long moment. "You did good calling me. But this is a dangerous situation, and I want you out of there as soon as my men arrive."

Rachel stiffened. "I'm not leaving. Dirk needs medical care, and I'm not going to abandon him."

"Rachel—"

"No, Jaxon," she said. "I won't leave until I'm sure he's stable enough to be moved or taken to a hospital. That's final."

Jaxon growled. She could picture him raking a hand through his hair, torn between concern for her safety and respect for her dedication to those in her care.

Finally, he sighed. "Stubborn woman. Fine, you can stay until Dirk's out of the woods. But I'm posting guards on you, and you do exactly as they say. No arguments."

"Understood," she said, relief flooding through her. At least now she'd have backup and a way to ensure everyone's safety. "Thank you, Jaxon. For everything."

"Just keep yourself safe," he said gruffly. "That's all the thanks I need."

13

Rachel's heart pounded as the roar of motorcycles outside grew louder. Not just one or two bikes—at least a dozen. Through the narrow slit of a window, she could see the Wolverine MC pulling up, armed with baseball bats and chains.

"Shit," Marcus hissed. He slammed the butt of his pistol against the wall, leaving a dent in the rotting wood. "They're not alone."

Rachel clutched her trembling hands together, her knuckles turning white. She was trapped. Again.

"We need backup," Dirk said. "Now."

Marcus yanked out his phone and barked an order to someone on the other end. His gaze flickered to Rachel, and she glimpsed the apology in his eyes. They had promised to keep her safe. But even the formidable Green Devils were no match for the Wolverines right now.

The rumble of engines cut off, followed by the slam of doors. Voices drifted through the walls, harsh and demanding. "We want Rachel now."

Rachel's stomach dropped. They knew she was here. Of course they did.

"Like hell," Marcus shouted. He strode to the barricaded door, pistol raised.

Dirk grabbed his arm. "Wait for backup."

"I'm not handing her over." Marcus shook him off, jaw clenched.

Rachel's breath caught. Never in her life had anyone fought for her. The Wolverines would tear Marcus apart, and it would be her fault. She couldn't let that happen.

Summoning her courage, she approached Marcus and touched his arm. "It's okay."

He stared at her, eyes gleaming with rage and regret. "I'm not giving up that easy. Jaxon will kill me if something happens to you."

The sound of gunfire exploded outside. Rachel screamed, but Marcus pulled her against him, shielding her with his body. His heart slammed against her cheek, as rapid as her own.

Over the chaos, a familiar roar rang out. "Green Devils!"

Jaxon. Her pulse leapt with relief and something more, a feeling she couldn't name.

The gunfight intensified, but Marcus's arms remained locked around her. "You're safe," he murmured. "We've got you."

She closed her eyes, daring to believe him.

The air in the room felt charged with electricity. Marcus kept Rachel tucked behind him, his body a shield against the Wolverines and their guns.

One Wolverine stood by the door, pistol trained on Marcus. The other two were on opposite sides of the room, rifles aimed and fingers on the trigger.

Trapped. Rachel's heart rammed against her ribs. They were outgunned and outnumbered, with no way out.

Except Jaxon. He'd come for them. He had to.

A shout rang out, followed by a grunt of pain. The Wolverine by the door crumpled to the ground, revealing a familiar figure in the doorway.

Jaxon's gaze locked on Rachel, ice-blue eyes blazing with fury and something more—something that made her stomach flip.

Then he smiled, slow and lethal. The Wolverines swung their rifles toward him, but Jaxon didn't slow.

"Let her go," he growled, "or you'll regret the day you ever joined this pathetic excuse for a club."

14

Jaxon stepped forward, grabbing Rachel from Marcus. The Wolverines tensed, fingers tightening on their triggers, but they didn't fire.

Not yet.

The sounds of boots and shouts echoed from down the hall. Jaxon's men coming to back him up.

The Wolverines glanced at each other, unease flickering in their eyes. They were outnumbered.

"Here are your options," Jaxon said. "You let us all walk out of here unharmed, or my men fill this room with bullets. Your choice."

The Wolverines scowled but didn't protest as the rest of the Green Devils filed in, an assortment of guns and knives in their hands.

Game. Set. Match.

Jaxon smirked, pulling Rachel flush against his side. "Negotiation over."

The leader of the Wolverines, Dom, stepped forward. "Not that easy, Jaxon. We'll do as you say, but in exchange, you give us the west side of your territory. Everything west of Route 66, all the way to the state line."

Jaxon tensed, his arm tightening around Rachel's waist. Giving up that much land would weaken the Green Devils' stronghold over the county. But if he didn't take the deal, who knew what the Wolverines might do to Rachel before he got another chance to save her?

His heart twisted as Rachel lifted her gaze to his, her eyes soft with trust and understanding. She knew, as he did, that her safety was more important than any amount of land or power.

"Done," Jaxon said. "Now get the hell off my territory."

Dom bared his teeth in a vicious smile and nodded to his men. The Wolverines holding the pledges released them, shoving them toward the Green Devils.

As more of his brothers showed up to help, Jaxon knew that giving up territory might make him look weak, but most of his brothers would understand.

"The west side of our land, everything west of Route 66 to the state line, now belongs to the Wolverines," Jaxon told his men, his arm securely around Rachel's shoulders. "In return, they've released Rachel and the pledges, mostly unharmed."

Murmurs of anger and unease rippled through the group, but no one protested. They all knew, as Jaxon did, that some things were more valuable than land or power.

"Anyone have a problem with that?" Jaxon demanded, his tone daring dissent.

No one spoke up.

Jaxon nodded. "Then let's get the hell out of here."

The Green Devils turned as one, marching out of the room with Rachel, the pledges, and their leader in the center.

They'd given up territory today, but gained something far more precious: loyalty, family, love.

For Jaxon, that was a win he'd take any day.

Jaxon hustled Rachel onto his bike, settling her in before kicking the engine to life. "You okay?" Jaxon asked Rachel, raising his voice to be heard above the roar of the bikes.

She nodded, but he didn't miss the way she flinched at every loud noise, her knuckles turning white where she gripped his arms.

He took her hands in his, gently prying her fingers loose. "You're safe now. I won't let anything happen to you."

As they rode back to the clubhouse, Jaxon felt the resentment simmering within the ranks. Giving up territory to the Wolverines went against everything they stood for, and he didn't blame his brothers for questioning his decision.

When they arrived, Jaxon cut the engine of his bike and helped Rachel dismount. Before he could say a word, one of the newer members, a troublemaker named Luke, stepped forward.

"Why'd we give up our land for a woman and a couple of kids? The prez has gone soft." Luke sneered, crossing his arms over his chest. "Guess all it takes is a piece of ass to get Jaxon on his knees."

The implication was clear. Jaxon saw red rage flooding his veins like molten lava. In two quick strides, he was in front of Luke, grabbing him by the collar of his cut and slamming him against the nearest wall.

"The only reason you're still breathing is because you wear that patch," Jaxon growled, face inches from Luke's. "But if you ever disrespect Rachel again, cut or no cut, I will beat you to within an inch of your life. You got that?"

Luke sputtered, eyes wide with fear as he nodded.

"She is not a piece of ass," Jaxon hissed. "She's mine. And I protect what's mine."

Jaxon released Luke, shoving him away in disgust. His chest was heaving, rage still simmering in his veins, but one look at Rachel's stricken face cooled his anger.

"I'm sorry you had to see that, baby," he said, wrapping an arm around her shoulders and pressing a kiss to her hair. "But no one disrespects my woman. No one."

Rachel nodded against his chest, and Jaxon felt the tension seep from her body once more. His woman understood. She was his, just as he was hers, and he would tear the whole world apart before he let anyone hurt her.

"The next person who questions my decisions will get worse than what Luke just did," Jaxon announced to the silent crowd. "Rachel and those pledges are family now. We protect our own."

A chorus of "Amen" and "Yes, prez" followed his proclamation. The resentment hadn't fully disappeared, but Jaxon's show of force reminded them exactly who was in charge.

His gaze met Rachel's, full of warmth and understanding and something more - love. She was worth every inch of territory, every drop of blood. Rachel was his everything, and these men would do well to remember that.

15

Rachel gripped the doorknob, her knuckles turning white, and began to swing the heavy wooden door shut. But before the bolt could slide into place, a steel-toed boot jammed between the frame and the door.

Jaxon.

Her heart leapt into her throat as the door burst open with a bang that rattled the windows.

"What the hell do you think you're doing?" he growled, crowding into her space.

Rachel stumbled back, panic rising in her chest. She searched his face—the sharp cut of his jaw, the piercing blue eyes that seemed to see straight through to her soul—but found no warmth there now. Only a storm brewing.

"I—I was just—"

"You were just going to lock me out?" Each word was clipped, biting. "After everything we've been through, you were gonna shut me out like I'm nothing to you?"

"No, of course not, I just—"

"Do you have any idea what I risked to get here? What I

sacrificed?" He slammed a fist against the wall, the crack of it like a gunshot in the silence. "Dammit, Rachel."

Rachel flinched at the outburst, instinctively raising her arms to shield herself. She knew he would never hurt her, not physically, but in that moment her body remembered a different time, a different place. A past that still haunted her dreams.

Jaxon's face crumpled. "Shit. I'm sorry." He ran a hand through his hair, looking away. "I didn't mean to scare you. You just—you drive me crazy, you know that?"

When he finally met her gaze again, the fury had vanished, leaving something else in its wake. Something fragile and broken that made her chest ache.

Rachel took a tentative step forward, then another, until she could reach out and take his hand. She gave it a gentle squeeze. "I'm sorry too. I should have known you would never—" Her voice caught in her throat. "I trust you, Jaxon. I do. My head's just taking a while to catch up with my heart."

Jaxon's eyes darkened, flickering to her lips. He pulled her closer, his hands settling on her waist in a possessive grip. Even through her shirt, his touch seared her skin.

"You can't do that again," he said. "Scare me like that. I thought I was going to lose you."

Rachel's breath hitched as he dipped his head, nuzzling against her neck. She could feel the warmth of his breath, the brush of stubble against her throat. Her pulse raced under his lips.

"I'm right here," she whispered. She slid her arms around his shoulders, anchoring him to her.

He shuddered against her, his embrace tightening. The raw emotion in it made her eyes sting. How had this man broken through her defenses so easily? Stripped away the layers of armor she'd built up over years?

"I couldn't handle it if something happened to you," Jaxon said. "You're the best thing that's ever been mine. The only good thing."

Rachel closed her eyes, a tear sliding down her cheek. She thought of the tattoos on his back, the secrets they held, the grief and guilt he carried with him always.

Her fingers curled into his hair as she held him close. "You have me," she said. "For as long as you want me. As long as you'll let me stay."

Jaxon pulled back to look at her, his eyes glassy with tears. Rachel's heart clenched at the sight. She reached up to cup his cheek, brushing her thumb over the rough stubble.

"Talk to me," she said. "Tell me what's wrong."

He swallowed hard, struggling to compose himself. "You can't do that again," he repeated hoarsely. "Put yourself in danger like that. I can't lose you too."

Too. The word echoed in Rachel's mind, realization dawning. She thought of the angel wings on his back, the secrets etched into his skin.

"Who did you lose?" she asked softly.

Jaxon's jaw tightened. His hands curled into fists at his sides for a moment before he turned away, shoulders hunching. Rachel waited patiently, giving him the space to gather himself.

When he finally spoke, his voice was raw with pain. "My sister. She was killed five years ago." He paused, drawing a shaky breath. "It was my fault. I was supposed to protect her, but I failed."

Rachel's heart broke at the anguish in his tone. She

moved to stand beside him, slipping her arm through his and leaning her head against his shoulder.

"I'm so sorry," she said gently.

Jaxon's hand came up to cover hers, his grip almost bruising. But she didn't pull away. She only held on tighter, offering what little comfort she could.

They stood in silence for a long moment, the only sound their mingled breaths. A profound sadness filled the space between them, tinged by the ghosts of loss and regret. But beneath it all was a fragile tendril of hope-the promise of solace in shared grief, of healing in the light they had found in each other.

Jaxon swallowed hard, staring unseeingly ahead. "Her name was Sophia. There was a fight over territory with the Wolverines that got out of hand. Sophie...she jumped in to defend me. Took a bullet meant for me."

His voice broke on the last word. Rachel felt her own eyes burn with tears at the image he painted. She couldn't imagine the pain of losing a sibling that way, or the guilt that must have haunted him ever since.

"I'm the reason she's not here anymore. If I hadn't gotten her involved in this life..." He trailed off with a ragged sigh.

"You can't blame yourself," Rachel said. She turned to face him, gripping his arms. "You didn't pull the trigger. You loved your sister, and she loved you. That's why she did what she did--to protect you. Not because of the life you led, but because of who you were to each other."

Jaxon stared at her for a long moment, eyes shadowed. "Can't I?" His eyes flashed, anger and grief twisting his features.

But she could see the first glimmers of hope peeking through, the beginnings of absolution in her words. He drew a shaky breath and pulled her close, wrapping his arms around her in a bone-crushing embrace.

Rachel held him just as tightly, a pillar of strength against the tide of anguish and regret. She understood now the meaning behind the angel wings, a memorial to the sister he had lost and a reminder of the sacrifice borne of love.

"Thank you," he whispered, lips brushing her hair. She smiled, nestling closer to his chest.

"You don't have to walk this path alone anymore," she said. "I'm here."

Jaxon's arms tightened around her, and she could feel the subtle tremor that ran through him. The first cracks in the walls he had built, giving way to the light that streamed between them—a light to guide him out of the darkness, and lead them both home.

"After she died, I swore I'd dismantle the Wolverines, piece by bloody piece. But taking revenge wouldn't bring her back. Nothing would." His voice cracked on the last word.

Rachel stroked his cheek, her heart aching for his loss. "You loved her so much," she said. "Of course, her death left a hole inside you. But she wouldn't want you to destroy yourself over it, Jaxon. She'd want you to heal. To find peace."

Jaxon was silent for a long moment. Then he gazed at Rachel with eyes full of wonder, as if seeing her for the first time. "How did you get to be so wise?"

Rachel smiled. "I'm not wise. I just know a thing or two about loss." Her smile faded. "And about holding onto pain for too long. It's like a poison - the only way to survive is to let it go, before it destroys you."

Jaxon nodded. "I spent years telling myself I didn't deserve to move on. That the only way to honor my sister's memory was to stay mired in the past, crippled by guilt and regret." His voice dropped. "Until I met you, and for the first time, I saw a future worth living for."

Rachel's heart swelled. She reached up and cradled Jaxon's face in her hands. "The past can't be changed," she said. "But the future is ours to write. Together."

Jaxon covered her hands with his own eyes shining with promise. "Together," he echoed. And sealed it with a kiss.

Jaxon pulled back to look at her, eyes shining with emotion. "I don't deserve you, Rachel. The things I've done..."

She reached up and cupped his face between her hands. "The past is behind us. All that matters now is the future we're building together."

He turned his head to press a kiss to her palm, the rough scrape of his beard igniting sparks along her skin. "You're my light in the darkness. My angel."

Rachel smiled, brushing her thumbs over his cheekbones. "And you're mine. My fierce, beautiful man."

Jaxon's eyes darkened, pupils dilating with desire. He lowered his head and captured her mouth in a searing kiss, all heat and passion and tender reverence. Rachel melted into him, her heart overflowing with love for this complicated, wounded soul.

"I have a confession to make, too. The car accident that killed my mother..." Her voice trailed off, and she looked away.

"It's okay," Jaxon said gently. "You can tell me."

Rachel met his gaze. "My parents were fighting because my father was drunk. He crashed the car on purpose, to spite my mother. And she died, just like that."

A tear rolled down Rachel's cheek. "Since then, I hated him for it. But holding onto that hate only made me miserable. I finally realized the only way to move on was to forgive him. Even though he doesn't deserve it."

Jaxon pulled Rachel close, cradling her head against his chest. "You're amazing, you know that? You've been through hell, but you still have so much love and compassion in you." He pressed a soft kiss to her hair. "Loving you is making me want to be a better man."

Rachel smiled through her tears. "You already are a good man, Jaxon Jones. The best I've ever known."

16

Jaxon drew Rachel into his arms, pressing a tender kiss to her forehead. "Ready for that bath now, baby?"

Rachel nodded, a flush of warmth spreading through her at the thought of sharing such an intimate moment. "Yes, I'd like that."

Jaxon scooped her up into his arms, carrying her down the hall to the master bathroom. He set her on her feet, turning to start the water. Steam soon billowed up as he added her favorite lavender bath oil, the floral scent filling the room.

Rachel watched as Jaxon undressed, desire stirring anew at the sight of his powerful body. She still couldn't quite believe he was hers now, to hold and cherish as she'd always longed to.

Jaxon slid into the oversized tub, holding out his hand. "Come here, beautiful."

Rachel stepped into the tub, settling between his legs. The hot water enveloped her, soothing her pleasantly aching body. She sighed, leaning back against Jaxon's chest.

Jaxon wrapped his arms around her, dropping a kiss on her shoulder. "Comfortable?"

"Very," Rachel said. "This is nice."

"It is." Jaxon nuzzled her neck, his hands gliding over her stomach beneath the water. "Being here with you like this, it's perfect."

Rachel smiled, tilting her head up to meet his gaze. "You're perfect for me, Jaxon Jones."

Jaxon's eyes softened, filled with a tenderness that made her heart ache. "And you're perfect for me, Rachel Lewis. My missing piece."

The warm water lapped at Rachel's skin as she sank into the bathtub, her body melting against Jaxon's. His arms wrapped around her, holding her close.

"I've never felt this way about anyone before," Rachel whispered.

Jaxon's lips grazed the curve of her neck. "Me neither, baby. You're it for me."

A lump formed in Rachel's throat. She turned in his arms to face him, tracing the lines of his tattoo with her fingertip. "After everything I've been through, I never thought I'd find this." Her eyes welled with tears. "I never thought I'd find you."

Jaxon cupped her face, wiping away a stray tear with his thumb. "I'm here now. I'm not going anywhere." He kissed her then, slow and deep, igniting a fire within her.

Rachel slid her hands over the hard planes of his chest, desire pooling low in her belly. She wanted nothing more than to lose herself in his embrace, to forget about everything but this moment.

Jaxon's hands drifted down to her hips, clutching her close. She could feel his need pressing against her, awakening her own. "I want you, Rachel. In every way." His voice was rough with longing.

Jaxon's eyes darkened with passion. He lifted her onto his lap, her legs straddling his hips as the water sloshed around them.

Rachel claimed his mouth again, her kiss conveying what words could not. That she was his, now and forever.

Jaxon slid inside her then, inch by delicious inch, stretching her, filling her, completing her in a way she had only dreamed of. Rachel gasped at the intrusion, clinging to him as a dizzying rush of pleasure overwhelmed her senses.

"Rachel," Jaxon groaned, clutching her hips. "My Rachel."

She began to move, finding a rhythm that brought them both to the edge of bliss. The world around them faded away until there was only this, only them, joined in body and soul.

Jaxon quickened the pace, his breaths coming fast and hard. Rachel arched into him, trembling on the brink of release.

"I love you," Jaxon rasped, gazing into her eyes. "Come for me, baby."

His words sent her tumbling over the edge, pleasure radiating through every nerve in her body. Rachel cried out his name as the waves crashed over her, clinging to him as he found his own release. They held each other for a long moment, hearts pounding as one. Rachel had never felt so complete. So loved. She smiled up at Jaxon, brushing a damp lock of hair from his forehead. "I love you too." She kissed him then, slow and deep, pouring all the love in her heart into that kiss. They had found each other through heartbreak and longing, and now they would never again be apart.

Jaxon's hands drifted lower, caressing her inner thighs. Rachel gasped into his mouth, desire igniting within her once more.

"I want you again," Jaxon rasped against her lips. "I'll never get enough of you."

"Then take me," Rachel whispered. "I'm yours, Jaxon. Always."

Jaxon lifted her easily, positioning her to straddle his lap. The feel of his hard length against her made her ache with need.

One hand grasped her hip, the other palming her breast as his mouth closed over her nipple. Rachel cried out, arching into him.

"That's it, baby," Jaxon murmured. "Give yourself to me."

Rachel rocked her hips, taking him inside her inch by inch. They groaned in unison as he filled her, their bodies joining as seamlessly as their souls.

Jaxon set a slow, deep rhythm, his hands roaming her body. The water sloshed around them, steam rising in wisps.

Rachel rode him, clinging to his shoulders. His name fell from her lips like a prayer as ecstasy built within her.

Jaxon's thrusts grew harder, more urgent. "Come for me, Rachel. I've got you."

The world shattered around her as she came apart in his arms. Jaxon surged up within her, finding his own release with a hoarse shout.

They clung to each other, hearts pounding as the ripples in the water gradually stilled. Rachel had found her home, her shelter, her eternally safe place in Jaxon's embrace. Together, they had forged something rare and precious.

Rachel rested her head on Jaxon's shoulder, savoring the

feel of his arms around her. The bath water had cooled, but she felt warm and content in a way she never had before.

Jaxon pressed a kiss to her temple. "You okay?"

"Mmm." Rachel smiled, trailing her fingers through the hair on his chest. "More than okay."

A low, pleased rumble vibrated in Jaxon's chest as the last of the water gurgled down the drain.

Silence fell over them, broken only by the soft sounds of their breathing. A heaviness had settled into Rachel's limbs, a bone-deep relaxation she wanted to hold on to forever.

Jaxon shifted, pulling her more firmly against him. "We should get out before we turn into prunes."

"Don't wanna move," Rachel mumbled, nestling closer.

Jaxon chuckled. "As much as I'd like to stay here with you, we'll be more comfortable in an actual bed."

Rachel sighed, knowing he was right. She sat up, the loss of his warmth leaving her bereft for a moment.

Jaxon stood and stepped out of the tub before turning to offer her his hand. Rachel took it, the rough calluses and strength in his grip grounding her.

He helped her out of the bath and wrapped her in a fluffy towel, rubbing her arms to ward off the chill.

"Thank you," Rachel said, "for tonight. For...everything."

Jaxon cupped her face in his hands, his eyes reflecting the depth of his emotion. "You're the one who's given me something I never thought I deserved."

Rachel's heart swelled, overflowing with love for the man in front of her. "We deserve each other," she whispered.

Jaxon's answering smile lit up his face. "That we do, sweetheart."

17

Rachel was in the kitchen making coffee when Jaxon came up behind her and wrapped his arms around her waist.

She leaned back into his embrace, covering his hands with her own. "Good morning."

"I was thinking we could take the bike out today, maybe ride up to the lake and have a picnic. If you want to, that is."

The thought of a romantic getaway with Jaxon. "That sounds perfect."

His smile widened. "Great. Be ready to go in an hour?"

She nodded. "I'll be ready."

He squeezed her waist before stepping back, a new lightness in his eyes. "See you soon then, sweetheart."

As he walked off, Rachel's heart swelled. She couldn't wait to spend the day with the man she loved, strengthening the bond they now shared.

Rachel stood in front of the mirror, admiring the black dress she'd chosen. It accentuated her curves in all the right places, the hem ending mid-thigh to show off her toned legs. She knew Jaxon would appreciate the view.

A knock on the door interrupted her musings. "You ready, darling?" Jaxon's voice rumbled from the other side.

"Just a minute!" She gave herself a final once-over, satisfied with her appearance, and opened the door.

Jaxon's eyes darkened as he took her in, pupils dilating with desire. "Damn, you look good enough to eat."

Heat pooled low in her belly at the hunger in his gaze. She stepped forward and traced a finger down his chest. "Well, I was rather hoping you'd devour me tonight."

A low growl escaped him as he crushed her to him, lips claiming hers in a searing kiss. His hands roamed over her body, squeezing and caressing, stoking the fire inside her.

When they finally broke apart, chests heaving, Rachel could barely form a coherent thought. "Take me to bed," she whispered.

Jaxon scooped her into his arms, kicking the door shut behind them. He laid her on the bed and stripped off his clothes with eager hands, gaze locked on her. Rachel shimmied out of her dress, anticipation thrumming through her veins.

Finally, gloriously naked, Jaxon covered her body with his. The solid weight of him was intoxicating. His arousal pressed against the apex of her thighs.

"I love you," he rasped, voice rough with passion. "So damn much."

She lifted her hips, wordlessly begging him for more.

With a groan, Jaxon entered her in one smooth thrust. Rachel cried out at the sweet invasion, nails digging into his back. He began to move, slowly at first, then picking up speed as ecstasy mounted inside them.

The world faded away until there was only Jaxon-his hands, his lips, his body joined with hers. Rachel let herself drown in the sensations, in the love and intimacy passing between them.

When release came, it was shattering, leaving them breathless and sated in each other's arms. Rachel smiled up at Jaxon, utterly content.

"Best picnic ever," he said with a grin, kissing her.

She laughed. "I couldn't agree more."

Rachel nestled against Jaxon's chest, relishing the warmth and solidness of his body. His arms came around her, holding her close.

A deep peace settled over her, borne of sated passion and profound love. Here, wrapped up with Jaxon, she felt safe and whole-as if she could stay in this moment forever.

"You're quiet," Jaxon said after a while, his hand stroking her hair.

"Just thinking." She tilted her head up to meet his gaze. "About how much I love you. How you make me happier than I ever dreamed I could be."

His eyes softened. "You do the same for me, sweetheart. You're the best thing that's ever happened to me." He kissed her gently. "With you, I can be the man I want to be. The man you deserve."

She smiled, blinking back tears. "You already are that man, Jaxon. You have the biggest heart of anyone I know. I'm the lucky one."

"We're both lucky," he said gruffly. "To have found each other. To have this."

She nodded, throat tight. They had overcome so much to arrive at this place of peace and joy. The scars of their pasts would never fully fade, but together they had healed in ways she hadn't thought possible.

"I want this forever, Rachel," Jaxon said softly. "You and me. If you'll have me."

Joy bloomed inside her, as radiant as the sunrise. "Yes," she whispered.

She drew lazy circles on his skin with her fingertips, marveling at how far they had come. At how he had stormed into her life and turned everything upside down, shaking free the constraints of the world she had so carefully built around herself.

At first, it had been overwhelming. Terrifying, even. But Jaxon had been patient, helping her open up to new experiences. Showing her that there was more to life than the predictable routine she clung to.

With him, she had learned to embrace the unknown. To welcome adventure and follow her heart. She had discovered strength and passion she never knew she possessed, and a capacity for love deeper than any ocean.

"You helped me break free. Showed me that it was okay to want more, to reach for it." Her eyes shone with tears. "You gave me my wings, Jaxon. You taught me how to fly."

His expression softened. "You always had it in you, sweetheart. I just helped you see what was already there."

"You did more than that," she said. "You changed my life. You made me want to live it fully, fearlessly, the way you do. I'm so grateful for you, for us, for the woman I've become because of you."

Jaxon cupped her face, wiping a stray tear from her cheek. "The woman you are is amazing, Rachel. You did that. I just stood by your side while you blossomed."

"We did it together," she said. "Like we do everything else."

"Together," he echoed, and kissed her with tender promise. The future was theirs to explore, side by side, and she couldn't wait to see all the wonders it held in store.

18

The Green Devils had finally gotten some intel and the Wolverines would pay for their mistakes. The harsh growl of motorcycles roared outside as Jaxon stared at the map spread across the scarred oak table. His knuckles were white where they gripped the edge, rage simmering in his gut like acid.

The Wolverines had crossed a line this time. They'd ambushed Slick as he was leaving the clubhouse, brutally beating him before he could get a swing in. Now his best friend was fighting for his life in the ICU, and Jaxon was out for blood.

"We've got their location," Marcus said, tapping a spot on the map. "According to Dirk, they've been receiving shipments of illegal firearms for months. Probably stockpiling them."

Jaxon's jaw clenched, rage spiking. The bastards were gearing up for war. He should have seen this coming.

"We'll hit 'em with everything we've got," he said, voice rough. "Take out as many as we can and destroy their supplies. They won't be causin' trouble for a long damn time after this."

Marcus's eyes glinted with grim satisfaction, loyalty etched into the lines on his weathered face. "You got it, boss."

Jaxon stared at the map, heart pounding as he imagined the chaos that would ensue. The sting of smoke and gunpowder, the shouts and screams, the metallic taste of blood.

The Wolverines had left him no choice. They would learn not to fuck with the Green Devils.

And if a few of his own men didn't make it out alive? That was the price of protecting what was his. Jaxon gritted his teeth, knuckles cracking.

The Wolverines signed their own death warrant. Now it was time to deliver.

Jaxon stood, pushing away from the table with a scrape of wood on concrete. "Mount up," he ordered, gaze sweeping over his men. "We roll out in ten."

The room erupted into action as the bikers jumped to obey. Jaxon stalked outside, tugging on his cut and sliding a cigarette between his lips. His arm stung where a bullet had grazed him during their last run-in with the Wolverines when they tried some shit, a reminder of how dangerous this life could be.

How dangerous he could be.

Jaxon lit his cigarette and took a deep drag, exhaling a cloud of smoke. Once they hit the Wolverines' clubhouse, there would be no going back. They would be at war, a point of no return that would likely end in blood and death.

But some things were worth fighting for. Worth dying for.

Like family. Like honor. Like the cut he wore, the patch that bound him to something greater than himself.

Jaxon flicked away his cigarette as the rumble of motorcycles shattered the night. His men pulled up, an army of leather and chrome, weapons glinting under the pale glow of the moon.

"Time to go to work," Marcus said, face obscured by his helmet. Jaxon nodded and swung onto his bike, the familiar power thrumming between his legs.

"Move out!" he bellowed, twisting the throttle. The formation of bikes surged forward as one, tearing off into the darkness. Toward their destiny.

Toward war.

The Wolverines' clubhouse came into view, a ramshackle building at the end of a long dirt road. Jaxon killed his headlight and rolled to a stop, the rest of his men flanking him. An eerie silence hung over the compound, as if the enemy were lying in wait.

Jaxon's instincts screamed danger. His arm throbbed in warning.

"Something's not right," Marcus said, voice low. "Place looks deserted."

Before Jaxon could respond, a shot rang out, shattering the quiet. A bullet whizzed past his head as all hell broke loose.

"Ambush!" someone shouted as the Wolverines emerged from the darkness, unleashing a hail of gunfire.

Jaxon dove behind his bike for cover, peering around the back tire.

Pain exploded in his arm and he jerked back, cursing. Hot blood seeped between his fingers—he'd been hit. The bullet grazed him, but it was enough. He gritted his teeth against the pain, refusing to show weakness. His men were counting on him.

The familiar rage bubbled up inside, blinding him. How dare these bastards attack his family? He would make them pay. Jaxon grabbed his spare gun from his saddlebag and leapt up, squeezing off several shots. Two Wolverines dropped as the rest scrambled for cover.

They wanted a war? He'd give them one.

Jaxon ducked behind a stack of crates, reloading his gun with a practiced hand. His arm was on fire, but he pushed the pain aside. Staying alive was all that mattered now.

"We're pinned down!" Marcus shouted over the roar of gunfire. "What's the play?"

Jaxon peered around the crates, searching for an opening. They were outnumbered, but he wasn't about to surrender. Not when lives were on the line.

"Flank 'em from the left," he ordered. "Move!"

Marcus nodded and waited for an opening, then sprinted along the side of the warehouse. Jaxon unleashed a barrage of bullets, forcing the Wolverines to take cover.

A scream rang out as Marcus's gun barked twice in succession. Jaxon's lips curled into a snarl. One less bastard to deal with.

The gunfire slowed as both sides regrouped. An eerie silence descended over the compound, broken only by the moans of the wounded. The smell of blood and gunpowder hung heavy in the air.

Jaxon's chest heaved as he caught his breath. He spared a glance at the bodies littering the ground, a mixture of his men and the enemy. They'd paid dearly for this fight.

"Bastards retreated," Marcus said, emerging from the shadows. "Guess they've had enough for one night."

Jaxon nodded, jaw clenched. "We won tonight, but the war's just begun."

His gaze hardened as he stared into the distance.

Something's not right...

19

Rachel sighed as she just finished checking on Slick, knowing this wasn't going to stop anytime soon. This war between the Green Devils and the Wolverines was never ending.

As Rachel cleaned up the emergency room, a loud bang rang out in the distance, followed by shouting and screaming. Her heart dropped as she ran outside to see members of the two gangs exchanging gunfire right in the middle of the hospital parking lot, bullets ricocheting off walls and vehicles.

Panic rose in Rachel's chest as a bullet whizzed past her head, the sound of its trajectory ringing in her ears. She ducked behind a car, her breathing rapid. When would she learn to stay out of trouble?

Rachel risked a glance around the car, only to see a massive brawl break out, gang members tackling each other to the ground as they swung punches and kicked wildly. She flinched as the sounds of grunts and yells filled the air, along with the metallic scent of blood.

Her heart pounding, Rachel weighed her options. She couldn't stay here, but she didn't know if she could make it back inside without getting injured in the process. As another bullet ricocheted off the car near her head, she made up her mind. She had to risk it. Taking a deep breath, Rachel prepared to run back into the safety of the emergency room, hoping to avoid the line of fire. She just wanted to escape this chaos alive.

Rachel bolted from behind the car. A scream caught in her throat as a bullet grazed her leg, slicing through her flesh. She stumbled but kept running, fueled by adrenaline and terror.

She dragged herself toward the emergency room, gritting her teeth.

Rachel took a deep, shuddering breath and steeled herself. She couldn't fall apart now, not when there were people counting on her. People who needed her help.

She pushed off the wall and went back inside the clinic, grabbing supplies from the cabinets and shelves. Antiseptic, gauze, bandages, stitches, painkillers—her hands flew over the instruments of her trade with practiced efficiency.

When she returned to the waiting area, the rest of the injured club members fell silent, watching with a mixture of wariness and respect as she approached.

Rachel ignored them, focusing only on the injuries that needed tending. A gash across a forehead, already crusted with blood. Bruised knuckles and split skin. A dislocated shoulder that needed to be set.

She worked methodically on each wound, cleansing and bandaging, setting bones with a sharp tug that made her patient grunt in pain. The familiar routine helped calm her frayed nerves, and soon she sank into the task at hand, losing herself in the details of each injury.

Cleanse. Bandage. Stitch. Repeat.

Gradually the waiting area emptied, until only Jaxon remained, slumped in a chair in the corner. His gaze was heavy on her as she worked, but he didn't speak, allowing her the space she so desperately needed.

When she finished wrapping a bandage around his ribs, her hands lingered on his bare skin. She felt the steady thump of his heartbeat beneath her palms, and warmth flooded her at the intimacy of the contact.

As she sorted through the mess of gauze and antiseptic, a wave of dizziness washed over her. She gripped the edge of the table, knuckles turning white, and sucked in a sharp breath.

Not now. Please, not now.

But it was too late. The familiar panic rose in her chest, clawing at her insides like a wild beast. Memories flashed behind her eyes, images of blood and broken glass and her mother's lifeless body—

Rachel stumbled back, chest heaving. She couldn't breathe. She was going to be sick.

She had to get out of here. Now.

Before she could stop herself, she turned and fled from the room.

20

Jax lunged forward as Rachel bolted, agony ripping through his battered body. "Rachel, wait!"

But she was already gone.

Jax collapsed back against the chair with a grunt, cursing under his breath. He should have seen this coming. He knew about her past, her trauma—he should have realized this would be too much for her.

Guilt and concern twisted in his gut as he thought of her out there, distressed and alone. He had to go after her. Now.

Summoning his strength, Jax pushed to his feet. The room tilted and spun, his injuries screaming in protest, but he gritted his teeth and stumbled toward the door.

Rachel needed him. He would crawl to her on his hands and knees if he had to.

Jax lurched outside, scanning the parking lot for any sign of her. Panic clawed at his throat when he couldn't spot her right away.

Then he saw a flash of movement near the tree line.

Rachel was leaning against a large oak, shoulders hunched as she hugged herself tightly.

Jax limped toward her as fast as he could, wincing with every step. By the time he reached her, he was breathless and trembling.

Rachel's eyes were squeezed shut, her chest rising and falling rapidly. "I'm sorry," she whispered. "I'm so sorry."

"Shh, don't apologize." Jax cupped her face in his hands, tilting her chin up so she had no choice but to meet his gaze. "Just breathe for me, okay?"

She nodded jerkily and drew in a shaking breath. Jax stroked her cheek with his thumb, his touch gentle and grounding. "That's it," he murmured. "Nice and slow. I'm right here."

Gradually, Rachel's breathing evened out. She sagged against him, the panic fading from her eyes, and Jax wrapped his arms around her in a fierce embrace.

Jax held Rachel until her trembling subsided and her breathing returned to normal. Only then did he speak again.

"You've been through hell."

Her eyes welled with tears at his words. "You're too good to me," she whispered. "Far better than I deserve."

"That's not true." Jaxon cupped her face again and leaned down so their foreheads touched. "You deserve the world, Rachel Lewis, and I'm going to make damn sure you get it."

She let out a shaky laugh. "You're impossible."

"So, I've been told." He smiled and brushed his lips over hers in a feather-light kiss. "Now, do you want me to take you home?"

Rachel was silent for a long moment. Then she took a

deep, steadying breath and lifted her chin, meeting his gaze with quiet determination.

"No," she said firmly. "I want to finish what I started."

Jax's heart swelled with pride at her words, and she walked back into the hospital.

Coming up beside him, Marcus let out a low whistle. "She's something else, alright."

Jax, eyes tracking Rachel's retreating figure until she disappeared from view. Only then did he turn back to the task at hand, shaking off the emotions swirling inside him. There would be time for that later, in the privacy of his own thoughts.

For now, he had a job to do. They all did.

21

The next day, before she could take two steps, a dozen pairs of eyes swiveled to face her, wide with shock and condemnation.

Her supervisor, Janine, stood up so fast her chair tumbled backwards. "Rachel, did you really think you could get away with this?"

Rachel froze, her heart pounding. She struggled to keep her expression neutral even as panic rose in her chest. "I don't know what you mean."

"Don't play dumb!" Another nurse, Mel, jabbed a finger at her. "How could you get mixed up with those criminals?"

"They're not criminals," Rachel said through gritted teeth. She balled her hands into fists, digging her nails into her palms. *Stay calm. Don't lash out.*

Janine strode over until she loomed over Rachel, fury etched into the lines on her face. "You've jeopardized everything we've worked for. The reputation of this hospital, the trust of our patients, all for what? Some two-bit biker?" She shook her head. "I expected better of you."

The words struck deep, reawakening Rachel's old insecurities. But beneath the hurt, anger sparked. She lifted her chin and met Janine's gaze squarely. "You don't understand. Jaxon isn't a criminal and who I choose to date in my personal life has no bearing on my work or my ethics."

"Perception is reality," the chief of staff said. "Your involvement with that man reflects poorly on this hospital. We're asking you to end the relationship, for the good of your career and this institution."

Rachel stared at the three of them, anger burning in her chest. They thought they could control her personal life, dictate who she could and couldn't care for. She wouldn't let them.

"I will not end my relationship with Jaxon," she said, her voice trembling with emotion. "And any judgment you make about my character or abilities as a nurse based on that relationship would be unfair and unjustified. Now, if there's nothing else, I have patients to attend to."

She turned on her heel and strode from the room, holding her head high. They could disapprove all they wanted, but she would stay true to herself. And to Jaxon.

Rachel walked onto the floor of the emergency room, her heart pounding. She knew her colleagues were watching, judging. Whispers and sideways glances followed her as she moved between patients.

"I heard she's dating the president of the Green Devils," someone said not-so-quietly. "How can she work here, with criminals and thugs crawling all over the place?"

Rachel bit her tongue until she tasted blood, refusing to give them the satisfaction of a reaction.

As she checked a young boy's blood pressure, her mentor, Dr. Singh, approached her. "Ignore the gossip and judgment,

Rachel. You're a fine nurse, and you know where your loyalties lie."

Rachel offered her a shaky smile. "Thank you. I appreciate your support."

Dr. Singh squeezed her shoulder. "You're welcome. And if anyone gives you trouble over this, you let me know."

Despite the condemnation from her supervisors and colleagues, Dr. Singh's faith in her lifted her spirits. Not everyone had turned against her. She still had an ally here, and she was grateful for that.

Rachel continued her rounds, holding tight to her resolve. She would weather this storm, just as she had so many others in her life. And when she was with Jaxon again, in the comfort and solidarity of his arms, she would know that she had made the right choice. She always had.

22

This was for Rachel. No matter what shit went down, he'd do this for her.

Jaxon rapped sharply on the scarred wooden door, the sound echoing in the musty hallway. His pulse thrummed in his veins, a mix of anticipation and dread.

When the door creaked open, he came face to face with a ghost from Rachel's past. Her father's bloodshot eyes widened in surprise and dismay.

"You've got some damn nerve showing up here after everything on the news... and dragging my daughter into the middle of it," the man growled.

Jaxon curled his lip, fists clenching. "And you've got some making up to do."

"What do you want?" he demanded, scratching at the gray stubble lining his jaw.

Jaxon crossed his arms over his chest, refusing to be baited. "To talk some sense into you. You need to go see Rachel."

"I don't need to do shit," Rachel's dad spat. "Especially not for that ungrateful bitch."

A flare of anger ignited in Jaxon's gut, but he tamped it down. Losing his temper wouldn't do Rachel any favors.

"She's been through hell," he said. "The least you can do is show up for her, if only for a day. Be a man and take some responsibility."

Rachel's dad scowled, sinking into a ratty armchair that let out a puff of dust. "You don't know anything about responsibility. Or about me and Rachel." His lips twisted. "Always sticking your nose in other people's business. Just like your old man."

Jaxon stiffened at the mention of his father, but didn't rise to the bait. He stared at Rachel's dad, willing him to understand. "She needs you. Whether you believe it or not."

Silence fell over the room, thick and cloying. Then Rachel's dad sighed, scrubbing a hand over his face. "I'll think about it," he muttered. "Now get the hell out of my sight."

Jaxon nodded, a flicker of satisfaction curling in his chest. It wasn't much, but it was a start.

He strode to the door, pausing on the threshold. "Don't let her down again," he said. "Or you'll have me to answer to."

With that, he stepped out into the sunlight, a weight lifting from his shoulders. Rachel's dad would come around. He had to.

Jaxon swung a leg over his motorcycle and fired up the engine, welcoming the familiar roar that drowned out his turbulent thoughts. He'd said his piece, planted the seeds—now all he could do was hope that they took root.

Jaxon's grip tightened on the handlebars as he rode away.

He wanted to believe he'd gotten through to the stubborn old man. That Rachel's dad would put aside his pride and do what was right.

The traffic seemed to melt away around him as Jaxon rode back to the clubhouse, lost in his thoughts. He couldn't force Rachel's dad to change as much as he might want to. But if the old man didn't step up...Jaxon would just have to be enough for Rachel.

He'd give her the family she deserved, blood relation or not. His brothers in the MC already considered her one of their own. And Jaxon...

His hands tightened again on the handlebars, but this time in anticipation. From the moment he'd first seen Rachel, he'd known she was special. Known that she could be his if he was patient and played the long game.

And now, it seemed, the pieces were finally falling into place. Rachel's dad was the last obstacle standing between them.

Jaxon hid a smile behind the shield of his helmet. The old man would come around—or Jaxon would make damn sure he regretted the day he'd pushed his daughter away.

Jaxon pulled up outside the clubhouse, gravel crunching under his tires. His brothers were gathered on the front porch, shooting the shit and passing around beers.

Wolf whistled when he saw Jaxon. "Well, look who finally decided to join the party. How'd it go with the old man?"

Jaxon killed the engine and swung off his bike, peeling off his helmet. "He's gonna visit Rachel, I think."

A cheer rose up from the others. Jaxon accepted the beer Thrash pushed into his hands, grinning. It was good to know his brothers had his back. And Rachel's.

"Just like that, huh?" Thrash said. "Bet you had to do some persuadin'."

"A little." Jaxon shrugged, gaze drifting to the line of Harleys parked along the side of the building. His mind was already leaping ahead, trying to guess Rachel's reaction when she opened her door to find her father waiting on the other side.

Would she cry? Throw her arms around the old bastard in joy? He hoped to God she'd call him after, happiness bubbling in her voice as she told him the news.

"You did good, brother," Wolf said, clapping him on the shoulder. "Real good."

Jaxon nodded, swallowing a mouthful of beer. Maybe he had. But until he saw the results with his own eyes, he'd reserve judgement.

For Rachel's sake, he hoped her father wouldn't let her down again. But if he did...Jaxon would be there to pick up the pieces.

Always.

23

Rachel walked into the cozy cafe, her thoughts still consumed by Jaxon. She closed her eyes for a brief moment, remembering the feel of his calloused hands on her skin and the warmth of his breath against her neck.

A familiar voice called out, "Rach, over here!"

Daphne waved at her from a table by the window. Rachel wove through the tables and chairs until she reached her friend, giving her a quick hug before sliding into the seat across from her.

Rachel set down her cup, her coffee now cold and forgotten. "I was surprised you wanted to meet her."

"I've got something to tell you!"

Rachel's brows knitted together. "What is it?"

"I'm pregnant! Can you believe it? A little Daphne or Slick running around..."

"He's going to be stoked. Do you wanna know what I'm doing today?"

She cocked her head. "Please tell."

Daphne's eyes lit up with excitement. "A tattoo!"

She had never considered getting a tattoo before. The idea seemed so foreign, yet...appealing. A permanent mark to symbolize her devotion to Jaxon.

"I know a great tattoo parlor downtown," Daphne said. "We could go there right now if you want."

Rachel glanced out the window at the gloomy sky, steeling her nerves. "Let's do it."

The rain was pouring down in sheets by the time they left the coffee shop, the cold seeping into Rachel's bones. Her anxiety spiked at the thought of getting a tattoo, but she steeled her resolve. This was for Jaxon. She would endure any pain for him.

After a harrowing drive through the storm, they finally arrived at the tattoo parlor. Rachel's heart hammered as she walked through the doors, gripping Daphne's hand like a lifeline.

The tattoo artist, a burly man covered in intricate tattoos himself, greeted them with a friendly smile. "Welcome to Ink & Roses Tattoo Parlor. What can I do for you ladies today?"

Rachel took a deep breath and squeezed Daphne's hand. "I'd like to get a tattoo."

"Wonderful!" The artist rubbed his hands together. "Did you have a design in mind?"

Rachel described the tattoo she envisioned: two red hearts intertwined with green ivy. The red and green represent the passion Jaxon had brought into her world.

"A beautiful design," the artist said. He sketched a draft on the parchment for her approval.

Rachel's eyes welled with tears at the sight of it. "It's perfect."

"Have a seat and we'll get started." The artist prepared

his tools, the buzz of the tattoo gun filling Rachel with trepidation.

She sat in the chair and extended her arm, glancing over at Daphne for support. Daphne smiled encouragement. "You've got this."

The first prick of the needle sent a spike of pain through Rachel's arm. She gritted her teeth, clutching the armrests. *You're doing this for Jaxon. The pain will be worth it.*

With every pass of the needle, she thought of Jaxon. His kind eyes, his warm smile, the way he made her feel cherished and alive. The pain began to fade into the background, overshadowed by her love for the man who had captured her heart.

When the artist finally finished, Rachel gazed in wonder at the tattoo adorning her arm. Two red hearts intertwined with green ivy, the symbol of her eternal love for Jaxon Jones.

Rachel and Daphne stepped outside the tattoo parlor, sunlight warming their faces as they emerged from the dim interior.

"We can celebrate with margaritas!"

Daphne pointed to her stomach. "Pregnant, remember?"

"Oh yeah, then mocktails!"

They headed to Daphne's car.

Just as they reached the car, a black van screeched to a halt beside them. The doors flew open and three men leapt out, grabbing Rachel and Daphne.

Rachel screamed, terror flooding her senses, but a meaty hand clamped over her mouth. She scratched and bit at her captor, panic overwhelming her usual need for control.

Daphne was putting up a fight too, kicking and punching, but the men easily subdued them both. As Rachel was dragged into the back of the van, she caught a glimpse of Daphne, her eyes wide with fear.

The doors slammed shut, enveloping them in darkness. Rachel pounded on the walls, screaming for help even as rough hands pinned her down.

Her heart raced as the van accelerated forward. Where were they taking them? She struggled against her captors, but she was no match for their strength. All she could do was pray for rescue, her new tattoo burning on her arm like a beacon, calling out for Jaxon through the inky blackness.

Rachel refused to give up hope. Jaxon would come for her. She knew it in her bones.

The van swerved around a corner, sending her tumbling across the floor. Her shoulder slammed into something hard, pain exploding through her arm. She bit back a cry, not wanting to give these bastards the satisfaction.

The van finally slowed and came to a stop. Doors opened, light flooding in, and rough hands hauled her out.

She squinted against the glare, taking in her surroundings. An abandoned warehouse, crumbling brick and broken windows. And Jaxon - oh thank God, Jaxon was here, fury etched into every line of his face.

Her heart nearly burst with relief even as confusion filled her. Why was Jaxon here? How had he found them so fast?

But as her eyes adjusted to the light, she realized with dawning horror that it wasn't Jaxon at all. This man was a stranger, tall and broad, his cold eyes glinting with menace. Her stomach dropped, icy fear flooding her veins.

"Welcome," the man said. "You'll be staying here for a while."

Rachel renewed her struggles, panic threatening to overtake her, but escape was impossible. They were well and truly trapped.

She exchanged a terrified glance with Daphne, who was pale and shaking, her eyes wide with fear.

The man stepped closer, reaching out to grasp Rachel's chin. She jerked away, but strong hands held her in place.

"Feisty," the man purred. "I like that in a woman."

Revulsion rolled through her and she spat in his face.

He backhanded her so hard her head snapped to the side, pain exploding across her cheek. "You'll learn respect, little girl."

She surged forward, slamming her forehead into his nose. There was a satisfying crunch and a howl of pain. Blood gushed between his fingers as he clutched at his face.

The men holding Daphne let go, rushing to help their leader. Daphne stumbled back, grabbing Rachel's arm. "Come on!"

They ran for the open doorway, heart pounding. If they could just make it outside, get help...

A gunshot rang out, the bullet whizzing past Rachel's head.

"Stop right there," the man snarled, pistol aimed at them. His nose was a mangled, bloody mess, eyes blazing with fury. "You'll pay for that, bitch."

Rachel and Daphne froze in their tracks, chests heaving. There was no escape, not now. They were well and truly at this psycho's mercy.

24

Jaxon's heart dropped to his stomach as his brother slammed the door of the clubhouse open. His eyes were wild, chest heaving.

"They took Rachel and Daphne."

The words echoed in Jaxon's mind. His hands curled into fists, knuckles cracking.

"Who?" he growled. Though he already knew.

"The Wolverines. Jasper from the tattoo shop just called me."

Jaxon saw red. His blood roared in his ears as a maelstrom of emotions tore through him—rage, fear, desperation. Rachel. He had to get to her.

He stalked to his bike, fingers tight around the handlebars. She was out there, in the hands of those animals. Cold terror seized his heart at the thought of what they might do to her.

Rachel.

He kicked the bike to life, the engine snarling beneath

him. Whatever it took, he would shred every last Wolverine to pieces to get her back.

The bike shot forward, a bullet racing toward its target. His brothers followed close behind, a thunder in his wake.

Rachel. Her name was a chant in his mind, a prayer on his lips. He'd burn the whole world down before he'd let them hurt her. She was his, and he would come for her.

Always.

Jaxon pulled up outside the Wolverines' warehouse, gravel spraying under his tires. His brothers fanned out behind him, headlights cutting through the darkness.

He killed the engine and dismounted, the air heavy with the scent of smoke and gas. His men had done their job well. Flames licked up the side of the building, tendrils of fire dancing behind the windows.

Shouts and curses rose from inside, accompanied by the crackle of gunfire.

Jaxon strode toward the entrance, adrenaline and purpose steeling his nerves. He signaled his men forward and kicked in the door.

The interior was chaos. A dozen Wolverines scrambled to evacuate, coughing and swearing. Jaxon raised his gun and fired, the retort of the shot echoing off the metal walls.

A dark figure dropped to the ground, the others whirling with weapons drawn.

Jaxon's men flooded in behind him, returning fire. He ducked behind a stack of crates, scanning the room. Where was she?

"Jaxon!" a familiar cry rang out. His head snapped up, gaze searching. There, on a catwalk above—Rachel. Her hands were bound, her face pale and terrified. Beside her stood Dom with a gun to her head.

Dread flooded Jaxon's veins, cold and sharp. He straightened, raising his hands.

"That's far enough, Jones," he growled, "or the bitch gets a bullet in the brain."

Jaxon's heart slammed against his ribs. After everything, he couldn't lose her, just like his sister.

"Let her go," he said, voice low and steady. "This is between us."

The man bared rotten teeth in a sneer. "I don't think so." He ground the muzzle of the gun into Rachel's temple, and her eyes fluttered shut.

Jaxon's world tilted on its axis. No. He wouldn't—he couldn't—

"Please," he rasped. All his life, he'd never begged for anything. But for Rachel, he'd get on his knees.

He met her gaze, willing her to look at him. To stay with him.

"I'm here," he said softly. "I'm right here."

Her eyes opened, luminous in the firelight. A tear slipped down her cheek.

Jaxon held her gaze, his heart in his throat. They had come so far, survived so much. It couldn't end like this.

He took a step forward, hands still raised. "Take me instead."

The scarred man sneered. "How noble. But I think I'll keep the girl."

He yanked Rachel against him, pressing the gun to her head—

A shot rang out, and he crumpled, lifeless. Rachel tumbled forward.

Jaxon lunged to catch her as she fell, clutching her to his

chest. She was shaking, sobbing into his neck. He smoothed her hair, murmuring in her ear.

"Shh, baby, it's over. I've got you now. You're safe."

The fire raged around them, but in the circle of his arms, all was still. Rachel lifted her head, eyes shining.

"You came for me," she whispered.

He brushed the tears from her cheeks. "Always."

Stepping out, Jaxon stumbled upon the gruesome scene, his boots splashing in the puddles of crimson blood seeping into the cracked concrete. Dirk and Slick lay motionless, eyes glassy and unseeing, bullet holes marring their foreheads.

Daphne was huddled over Slick's body, sobs wracking her petite frame. Her hands fluttered uselessly over his chest, as if she could will his heart to beat again through the sheer force of touch.

Jaxon's stomach roiled at the sight, bile and rage churning into a toxic slurry. He'd known Dirk and Slick since they were kids running wild in the streets. They were family.

And now they were gone.

He dropped to his knees beside Daphne, pulling her into his arms. She clung to him, her tears soaking into his cut. "Shh, I got you," he murmured. But his gaze remained fixed on Marcus's pale, lifeless face.

The crunch of boots on gravel made him look up. Liam strode toward them, his face grim. As the new president of the Wolverines, he was the only one who could have pulled off something like this.

Jaxon gently extricated himself from Daphne's hold and rose to his feet. Liam was the one who shot Dom. His own brother. "You better have a damn good explanation."

Liam's mouth twisted. "Dominic was never going to stop,

and neither were you. You wanted him dead for murdering your sister. That's done. Now, we need to move forward and put all the ambiguity between us in the past. Now that I'm the President, things will be done differently."

Jaxon turned to Daphne. She was still huddled on the ground, her body wracked with sobs.

He reached down and grasped her elbow, pulling her to her feet. "Let's get you home."

She sagged against him, her tears soaking into his shirt. He held her close.

"We should get out of here." He nodded at his bike. "Can you ride?"

Daphne nodded shakily. Jaxon helped her onto the back of Thatcher's bike as the engine roared to life. "Let's get you home."

25

After everything, Rachel's heart raced as she caught sight of Jaxon sitting alone on their usual bench at the park, his broad shoulders silhouetted against the dusk.

She quickened her pace, a tumult of emotions surging through her. Love and longing. Fear and uncertainty. But beneath it all was a deep-rooted certainty — she couldn't imagine her life without Jaxon.

"Jaxon." His name escaped her lips in a soft whisper as she came to a stop before him.

He looked up, his piercing blue eyes locking onto hers. A slow smile spread across his face and he stood, pulling her into his arms. "You came."

"Of course I came." She breathed in his familiar scent of leather and spice, melting into his embrace.

He cupped her chin and tilted her face up to his. "It's been a chaos of a week for both of us, it seems."

Tears sprang to her eyes as she gazed into his eyes.

"You'll always have me." He brushed his lips over hers, a feather-light touch that sent sparks dancing across her skin.

"We'll get through this together, just like we get through everything else."

She smiled, winding her arms around his neck to pull him closer. "Together," she whispered, before claiming his mouth in a searing kiss.

She pulled away, heart pounding as she gazed into his eyes. Now was the moment of truth.

"Look," she said, raising her arm to show him the tattoo. "I got this for you. A symbol of my love, and my commitment to facing my past so I can build a future with you."

His eyes widened as he took in the tattoo, fingers gently tracing the ink on her skin. "Rachel," he breathed, emotion thickening his voice. "You didn't have to do this."

"I wanted to." She smiled up at him.

Jaxon tensed, his hand dropping from her wrist. She could see the conflict in his eyes.

"I know it's difficult to face our pasts," she said gently. "But we can't move on until we do."

He pulled her close again, enveloping her in his warmth. She could feel the tension easing from his body as he relaxed into her embrace. "You're right. I'm ready to face him."

"When?" Jaxon asked.

"Now."

"That's my girl," Jaxon said with a grin. He slung an arm around her shoulders, pulling her close against his side as they began the walk to her car.

Rachel relaxed into his embrace, drawing strength from his solid presence. The path ahead would not be easy, but Jaxon would be there to guide her. Together, they could face any challenge. Even the ghosts of the past.

They reached Rachel's car, but neither of them moved to

get in. An awkward silence fell as the weight of what was to come settled over them.

Rachel bit her lip, anxiety churning in her stomach. What if her dad didn't want to see her? What if the wounds of the past were too deep to heal? She stared unseeing at the ground, her breaths coming in short, sharp gasps.

A finger tilted her chin up. Jaxon gazed down at her, his eyes filled with understanding and compassion. "It's going to be okay."

She threw her arms around him, clinging to his solid strength. He wrapped her in a fierce embrace, his warmth seeping into her bones and calming her frayed nerves.

After a long moment, Rachel pulled back with a shaky smile. "Thank you. I don't know what I'd do without you."

Jaxon brushed a stray lock of hair from her face. "You'll never have to find out." His lips curved into a teasing grin.

Rachel laughed, the tension in her chest easing. Trust Jaxon to know exactly what to say to lift her spirits. She squeezed his hand and moved to get into the driver's seat, determination overriding her anxiety. This was a new chapter waiting to be written. And she was ready to face it with her heart full of love - for herself, for her past, and for the man who made her whole.

"See you after," Jaxon said, closing the door behind her.

She started the engine, meeting his gaze through the open window. A soft smile curved her lips.

Rachel drove off, her hands tightening around the steering wheel. She took a deep breath, centering herself. *You can do this.*

In the rearview mirror, she saw Jaxon's figure grow smaller until he disappeared from view. The loss left an ache in her chest, but also a quiet strength. She wasn't alone. Not anymore.

The road stretched endlessly ahead, both familiar and strange. So much had changed since the last time she traveled down this path. She was no longer the frightened girl running from her past, with no one to turn to and nowhere to go. Now she had a home. She had love. And she was ready to face the ghosts that had haunted her for far too long.

Rachel arrived at the old farmhouse as the sun dipped below the horizon, painting the sky with vibrant shades of red and gold. The familiar sight evoked a swell of bittersweet nostalgia. So many memories, good and bad, were etched into the weathered wood and stones of her childhood home.

She got out of the car on unsteady legs, her heart pounding. For a long moment, she simply stood there drinking in the sight. Then a figure emerged from the house, and she froze.

It was her dad. Older, more careworn, but unmistakably him. He paused at the top of the steps, staring at her with a complex mix of emotions flickering over his face.

Rachel opened her mouth, a thousand thoughts and feelings crowding her mind, but only one word came out.

"Dad?"

26

Rachel walked through the sliding glass doors, filling her with a surge of purpose. She was home. After weeks of uncertainty, the familiar routines of the ER soothed her frayed nerves. The controlled chaos, the steady beep of monitors, the purposeful rush of nurses and doctors moving from one critical patient to the next—it all gave her a sense of belonging.

Rachel moved to the nurse's station and reviewed the files. Gunshot wound in room 3, heart attack in room 4, multi-car accident victims in rooms 6 through 8.

Her fingers tightened around the files as a spike of adrenaline shot through her. This was what she lived for. The chance to help people at their most vulnerable, to use her skills to save lives and stitch broken bodies back together.

She hurried to room 3, her sensible heels clicking efficiently against the linoleum floors. "How's he doing?" she asked the doctor, stitching up the gunshot victim.

"BP is stabilizing. We need to monitor for internal bleeding."

Rachel nodded, all business. "I'm on it."

As she helped prep the patient for a CT scan, a fierce joy bloomed inside her chest. Jaxon had shown her a side of life she'd never known, a wildness and passion that both thrilled and frightened her. But this—this was her true calling. Helping those who needed it most. Using her gifts to make a difference. Rachel smiled, feeling more at peace than she had in a long time. She was exactly where she was meant to be.

That evening, Rachel's phone buzzed with a text from Jaxon. "Meet me outside."

She found him waiting on his motorcycle, his piercing blue eyes peering out from under his leather cut. Her heart skipped a beat at the sight of him.

"Get on," he said with a jerk of his chin.

"What are we doing?" But she was already swinging her leg over the seat behind him, wrapping her arms around his waist.

The engine roared to life beneath her, vibrating through her body. "You'll see."

Jaxon took them to the poorer side of town, where run-down tenements crowded together and trash littered the streets. He pulled up outside a community center and killed the engine.

"What is this place?" Rachel asked.

"They provide meals and services for homeless folks and poor families. But they're short-staffed tonight. I thought we could volunteer to help serve dinner."

Rachel stared at him, stunned. "You want to volunteer?"

He shrugged. "We're gonna change things around here. Might as well start now."

Joy and purpose flooded Rachel again, mingling with her

affection for this complicated man. She leaned in and kissed him soundly. "Let's get to work."

Inside, they donned aprons and helped ladle stew into bowls, carry trays for those who couldn't, and clear away dirty dishes when people had finished eating.

Rachel looked at the hope and gratitude on people's faces and felt Jaxon's hand squeeze hers, his eyes reflecting the same emotions.

They were making a difference together. And in that moment, Rachel knew this was exactly where they were both meant to be.

Epilogue

Three years later...

The rev of Rachel's motorcycle rumbled through her as she pulled up outside the steel door of the Green Devils' clubhouse. She killed the engine and swung her leg over the bike, the familiar ache in her lower back barely registering.

After a twelve-hour shift at the medical center, her scrubs were wrinkled and stained with traces of antiseptic, a far cry from the tailored leathers she now wore as an old lady of the club. She ran a gloved hand through her windswept hair and took a deep breath of the crisp night air, scented with the aroma of cigarettes, motor oil and stale beer that meant she was home.

Home. The word still felt foreign to her tongue, eliciting a mix of fear and longing in the pit of her stomach. She shook off the feeling and walked towards the door, the heavy thud of her boots grounding her in the present.

The clubhouse was smoky as always, filled with the raucous laughter and drunken shouts of her brothers. Their eyes followed her as she made her way to the bar. A sea of respect, lust and brotherly affection. She nodded at a few of them; her gaze settling on Jaxon in the corner.

He was watching her with those piercing blue eyes, a slow smile curving his lips. Her heart skipped as warmth flooded her cheeks. After all these years, his gaze still had the power to unravel her, stripping away the layers of control and composure she clung to.

"Hard day at work, darlin'?" His gravelly voice was laced with concern as he enveloped her in a hug, the familiar scent of leather and spice enveloping her senses.

She sighed and sank into his embrace, the tension seeping from her body. "Nothing I can't handle."

His chest rumbled with laughter. "That's my girl."

A smile tugged at her lips as she breathed him in. She was home.

Jaxon pulled away reluctantly, his hands lingering on her waist. His eyes were soft with affection as he gazed down at her, a hint of nervousness flickering in their depths.

Her brow furrowed. "What is it?"

He cleared his throat, shoving his hands into the pockets of his leather cut. "There's something I've been meaning to ask you."

Her heart lurched. "Yes?"

For a moment, he seemed at a loss for words. Then he steeled himself and dropped to one knee, grasping her hands. A hush fell over the rowdy crowd as all eyes turned to them.

Jaxon took a deep breath, his piercing gaze holding hers. "Rachel, from the moment I saw you, I knew you were the one for me. You crashed into my life and turned it upside down, in the best way possible." His voice shook slightly as he continued. "You bring out the best in me and inspire me to be a better man. I want to share my life with you, through all the ups and downs, as your partner in crime, and as the man who will always be there to hold you when you fall."

Her vision blurred as tears welled up in her eyes. Her heart swelled, overflowing with love for the man kneeling before her.

"Rachel Lewis, will you marry me?"

She smiled through her tears, joy suffusing every inch of her being. "Yes, Jaxon. Yes, I will marry you."

The clubhouse erupted into cheers and whistles as Jaxon surged to his feet, crushing her in a searing kiss. Their future was uncertain, but as long as they were together, she knew they could weather any storm.

Rachel was dimly aware of the raucous congratulations around them, the Green Devils swarming forward to clap Jaxon on the back and hug her tightly. But at that moment, all she could see was Jaxon, his eyes alight with joy and love as he gazed at her.

He cupped her face in his hands, brushing away the tears with his thumbs. "I love you so damn much," he rasped, his voice thick.

She reached up and curled her hands around his wrists, anchoring herself to him. "I love you too. More than I ever thought I could love anyone."

Jaxon crushed her against him again, nearly lifting her off her feet. The ring on her finger glinted under the dim lights of the clubhouse, a symbol of the new life they would build together.

Rachel closed her eyes and breathed in the familiar scent of leather and spice, her heart full to bursting. They had a long road ahead, filled with challenges and obstacles to over-come. But they would face it all together, side by side, bonded as partners against the world.

Jaxon pulled back and took her left hand, gazing at the engagement ring now adorning her finger. He brushed his thumb over the diamond, a soft smile curving his lips.

"It's perfect," he said, his voice rough with emotion. "Just like you."

Rachel's heart skipped a beat at the tender look in his eyes. She curled her fingers around his, clinging to the solid warmth of his hand. "I love it. And I love you."

Jaxon's smile widened. "C'mon, let's get out of here." He tucked her hand into the crook of his elbow and guided her toward the exit, the Green Devils whistling and catcalling behind them.

Rachel ducked her head to hide her blush, feeling almost dizzy with happiness. The cool night air was a shock to her overheated skin as they stepped outside, the sounds of the clubhouse fading into the distance.

Jaxon swung her up onto his bike, sliding on behind her and kicking the engine to life with a roar. The familiar vibra-tion sang through her veins as they sped off into the night, the ring on her finger glinting under the moonlight.

Rachel leaned back into Jaxon's embrace, her hands covering his on her waist. The wind whipped her hair and stung her eyes, but she didn't care.

She was going home with the man she loved. The future had never seemed so bright.

The house was dark when they pulled up, but warmth flooded through Rachel at the sight of it. Their home. The place they'd built together through hard work and sacrifice.

Jaxon cut the engine and helped her off the bike, his

hands lingering on her waist. "You ready to celebrate, darlin'?" His voice was low and rough, his eyes gleaming in the faint light from the moon.

Rachel's heart stuttered. "Yes," she whispered.

Jaxon scooped her up into his arms, kicking the front door open. He carried her over the threshold as if it was their wedding night, not stopping until they reached the bedroom.

Moonlight filtered through the window, bathing the room in a silvery glow. Jaxon set her on her feet, his hands coming up to cradle her face. "I love you," he said. "You're the best thing that's ever happened to me."

Rachel's eyes stung. "I love you too." She wrapped her arms around his neck, pressing herself against him. "Thank you for saving me."

"You saved yourself," he said. "You're the strongest, most incredible woman I've ever known. And now you're mine." He kissed her then, deep and slow and thorough, and Rachel gave herself over to the joy and passion of the moment.

The ring on her finger was a sweet, heavy weight, binding them together in a way that went far deeper than any piece of jewelry. They'd walked through the fire to get here, but they'd survived.

Brooks

BROOKS

USA TODAY BESTSELLING AUTHOR
ASHLEY ZAKRZEWSKI

1

Sweat dropped down my brow as I rode my Harley alongside Dax, my Red Devil's brother. We were on a mission to get the debts owed to us by the local merchants, who needed us for their protection.

The weight of my responsibilities bared down on me, like the heavy leather cut I wore on my back. I had an ardent loyalty to the Red Devils and the family we'd built, and I was committed to safeguarding them regardless of the cost.

The shop owner peered out the window as we arrived. He was an older man, balding, with a permanent frown. The bell above the door jingled as we entered, the sound cheerful given the circumstances.

"Good morning, gentlemen," the merchant said, wringing his hands together. "What can I do for you today?"

Dax stepped forward, his voice firm but not unkind. "You know why we're here, Tony."

Tony swallowed hard, beads of sweat forming at his temples. "Well, see...that's the thing. The Pistons came by last week, offering their protection for half the price you guys charge."

My blood boiled at the mention of the Pistons. Those bastards had been encroaching on our territory for months now, trying to undermine our authority and steal our business.

"Is that so?" I asked. Tony flinched at the tone, regretting bringing them up.

Dax's voice, steady and relaxed, cut through the tense silence. "Look, Tony, we've been protecting your business for ten years now. You haven't had a single robbery or break-in under our watch. Can you put a price on that kind of security?"

I watched as Tony's eyes darted between us, his mind wrestling with the decision. He wasn't a bad guy - just another merchant trying to make ends meet. But in this world, loyalty was everything.

"Besides," Dax continued, "you know what happens when people switch sides. The Pistons might offer you a better deal now, but when they can't hold up their end of the bargain, it'll cost you more than money."

The harsh reality of Dax's words hung heavy in the air. The scales were tipping in Tony's mind as he weighed up the pros and cons of sticking with the Red Devils. I clenched my fists, willing him to make the right choice.

Tony let out a shaky sigh and nodded. "You're right. I don't want to risk my livelihood over a few bucks. The Red Devils have always kept me safe, and I don't want to gamble with that." He rummaged behind the counter and pulled out an envelope, handing it over to Dax.

"Good choice, Tony," Dax said, patting the man's shoulder before pocketing the envelope. It wasn't a warm gesture, but it spoke volumes about the bond between the Red Devils MC and the merchants we protected.

"Thanks, fellas," Tony murmured. "I appreciate what you do for me." As much as I wanted to offer him some reassurance, actions spoke louder than words.

"Stay safe, Tony," I said before turning and walking back towards the door. The bell jingled again as we stepped out into the sunlight, the tension of the situation dissipating.

"Another one down," Dax muttered as we mounted our bikes. I nodded, revving my engine in agreement. It was a small victory, but every bit counted in the ongoing battle against the Pistons.

"Damn Pistons," I growled, my grip tightening on the handlebars of my bike. "They're getting bolder by the day."

Dax glanced over at me, his brow furrowed. "You're damn right, brother. We can't let them keep trying to push us out like this. They think they can just waltz in and steal our territory? Not on my watch."

A burning anger resonated deep within my gut. The Pistons were trying to undermine everything we'd built over the years... it was infuriating.

"Tony's been with us for years, and now they want to take him away from us?" I shook my head, disbelief coursing through me. "What happened to loyalty, huh?"

"Seems like money talks louder than loyalty these days," Dax said bitterly. "But not everyone can be bought, Brooks. Tony made the right choice in sticking with us. We've proven time and time again that we can protect him and his business."

"Still, it's not enough," I grumbled, my jaw clenched. "We need to put an end to their little games before they cause actual problems for us."

"Agreed." Dax nodded. "We'll bring it up with Hawk when we get back to the clubhouse. He needs to know what's going on."

The thought of facing our President with this news wasn't comforting, but we had to do something about the Pistons' encroachment. Our club's reputation and livelihood were at stake.

"Let's hit the road," I said, eager to put some distance between us and the merchant's shop. We needed to focus on the task at hand, and that meant making sure the rest of our merchants knew who they could truly rely on.

"Right behind you, brother," Dax replied, his tone resolute. With a roar of our engines, we sped off down the street, our determination fueling us forward.

As we rode, a nagging feeling came over me. This would not be an easy fight. The Pistons were becoming bolder, and it was only a matter of time before they crossed a line that would lead to bloodshed. We'd have to stand strong and united if we wanted to protect what was ours—no matter the cost.

Dax and I pulled into the Red Devil's MC clubhouse. The weight of the day's events bore down on me, my fists clenching around the handlebars. We'd gone to collect debts from local merchants, only to find that our rival gang, the Pistons, had been encroaching on our territory.

"Damn Pistons," Dax muttered under his breath as we parked our bikes. The sound of our engines echoed in the parking lot, a low growl fading away until it disappeared. The gasoline odor mixed with sweat and leather permeated the room.

"Let's get this over with," I said, my voice heavy. I knew we needed to inform our President about the Pistons' bold move, but part of me dreaded his reaction. The tension between our clubs had been steadily building for the better half of two years, and this could be the spark that ignited an all-out war.

Dax nodded, and together, we entered the clubhouse. The familiar sights and sounds filled my senses - the low murmur of conversations, the clink of glass bottles, the flicker of neon lights. But the atmosphere was charged.

"Brooks, Dax," our President, Hawk, called out, motioning us over to where he sat. His dark eyes narrowed as he studied our faces, sensing the urgency in our approach. "What's going on?"

"The Pistons have been offering protection to our merchants at a lower price. They're trying to take our turf." I said, struggling to keep my anger in check.

Hawk's eyes flashed with cold fury. The space we were in seemed to get smaller, the air growing thicker and hard to take in.

"Those bastards," Hawk growled, slamming his fist on the bar top. The sound echoed through the clubhouse like a gunshot, silencing all other conversations. "We've been protecting these people for years, and they think they can just waltz in and steal what's rightfully ours?"

"We reminded him of our record," Dax interjected, his voice tight. "He agreed to stick with us, but we need to make sure this doesn't happen again."

Hawk nodded, his jaw clenched as he considered our words. "We need to send a message to the Pistons that we won't back down."

His gaze swept over both Dax and me, and a surge of adrenaline coursed through my veins. We were the Red Devils, and we would not be pushed around.

"Let's show them who they're messing with," I said, my anger boiling over. The tension in the room was palpable. Every member of our club united in their determination to protect our territory and our family.

"Damn right," Hawk agreed, rising from his chair. "We'll plan our next move tonight. They'll regret crossing us."

As we prepared for the confrontation ahead, my thoughts turned to Tina and Kennedy, the two most important people in my life. I'd do anything to keep them safe, even if it meant going to war. For them, for the Red Devils, we'd face whatever challenges lay ahead, our brotherhood unbreakable. And together, we'd make the Pistons pay.

2

The sun was setting as I stood in front of the Red Devils clubhouse, my heart pounding. It hadn't been an easy decision to make, but it was necessary. Our club's survival depended on it. I took a deep breath and clenched my fists, knowing that what I was about to do would test every ounce of my loyalty and determination.

"Brooks," Hawk called out to me from behind, his voice tense but steady. "You sure you're up for this? Delivering the message to Scar ain't gonna be a walk in the park."

I turned to face him, meeting his concerned gaze. "I'm good," I replied, my voice firm. "The Pistons need to know we won't back down. They've been pushing us too far for too long."

Hawk nodded. "All right, then. We'll have your back, just in case things go south. But I'd rather not spill any blood tonight if we can help it."

"Me neither," I agreed. The weight of responsibility settled onto my shoulders. "But they need to understand that we won't give up our territory without a fight."

"Damn straight," Hawk said, slapping me on the back. "Now let's get ready. The meeting's set for tonight at that old warehouse on the outskirts of town. Neutral ground."

"Neutral ground" - I couldn't help but snort at the idea. There was nothing neutral about the tension between the Red Devils and the Pistons. This meeting would be anything but friendly.

"Let's arm up, boys!" I shouted to the rest of the gang, who were gathered around, watching us. "We're heading into enemy territory, and I don't want anyone caught off guard."

As the men dispersed to grab their weapons, I glanced at my own holster, feeling the reassuring weight of my pistol tucked securely against my side. It wasn't that I wanted to use it, but I knew the Pistons wouldn't hesitate if they saw an opportunity.

"Hey," Hawk said, his voice low as he approached me. "I know you've got a lot on your mind with all this, but remember, we're doing this for our family. For the club."

I nodded, swallowing hard. "Yeah, I know. I just... I hope this is the right move."

"Me too," he admitted, his eyes dark and serious. "But I trust you, Brooks. And I know the rest of the guys do, too. We'll get through this. Together."

With that, we turned and followed the rest of the Red Devils out of the clubhouse, each step bringing us closer to the unknown dangers that awaited us at the warehouse - and to the man who could either be our salvation or our downfall: Scar.

The roar of our engines echoed through the night as we rode down the desolate stretch of highway. The wind whipped against my face, but it did nothing to alleviate the unease that settled in my gut. Hawk rode beside me, his unwavering presence a reassurance I couldn't put into words.

"Almost there," he shouted over the noise.

"Hope Scar's ready for this," I muttered.

The warehouse loomed ahead, its hulking shadow falling across the cracked pavement like a dark omen. As we cut our engines and coasted to a stop, I could feel the tension among the Red Devils thickening, an electric charge pulsing through the air.

"Stay sharp," I warned them, my eyes scanning the perimeter for any signs of danger. "And remember, we're here to talk. Don't start something unless they do."

"Got it, Brooks," one guy grunted, his hand resting on the butt of his gun.

We dismounted, boots crunching on gravel, and approached the entrance to the warehouse. As the massive metal door creaked open, I steeled myself for whatever lay inside, my heart hammering in my chest.

"Showtime," Hawk muttered, and I nodded.

The Pistons were already waiting for us, their icy stares fixed on our approaching group. Scar stood at the forefront, arms crossed over his chest, an unreadable expression on his face. My fingers twitched near my holster, instincts screaming at me to be ready.

"Brooks," Scar said, his tone icy. "Didn't think you'd have the balls to show up."

"Cut the crap, Scar," I shot back, not allowing him to rile me up. "You know why we're here."

"Of course I do," he replied, smirking. "But that doesn't mean I have to like it."

"None of us do," I pointed out, feeling the weight of my

responsibility as I faced off with our rivals.

"One of us has to back down," he countered, his eyes narrowing.

"Is that what you're suggesting?" I asked, my voice tight with barely-contained anger.

"Maybe," Scar said, glancing at the Raptor, their President with a wicked smile playing on his lips. "Or maybe I just wanted to see how far you'd go to protect your precious club."

"Farther than you can imagine," I growled, my hand moving closer to my gun as the tension between us reached a boiling point.

"Enough with the posturing," Hawk interjected, stepping forward alongside me. "We're here to talk territory."

"Talk? You mean demand?" Scar sneered, his voice dripping with disdain.

"Call it what you want," I replied, my jaw clenched. "Fact is, we won't give up an inch of our territory. Stay out of it, or there'll be consequences."

"Is that a threat?"

"Consider it a promise," Hawk spat back.

Scar studied us for a moment, his eyes flicking between Hawk and me. The air between the two groups was thick with tension, like a powder keg waiting for a match. I could feel the Red Devils behind me, their presence a solid wall of support.

"Don't think we'll just sit back and let you control everything. If you won't share, we'll take."

"Over my dead body," I muttered, my heart pounding.

"Maybe it'll come to that," Scar said, a sinister smile spreading across his face.

As if on cue, the distant wail of sirens pierced the night.

Both groups glanced nervously in the direction of the approaching sound, the tension momentarily forgotten.

"Damn it," Hawk cursed, his eyes darting between the Pistons and the direction of the sirens. "This isn't over."

"Agreed," Scar said as he signaled for his gang to mount up. "Next time we meet, it won't be so... civil."

"Let's get out of here," I said to my brothers, feeling a mixture of relief and frustration. We had avoided bloodshed tonight, but the war between our clubs was far from over.

As we sped away from the warehouse, the sirens growing louder, I couldn't help but think about what lay ahead. The Pistons were relentless, and they wouldn't stop until we were defeated. Hawk and I needed a plan to put an end to this once and for all.

"Next time won't be so easy," I murmured to myself, my resolve hardening. "We'll finish this."

The clubhouse door slammed shut behind us, its echo the only sound breaking the hushed tension that had followed us from the warehouse. My boot heels clicked on the concrete floor as I walked to the bar, pouring myself a shot of whiskey. The burn in my throat felt insignificant compared to the fire burning within me; my heart pounded with anger and frustration.

"Brooks," Hawk said, joining me at the bar. His face was grim, mirroring my own feelings. "We can't let those Pistons bastards keep pushing us around. We need to make a stand."

I downed another shot before responding. "You're right. But what's our next move?"

"Hit 'em where it hurts," Hawk suggested, his eyes narrowing. "We need to show them that the Red Devils aren't to be messed with."

"Agreed," I said, slamming the empty shot glass onto the

counter. The sound echoed through the room, drawing the attention of our brothers, who were scattered throughout the clubhouse. They looked at us expectantly, waiting for direction. "But we have to be smart about this. No more wasted opportunities."

"Exactly," Hawk nodded, rubbing his chin thoughtfully. "What if we went after their supply chain? They've been moving in on our territory, trying to cut into our profits. If we hit them there, they'll know we mean business."

"Cut off the head of the snake," I murmured, the idea taking root in my mind. "If we cripple their income, they won't have the resources to keep this up."

"Damn straight," Hawk agreed, a fierce determination settling over him. "They think they can just waltz in and take what's ours, but we'll show them what happens when you mess with the Red Devils."

"Alright then," I said, raising my voice so that everyone could hear. "Listen up, brothers. We've got a plan to put those Pistons in their place. It's time to remind them that this is Red Devil's territory, and we won't back down without a fight."

"Damn right!" came the chorus of voices, our brothers rallying around us, ready to defend our family and our club.

"Let's get to work," I said, my heart swelling with pride and determination. "We'll show them what happens when you mess with the Red Devils."

As we began to strategize and prepare for our next move, the room filled with the energy of purpose. We were united, our bond stronger than ever. The Pistons had underestimated us, but they would soon learn the true strength of the Red Devils. And when all was said and done, there would be no question who ruled these streets.

3

I watched my little girl, Kennedy, twirl around in her princess dress. Today was her fourth birthday, and we'd gone all out for our princess. She giggled, running toward me with open arms.

"Look, Daddy!" she exclaimed, tripping over the hem of her gown. I caught her just in time, lifting her into the air.

"Careful there, sweetheart," I said, a smile spreading across my face. "You're the star of the party. Can't have you taking a tumble."

Kennedy beamed up at me, her eyes sparkling with excitement. "Thank you for the bestest birthday ever, Daddy!"

I hugged her tight, a warmth in my chest that only my family could bring. I set her down, watching as she raced off to join the other kids in the bouncy house.

The backyard was alive with color, laughter, and the unmistakable scent of freshly baked cupcakes. Tina, my wife, had outdone herself. Streamers hung from tree branches, creating a magical canopy above the tables filled with finger foods, drinks, and an assortment of sweets. Balloons dotted the landscape, their vibrant hues lending an air of whimsy to the celebration.

The centerpiece of the party was the bouncy house, a fortress constructed entirely of inflatable walls and floors. The children's laughter rang through the air as they bounced and played within its confines. Kennedy's friends, dressed in their own princess gowns and superhero capes, ducked and weaved through the castle.

Nearby, a long table draped in a pastel pink tablecloth held stacks of plates, cups, and utensils. Parents mingled amongst themselves, sipping on cold lemonade or snacking on the treats Tina had prepared. A sense of joy and contentment filled the air, and for a moment, I could almost forget the harsher realities of life.

"Hey, Brooks," Tina called from across the yard. She was standing behind the cupcake table, her apron covered in a dusting of powdered sugar. Her eyes were bright, her smile infectious. I couldn't help but grin back as I made my way over to her.

"Need some help?" I asked, already reaching for a tray of cupcakes.

"Always," she replied, nudging me with her hip. "Just be careful not to drop them."

"Me? Drop something?" I feigned offense. "I'll have you know I have the steadiest hands in town."

She rolled her eyes, laughing softly. It was moments like these that I cherished the most—just being able to enjoy each other's company without any outside interference. Together, we carried the trays of cupcakes to the main table, the sweet aroma wafting through the air as we walked.

The moment the cupcakes were set down, I felt a strong

slap on my back and turned to see my brothers, Dax, Ryder, and Ace. Their leather jackets bearing the Red Devils MC insignia seemed out of place amidst the pastel-hued birthday decorations, but their grins were as genuine as ever.

"Happy birthday, little princess!" Dax boomed, bending down to give Kennedy a bear hug. She giggled, squirming in his arms until he set her down with a chuckle.

"Thanks for coming, guys," I said, clapping each of them on the shoulder. "Means a lot."

"Wouldn't miss it for the world, brother," Ryder replied, his eyes softening as he looked at Kennedy bouncing excitedly between her uncles. "She's growing up so fast."

"Too fast," I agreed, feeling a pang of melancholy mixed with pride. My little girl was getting older, and there was nothing I could do to slow down time.

"Ah, don't go getting all sentimental on us now," Ace teased, punching me lightly in the arm. "We're here to celebrate, remember?"

"Of course," I snapped back into the present, allowing a smile to spread across my face. "Let's get this party started."

Tina joined me, slipping her hand into mine and intertwining our fingers. She leaned in for a quick kiss, whispering, "I love you" before pulling away. Our connection was electric, even after all these years, and I couldn't help but feel grateful for the life we'd built together.

"Alright, everyone!" Tina called out, garnering the attention of the children and adults alike. "It's time to sing 'Happy Birthday' to Kennedy!"

As our family and friends gathered around the table, arms' draped over shoulders, I felt my daughter's small hand grasp mine. She looked up at me with those big, innocent eyes—the same ones that reminded me every day of what I was fighting for.

"Ready, sweetheart?" I asked her, my voice cracking slightly under the weight of emotion.

"Ready, Daddy!" she exclaimed, her excitement infectious. The room filled with the sound of laughter and singing as we celebrated Kennedy's birthday. For a moment, the outside world ceased to exist, and all that mattered was the love between us.

It was a fleeting sense of peace, one I knew wouldn't last forever. But in that moment, surrounded by family and friends, I allowed myself to truly cherish it. We were in this together, and no matter what challenges lay ahead, our love would keep us strong.

With the sound of "Happy Birthday" fading, Kennedy's excitement shifted to the bouncy house that I'd set up earlier in the backyard. She dragged me by the hand, her eyes shining with anticipation.

"Come on, Daddy! Bounce with me!" she squealed as we approached the massive inflatable castle. The other children had already begun to jump around, their laughter ringing through the air like a chorus of happiness.

"Alright, sweetheart," I agreed, feeling my own heart swell with joy at the sight of her beaming face. We stepped into the bouncy house together, and as I watched her bounce up and down with unbridled enthusiasm, I knew that these were the moments I lived for.

"Higher, Daddy, higher!" Kennedy shouted, giggling as I tossed her into the air. She soared before landing among the cushions, her laughter infectious. I couldn't help but join in, forgetting for a moment the darkness that loomed beyond this celebration.

"Look at you two," Tina called out from outside the bouncy house, snapping a photo of us mid-air. Her smile was genuine, a testament to the love we shared as a family. I caught her eye and grinned, silently thanking her for capturing this memory.

"Your turn, Mommy!" Kennedy insisted, pulling Tina into the bouncy house with us. As the three of us jumped together, our laughter mixing with that of the other children, I felt an overwhelming sense of love and contentment. This was our sanctuary, a place where we could briefly escape the chaos and danger that threatened to consume us.

"Alright, gang, time for another game!" Dax shouted, clapping his hands and herding the kids out of the bouncy house. They squealed with excitement, their faces flushed from exertion and pure joy. I held Kennedy's hand as she stumbled out, her energy seemingly endless.

"Did you have fun, sweetheart?" I asked, my voice warm with affection.

"Best day ever, Daddy!" she beamed, wrapping her small arms around my neck. As I hugged her tightly, I knew that I would do anything to protect this little girl and the love she brought into our lives.

"Promise me something, Kennedy," I whispered in her ear.

"Promise what, Daddy?" she asked, her eyes wide and curious.

"Promise that you'll always keep smiling," I told her, a lump forming in my throat as I considered the uncertain future we faced.

"Promise, Daddy," she whispered back.

As we gathered around the picnic table, all eyes on Kennedy as she excitedly tore into her presents, I couldn't help but chuckle at the pure joy radiating from her little face. The sun cast golden rays across the backyard, dappling the grass with warm light. The sound of children's laughter filled the air, along with the sweet scent of vanilla frosting from the freshly baked cupcakes.

"Man, she's really racking up the gifts, huh?" Ryder teased, playfully nudging me in the ribs.

"Looks like you've gone soft on us, Brooks," Ace added, smirking beneath his beard.

"Hey, it's just a birthday party," I replied defensively. "Can't a man spoil his daughter a little?"

"Of course, brother," Dax chimed in, slapping me on the back. "Just don't forget who you are. Red Devils MC and all that."

"Trust me," I said, meeting each of their gazes with a smile. "I haven't forgotten."

Kennedy let out a delighted squeal as she unwrapped yet another toy, her happiness contagious. My brothers and I exchanged grins, our rough exteriors momentarily softened by the affection we felt for this little girl.

"Alright, enough teasing," Tina said, shooting a playful glare at my brothers as she approached. "Brooks may be a tough biker, but he's also an amazing father, so lay off."

"Relax," Ace replied, raising his hands in surrender. "We're just messing around."

"Besides," Dax added, winking at Tina, "we know how much you two lovebirds adore your little princess."

"Damn straight," I agreed, reaching out to squeeze Tina's hand. I couldn't deny the love that bound the three of us together — a fierce, unbreakable bond that gave us strength in even the darkest of times.

"Alright, everyone," Tina announced to the gathered children. "Time for cake and ice cream!"

The kids cheered, racing towards the table where a beautifully decorated cake awaited. Kennedy's bright blue eyes sparkled with anticipation as she stood on her tiptoes to get a closer look. The backyard hummed with a sense of serenity, a calm oasis that seemed far removed from the brewing storm that lay just beyond our reach.

"Happy Birthday, Kennedy," I whispered, brushing my thumb across her soft cheek. Her giggle was a balm to my soul, reminding me of all that I had to fight for—and all that I would risk to protect this family that meant everything to me.

The laughter of Kennedy and her friends filled the air as they excitedly devoured their cake and ice cream. I couldn't help but smile at the sight, my heart swelling with pride for my little girl. Tina stood beside me, her hand resting on the small of my back, a comforting presence.

"Hey, Brooks! Toss me a beer, will ya?" Ryder called out from across the yard, disrupting our intimate moment.

"Sure thing!" I shouted back, grabbing a cold one from the cooler and lobbing it over to him with ease. His hand shot out, catching it effortlessly before he cracked it open and took a swig.

"Nice throw," he said with a nod of approval.

"Years of practice," I admitted with a chuckle, watching as my brothers joked around and chatted with the other party guests. It was moments like these—when we were all together, not a care in the world—that I cherished the most.

My phone buzzed in my pocket, and I frowned at the unfamiliar number on the screen. "Excuse me, babe," I murmured to Tina, stepping away to answer the call.

"Brooks, it's Marty from the shop," the voice on the other end said urgently. "We've got a problem."

"Spit it out, Marty. What's wrong?" I asked, my grip on the phone tightening as my gut churned with unease.

"Someone hit the shop last night, broke in and cleaned us out," he explained, his voice shaky with fear. "They left a message, Brooks. It's the Pistons."

My heart raced, my blood boiling with anger as my mind raced through the implications of this betrayal. The Pistons had just declared war, and I'd be damned if I let them get away with it.

"Alright, Marty," I said, struggling to keep my voice level. "I'll take care of it. Sit tight."

As I hung up the phone, I felt the weight of the situation settle on my shoulders. Our peaceful oasis had been shattered, and now I had to face the storm that was about to descend upon us all.

"Brooks?" Tina questioned, concern etching her face as she noticed the change in my demeanor. "What's wrong?"

"Nothing we can't handle, babe," I replied, forcing a smile for her sake. But as I looked around at the joyous faces of our family and friends, I couldn't shake the feeling that everything was about to change—and not for the better.

4

The sunset cast an array of colors as I stood on the porch, feeling the weight of my Red Devil's MC cut on my broad shoulders. The worn leather and the emblem on my bicep were constant reminders of the brotherhood I belonged to - the life I led outside these walls.

"Daddy!" Kennedy squealed, rushing over to wrap her tiny arms around my leg. Her laughter was music to my ears, soothing the rough edges of my soul.

"Hey there, princess," I said, ruffling her hair.

"Uh-huh," she nodded. "Uncle Zane is here!"

My brother-in-law was in the MC with me and was one of the few people I shared a bond that ran deeper than blood. As I entered the dining room, I found Zane leaning back in his chair, grinning at me.

"Long time no see, bro," he said, reaching out for a fist bump. I obliged, smirking as we knocked knuckles together.

"Good to see you too, man," I replied, taking my seat at the head of the table. Tina placed a steaming dish of lasagna in front of us, the aroma making my mouth water. We bowed our heads as she said grace, then dug into the delicious home-made meal.

"Hey, Zane," I started, my fork clattering against my plate. "How's life treatin' ya?"

"Same old, same old," he replied, wiping sauce from his bearded chin. "Can't complain."

"Good to hear," I said, raising an eyebrow at him. I knew there was more to it than that, but now wasn't the time to pry. Instead, I focused on enjoying this peaceful evening with my family.

"Brooks," Tina said, placing a hand on my forearm. "Are you okay? You seem...distracted."

"Me?" I shook my head, forcing a smile. "Nah, I'm good. Just tired, is all." My gaze met hers, and for a moment, I felt a flicker of concern hidden behind her beautiful eyes. But just like that, it was gone, replaced by a reassuring smile.

"Alright," she whispered, squeezing my arm before turning back to her meal.

As the evening wore on, my thoughts couldn't help but drift to my responsibilities beyond this peaceful sanctuary. Being a slinger for the Red Devils MC meant I had to collect debts from those who owed the club—a necessary task that provided financial stability for my family. It wasn't the kind of job I ever pictured myself doing, but it demanded my unwavering loyalty and fierce protectiveness toward those I loved.

"Brooks," Tina called out, breaking me out of my reverie. "Can you help me clear the table?"

"Sure thing, darlin'," I replied, rising from my seat and stacking plates in my arms. As I carried them over to the sink, I noticed Kennedy playing with her toys by the fireplace, her laughter filling the room like music. My heart swelled with love, and I knew I would do anything — face any danger — to keep her safe.

"Is everything all right?" Zane asked, his voice low as he leaned against the kitchen counter, concern etched on his face.

"Never better," I responded, setting the plates down with a clatter. "Just got a lot on my mind."

"Club stuff?" he inquired, his brow furrowing.

"Always," I said with a sigh, knowing there was no point in hiding it from him. "But it's nothing I can't handle."

I glanced over at Tina as she wiped down the table, her delicate hands moving with grace. Even though she didn't know the extent of my involvement with the club, she could sense when something weighed heavily on me. But she never pushed; she trusted me enough to handle whatever came our way.

"Promise me you'll be careful," Zane urged, his voice barely audible.

"Of course," I reassured him, clapping a hand on his shoulder. "I'm not going anywhere."

My phone buzzed in my pocket. Glancing down, I saw an incoming call from the President. My heart raced as I excused myself and stepped onto the back porch to take the call.

"Brooks," Duke greeted me. "We've got a situation brewing. We need you down here."

"Understood," I replied, my grip tightening on the phone.

"Good," he said, ending the call.

As I pulled on my leather jacket again and prepared to leave, I couldn't help but feel the weight of my responsibilities—not just to the Red Devils MC, but to my family as well. It was a delicate balancing act, and one wrong move could send everything tumbling down.

But for now, all I could do was face whatever challenges lay ahead, hoping that my loyalty and determination would be enough to keep my loved ones safe from harm.

As I mounted my Harley, the foreboding darkness enveloped the once peaceful evening. It hung heavy in the air, like a storm cloud threatening to unleash its fury upon us.

"Whatever's coming," I thought to myself, "I'll face it head-on."

With a deep breath, I revved the engine and sped off into the uncertain future.

5

I was sitting at the worn wooden bar, the steady hum of conversations and laughter filling the Red Devils MC clubhouse, when my phone buzzed in my pocket. Pulling it out, I saw Tina's name flash on the screen. My gut tightened -- she knew better than to call me while I was at the clubhouse, unless it was important.

"Hey, babe," I said, trying to keep my voice casual. "What's up?"

"Brooks," Tina's voice trembled, raw with fear. "They're here. There are three men, masked, with guns. They broke into our house."

My heart slammed against my ribs, adrenaline flooding my veins. I could hear her labored breathing, punctuated by muffled sobs. The surrounding room seemed to fall away, replaced by a cold, primal need to protect my family.

"Where are you?" I asked, my voice low and urgent. "Are you safe? And where's Kennedy?"

"I'm hiding in the closet with Kennedy. She's terrified,

Brooks." A sob cracked her voice. "I don't know what they want. They're tearing through the house–"

"Stay hidden, stay quiet," I instructed, gripping the phone so tightly it threatened to crack. My mind raced, already calculating how fast I could get home. "I'm coming, Tina. I'll be there as fast as I can."

"Please hurry, Brooks. I–" Her words were cut off by the sound of a door slamming open, followed by a man's gruff voice shouting orders. The line went dead, leaving only a high-pitched tone echoing in my ear.

"Shit!" I cursed, jumping to my feet and slamming my fist against the bar. Panic clawed at my chest, threatening to consume me whole. My wife and daughter were in danger, and there was nothing I could do but pray that I'd make it in time.

I stormed out of the clubhouse. My bike roared to life beneath me, its familiar vibrations anchoring me to reality.

"Please be okay," I whispered into the wind, willing my bike to fly faster than ever before. "Both of you, just hold on."

The wind roared in my ears as I tore through the streets, pushing my bike to its limits. Every red light was another obstacle between me and my family, but there was no time for caution—only speed and raw desperation.

"Damn it!" I snarled, weaving through traffic like a man possessed. Images of Tina and Kennedy, terrified and alone, flashed through my mind, fueling my determination to reach them.

I rounded the final corner, the tires screeching beneath me, and my heart plummeted at the sight of our home. The front door hung open, splintered wood strewn across the porch like a cruel invitation. I killed the engine and leapt off my bike, sprinting towards the wreckage.

"Kennedy! Tina!" My voice echoed through the empty house, a desperate plea met with silence. Panic clawed at my chest as I took in the chaos surrounding me—overturned furniture, shattered glass, and drawers ripped from their hinges.

"Where the hell are they?" I muttered under my breath, rummaging through the debris. My fingers closed around a small, stuffed unicorn—Kennedy's favorite toy. It was torn and dirty, a testament to the violence that had unfolded in our once safe sanctuary.

"Please, God," I whispered, clutching the tattered toy to my chest. "Don't let them be hurt."

My hands shook with anger and fear as I dialed the police, the cold metal of the phone pressing against my cheek. "My wife and daughter's been taken," I told the operator, voice raw from barely suppressed emotions. "Three men with guns broke in."

"Can you give a description of the men?" The voice on the other line was calm and professional, but it grated on my nerves.

"Masked. That's all I know," I replied, frustrated at how little information I had to offer.

"Stay where you are, sir. Officers are on their way," the operator instructed. I clenched my jaw, the need for action churning inside me like a storm. But I knew that if I wanted to get them back, I'd have to work with the police, at least for now.

Within minutes, sirens wailed in the distance, growing louder as the red and blue lights cut through the dark night. I opened the front door just as the officers stepped out of their cars, their faces grim and focused.

"Brooks?" one of them asked, extending his hand. I nodded, shaking it before getting to the point.

"Three masked men with guns broke into my house and took my wife and daughter,," I said, my voice cracking with the effort it took not to break down completely. The officer's face hardened, and he signaled for his partner to start investigating the scene.

As the second officer started dusting for fingerprints and snapping photos of the chaos that surrounded us, the first officer turned back to me. "Did your wife say if they mentioned anything about what they were looking for?"

I shook my head, memories of Tina's trembling voice playing on repeat in my mind. "No, she didn't. They just took them and left."

"Is there any reason someone might want to target your family?" the officer inquired, watching me closely.

"None that I know of," I replied, my thoughts racing back to the Red Devils MC and wondering if our enemies had somehow found out about my connection to the club. But no, that couldn't be it. The life I led within the MC was separate from my family—I'd made sure of it.

"Alright, we'll do everything we can to find them," the officer promised, his voice steady and reassuring. "We'll be in touch with any updates."

"Thank you," I muttered, my throat tight with a mixture of gratitude and desperation. As the officers finished their investigation and left, I stood alone in the wreckage of my home, the weight of their abduction crushing down on me like a thousand tons.

"I swear, I'm gonna find you," I whispered into the silence, my resolve steeling itself against the darkness.

I paced back and forth in the wreckage of my home, my boots crunching on shattered glass as I clutched my phone like a lifeline. With each step, my heart pounded harder in my chest, filling my ears with a staccato rhythm that mirrored the desperation coursing through me. I could feel the oppressive weight of helplessness bearing down, threatening to crush me beneath its suffocating mass.

"Come on, come on," I muttered under my breath, willing my phone to ring with news of Tina and Kennedy's whereabouts. The silence was deafening, amplifying the void their absence had left behind.

"Brooks!" a familiar voice called out from behind me, shattering the silence like a gunshot. I spun around to see Zane striding toward me, his face etched with concern. "What the fuck happened?" he demanded, his eyes scanning the chaos before him.

"Someone took them, Zane," I replied, my voice breaking with the weight of unshed tears. "Tina called me, said there were three guys wearing masks and carrying guns... and then the line went dead."

"Shit," Zane cursed, running a hand through his hair as the gravity of the situation settled over him. "Have you heard anything since?"

"Nothing," I admitted, shaking my head, frustration boiling over into anger. "The police were just here, but they don't know anything yet either."

"Alright," Zane said, his voice steady and reassuring. "We'll find them, Brooks. I swear it."

"Damn right we will," I agreed, the embers of determination beginning to burn within me. "No one gets away with hurting my family."

Zane clenched his jaw. His eyes filled with a silent promise of retribution.

"Whoever these guys are," I growled, my hands curling into fists, "they just made the biggest mistake of their lives."

6

My heart pounded, a heavy drumbeat as I paced back and forth in the garage. The smell of oil and gasoline hung in the air like a dark cloud, suffocating me with every breath. It had been hours since Tina and Kennedy had disappeared, and all I wanted to do was tear down every door in the city to find them. But I couldn't shake the gnawing feeling deep inside that involving the Red Devils MC could put them in even more danger.

"Damn it," I muttered under my breath, clenching my fists until my knuckles turned white. I leaned on the workbench, feeling the cool metal press against my heated skin. The weight of my decision was crushing me, but I couldn't afford to be reckless. My family's lives were at stake here.

"Brooks." A voice echoed through the garage, snapping me out of my thoughts. I looked up to see Zane, Tina's brother, and one of my closest friends, standing in the doorway. His eyes were filled with concern as he approached me. "Any news?"

"Nothing yet," I replied. I hated the feeling of helplessness that washed over me, but I knew involving the MC could bring hell upon us. If word got out that those bastards took my wife and daughter, there would be no stopping the bloodshed that would follow. The retaliation from the rival gang who kidnapped Tina and Kennedy could escalate the situation into something far more dangerous than anything we'd ever faced before.

Zane studied me for a moment before speaking again. "You know, the MC can help, Brooks. We've got connections all over the city, and they'll do whatever it takes to get them back."

"Or get them killed," I snapped, glaring at him. I knew he meant well, but I couldn't risk it. Not with the lives of my family at stake. "You know what they're capable of, Zane. If we bring the MC into this..."

"Brooks, think about this logically," Zane urged, his eyes pleading with me. "We don't know how much time we have left before... before..." He trailed off, unable to finish the thought.

"Before what?" I demanded, my voice shaking with anger and fear. "Before they hurt them? Kill them? Is that what you were going to say?"

"Of course not!" Zane shot back, his voice strained. "But doing this alone... it's just too risky. We need help, Brooks. We need our brothers."

My chest tightened as I stared into Zane's eyes, searching for any sign that he was wrong. But deep down, I knew he was right. As much as I hated the idea of putting my family in danger, the clock was ticking, and I couldn't waste any more time.

"Brooks, listen to me," Zane began, his voice steady and firm. He grasped my shoulder with a strength that forced me to look at him. "I understand your fears, but we don't have the luxury of time. Tina and Kennedy need us to act now."

I clenched my jaw, bitterness rising within me like bile. I knew he was right, but the idea of involving the MC made my stomach churn. The brotherhood would have my back without so much as a second thought, but I had seen first-hand what happened when you messed with one of our families.

"Think about it," Zane continued, his gaze never leaving mine. "The Red Devils have connections all over the city. They can get us information that the police could never find on their own." He paused for a moment, letting his words sink in before going on. "And you know as well as I do that they're not afraid to get their hands dirty. If things go south, we'll need backup."

"Backup?" I scoffed, shaking my head. "You mean cannon fodder. I'm supposed to send our brothers into this mess just so they can take the bullets meant for my family?"

"Brooks," Zane said, his voice softer now. "What if it were me? What if someone snatched me up, and you had no idea where I was? Would you hesitate to call in the MC then?"

The question hit me like a punch to the gut. My heart raced as I imagined Zane in danger, and I knew without a doubt that I'd do anything to protect him—just like I would for Tina and Kennedy.

"Dammit, Zane," I muttered. "This isn't fair."

"Life's not fair, brother," he replied, his hand still gripping my shoulder. "But we have a chance to make things right. With the help of the MC, we can bring Tina and Kennedy home safely."

As much as I hated to admit it, I couldn't deny the truth

in his words. The Red Devils had resources and manpower that we desperately needed, and time was running out. My hands trembled with a mix of fear and anger as I finally nodded.

"Alright," I whispered, my voice hoarse. "We'll get them involved."

Zane's eyes softened, and he gave me a small nod of understanding. It wasn't an easy decision to make, but it was the one that gave us the best chance at finding my family and bringing them home. With the Red Devils behind us, I felt a glimmer of hope pierce through my despair.

"Let's go find our girls, brother," Zane said, determination etched on his face.

"Damn right we will," I agreed, pushing past my fears and focusing on the task at hand. Together with the help of the Red Devils, we would find Tina and Kennedy and bring them home—no matter the cost.

Sweat dripped down the sides of my face as I stood in front of my brothers. Zane stood beside me, an unwavering pillar of support. The roar of their engines echoed through the garage, a steady rumble that ignited a fire within me.

"Listen up!" I yelled over the noise, my voice cracking with emotion. "My wife and daughter have been taken. We've got reason to believe it might be the Pistons or others that we have pissed off. They won't hesitate to harm them." I paused, letting my words sink in before continuing. "I've always been one to handle my own problems, but I need your help this time. Time is running out, and we can't waste any more of it."

A chorus of murmurs rippled through the group. I could see the concern etched on their faces, their loyalty shining through. These men were my family, and now they'd be helping me save mine.

"Alright, brothers," Zane took over, his authoritative voice cutting through the chatter. "We're going to split up into teams. Some of you will hit the streets. The rest of us will work on tracking down any leads we find."

"Bullet, you and your crew check our contacts. They might have heard something about who's behind this," Zane continued. Bullet nodded, a solemn expression on his face, and gestured for his group to follow him.

"Razor, you take another team and keep an eye on known enemies. See if anyone's acting out of the ordinary or making moves they shouldn't be." Razor, a tall, lanky man with a shock of red hair, saluted before gathering his crew.

"Brooks and I will coordinate everything," Zane said, looking at me for confirmation. I nodded, gripping his shoulder in gratitude. "We'll work together, and we won't stop until we've found Tina and Kennedy."

"Let's ride!" I shouted, my voice filled with determination. My brothers responded with a deafening roar of their engines, the sound sending shivers down my spine.

The smell of stale beer and cigarette smoke lingering in the air. I couldn't help but feel a surge of hope. The Red Devils MC was a force to be reckoned with when united, and seeing them all gathered around me, ready to fight for my wife and daughter, gave me strength.

"Brooks," Zane's voice broke through my thoughts. "You okay, brother?"

I looked into his eyes, which held concern mixed with determination. "Yeah, just...thankful for all of you."

"Hey, we're family," he said, pounding his chest over his heart. "Now, let's go find Tina and Kennedy."

We split up, each team taking their designated routes. As I revved my motorcycle, the roar of the engines around me felt like a battle cry. We were going to war, and I wouldn't rest until I had my family back.

The streets flew by as we raced through the city, our bikes cutting through the night like metallic predators. My mind kept returning to Tina and Kennedy—what they must be going through, how much I missed them.

"Damn it," I muttered under my breath as I took another sharp turn. My resolve hardened, every mile bringing me closer to finding my family.

"Brooks!" Zane shouted through the helmet comms, snapping me out of my inner turmoil. "We got a lead. Sounds like one of Bullet's contacts knows something."

"Where are we meeting?" I asked, my pulse quickening.

"Abandoned warehouse off 5th Street. Let's move!"

We raced through the city, adrenaline pumping through our veins. As we approached the warehouse, I saw Bullet and his crew waiting for us, their faces grim.

"Talked to one of my guys," Bullet began, his voice tense. "He says there's been chatter from the Pistons wanting to make us pay. Who else would be stupid enough to kidnap our Vice President's family?"

"Raptor has no idea what he's done." My hands clenched into fists. "Did you get a location?"

"Still working on that," he replied. "But we're getting closer."

"Good. We won't stop until we find them and make them pay." My voice was a low growl, every word filled with fierce resolve.

"Damn right," Zane chimed in. "We'll tear this city apart if we have to, but we're bringing your family home, Brooks."

As I looked around at the faces of my brothers, their expressions mirroring my determination, I felt an unshakeable sense of purpose. The Red Devils MC were united, and together, we would bring down hell on whoever dared to harm my family.

"Let's ride!" I shouted, the roar of our engines echoing through the night as we set off once more, a relentless force bent on justice.

7

The distant hum of motorcycles filled the air as I stood beside my brothers, Ryder and Zane, in the garage of the Red Devils Motorcycle Club. My gaze traveled from one face to the other, both men worn with worry, their eyes reflecting the weight of the situation.

"Alright, listen up," Ryder said, taking control as the strategic mastermind he was known to be. "I'll use my informants and surveillance equipment to help you find Tina and Kennedy."

"Thank you, Ryder," My gravelly voice was filled with gratitude but laced with a hint of desperation. This wasn't the first time I had relied on Ryder's skills, but this was different. The stakes were higher than ever.

"Let's start with what we know and work our way from there," he suggested, knowing that every second counted. We retreated to his makeshift war room, where maps and photographs covered the walls, and multiple monitors displayed feeds from his extensive network of cameras.

"Ryder, you got eyes all over town, huh?" Zane

remarked, raising an eyebrow at the sheer scale of my operation.

"Information is power," he replied, tapping his fingers against the table. "Now, let's start tracking down leads."

"First things first," I chimed in, eyes scanning the images on the monitors. "We need to gather information about the Pistons'."

"Agreed," he said. "The guys are already working on it. They've been hitting the streets, talking to contacts, anything they can do to get us closer to finding Tina and Kennedy."

"Any luck so far?" Zane asked, his tone anxious.

"Nothing concrete yet, but we're narrowing it down," Ryder reassured him. "We'll find them."

"Alright," I said, determination setting in. "When did they get bold enough to kidnap rivals families?"

"Let's split up and follow different leads," Zane proposed. "We'll cover more ground that way."

"Good idea," Ryder agreed. "I'll keep an eye on things here and coordinate with my informants. You two hit the streets and see what you can dig up."

Hours turned into days, and we were still no closer to finding Tina and Kennedy. Each lead we followed seemed to dissolve into a frustrating dead end. I could feel the desperation mounting with every fruitless search, every useless tip from an informant. There are too many places they could be and as much as I wanted to just bust down doors until I find them, being stupid and jumping the gun won't make things any better. I have to do this right.

"Dammit," I cursed as I slammed the door of our latest false lead, an abandoned warehouse on the edge of town. "This is getting us nowhere."

"Keep your head up. We'll find them," Ryder said.

"Easy for you to say," Zane muttered under his breath.

As the three of us dove back into the investigation, The weight of responsibility was heavy on my shoulders. We were up against a dangerous rival club led by a ruthless man, and the stakes were higher than ever. But I knew that together, we would stop at nothing to bring Tina and Kennedy home safely. Plus, I'm not one to be scared to get my hands dirty.

The air was thick with tension as we gathered around the table, our eyes locked onto one another. Anger radiated off my brothers, a palpable energy that threatened to consume us all if we didn't channel it into something productive.

"Alright," Ryder said firmly, clenching his fists on the table. "We know The Pistons are behind this, and territory is their motive. But that doesn't mean we go charging in guns blazing. We need a strategy, a plan that'll get Tina and Kennedy back without putting more lives at risk."

"Easy for you to say," I spat, eyes burning with fury. "Those bastards took my family, Ryder. I won't rest until I make them pay."

"Brooks, I understand your pain," he replied, trying to keep his voice steady. "But we can't afford to be reckless. Raptor is a dangerous man, and The Pistons won't hesitate to kill anyone who gets in their way."

"Ryder's right," Zane chimed in, his fists clenched as well. "We all want to bring down Raptor and save Tina and Kennedy. But we have to be smart about it."

"Smart?" I scoffed, slamming my hand down on the table. "While we sit here 'being smart,' my wife and daughter are suffering at the hands of those animals!"

"Enough!" he shouted, silencing the room. "We're not

getting anywhere by arguing. Let's focus on what we do know and work from there."

"Fine," I muttered, still seething but willing to listen. "Let's hear your brilliant plan then."

"First, we need to gather intel on The Pistons' operations and find out where they're holding Tina and Kennedy. If we can pinpoint their location, we'll have a better chance of getting them out alive."

"Okay," Zane said, nodding. "But what about Raptor? The guy's a madman, and he won't go down without a fight."

"True," he acknowledged, mind racing with possibilities. "But if we can find a weakness, something to use against him, maybe we can force his hand and end this without bloodshed."

"Or," I interjected, eyes narrowing, "we could just storm their hideout and take them all out. No more Pistons, no more problems."

"Brooks, you know that's not how this works," he replied, exasperated. "Even if we take them down, another rival club will just fill the void. We need a long-term solution, not a short-sighted act of revenge."

"Ryder's right," Zane agreed, looking at me solemnly. "We need to think bigger than just settling scores. We have to protect our territory, our families, and our future. But we also need to be smart about it, or we risk losing everything."

"Fine," I finally conceded, my anger simmering below the surface. "Let's do this your way. But if any harm comes to Tina and Kennedy... there'll be hell to pay."

They both nodded, understanding the weight of my words. As we moved forward with our plan, the danger of confronting Raptor and The Pistons loomed over us like a dark cloud. But there was no turning back now. We had to save my family, and we had to do it together.

The smell of burnt coffee and cigarette smoke hung heavy in the air as we huddled around a small table, littered with maps, photographs, and hastily scribbled notes. The dim light cast eerie shadows on our faces, highlighting the desperation etched into each of our expressions.

"Alright," Ryder began. "We know that Raptor has Tina and Kennedy in The Pistons' hideout. Our best chance at getting them back alive is to exploit their weaknesses."

"Which are?" I growled, my knuckles white.

"First," Zane chimed in, tapping his finger on a photograph of Raptor, "he's arrogant. He thinks he's untouchable. We need to capitalize on that overconfidence."

"Agreed," he nodded. "If we can catch him off guard, it might give us the window we need to get in and out without being detected."

"Second," Zane continued, "their security system. It's good, but it's not perfect. Ryder, you mentioned knowing someone who could help us bypass it?"

"Right," he confirmed, recalling the conversation he had with his informant earlier. "He's an expert in electronic surveillance, and owes me a favor. He can help us disable their alarms and cameras long enough for us to slip inside."

"Good," I said, my eyes never leaving the photographs. "And once we're in?"

"Divide and conquer," Ryder suggested. "Zane, you focus on finding Tina and Kennedy. Keep your head down and move quickly. Brooks, you and I will create a distraction, keep The Pistons busy so they don't notice Zane slipping through."

"Sounds like a plan," Zane agreed, rubbing his palms together.

"Wait," I interjected, my brow furrowing as I studied the map. "What about their patrols? We need to bypass them too."

"Right," he agreed, leaning in closer to examine the map. "If we can figure out their patrol patterns, we can time our approach to avoid being spotted."

"Or," Zane proposed, his eyes lighting up with an idea, "we can create a diversion elsewhere, something big enough to draw their attention away from the hideout."

"Either way, we'll need eyes on the ground," he said, considering our options. "Someone to keep us informed of any changes in their movements."

"Leave that to me," I offered, determination shining in my eyes. "I know a few guys who owe me a favor. They won't let us down."

"Alright then," he concluded. "We've got our plan. Let's put it into motion and bring Tina and Kennedy home safely."

As we stared at the makeshift battle plans before us, I wondered if we were signing our own death warrants. But there was no other choice. We had to save my family, even if it meant walking straight into the lion's den.

8

The roar of engines reverberated across the desolate landscape as our band of Red Devils MC members, with me at the helm, ventured deeper into enemy territory. The Pistons' turf was a dangerous place for us to be. Zane rode alongside me, his eyes flicking back and forth between the road and the shadows cast by decrepit buildings.

"Stay sharp, boys," I called out. "We don't know what we're walking into here."

"Trust me, I'm ready," Zane replied, his jaw clenched. I knew how much it killed him to think of his sister in danger, and I admired his courage and loyalty to both his family and the club. My heart burned with a fierce determination to protect those I loved—my brothers in the Red Devil's MC and my blood family alike.

As we delved further into The Pistons' territory, the tension between our two rival clubs became palpable. The Pistons had always been angling for control over our lands, and there was no love lost between our two families. We all knew that one wrong move could escalate the situation into an all-out war, and nobody was itching for that kind of blood-shed. But we had to find our missing girls, and if it meant crossing into hostile grounds, then so be it.

"Brooks, you sure about this?" asked one of our brothers, Tank, his burly frame hunched over his bike. I could hear the concern lacing his words, and I knew he wasn't the only one who felt uneasy.

"Nobody's ever sure about anything, Tank," I said, trying to inject some confidence into my voice. "But we've gotta try. For Tina and Kennedy."

"Damn right," Zane chimed in, his voice hard as steel. "No one messes with our family and gets away with it." The others grunted their agreement, and I could see the resolve etched on each of their faces.

As we continued down the desolate road, I couldn't help but feel a gnawing anxiety in my gut. We were in uncharted waters, and every passing minute brought us closer to potential danger. But there was no turning back now—we had come too far, and the stakes were too high. Our loyalty to our family and club demanded that we see this through, no matter the cost.

"Keep your wits about you, boys," I warned as we rode deeper into the heart of The Pistons' domain. "We're in their world now. Let's just hope we can find what we're looking for before they realize we're here."

We neared The Pistons' headquarters. My heart hammering in my chest, and I knew the others felt it too. We were riding straight into the lion's den, but there was no other choice—we had to find Tina and Kennedy before it was too late.

"Keep your eyes peeled, boys," Zane whispered through

the comms, his voice tense. "We don't know what kind of welcome party Raptor has planned for us."

As if on cue, the rumble of approaching engines filled the air, and a group of Pistons appeared from behind a bend in the road, their faces twisted into snarls of pure hatred. They had been lying in wait, and now they had us surrounded.

"Looks like we found our welcome party," I muttered, gripping the handlebars tighter.

"Red Devils," sneered one of the Pistons, a tall man with a scar running down the side of his face. "You've got some balls coming into our territory."

"Give us Tina and Kennedy, and we'll leave without any trouble," I said, trying to keep my voice steady. "We're not here to fight."

"Too bad," spat the scarred biker, pulling out a knife and brandishing it menacingly. "Ace wants you all dead."

"Enough talk," growled Tank, reaching for the shotgun strapped to his bike. "Let's do this."

Shots rang out, metal clashing against metal as we charged toward our enemies. I ducked and weaved through the chaos, adrenaline fueling my every move. I'd been in fights before, but this was different—this was war.

My thoughts raced as I tried to make sense of the battle-field. We needed a plan, something that would give us an advantage in this unfamiliar territory. I remembered a tactic we'd used in the past, one that required precision and timing but had saved our asses more than once.

"Zane," I shouted over the din of battle, "get some of the boys and flank them from the right. We'll hit them from both sides."

"Got it," he replied, nodding before barking orders at a few nearby Red Devils.

As our brothers moved into position, I focused on keeping the Pistons' attention on us. Tank unloaded round after round, forcing them to take cover behind their bikes. The air was thick with the smell of gunpowder and sweat, a potent reminder of how close we were to death.

"NOW!" I yelled, my voice raw as Zane and his team burst from their hiding spots, catching the Pistons off guard. They never stood a chance.

In the skirmish's aftermath, I surveyed the wreckage with a heavy heart. We had won this battle, but at what cost? How many more of these confrontations would we have to face before we found Tina and Kennedy?

But even as the weight of our situation bore down on me, I knew there was no other choice. We would face whatever dangers The Pistons threw at us, using our knowledge and experience to navigate this perilous territory. Because we were the Red Devil's MC—loyal, determined, and willing to do whatever it took to protect our own.

Weary and bloodied, but still standing, we pushed deeper into Pistons' territory. The persistent growl of our Harleys was the only sound that cut through the cold night air, a haunting reminder we were alone in this treacherous land.

"Brooks!" Zane shouted over the rumble of engines, drawing my attention. "Ryder got intel on another possible location. We're heading there now."

"Let's hope it's the right one," I muttered under my breath, my grip tightening on the handlebars.

As we approached the derelict warehouse, I couldn't help but notice the unusual silence that enveloped the area. It sent an unsettling shiver down my spine.

"Something's not right," I whispered to Zane. "Stay sharp."

"Always am," he replied, his eyes scanning the perimeter. With caution, we dismounted our bikes and crept towards the warehouse, my heart hammering in my chest as if trying to break free. As we reached the entrance, Ryder signaled for us to halt.

"Tripwire," he mouthed, pointing at the thin line stretched across the doorway. I nodded, understanding the gravity of the situation. One wrong move, and we'd be blown to bits.

"Tank, can you disable it?" I asked, my voice barely above a whisper.

"Piece of cake," Tank replied confidently, pulling a pair of wire cutters from his vest. With steady hands and expert precision, he snipped the wire, causing my muscles to relax ever so slightly.

"Good work," I praised, clapping him on the back.

"Let's move," Zane urged, taking the lead as we slipped inside the warehouse.

"Keep your eyes peeled for more traps," I warned, my senses on high alert.

"Brooks, look out!" Ryder shouted, his voice echoing through the cavernous space. I barely had time to react before a makeshift net dropped from the ceiling, narrowly missing me. I glanced at Ryder, grateful for his keen eye.

"Thanks," I grunted, my heart pounding as adrenaline surged through my veins.

"Looks like Raptor ain't playing around," Zane muttered, shaking his head.

"Neither are we," I replied with steely determination.

As we searched the warehouse, Raptor would not make

this easy for us. But for every obstacle we faced—tripwires, snipers, even a pit filled with broken glass—we overcame them, using our skills and resources to their fullest extent.

"Damn it," Zane cursed as we reached the final room, only to find it empty. "This isn't where they're holding Tina and Kennedy."

"Then we keep looking," I said, my resolve unwavering. "We won't stop until we find them."

"Agreed," Zane nodded, gripping my shoulder in solidarity.

"Ryder, get us another location," I ordered, my voice laced with urgency. "We're running out of time."

"Understood," he replied, his eyes reflecting the same fierce determination that burned within me.

As we mounted our bikes once more and roared off into the night, I couldn't help but feel the crushing weight of the stakes bearing down on us. Our enemies were relentless, but so too were we. And when it came to protecting our family, there was no challenge too great, no danger too dire, that we wouldn't face head-on.

We were the Red Devils MC, and we would not be defeated.

I pushed open the door to yet another dingy room. My heart raced with adrenaline and fear, each beat pounding in my ears like a war drum. This had to be it. It had to be where Raptor was keeping Tina and Kennedy.

"Damn it," Zane cursed beside me, echoing my own frustration. The room was empty—just like all the others we'd searched.

"Brooks, something's not right," he said, squinting at the floor. "There's no sign of struggle here. No scratches or marks on the walls."

He was right. From the moment we'd entered Raptor's territory, everything had felt off—from the seemingly abandoned warehouse to the eerie silence that hung in the air like an oppressive fog. But I couldn't—wouldn't—let doubt creep into my mind. I glanced over at Zane, his face etched with worry, and knew he felt the same way.

"Ryder, get us another location," I gritted out, my voice barely audible over the roar of blood in my ears. "This is a dead end."

"Copy that, Brooks," Ryder replied through the comms, his tone somber but determined. "Sit tight. I'll find you something."

As we waited, I leaned against the wall, my clenched fists shaking with suppressed rage. Every second we wasted was a second closer to losing Tina and Kennedy forever. The thought sent waves of nausea rolling through my gut, tightening around my heart like a vise.

"Hey," Zane said, placing a hand on my shoulder. His touch was warm, grounding—a lifeline in the storm of my thoughts. "We're gonna find them, man. We won't stop until we do."

I nodded, swallowing hard against the lump in my throat. "I know," I whispered, more to myself than to Zane. "I just can't shake the feeling that we're running out of time."

Ryder's voice crackled through the comms. "There's another building a few miles from your location—an old factory. It's worth checking out."

"Thanks, brother," I muttered, pushing off the wall and heading for the door.

The moon hung low in the sky as we thundered down the deserted road, its pale light casting eerie shadows across the road. The wind whipped through my hair, stinging my eyes and tearing at my clothes like icy fingers. But all I could think about was Tina and Kennedy—their faces, their laughter, their love.

"Stay focused," Zane called out. "We'll find them. We won't let Raptor win."

"Never," I vowed, gripping the handlebars until my knuckles turned white. "We're the Red Devils MC, and we won't back down."

As we raced toward the next location, my heart hammered with renewed determination, fueled by the fierce loyalty that bound us together. We would face whatever challenges lay ahead—and for the sake of our family, we would prevail.

9

The Pistons MC hideout loomed ahead like a fortress, surrounded by chain-link fences topped with razor wire. As I revved my motorcycle's engine, I couldn't help but feel a surge of adrenaline course through my veins.

"Brooks," called out Jake. "you ready for this?"

"Damn right," I replied, gritting my teeth. The thought of Tina and Kennedy being held captive by those Pistons bastards made my blood boil. This conflict had been brewing for far too long, and now it was time to set things straight.

"Remember, we're here to get your family back safe and sound," said Zane, my brother-in-law and fellow Red Devil, as he patted me on the shoulder. "Let's show these Pistons what happens when they mess with the Red Devils."

We approached the hideout. Their gang members sneered at us from behind their fence, itching for a fight. As we dismounted our bikes, their leader stepped forward to meet us.

"Red Devils," he spat, sizing us up with contempt. "Didn't expect to see you here."

"Cut the crap, Raptor. We know you've got Tina and Kennedy." I shot back, fists clenched so tight that my knuckles turned white. "You're gonna hand them over, or you'll wish you never crossed us."

"Ha!" Raptor laughed. "You think you can just waltz in here and make demands? You've got another thing coming."

With that, chaos erupted. The Pistons charged at us with wild abandon, swinging fists and chains. We retaliated with equal force, throwing punches and defending ourselves from their onslaught. The sound of fists connecting with flesh and the grunts of pain filled the air as both sides fought.

Amid the brawl, I glimpsed the building where Tina and Kennedy were being held. It was a dilapidated old warehouse with graffiti-covered walls and broken windows. They reinforced the door with steel, and there were armed Pistons patrolling the perimeter.

"Zane!" I shouted over the noise of the fight. "We need to break through that door!"

"Already on it," he replied, smashing a Pistons member in the face with his elbow before sprinting towards the door.

As I charged ahead, my thoughts raced, fueled by a desperate need to get my family out of there. The hideout may have been fortified, but the Red Devils were relentless. We'd break through, no matter what it took.

"Ready or not, Pistons," I muttered beneath my breath, "here we come."

"Regroup!" I yelled, as the chaos around us reached its peak. The Red Devils and Pistons clashed like two unstoppable forces, but we had to focus on our primary goal: rescuing Tina and Kennedy.

We retreated to a nearby alley, putting some distance between ourselves and the hideout. Zane took charge of outlining the plan. "Listen up, everyone. We need to get Brooks' wife and daughter out of there, and we know they're inside that warehouse."

"Brooks and I will go through the front door," Zane continued, his eyes locked on mine. "We'll use a distraction to draw out the guards. Once we're in, the rest of you will follow in pairs, sweeping the place for any Pistons and securing our escape route."

"Distractions?" asked one of our most experienced members.

"Explosives," I chimed in, feeling my heart rate increase at the thought. "We'll plant them around the perimeter. The explosions will draw the guards away from the warehouse."

"Sounds like a plan."

"Alright," Zane said, clapping his hands together. "Let's gear up."

The Red Devils gathered their weapons and equipment with a sense of urgency. Firearms were handed out, the cold steel a reassuring weight in our hands. We strapped on bulletproof vests, knowing we'd need all the protection we could get. Zane and I each grabbed a small supply of explosives—C-4, to be exact—along with detonators.

"Listen up," I called out, ensuring I had their attention. "We're heading into enemy territory, but we've trained for this. We've survived worse, and we'll survive tonight."

"Damn straight!" Raptor yelled, pumping his fist in the air.

"Remember our creed," Zane added, his voice steady and strong. "'Strength in brotherhood, loyalty above all.' That's what we're fighting for tonight — our family."

"Strength in brotherhood, loyalty above all!" the Red Devils chorused, revving their engines in unison.

With our spirits high, we set off toward the warehouse. A sudden rustling in the bushes caught my attention, and I reached for my pistol. A deer darted across the way.

As we neared the perimeter fence, I signaled for Dax and Tank to hang back. My heart pounded in my ears, drowning out the sound of their idling engines.

"Dax, you're up," I whispered into the comms. "Give us some cover."

"Got it, boss," he responded, lobbing a smoke grenade toward the far end of the compound. The canister hissed as it spewed thick, white clouds, drawing the attention of the guards and sending them scrambling.

"Go, go, go!" I shouted.

My pulse quickened with each step. The knowledge that Tina and Kennedy were so close driving me forward.

"Boss," Dax whispered, crouching behind a crate as two guards rounded a corner. "We got company."

"Leave it to me," I murmured, reaching for the collapsible baton at my side. I crept forward, staying low and silent until I was within striking distance. With a swift, practiced motion, I took them both out, their unconscious forms crumpling to the ground.

"Nice work," Tank said, helping me drag the guards out of sight. "Let's keep moving."

As we approached the warehouse where Tina and Kennedy were being held, I felt a cold knot form in the pit of my stomach. But this was no time for fear or doubt; my family needed me.

"Tank, keep watch," I instructed. "Zane, with me."

"Roger that, boss," they both replied in unison.

We reached the side door of the warehouse, and I couldn't help but think of the risks we were taking. Lives hung in the balance—not just Tina and Kennedy's, but our own as well. Was I leading my brothers into a trap? The thought gnawed at me, but I pushed it to the back of my mind. We had come too far to turn back now.

"Ready?" I asked, my hand on the door handle.

"Always," Zane responded, his eyes steely and determined.

With a deep breath, I turned the handle and slipped inside, my heart thundering with anticipation as we embarked on the final leg of our mission.

As we slipped into the warehouse, the air was thick with tension. The dim glow of a single flickering light overhead cast eerie shadows across the concrete floor. I could hear a distant banging from somewhere deeper in the building— was that the sound of my family fighting for their lives?

10

As we stormed the warehouse, the Red Devils moved with precision, their weapons drawn and ready for whatever the Pistons had in store for them. Their demeanor was everything I'd come to expect from my brothers in arms—focused, fearless, and unwavering in their loyalty to one another. Our bond as a club was stronger than anything the Pistons could throw at us, and we were prepared to lay down our lives if it meant saving Tina and Kennedy from their clutches.

"Brooks! Over there!" Zane yelled, pointing towards a group of Pistons guarding a door on the far side of the warehouse. It didn't take a genius to figure out that was where they were holding my wife and daughter.

"Cover me, I'm going in!" I called back, taking off towards the guarded entrance. My boots slammed against the concrete floor as I charged forward, adrenaline pumping through my veins. I knew the risks, but nothing mattered more than getting my family back.

"Right behind you, brother!" Zane responded, following closely. I could hear the gunfire and shouts of my fellow Red

Devils as they fought to clear a path for us. The weight of their loyalty and the knowledge that we were all in this together gave me the strength I needed to face whatever lay ahead.

"Come on! Is that all you've got?" Raptor sneered from across the warehouse, his voice dripping with contempt.

"Your days are numbered, Raptor!" I spat back, rage coursing through me. "You messed with the wrong family!"

"Your family belongs to us now!" one of the Pistons shouted, aiming his gun in my direction.

"Like hell they do!" Zane roared, firing back at the Piston who dared threaten our kin.

The air crackled with tension as bullets whizzed by and ricocheted off the metal beams above us. The smell of sweat and gunpowder filled my nostrils, a potent reminder of the high stakes we faced in this deadly showdown. My heart pounded in my chest with each step I took towards the guarded door, knowing full well the danger that awaited me.

"Brooks! Keep moving!" Ryder urged, muffled by the cacophony of gunfire and chaos.

"Covering fire!" I yelled out, signaling my brothers to lay down a barrage of bullets as I sprinted forward, dodging and weaving between crates and barrels.

"Watch your six!" Zane bellowed, taking out a Piston who had snuck up behind me. I nodded, reaffirming my resolve to get Tina and Kennedy back.

"Damn it, Raptor, you're going down!" I growled under my breath, cursing the man who had forced us into this perilous situation. But as much as I hated him, I knew I couldn't let my emotions cloud my judgment. Too much was at stake.

"Keep pushing, Red Devils!" Ryder commanded,

rallying our forces as we continued to exchange fire with the Pistons.

"Show these bastards what happens when you mess with our family!" Zane added, his fierce determination fueling our collective efforts.

As the firefight raged on, I couldn't help but think of the sacrifices we'd all made to be part of this brotherhood. The long nights away from our families, the constant struggle for survival—it was a hard life, but one bound by an unbreakable bond. And as bullets flew and bodies fell around me, I knew there was no other group of men I'd rather have by my side.

"Let's finish this!" I shouted, feeling a surge of adrenaline as we inched closer to the door where Tina and Kennedy were held captive. The sounds of gunfire were deafening, drowning out all thought and reason. But amidst the noise and chaos, one thing remained clear: nothing would stop us from saving the ones we loved.

I kept my focus on the door just ahead, pushing through the smoke and sweat of the gunfight. But my vision blurred as I saw a shadowy figure aiming straight for me—an enemy Piston, bent on ending my life.

"Brooks, watch out!" Zane's voice broke through the cacophony, filled with urgency.

Before I could react, Zane lunged forward, his body colliding with mine, shoving me to the ground. The pain in my side from slamming into the concrete was overshadowed by the realization that Zane had just saved me from taking a fatal shot.

"Zane, what the hell—" My words were cut short as the sound of gunfire rang out once more, and this time, I knew it had found its mark.

"Damn it," Zane whispered, clutching at his stomach. "Took one for you, brother."

As I looked into Zane's eyes, I could see the pain he was trying to push down, but also the unyielding determination in him. He'd made a choice—a sacrifice—to protect me, and there was no going back.

"Zane, don't you dare leave us!" I shouted, my heart pounding in my chest. But even as I said the words, I knew that this was the price we paid—the sacrifices we made for our brothers in the Red Devils MC.

"Take care of 'em... Tina... Kennedy..." Zane's breath hitched. "They're all that matters..."

"Zane, stay with me!" I pleaded, gripping his hand, desperate to keep him conscious. But despite my best efforts, I could feel his grip on my hand weakening, his eyes beginning to glaze over.

"Brotherhood... always..." Those were his final words before his eyes closed, and I knew he was gone. My friend, my brother, had given his life for mine—the ultimate sacrifice.

"Rest easy, brother," I choked out through my tears. "I will make this right. I promise."

As I cradled Zane's lifeless body, the weight of his sacrifice bore down on me like a crushing anvil. My eyes threatened to spill over with tears, but I couldn't afford that luxury right now. The battle was still raging around us, the deafening roar of gunfire and the acrid scent of smoke filling the air.

"Brooks!" Dax shouted above the cacophony, his face contorted with urgency. "We have to move! We can't let Zane's death be in vain!"

I nodded, swallowing the lump in my throat, and gently

laid Zane down on the cold warehouse floor. He deserved better than this—we all did. But it wasn't over yet. Tina and Kennedy were still trapped, still in danger. And I had promised Zane that I would protect them.

"Cover me!" I barked at the other Red Devils as I scrambled to my feet, my heart pounding like a jackhammer. With every step I took, the pain of losing Zane twisted inside me like a knife, threatening to tear me apart. But I couldn't fall apart now—not when my family needed me most.

"Damn it, Zane," I muttered under my breath as I darted from cover to cover, bullets whizzing past my head. "I hope you're watching over us."

As we pushed deeper into the Pistons' warehouse, the full extent of their wickedness became clear. The walls were adorned with sickening trophies, reminders of the lives they'd destroyed. It only fueled my determination to bring them down and save Tina and Kennedy.

"Over there!" Dax yelled, pointing to a door at the end of the hallway. I could hear muffled cries from behind it—the sound making my blood run cold.

"Stay focused, Brooks," I told myself, my hands shaking as I gripped my gun. "You can do this."

"Ready, brother?" Dax asked, his eyes filled with concern as he looked at me.

I nodded, taking a deep breath to steady myself. "Let's end this."

11

The stench of sweat filled the room as I kicked open the door, my heart pounding in my chest. It felt like a sick joke. There they were, Tina and Kennedy, bound to chairs. But they weren't alone—a man stood behind them, holding a knife to Tina's throat.

"Brooks," Tina gasped, eyes wide with terror. "Please, do something." The desperation in her voice sliced through me like a razorblade.

"Let 'em go," I growled, trying to hide how shaken I was by the sight before me. "Or I'll kill you where you stand."

"Brave words, Devil," the man sneered, pressing the edge of the blade into Tina's delicate skin. A drop of blood welled up, and I clenched my fists, knuckles white. "But I don't think you want your wife's blood on your hands."

I knew I had to get them out of this situation, even if it meant sacrificing myself. The thought of losing Tina and Kennedy tore at my soul, but I couldn't let them die. No matter what.

"Let 'em go and take me instead," I said, my voice cracking. The man laughed, low and cruel.

"Look at you," he taunted, turning his attention back to Tina. "Your husband's ready to die for you. Touching, really. Does that scare you?"

Tina stared him dead in the eye. "You don't scare me," she spat, the fierce love of a mother and wife burning bright within her.

"Really?" the man sneered, tightening his grip around Tina's throat. "How about now?"

"Enough!" I roared, unable to bear seeing her in pain any longer. "Take me, you bastard. Just let them go."

In that moment, I knew damn well what I was risking. Death wasn't something that scared me—not when it came to protecting my family. But I also knew Tina better than anyone. She had a strength inside her that could withstand anything. This man didn't scare her. And as long as she held onto that strength, I had faith that we'd make it out of this hell alive.

"Alright," the man said, his eyes locked on mine. "You've got yourself a deal. But remember... your wife's life is still in my hands."

As he spoke those chilling words, I steeled myself for whatever may come next. Whatever it took, I would save my family. At any cost.

As I prepared myself for whatever twisted game, the man had planned, a sharp crack echoed throughout the room. The man's grip loosened on Tina's throat, and I watched in shock as his lifeless body crumpled to the floor, blood leaking from the middle of his forehead.

"Damn good shot, Dax!" I exclaimed, relief flooding

through me as I registered my brother-in-arms at the doorway, pistol still smoking in his hand.

"Brooks, we gotta move," Dax urged, concern etched on his face, as he kept watch for any other threats that might lurk nearby.

"Right," I agreed, crossing the room to where Tina and Kennedy were tied up. My hands shook as I fumbled with the ropes, tears blurring my vision. "I've got you, baby. We're gonna be okay."

"Thank God," Tina whispered, choking back sobs as I freed her from her bindings. She wrapped her arms around me, holding on tight as if I might disappear at any moment. I held her just as fiercely, my heart swelling with love and gratitude for this strong, incredible woman.

"Daddy!" Kennedy cried out, her bright blue eyes shimmering with unshed tears as I moved to untie her next. Relief washed over Tina's face as she took our daughter into her arms, squeezing her close.

"Baby girl, you're safe now," she murmured, pressing soft kisses to the top of Kennedy's head as tears flowed freely down her cheeks. "We're all safe now."

I grabbed Kennedy in my arms and Dax took the frontline.

"Let's get out of here," I said, my voice rough with emotion as I turned to Dax. He nodded, his steely gaze scanning the perimeter one last time before signaling the all-clear.

"Lead the way, brother," I replied as I took Tina's hand.

As we made our way out of that nightmare, I knew that the road ahead wouldn't be easy. But as long as we had each other — my family and my brothers in the Red Devils — we could face whatever challenges life threw at us. Together.

———

The Red Devil's clubhouse as we gathered to honor our fallen brothers. The weight of loss hung heavy in the air, a tangible reminder of the price.

"Damn it, Zane," I whispered, my voice cracking as I stared at his empty chair, now draped with his kutte. He had fought like hell to protect Tina and Kennedy, but in the end, he'd paid the ultimate price. My heart ached for Tina—not only had she been through so much already, but now she had to face life without her brother.

"Brooks," Dax said, clapping me on the shoulder. "We're all feeling it, man. Let's remember the good times, huh?"

I nodded, wiping away the tears that threatened to spill. Drawing a deep breath, I turned to address the room. "Zane was one hell of a rider. I remember when he first joined the club, barely old enough to ride. He challenged me to a race on his first day. Damn kid almost won, too."

A murmur of laughter rippled through the crowd, soft smiles appearing on the faces of our brothers despite the pain we were all feeling. It was a welcome moment of levity amid the sorrow.

"Remember when Zane saved that stray dog?" one of the guys chimed in, shaking his head with a chuckle. "He insisted on bringing it back to the clubhouse, even though it had fleas. Named it Rascal, and it followed him everywhere."

"Never thought I'd miss the sound of that damn dog barking," another added.

"Zane always had our backs," Dax spoke up, his eyes glistening as he shared his own memory.

I nodded, remembering how Zane's fierce loyalty had been a driving force in our club. "And he loved his family more than anything," I added, thinking of Tina and their strong bond as siblings. "He'd do anything for them."

"Damn right," Dax agreed, raising his beer in salute. "To Zane—brother, friend, and one hell of a Red Devil."

"Here, here!" came the chorus of voices as we all raised our glasses, drinking deeply in memory of our fallen friend.

As the night wore on, we continued to share stories and memories of Zane and the others we'd lost. The pain of their absence would never fade completely, but together, we found solace in honoring their lives and the bonds that held us together as brothers.

"Zane would be proud of us," I whispered to myself, staring up at the stars above. "We'll keep fighting, brother. For you, and for our family." And with that vow, I knew we'd find the strength to carry on, no matter what challenges lay ahead.

12

The warm glow of the living room fireplace beckons as I pull into the driveway, its familiar flicker a beacon of comfort after the terrifying series of events that unfolded. The cozy two-story house stands tall against the dark sky, a sanctuary for my family and me. Shadows dance along the walls, cast by the flames licking at the hearth, as the night's chill lingers in the air outside.

"Alright, we're home," I say, my voice hoarse from the strain of the past few hours. I glance back at Tina and Kennedy, their faces pale and etched with fear. "Everything's going to be okay now."

I lead the way up the front steps, my boots heavy on the wooden planks. The door creaks open, revealing the familiar surroundings of our home. The large couch dominates the living room, inviting and plush, ready to envelop us in its comforting embrace. My family follows behind me, their footsteps hesitant and quiet.

"Go on, sit down," I tell them, guiding Tina and Kennedy toward the couch. Their eyes dart around the room, scanning for any signs of danger, but all they find is the safety of our haven.

"Brooks," Tina whispers, her fingers gripping my arm as if she's afraid I'll disappear. "I don't know what we would have done without you." Her gaze locks onto mine, and I see the love and gratitude shining through the remnants of terror.

"Family first," I murmur, pulling her and Kennedy close. "Always."

As we huddle together on the couch, the heat from the fireplace warming our chilled bones, I feel the weight of responsibility settle on my shoulders. The sacrifices I've made, the life I've chosen—it all comes with a price, one that almost cost me everything tonight. But seeing my family safe and sound, it's a price I'm willing to pay.

"Promise me, Brooks," Tina says, her voice trembling. "Promise me we'll never have to go through something like this again."

"I promise, baby," I reply, my heart pounding in my chest as I reaffirm my commitment to protect them at any cost. "I love you both so much, and there's nothing I wouldn't do for you."

As we sit together, the comforting warmth of our home surrounding us, I know deep down that I will do whatever it takes to keep the darkness at bay. For my family, for my club —I will fight until my last breath, ensuring their safety and happiness. And with that resolve, I find solace in the love we share, the bonds that hold us together, and the knowledge that no matter what, we will face the world as one.

The flickering flames in the fireplace cast moving shadows on the walls, their warmth seeping into my tired bones. The soft crackling and popping of logs breaking down into glowing embers is a welcome sound after the chaos we just endured. My body aches from the tensions of the night.

Kennedy's tiny hand reaches out to touch mine, her eyes fluttering closed as she snuggles against my side. Her breathing soon slows, even as her small chest rises and falls. As I watch her sleep, the weight of tonight's events presses on my heart. I'd almost lost them - my world, my everything. The thought sends shivers down my spine that have nothing to do with the cold outside. I wrap my arm around Kennedy, pulling her closer, vowing to protect her at all costs.

"Brooks..." She leans against me, her hand resting on my arm while her head finds its place on my shoulder. Her eyes close and I see her body finally relax, the stress of our ordeal melting away under the heat of the fireplace. I press a gentle kiss to her forehead, inhaling the familiar scent of her shampoo.

"Hey," I say, making sure not to wake Kennedy. "You okay?"

Tina nods, her words slurred by weariness. "Just...so tired."

"You and Kennedy are my world, baby. You are safe now. Get some rest." My heart swells with love for these two incredible women in my life, and I swear to let nothing happen to them again.

As I sit there, holding my family close, I can feel the weight of my responsibility as a husband, father, and member of the Red Devils MC. It's a burden I willingly bear, no matter the cost.

As I gaze down at their peaceful faces, relief washes over me like a tidal wave, leaving trails of salty tears streaming down my cheeks. My heart pounds like a jackhammer, each beat a testament to the love and devotion I have for my family. I've risked life and limb countless times as a member of the Red Devils MC, but nothing has ever shaken me to my core like almost losing them.

"Promise me," I whisper, choking on the words, "promise me we'll always be together."

Tina's eyes flutter open, meeting mine with an intensity that leaves no room for doubt. "I promise, Brooks. We're in this together, forever."

As she closes her eyes again, a sense of clarity and purpose fills my mind. This moment, right here, is all that matters. Saving them, protecting them—that's my true mission in life. All the rides, the fights, the brotherhood of the club... they all pale in comparison to the love I have for my family.

Silently vowing to never let anything happen to them again, I tighten my hold on Tina and Kennedy. This is what loyalty and sacrifice mean to me now. No matter the cost, no matter the danger, I will protect them with every fiber of my being.

"Sleep well, my loves," I murmur as their breathing becomes slow and steady. "I'll be here, watching over you."

The flames dance in the fireplace, casting a warm glow over our intertwined forms. With each flicker of light, I feel the strength of my resolve growing, fueling the fire within me that will never let our family be torn apart again.

Twisted Redemption

TWISTED
REDEMPTION

USA TODAY BESTSELLING AUTHOR
ASHLEY ZAKRZEWSKI

1

The alarm blared, jolting me out of bed, heart still pounding as images of Jason's lifeless body flashed through my mind. My t-shirt clung to my body, soaked, and I tried to slow my breathing. The nightmares were almost every night since I saw his body lying there on the cold, hard ground. Blood pooled around everywhere, but only one single gunshot. It wasn't my first time seeing a dead body, but seeing my partner's was different. My job was dangerous, always had been, but it showed me just how far down the rabbit hole we had to go to get the results our bosses wanted. Jason, my partner, literally gave up his life to seek of the evidence they were searching for, and at first, thoughts ran through my head. Was any job worth my life?

Coming to the FBI, at first, it was my dream. Ever since I was a little kid, watching crime dramas on the television, I knew exactly what I wanted to do. Take down bad guys. Clean up communities and make them safer for everyone. My job gave me that opportunity, but as a kid, the consequences of it never seeped in, but seeing Jason, there on that ground, put things into perspective.

My feet were like icebergs and I walked over to my dresser to grab a pair of socks. Breathing had slowed down a bit, and the images stopped. For now. A typical night's sleep for me was about three to four hours since that night. Always waking up with soaked sheets and an erratic heartbeat. My core was shook and something had to give.

A week of paid leave wasn't what I needed. My boss seemed to think staying at home and being alone with my thoughts was better for me, but if he only knew what I was dealing with here. Thank god, today was my first day back and I had plenty of things to do.

I had to do something! What kind of partner would I be if I just stood around and didn't try to find out who killed him? Who mutilated him? Being undercover was tricky, we had both done it more times than we could count, but it was different with the Twisted Jokers. They were known for being brutal, conniving, and cunning. What did Jason stumble upon that took his life?

The closet door opened and I grabbed a pair of jeans, white t-shirt and my leather jacket. As I got dressed, my mind kept going back to the club. Jason had gone undercover after I got out. I spent three years trying to find intel on how we could take them down, but the loyalty between the members was crazy. When Jason pulled me out and went in himself, I never imagined this was how it would end. And neither did he.

Maybe I could go back. When they moved into the city, wreaking havoc, I came up with a fake story about how my mother was ill, and I had to stay behind to take care of her, but would come up and join them when I could. Typically, things like that didn't happen, but weirdly enough, they all had good relationships with their parents. So, it was the one thing that gave me an easy way out without being suspicious.

Wait till I get my hands on you bastards.

The stairs creaked under my weight and I grabbed my car keys off the ring by the door, and went straight to the car, heading for the office. My thoughts turned to the plan - infiltrate the Twisted Jokers again. I would have to immerse myself in their world, become one of them, but the price was worth it for the chance at vengeance. The nightmares would soon return, after the things I had to do last time, but eventually they would be taken off the streets and Jason's murderer would face justice. I had to keep reminding myself of that. The end goal.

I won't let you down.

The streets were nearly deserted at this hour, only the occasional stray cat or distant siren breaking the quiet. With the plan, I must tread lightly, gather information bit by bit, and regain the trust of these hardened criminals. Some were worse than others, and many just ended up falling into the wrong crowd or wanting somewhere to fit in and the Twisted Jokers suckered them into joining their club. Not everyone did illegal things, but the ones who did were close to the leader. They knew what needed to be done without him saying a word. And at one point, I was that guy. I had to get my hands dirty or else they would know something was up, but it gave me nightmares. It reminded me of that saying, "Sometimes good people do bad things. It doesn't make them bad people." Was that true though? How could you determine who was a good person or a bad person?

When I pulled into the parking lot, not many cars were there given the hour. For my first day back, being able to go through files without everyone hounding me with condolences was exactly what I needed. They didn't need to worry about me, but instead focus on catching the motherfucker responsible. Knowing whoever did this was still out there, living their life, while Jason was in the ground killed me.

My knuckles hit the steering wheel. The rage boiling up inside me might consume me if I don't get started soon. The longer I waited, the more this person would think they got away with it. The twisted truth was: it was someone within the Twisted Jokers. That was undeniable. If I could figure out the events that led up to his death, than it might open some doors to the truth. He was too far up in the ranks to suddenly be murdered, so the only logical explanation was that somehow they found out that he was undercover, but how? It just didn't make any sense. We were careful with our interactions. I ran my fingers through my hair at this grappling thought.

I opened the car door and slammed it behind me. There was so much to figure out before I could just go back in. Review all the briefings from Jason. Find out everything there was to know about the new members of the club. The most important thing was to go in with as much details as possible.

I went straight to the break room area to make a pot of coffee, because it would be necessary. My eyes were already hanging heavy and the exhaustion was starting to set in. After filling the cup with the amber liquid, I traveled to my desk and immediately I growled.

It was covered in cards and even flowers. Over the course of the week I've been gone, fellow agents had left things on it. I take each item and dump it into a trashcan at the far side of my office. *I don't have time for this bullshit right now. My grief will have to wait.*

My fingers tapped a staccato rhythm on the desk, eyes scanning the array of photographs and case files that cluttered its surface now. A beat of sweat trickled down my jaw, and I absentmindedly wiped it with the back of my hand. The small, cramped office was suffocating, but I hardly noticed; the weight of my partner's death heavy on my shoulders.

Over Ten years in the field and now this.

At thirty-five, I was a seasoned undercover Special Agent, having put away countless criminals during my career. But the Twisted Jokers motorcycle club proved to be a formidable adversary, and Jason's death only further fueled my determination to bring them down and find out who was responsible. There must be something in these files to help me. The leader rarely got his own hands dirty, and with Jason being his right hand man at the time of his death, who does that even leave? Fuck! I pulled at the collar on my shirt. Why was so it so fucking hot in here? It was a small discomfort compared to the gnawing pain in my chest whenever I thought about Jason. We'd been through so much, and now I found myself alone, facing an organization hell-bent on wreaking havoc in the city.

When we were tasked with the assignment on the Twisted Jokers eleven years ago, it was led up by someone else. A ruthless man who did nothing but tear down the city, and then when they moved here, he was killed. We never did find the person responsible, but everyone was almost sure it was a rival club trying to make a statement. Gunner, who was barely an adult, at the time, took over in his father's place. He was on track to do great things, and get away from the destruction, but somehow that life pulled him in. Within one year, he was going down the same path his father did. His morals went right out the window.

Gritting my teeth, I forced myself to focus on the task at hand: gathering evidence. Grief couldn't consume me; there would be time for mourning later. For now, I owed it to Jason to seek justice and closure. After all, if the roles were reversed, Jason would do the same for me.

Dammit, Jason. Why'd you have to go and get yourself killed like that? Anger and sadness clashed within me, leaving me hollow. I took a deep breath, trying to push my emotions aside and concentrate on the case.

As I flipped through the pages, my mind raced. Infiltrating the Twisted Jokers was the only way to figure out who was responsible for Jason's death. It wouldn't be easy, but I was ready to take on the challenge. After all, this was the work I'd committed myself to for the past decade, and I wasn't about to back down now.

Ten years... ten years they have been bringing down this city and it's time to make this right.

"Eli," came a gruff voice from behind. "You're in early."

Detective Tripp Clark, a seasoned detective with salt-and-pepper hair and warm brown eyes, leaned against the edge of my desk. A mentor figure to me for the past year, Tripp's wisdom and compassion was invaluable in helping me navigate the darker aspects of our profession.

"Couldn't sleep," I replied, my gaze still locked on the evidence before me. "Every minute we waste is another opportunity for these bastards to hurt someone else."

"Your dedication is impressive, kid," Tripp said, a hint of admiration in his voice. "But it's important not to let this case consume you. We'll bring them down together."

"Thanks, Tripp," I murmured, taking a moment to acknowledge the support. "I just... I can't shake the feeling that we're so close, you know? He did all that work undercover and then he got murdered. We have no idea why and who is responsible. I'm done tiptoeing around."

He nodded, understanding the frustration that gnawed at my heart. The relentless pursuit of justice that drove agents to the brink of obsession.

"Listen," Tripp began, gesturing towards the photographs spread out on the desk. "I've been going over the intel you and Jason gathered during your time undercover, and your instincts are spot-on. The Twisted Jokers are more dangerous than we initially thought, but your work has given us a real shot at taking them down. Jason's time undercover might not have ended the way we thought, but his intel gives us a leg up to do exactly what he wanted. Take them down."

My chest swelled, though I knew there was still much to be done.

"I can't help but feel like I'm missing something crucial," I confessed, brow furrowing. "Something that could break this case wide open." I ruffled through all the papers scattered around the desk. "What are we missing? What did Jason uncover that got him killed?"

"Sometimes the answers we want aren't found in the evidence, but in the relationships we forge," Tripp said, placing a reassuring hand on my shoulder. "Trust your instincts, and don't be afraid to dig deeper. There is a chance that Jason wasn't telling us everything. He could've gotten close to someone within the group or slipped up and got made."

I nodded, absorbing Tripp's advice like a sponge. The key to bringing down the Twisted Jokers lay not just in the photographs and files that littered the desk, but in the bonds he'd formed while working undercover. Somewhere, hidden in the shadows of their twisted world, was a traitor – one who held the power to bring the entire operation crashing down. I needed to find whoever the person was and use them to our advantage.

"Alright, let's get to work."

As we delved into the case together, I was grateful for Tripp's guidance and support. In this treacherous game of cat and mouse, every ally counted, and I was determined to get justice served – for Jason, for the city, and for all those who suffered at the hands of the Twisted Jokers.

My fingers danced across the keyboard, eyes never leaving the screen as I compiled a digital dossier on the Twisted Jokers. Finding the traitor would require drawing connections between members, and I was working tirelessly to gather evidence against each one. The lit office cast an eerie glow on my face, revealing the dark circles under my eyes – a testament to the countless hours spent poring over every scrap of intel and barely sleeping over the last week. I missed something crucial and I needed to find out what that was as soon as possible. Jason and I worked undercover together for years, but taking down the Twisted Jokers was our ultimate case. The one that would finally net the promotion and accolade we were seeking since joining the department.

"Got another name for you," Tripp said, his voice low as he handed me a small, crumpled piece of paper. "He goes by 'Razor.' This guy's been with the club since its inception."

I nodded, entering Razor's name into the database. My focus was unwavering, fueled by memories of Jason's lifeless body lying in a pool of blood. I couldn't shake the image, nor did I want to; it served as a constant reminder of what I was fighting for.

"I know this is hard for you," Tripp began. "But remember, keep a clear head."

"Of course." I managed a weak smile, my thoughts briefly drifting to the bond I shared with the seasoned detective. Our mutual trust and respect was a beacon of light amidst the darkness that surrounded the investigation. But even in our camaraderie, I felt the responsibility resting heavily on my shoulders. It was my mission to bring the Twisted Jokers down, and I wouldn't let anyone else suffer the same fate as Jason.

"Okay, back to work then," I muttered, returning my gaze to the computer screen. As I clicked through files and cross-referenced names, my mind raced with possibilities. Who among these hardened criminals could be the traitor? Who held the key to dismantling their entire operation?

My eyes narrowed as I stumbled upon a piece of information that caught my attention. Razor had a history of dealing with undercover agents, and there was evidence suggesting he may have been involved in exposing their identities in the past.

"Tripp," I called out. "I might have something."

"Really?" Tripp moved closer, intrigued. "What'd you find?"

"Look at this." I pointed to a series of transactions and coded messages. "Razor has been in contact with someone outside the club – someone who might know about our operation. Is it possible that someone in our organization is working against us?"

"Interesting," Tripp mused, rubbing his chin. "We need to

keep an eye on him. He could be our ticket to finding the mole."

"Agreed," Eli said.

"You feel like having a drink?" Tripp asked.

I knew exactly where he was going with that. "On it."

Later that night, I sat with my back pressed against a cold brick wall in the alleyway. There was a distant rumble of motorcycles echoing through the city streets, a chilling reminder of the Twisted Jokers' presence. A chill ran down my spine, but I remained focused on the task at hand. Eyes flicked between the shadows and the mouth of the alley, ready to pounce at the first sign of danger.

"Anything yet?" Detective Tripp Clark's voice crackled in my earpiece.

"Nothing," I whispered, adjusting the tiny microphone embedded in my collar. "I'll keep you posted."

Tripp was the one to suggest this stakeout, knowing it would give us a chance to observe the Twisted Jokers up close without drawing attention to themselves. It was a risky move, but I trusted Tripp implicitly – I knew that the older detective wouldn't send me into harm's way without good reason.

"Stay sharp, kid," Tripp said, his voice tinged with concern. "This case means a lot to both of us, but I don't want you taking unnecessary risks."

"Understood." This case wasn't just about putting criminals behind bars; it was about bringing peace to a city plagued by fear.

As I scanned the area, there was a flicker of movement near the entrance of the alley. Two men emerged from the shadows, one tall and lanky, the other short and stocky. They were dressed in the unmistakable black leather jackets of the

Twisted Jokers, their faces obscured by the darkness. My heart hammered as adrenaline coursed through my veins.

"Tripp, two members just entered the alley," I reported, voice steady despite the tension building.

"Keep your distance," Tripp advised. "We need more intel."

I watched the men intently, taking note of their every gesture and word. Even the smallest piece of information could be crucial in bringing down the dangerous biker gang. As they conversed, I committed their faces to memory, determined to unmask them and bring them to justice.

"Looks like they're meeting someone here," I said, eyes narrowing as a third figure approached the pair. "Wait... I recognize him. That's Razor."

"Stay on them, but don't get too close," Tripp warned. "We can't afford to spook them."

"Copy that," I acknowledged, my muscles coiled like a spring, ready for action.

Observing from my vantage point, the meeting unfolded before me, my resolve hardened. Together, Tripp and I would dismantle the Twisted Jokers' reign of terror, brick by brick, if necessary. It wasn't just about avenging Jason's death – it was about restoring hope to a community that had been held hostage by fear for far too long.

"Tripp," I murmured, gaze never leaving the trio, "we've got this. We're going to make this city safe again."

With him by my side, we would face down the darkness and emerge victorious – not just for ourselves, but for everyone who ever suffered at the hands of the Twisted Jokers.

2

The door to the bar creaked open, casting a sliver of light across the worn wooden floor. I stepped inside, my heeled boots clicking against the scuffed planks as I surveyed the domain. As the younger sister of the Twisted Jokers motorcycle club leader, I grew up in the shadow of this notorious world, but I was anything but a feeble wallflower.

"Hey, Zoe!" a gruff voice called out from behind the scarred counter where a row of liquor bottles stood like silent sentinels. I offered a half-smile, more out of habit than actual warmth. In truth, I trusted few people within these walls, my past experiences having taught me that even the most familiar faces could hide dark intentions.

"Hey, Eddie," I replied, making my way to the bar with an air of confidence that left no room for doubt about my place here. I took a seat on one of the rickety stools, my eyes scanning the room as the jukebox crackled to life with the opening chords of an old rock song.

It was a typical evening at the Twisted Jokers' typical hangout: a handful of patrons huddled in corners, nursing their beers and murmuring in hushed tones; the pool table in the far corner, bathed in the glow of a flickering neon light, drawing the occasional curse or jeer from its players; and the ever-present scent of stale beer and cigarette smoke clinging to every surface like an unwanted guest.

"Usual?" Eddie asked, already reaching for a glass and filling it with amber liquid. I nodded, my gaze drifting back to the door. There was something about tonight. The air was charged, the shadows deeper, and my instincts told me to be on guard. But then again, my instincts were always on high alert these days.

"Thanks," I said, accepting the drink and taking a slow sip, the bitterness settling on my tongue as a familiar comfort. I learned to revel in small pleasures like this, knowing that life could turn on a dime and snatch them away. But for now, I was content to sit at the bar and watch, my presence alone enough to deter any troublemakers who might have otherwise been tempted to cause a scene.

The jukebox crooned an old blues tune, the sultry notes weaving through the dimly lit bar like tendrils of smoke. I leaned against the worn pool table, eyes scanning the room with a keen intensity that pierced through the haze. I was a force to be reckoned with, my confident demeanor and no-nonsense attitude both a magnet and a warning to those around me.

"Hey, Zoe," called out a regular from across the room, raising his glass in salute. "You look like you're ready for war."

"Isn't that always the case?" I replied, voice laced with a sharp wit that drew chuckles from the nearby patrons. My long, curly hair tumbled over my shoulders like a cascade of auburn silk, framing the full lips that curved into a knowing smile. Even as I bantered with the familiar faces in the bar, my thoughts turned inward, mulling over the undercurrents that thrummed beneath the surface tonight.

"Nice shot," someone said as I expertly lined up my cue and sunk the ball into the corner pocket. The click of the ball hitting the back of the pocket echoed through the bar, capturing the attention of several onlookers.

"Thanks," I responded with a casual shrug, gaze never wavering from my next target. Every movement I made was fluid, decisive, my body language radiating an unspoken challenge that dared anyone to underestimate me.

As the game progressed, my mind continued to race. A shiver ran down my spine, a whisper of unease that I tried to shake off. But the feeling persisted, gnawing at the edges of my consciousness like a thorn lodged deep in my side.

"Zoe," my brother Gunner called. "You alright?"

"Fine," I answered, too quickly. I forced a smile, hoping to reassure him.

"Keep your head in the game," he teased, ruffling my hair affectionately. But the concern in his eyes lingered, a silent reminder of the protective bond we shared.

"Always do," I murmured, sinking the final ball with a satisfying thunk. As I straightened up, my gaze locked onto a figure near the door—a newcomer whose presence shifted the balance of the room. My instincts flared to life, my heart pounding as I braced for whatever storm was brewing on the horizon. I headed back to the bar to get another drink.

I leaned against the worn wooden counter, eyes scanning the room as I sipped my beer. There were several gazes on me, drawn to the way my hair cascaded down my back and framed my high cheekbones.

"Hey there," a voice drawled from beside me, breaking into my thoughts. A man in his thirties appeared, dark hair and a sly grin spreading across his face. "I couldn't help but notice you from across the room. Mind if I buy you a drink?"

I arched an eyebrow, letting my gaze drift languidly up and down his form before meeting his eyes again. "Thanks, but I prefer not to mix business with pleasure," I replied coolly, taking another sip of the beer.

What was it about me that made guys constantly hit on me? Newcomers were so quick to do it, but everyone in this bar watched me like a hawk. They were protective. Most knew I could handle myself in these situations, but my brother always loved a chance to step in and bloody his knuckles.

"Business?" he asked, momentarily taken aback by my quick retort. "What kind of business are you in?"

"Keeping fools like you at arm's length," I shot back, a wicked smile playing at the corners of my full lips as I watched him bristle with indignation.

"Feisty, aren't you?" he said. "I like that in a woman."

"Then it's a shame I don't care what you like," I responded without missing a beat, turning away from him to focus once more on my beverage.

As I savored the bitter taste of the beer on my tongue, my mind wandered to darker times, when trust had been a luxury I couldn't afford. Images of cold, unyielding walls and the iron grip of captivity tightened around my heart, threatening to steal my breath. It was several months since I'd escaped the clutches of a rival gang, but the scars they'd left behind still lurked beneath the surface, making me hesitant to let anyone get too close.

"Hey," the man persisted, leaning in closer as if trying to regain my attention. "I've got money, you know. I could show you—"

"Save it," I cut him off, voice low and dangerous. "You're barking up the wrong tree. Now, unless you want to find out what happens when you push me too far, I suggest you take your pathetic ass pickup lines elsewhere."

He stared at me for a moment, jaw clenched with anger, before finally storming away in a huff. As he disappeared into the crowd, I took a deep breath, heart pounding. Opening myself up to others was risky, but there was a part of me that longed for connection, for the chance to reclaim the life that was stolen.

As the night wore on, something was about to change. The air was charged, as though the universe itself was holding its breath. And as the door to the bar swung open once more, the first stirrings of a storm brewing, one that would soon sweep me up in its wake.

It was time for my shift to start, but I only worked a couple of hours a night. Just enough to pay my measly rent on my run down apartment. I drank the last sip of my beer and walked behind the bar, picking up a rag to wipe down the counter.

The jukebox crooned softly in the background, providing a comforting soundtrack to the low murmur of conversation that filled the air. I spotted a regular, Jake, nursing a whiskey at the far end of the counter.

"Hey," I called out, smirking. "That drink treating you well, or are you two breaking up tonight?"

Jake chuckled, raising his glass in a mock toast. "Oh, we're still going strong, Zoe. But if I ever need a rebound, I know where to find you."

"Very funny," I shot back, rolling my eyes but smiling nonetheless. The men that frequented the bar knew I was off-limits. Gunner would kill anyone who tried so much as lay a hand on me. That was a fact. So, I hadn't had much of a love life.

My smile faded as I noticed a pair of newcomers enter the bar, their rowdy laughter drawing unwanted attention. Already on edge, I braced myself for trouble.

"Alright, guys, let's keep it down, okay?" I said, giving them a stern look. "We're here to have a good time, not start a riot."

The taller of the two men sneered. "You got a problem with us having fun, sweetheart?"

"Only when it involves disturbing the peace," I replied coolly, eyes never leaving his. "Now take a seat and behave, or you'll find yourselves outside faster than you can say 'last call.'"

"Fine," the man grumbled, clearly taken aback by my unflinching attitude. They slunk off to a booth in the corner, muttering under their breath.

"What was that?" I asked, perking her ears up toward the men. I had been brought up to be strong minded and not many people talked back to me because of what I was. These guys must be new around here.

"Zoe, you okay?" Gunner appeared, his brow furrowed. He was watching from his usual spot near the pool table, always ready to step in if needed like the big overprotective big brother he was.

"I'm fine," I reassured him, heart still racing. "I can handle myself, you know that."

"Right," he replied, his dark eyes serious. "But after everything you've been through..."

Gratitude and frustration washed over me. I appreciated my brother's protectiveness, but sometimes it was suffocating. He didn't need to watch over me every minute of the day. Sometimes, he treated me like a child, not the thirty-five-year-old I was.

"I need you to trust that I'm strong enough to face whatever comes my way," I said, meeting his gaze. "That's the only way I can start to heal. Treating me like a lost puppy isn't helping things."

He hesitated, then nodded. "Okay, I'll back off."

As I poured another round of drinks for the patrons, there was the weight of my past pressing down. I longed to break free from its grasp, to find a sense of normalcy in the chaos that became my life. And as I caught sight of a stranger lingering near the door, a shiver ran down my spine, heralding the approach of something far beyond my darkest fears.

I expertly navigated my way through the crowd, eyes scanning the room as I balanced a tray of frosty amber pints in one hand. I prided myself on my ability to read people, a skill honed from years behind the bar and a past I'd rather forget. As I approached a rowdy table of bikers, I kept my eyes on the man in the corner, his gaze never straying far from me.

"Here you go, boys," I said with a smirk, setting the drinks down with a satisfying thunk. "Drink up before they get warm."

"Thanks," one of the men replied. "You always know how to keep us happy."

"Someone's got to," I shot back playfully, wiping my hands on my jeans. My fingers brushed against the sticky residue that clung to the denim—a familiar sensation in this place.

"Hey," another biker called out as he approached the bar,

his tattooed arms flexing under the weight of his empty glass. "Can I get a refill?"

As much as I dreamed of getting far away from here and starting over fresh, the world kept dragging me back in. I came close a couple of times, but Gunner always needed me. I would never tell him about my thoughts of leaving, because he would take that as being disloyal which could turn him against me. After seeing the things he was capable of, I wasn't so sure that he wouldn't treat me like any other member. Blood or not.

"Sure thing," I replied, grabbing the glass from him and filling it to the brim with the bitter liquid.

As I handed the drink back to the biker, I caught a whiff of the stale cigarette smoke that clung to his clothes—a smell that became almost comforting in its familiarity. How did I end up here? Working in this bar for shitty tips and a bunch of horny men? I had dreams once. Dreams that were much bigger than the Twisted Jokers, but life had a funny way of dismantling them.

"Thanks, darlin'," he said, his eyes crinkling at the corners as he raised his glass in a toast. "You're a lifesaver."

"Anytime," I replied, thoughts drifting back to the stranger in the corner. I could feel his eyes on me, and it sent a shiver down my spine.

Who was that guy? I scanned the crowd for any signs of trouble. The bar was my sanctuary for years, and I wasn't about to let some outsider threaten that. Everyone knew this was the Twisted Jokers spot, except for out-of-towners. Although, they would quickly be able to tell once inside. The tattoos and leather jackets give it away pretty quickly. So, why was this guy in our bar?

He was dressed in dark jeans and a black leather jacket..

His brown hair was short and faded on the sides, revealing a scar on the left side of his head.

I kept my gaze fixed on the stranger. An invisible tension threading its way through the bar, as others began to take notice of the unwelcome visitor. Although it wasn't hard to notice someone that doesn't belong. Most of the members saw each other daily. He stood out like a sore thumb.

My mind whirred with questions and possibilities - *why was he here? What did he want?*

The stranger remained at the far end of the bar, nursing a drink and keeping to himself. But every so often, I would catch his dark eyes flicking in my direction, as if sizing me up. It unsettled me, reminding me of the predator-prey dynamic I had once been forced to endure during my captivity.

"Hey, sis, you okay?"

"Fine," I replied, focusing on my task at hand. "Just tired."

"Zoe," Gunner's voice held a note of caution, but I cut him off before he could continue.

"Really, Gunner. I'm fine," I insisted, forcing a tight smile. I recognized the worry in my brother's eyes, but I didn't want to burden him further. He had enough on his plate.

"Alright," he relented, though it was clear he remained unconvinced. "I'll be in my office if you need me."

As the evening progressed and patrons continued to filter in, I scanned the crowd for the mysterious stranger.

"Hey, beautiful," a voice interrupted my thoughts, drawing my attention toward the end of the bar where a regular, Tom, sat nursing a beer. "How's your night going?"

"Better before you showed up," I quipped without

missing a beat. Despite the unease, I refused to let my guard down or show any sign of weakness.

"Ouch," Tom feigned hurt.

My heart raced with each new face that appeared. Would he bring trouble for me and the Twisted Jokers? What was it about him that struck such a chord?

I took a deep breath, willing myself to focus. If the stranger returned, I'd be ready for him. And if not? Well, I'd cross that bridge when I came to it. For now, there was a job to do, and I refused to let fear dictate my actions.

3

The heavy door of the dimly lit bar closed behind me with a muted thud, sealing me off from the last remnants of daylight. I stood for a moment, allowing my eyes to adjust to the darkness, the pervasive scent of whiskey and cigarette smoke settling around me like a shroud. Every fiber of my being was focused on the mission: gathering information on the elusive Twisted Jokers motorcycle club, their secrets hidden within the shadows of this dingy establishment.

As I scanned the room, my eyes were drawn to a vision in the corner - a woman whose vibrant auburn hair cascaded like liquid fire down her back. Her piercing blue eyes met my gaze unflinchingly, capturing my attention like a moth ensnared by a flame. Zoe Mitchell, sister of the club's notorious leader. I recognized her from the files. She was much prettier in person.

I forced my concentration back onto the purpose, but the image of the fiery-haired woman lingered in my mind, an unexpected temptation that threatened to distract me from my objective. I walked toward the bar, every step measured and controlled, my body language exuding a calm confidence that belied the turmoil within. As I neared my destination, I reminded myself that I was here for answers, not entanglements. Jason's tragic death weighed heavily on my conscience, driving me to seek justice and protect those who could not protect themselves.

"Hey there," came a voice that cut through the low murmur of the bar like a knife, smooth and sharp. "Haven't seen you around before. You new in town?"

And so it begins...

I turned to find Zoe standing beside me, her friendly smile a stark contrast to the guarded expression in her eyes. She radiated a magnetic energy, drawing me in despite my best efforts to remain detached.

"Something like that," I replied cautiously, voice betraying none of the inner conflict.

"Ah," she said, nodding as if my answer confirmed some private suspicion. "Well, welcome to our little slice of nowhere. I'm Zoe." She extended a hand, her grip firm and confident when I shook it.

"Nice to meet you, Zoe," I responded, tone carefully neutral. "I'm Eli."

"Where are you from?" Zoe asked with genuine curiosity, her gaze never leaving my face. There was an intensity in her eyes that matched my own, hinting at a hidden depth beneath her amiable facade.

"Does it really matter?" I countered softly, a small smile tugging at the corner of my mouth. It was a dangerous game, this delicate dance of words and glances, but I found myself drawn into it despite himself.

"Maybe not," she admitted, her own smile widening. "But it's always nice to know where people come from."

"Fair enough," I conceded. "I'm originally from upstate, but I've been traveling for a while now."

"Upstate, huh?" Zoe mused, leaning closer as if sharing a secret. "I bet it's beautiful there this time of year."

"Nothing quite like it," I agreed, suddenly acutely aware of the warmth of her body, the faint scent of jasmine that drifted from her skin. "But every place has its own charm, don't you think?"

"True," she conceded, her eyes flickering over my jawline. Our attraction became a living, breathing entity between us; undeniable, unspoken, and utterly enthralling.

My gaze flickered around the bar, my trained eyes scanning for any sign of Gunner. My heart hammered, a reminder that I needed to stay focused on my mission. As tempting as it was to get lost in Zoe's eyes, I couldn't afford to let my guard down.

"Tell me something," I said, forcing myself to steer the conversation back towards the objective. "What do you know about the Twisted Jokers?"

Zoe raised a brow, her smile taking on a mischievous edge. "Aren't you full of surprises? Why are you so curious about them?"

"Can't a man have a few secrets?" I deflected smoothly, shifting in my seat to face her more fully. The pulse at the base of my throat quickened, betraying my unease at the direction our conversation took.

"Secrets make the world go 'round, don't they?" Zoe replied, leaning back and studying me intently. "You'll find my lips are sealed when it comes to certain...organizations."

"Really?" I countered, smirking despite the tension coiling in my gut. "So you're saying you don't like to share?"

"Sharing is overrated," she shot back, a playful glint in her eyes. "Especially when it comes to sensitive information."

Our banter was a high-stakes game, each move calculated and deliberate. I tried to ignore the way my pulse raced at her proximity and the thrill of our verbal sparring. This woman was dangerous, and I couldn't forget that.

"Sensitive information, huh?" I mused, weighing my options. I was walking a fine line, trying to gather intel while simultaneously not revealing my true intentions. "What if I told you that I have a particular interest in the Twisted Jokers? Would that change your mind?"

"Interest or not," she replied, her voice low and tantalizing, "I'm afraid I can't help you with that." Her eyes locked onto mine, daring me to push further.

My resolve wavered, caught between the mission and the magnetic pull of Zoe's presence. I needed to stay focused, but something about her made it nearly impossible for me to resist. Zoe sat down at the round table. "Mind if I join you?"

"Please, have a seat," I replied.

The lighting cast shadows across Zoe's face, accentuating the sharp lines of her cheekbones. Her arms were crossed tightly over her chest, and the muscles in her shoulders tensed with each passing second. It was obvious what was going on. She wanted to know why some stranger was coming around asking questions about the Jokers.

"You should know that the Twisted Jokers aren't ones to be messed with and this is their place... so if you are smart, you'd get the hell out of dodge before they find out you've been asking around about them."

She truly had no idea.

"Let's just say I have my reasons..."

"Even if it means digging up skeletons?" Zoe asked, her

eyes searching my face for any sign of hesitation. "Because trust me, if you go poking around in the Jokers' business, that's exactly what you'll find."

"Maybe I'm not afraid of a few skeletons," I countered. "Besides, if I let fear hold me back, I wouldn't be much of a man, would I?"

Zoe's blue eyes momentarily flickered before settling into an expression of genuine curiosity. She uncrossed her arms, leaning forward and resting her elbows on the table, but before she could say anything, she was interrupted.

"Eli, what the hell are you doing here?" Gunner yelled from across the bar, making my way over to me. Zoe's eyes went wide.

"You told me to stop in if I was ever back in town! Your sister here... she wanted to know why I was asking about you guys... she's a keeper."

Gunner eyed me. "Watch out now, she's off limits. You can have any other girl in her you want..."

The fact that he even said that out loud made my blood boil. Men like Gunner took what they wanted... women, money, and whatever else.

"Don't worry, she's not my type." I watched as Zoe switched from one foot to the other. It bothered her. "So, i'm only gonna be in town for about a week, but thought I'd stop in and see how you were."

My best bet right now was to play the old buddy card. I went undercover about a year and a half ago. Gunner and I used to do things together, things I wasn't proud of, but I did for the sake of the investigation. So, I already proved my loyalty to the Jokers.

"Well, you're welcome here anytime. You'll have to meet

my new right hand man... my old one... well he isn't around anymore."

This hit a nerve, because he meant Jason. I wanted so badly to tighten my fists and take Gunner out right there and then, but this was bigger than just my partner and I. If I did this right, the city could finally live without fear.

"Anytime. I'm gonna head out for tonight, but I'll catch you tomorrow maybe?"

"You know where to find me," Gunner said as I walked out of the bar and let the door close behind.

I headed straight back to my office to debrief the night into my notes. Being undercover and having a connection with the Twisted Jokers already would prove to be an advantage in this case. Gunner would never second guess someone who already proved themself time and time again, but then he got rid of Jason so quickly. Why? What happened that caused the Twisted Jokers to turn on him?

The steady hum of the overhead fluorescent lights filled my small, cluttered office. Stacks of paperwork and case files obscured most of the surfaces, leaving only a narrow path towards the window. Outside, the city's skyline stretched across the horizon, a canvas of steel and glass punctuated by cranes and construction sites.

"Eli," Tripp said, leaning against a filing cabinet, his salt-and-pepper hair glinting under the harsh light. "I've got an update on that shipment we've been tracking."

I looked up from the file I had been poring over, the intensity in my eyes betraying my unwavering focus. I had been working tirelessly.

"Tell me everything you know."

Tripp crossed his arms and recounted the new information he'd received. "Our informant says the shipment is coming soon. We still don't know the exact location or time, but it's going to be somewhere in the industrial district."

"Without a date, not sure how we can do anything yet." I clenched his jaw. This could be our best chance to catch the Twisted Jokers red-handed and finally put an end to their reign of terror.

"Let's go over the intel we have so far," Tripp suggested, picking up a marker and approaching the whiteboard mounted on the wall. As he began to write, I observed the seasoned detective's steady hand, a testament to his years of experience.

"First, we know the shipment contains a large cache of weapons," he continued. "Second, it's being transported by a group of high-ranking members within the gang. This means they'll have eyes on us, so we need to be discreet. And third, we suspect there's a mole in our department feeding them information."

"Who can we trust then?" I asked, frustration creeping into my voice. If was if I was were navigating a minefield, unsure of where to step next.

"Right now, it's just you and me," he replied, locking eyes with me. "We can't afford any missteps or leaks."

I nodded, understanding the gravity of the situation. Getting closer to the Twisted Jokers was crucial, but I also must balance the risks involved. As I absorbed the seasoned detective's words, an unwavering determination settled within me. I would not let Jason's death be in vain, nor would I allow the Twisted Jokers to continue their reign of terror.

"We'll be ready but there's something else we're missing," I said, rubbing my temples as I tried to piece together the puzzle. "We need more intel on their operations."

"Getting close to Zoe Mitchell might be our best shot at infiltrating the club," Tripp suggested. "She's not only the sister of the leader, but she's also trusted by many of the members. You've already managed to pique her interest, haven't you?"

I recalled the charged encounter I had with Zoe, her piercing blue eyes searing into my very soul. The magnetic pull between us was undeniable. Tripp was right, but a pang of guilt gnawed at me for using her to further the investigation.

"Guess it's time to get closer to our target," I agreed, my mind racing with plans and contingencies.

4

The warm aroma of freshly brewed coffee and sweet pastries enveloped me as I sat across from Lola enjoying the soft jazz playing in the background in the cozy corner of the local cafe.

Sometimes I had to get out. Being surrounded by the club twenty-four-seven wasn't healthy. Even though I was born into it doesn't mean I had to agree with them on everything. Especially with the path they seemed so hellbent on going down now. My brother scared me. I never thought he would become this kind of leader. And I'm scared that if I did find a way to get away from all this, he would only get worse. There would be no one to tell him he was going too far or to call him on his shit.

Lola asked to meet up and grab a coffee which was exactly what I needed right now. Someone to talk to. My head was all over the place with this new guy, Eli, and it killed me to second guess myself all the time, but when you have a past like mine, it was kind of hard not to. All my life I had been trained not to trust men. I had seen some of the things my father put my mother through and now I saw first-hand the things my brother put his groupies through. In my head, I knew not all men were like that, but how the hell did you find out for sure? Men were great liars, good at telling us what we wanted to hear, and I liked to be spared the bullshit act.

"Zoe, honey, what's got you so wound up?" Lola asked, sipping her cappuccino as she studied my troubled expression.

Honestly, I didn't know how to even put it into words to confide in Lola. It was ridiculous, right? How could I be so attracted to someone I didn't even know? More importantly, Gunner already knew him which means he was a member, and members were off-limits. Plus, the fact I knew absolutely nothing about this guy. Was it because he was mysterious?

He had gotten out once. Why the hell would he come back? He hadn't been around and everyone knew how my brother was, especially now. Once Jason was killed, everyone was on edge. I found it odd that he just showed back up, out of nowhere, and wanted to catch up.

But those eyes... since the moment I locked onto his, my whole body shook. I've never had that happen to where someone disrupted my whole world in a matter of seconds. Since my abduction, I hadn't even so much as thought that way about a man and then in walked Eli and everything changed. The rush of heat to my cheeks when I caught him staring at me. The butterflies in my stomach. So fucking juvenile.

Gunner would kill Eli if I were to pursue my feelings, but hell at this point, why should I let him run my life? I was a grown ass woman. Why should he have the ability to dictate who I could be with? At some point, I had to stand up for what I wanted, even if not in this instance. Until I did, Gunner would never let me live my fucking life. He would always think he had power over me, and maybe it was about high time he learned the truth. The only fucking reason I was still around was to keep him from going completely downhill. Without me, he would be in prison.

"Earth to Zoe? Did I invite you here to just stare off into space? What the hell is going on?" Her eyebrow was arched and her hand resting on my knee.

I hesitated for a moment before confessing, "I met someone... His name is Eli, and I can't get him out of my head. There's just something about him that draws me in."

Lola raised an eyebrow, intrigued by this new development. "Well, that's certainly a change from your usual 'trust no one' attitude. Tell me more about this Eli."

"I met him at the bar. Yes, I know what the fuck, right? He immediately couldn't take his eyes off of me. And yes, that's normal at the bar, but this guy didn't know anything about me."

As I delved into my encounter with Eli, I valued my friendship with Lola. In a world filled with deception and danger, the bond between us was a rare beacon of trust and loyalty. The only safe space to talk about anything without repercussions.

"His eyes, Lola," I began. "It's like he can see right through me, straight to my soul."

Lola leaned forward, her green eyes glinting with curiosity. "And that's a good thing?"

Fuck, I sound like one of those damn women from those shows. I bit my lip. "I don't know. There's something magnetic about him, but it scares me too.."

Everything from my past threw kinks into this daydream.

In another dimension, maybe it could be possible, but not in this one. There were just too many variable that could hurt both of us, and why even start something like this knowing how it had to end. Tragic!

"Sounds like you're intrigued," Lola said, taking a delicate bite from her croissant, crumbs tumbling onto her plate.

"More than intrigued," I admitted, twirling a strand of my auburn hair around my finger. "But I can't let my guard down. Not after everything that's happened." My gaze drifted to the window, where passersby strolled along the sidewalk, oblivious to the turmoil brewing in my heart. Why am I so fucked up?

Lola reached out, placing a reassuring hand on my arm. "You're stronger than you give yourself credit for. Just be cautious, okay? Get to know him better before making any decisions. Hell, it's not like you guys are getting married tomorrow."

"Maybe you're right," I conceded, offering a weak smile. "It's just been so long since I've had this pull towards someone, and it's both intoxicating and terrifying at the same time."

"Then trust your instincts, babe," Lola advised. "If something feels off, walk away. But if there's a chance he could be good for you, don't let fear hold you back."

I nodded, my resolve strengthening as I took a sip of my coffee. Around us, the cafe buzzed with life – the hiss of the espresso machine, the soft rustle of newspaper pages, and the hum of conversation creating a symphony of everyday normalcy. And for a moment, I allowed myself to believe that maybe, just maybe, I could find happiness in this chaotic world. What a fucking joke.

The real world would pull me back in and I could never

ask someone to risk their safety just to be with me. Showing interest in Eli was putting a target on his back. Gunner killed many members for less and I could imagine what he would do if it involved me. Eli wouldn't stand a chance. Fuck, why did he have to show up? Wreak havoc on my mind! I was going to get out in a couple of weeks and now he just showed up here and made me wonder.

"The one thing I haven't told you..."

"Oh god! What is it?"

"After all the sparks, and we sat down and joked back and forth, Gunner recognized him."

Lola shook her head. "That means he's in too. Oh, god. Don't get involved with someone in the Jokers. Not only for your sake, but theirs. If you ever do get the chance to sneak out and never look back, it'll be ten times harder if you are tied to another person inside."

There was something more to Eli and I must figure out what it was. He might be a member, but why had I never met him? Seen him around? It wasn't like my brother to let members just join and leave, so why was he such a special case? There was so much left to find out about this man.

"He's different. And maybe tomorrow I will wake up and not give a rat's ass about him, but right now I can't stop imagining his eyes. The way they devoured me."

Lola laughed so hard, coffee almost came out of her nose. "Fuck... for both situations. Just get it over with and the lust will be gone. One night. You know what this is? It's your body telling you it's been too damn long."

Was she right? Was it just lust? From the moment I laid eyes on him, it was like he was protecting me even from across the bar. Why would he do that? There were so many unanswered questions and yet Gunner might freak if he saw me talking to him too much. Did I really care about what Gunner thought? Not normally, but I didn't want to put Eli in danger.

"Promise me you'll be careful," Lola implored.

"Promise."

My fingers traced the rim of my coffee cup, gaze distant as I delved into the shadows of my past. "What happened with my ex... you know that really fucked me up. Hell, I'll never be the same, ever."

"We haven't really talked about it because I'm not one to pry." Lola leaned in to show support.

Taking a deep breath, I gathered my courage and continued. "Marcus hurt me in ways I never thought possible. Left scars on my heart that might never heal. Hell, he hurt me physically. He would never show his face around her again. Especially knowing my brother would kill him on sight."

I hadn't had the courage to explain things to her yet, but maybe it was time. She deserved to know.

"Marcus?" Lola's green eyes flashed with anger at the mention of his name. "That piece of garbage didn't deserve you. I knew something bad happened... why didn't you tell me this sooner?"

"Because of the way you are looking at me right now."

Lola straightened up her shoulders and then took another sip of coffee. "I'm sorry. You have been dealing with all of this by yourself. I feel horrible. I'm supposed to be your best friend..."

"I wanted to keep it to myself and focus on trying to heal, but the damage is done. That's why I struggle so much with trusting people now. I want to believe in the good in others, but it's so hard when you've seen firsthand how cruel they can be. And then not even two months later, those bastards kidnapped me... and did all those awful things before my brother came to my rescue... which he will never let me forget..."

Lola reached across the table, her fingers intertwining with mine in a gesture of solidarity. "I know it's difficult, babe, but you can't let that dictate your entire life. There are still good people out there – like Eli, maybe."

I smiled wistfully at Lola's optimism, but my mind churned with doubt. Could I really trust someone again, especially a man who already managed to burrow beneath my defenses? He could be just as bad as Marcus.

"Thanks girl," I murmured, squeezing my hand gratefully. "I don't know what I'd do without you."

"Hey, we're sisters by choice," Lola grinned. "Sisters look out for each other, no matter what."

Lola and I knew each other for a very long time. We spent most of our childhood together and she knew all of my deep dark secrets. Yet never once did she ever treat me differently because of it. Instead, Lola always told me that I would get out one day and when I did, I wouldn't be alone.

I didn't foresee myself sticking around with the gang after Gunner took over, but he kept asking me for help, and then a year turned into five, and then into over a decade. Now, here I was, thirty-five-years-old and still proving loyalty to the same Twisted Jokers.

Could this be the sign that propelled me into finally get away from Gunner and the club?

5

Perched on the edge of my stool, my fingers drummed on the sticky counter. The atmosphere was filled with the clinking of glasses and occasional bursts of laughter from the pool table. Zoe's enchanting presence behind the bar, coupled with her swaying auburn hair, had me captivated. She was a whirlwind, serving shots, making cocktails, and bantering with equally captivated patrons.

"Whiskey, neat," I muttered, not able to tear my eyes away from her. I couldn't afford distractions, not now. There was an irresistible allure to Zoe, causing my heart to race like a revving motorcycle. I'd never been one to let my guard down, but with her... it was tempting.

"Coming right up," Zoe replied with a smile that held a hint of mischief. Briefly, her blue eyes locked with mine before she continued with her task. Her fingers danced across the bottles, plucking one from the shelf, and the amber liquid splashed into a tumbler. As she slid it toward me, our fingertips brushed.

"Thanks," I mumbled, taking a sip of the smooth whiskey

that burned a trail down my throat. I observed her, fascinated by how she interacted with the regulars and dealt with the occasional overly enthusiastic admirer. There was no denying her resilience and courage.

Zoe apologized for the delay, leaning in as she cleaned the counter. "Busy night."

"No worries," I replied. Despite my efforts to concentrate, I found myself being irresistibly pulled towards her like a magnet.

"So how long have you known my brother?" Zoe asked, her eyes narrowing. "Haven't seen you before."

So this is the part where she grills me. Zoe might not want to know the answers. Although, this could help determine if she knew about all the horrible things her brother did. Was she aware of all the deaths surrounding the Twisted Jokers? Did she know that her brother was responsible? As I looked into her eyes, I prayed that she wasn't just pretending. Yet, she was still here in the city when she should have left a long time ago. How did she get mixed up in all of this?

"I'm not around much... but when I'm in town, I stop by and see what he's up to," I admitted, flashing her a half-smile. I hated lying to her, especially when she could be a great ally during this operation, but taking them down had to be my top priority. Lives were at stake here, and as much as her eyes captivated me, saving countless people was more important. Always.

"Ah, he doesn't let strangers anywhere near him, but he says he trusts you, so whatever you did to earn that trust must be huge," she said, straightening up and tossing the rag over her shoulder. "Enjoy your drink." With a wink, she moved down the bar to attend to other customers, leaving me to my thoughts.

What was it about her? The men in the bar were always staring her way and I bet they hated not being able to have a chance with her. She was the one no one could have which only made them that much worse. Hopefully Gunner knew that he put a target on his sister's back. Something like that was the first thing a rival club would go after.

There was more to Zoe than met the eye. But I must keep my distance, for both our sakes. The loss of Jason was a constant reminder of the danger lurking behind every corner. And yet... as I watched her glide across the room, laughing and engaging with everyone she encountered, I wondered what it would be like to let go, even just for a moment. To lose myself in the captivating spell, she casted on everyone around her.

Focus! Don't let her do this to you! Think with your head, not your dick. I took the last sip of my whiskey and turned to leave, but Zoe's eyes were fixed on me. This couldn't be my imagination. She was staring at me. I tried to resist the urge to smile like a goofy schoolboy, but it doesn't work.

"Another drink?" the bartender asked.

My gaze was still on Zoe as she slid a cocktail down the counter to a waiting patron. "Uh, sure. Why not? Not like I have anything better to do tonight."

Thank fucking god I wasn't wearing a earpiece because this could be a little awkward if Tripp were listening in. It gave me a little bit of leeway, because I could never harmlessly flirt with Zoe otherwise.

Being undercover doesn't exactly scream relationship worthy to a woman. So other than the one casual girlfriend I had about three years ago, I hadn't even really thought about women. Some might find that weird, but my focus was on my dream: taking down bad guys and cleaning up communities.

Relationships were complicated, messy, and sometimes downright exhausting. Someone calling every night wanting to talk about how their day went, wanting to go out and eat all the time, and the gifts... Nah, I would just stay single, enjoy my career, and get my needs met occasionally without all the strings. *Yes, please!*

"Rough day or just admiring the view?" the bartender inquired, smirking as he poured me another whiskey.

"Can't it be both?" I quipped, forcing a chuckle. I took a sip of my drink, the burn not enough to distract me from the internal conflict raging within. "She's something else, isn't she?"

Fuck. Did I just say that out loud? My head swiveled to see who was close enough to hear my stupid outburst but thankfully there was no one.

"Zoe?" the bartender nodded. "Yeah, she's quite the force of nature. But I'd be careful if I were you. She's off-limits, especially to someone like you."

"Someone like me?" My brow furrowed, defensive. "What the fuck is that supposed to mean?"

"Her loyalty to her brother and this club runs deep," the bartender warned, his voice low and serious. "She isn't going to lose it all for some guy."

"I get it," I muttered, draining my glass. "Loyalty is important. She isn't my type, but she's nice to look at."

It wasn't hard to lie to this guy, but she was more than nice to look at. She had wit, personality, and heart. Someone who could be loyal to a fault. Depending on the situation, this could be a flaw or a strength. For me right now, it was a strength.

"Did I hear my name being tossed around?" she asked, resting her hip against the counter.

"Nothing to worry about," the bartender assured her with a wink, moving away to help another customer.

"You know," she began, biting her lip, "You don't have to stare at me all night. If my brother catches you, you might not wake up tomorrow.."

"Really?" I faked my surprise, because I would love to see Gunner attempt to take me down. Honestly, I hoped it was him that was responsible because then I could finally do what I had been dreaming about since I first went undercover ten years ago.

"Not kidding," she confirmed, her voice softening. "My loyalty to my brother comes first."

Tripp wanted me to get close to her, to use her for the sake of the case, but I just wasn't that type of guy. Or was I? Why was I making this so difficult for myself? She was just some girl and this was only happening because it had been a while.

Zoe is just a woman that works at this bar. She can't be more than that. Give it up!

The way Gunner talked about his sister made me sick, like she was his property. Now, Zoe was telling me that her loyalty was to her brother. What happened that caused this beautiful woman to stake her life on a man like Gunner? She had to know what he did. All the people he murdered and reigned terror on. The person he was... and yet she was still so loyal to him? Was she just caught in the crossfire or a willing participant? Just the mere thought made my whole body tense up.

Surely, it's the first. She looked as if she was being held at gunpoint sometimes. Maybe this was the only life she knew, and I knew how hard it was to tear up roots and move away from a bad situation. Everyone thought it would be easy, just getting away, but from firsthand experience, it wasn't the case. Maybe she was just waiting for the perfect time to escape.

"I have to get back to work. My brother said he should be back before you head out for the night," she said.

Why would Gunner want to see me? Fuck. Well I had to stay now. Any time spent with Gunner was more insight to the club and what they might be doing in the coming days or weeks. The whole point of this was to finish what Jason started and find out who is responsible for his death.

Zoe headed back down the bar to serve another parched patron. My fingers drummed as my eyes darted from Zoe to the group of regulars huddled in a corner. They spoke in low voices, their heads bent close together as they shared the latest gossip about recent robberies plaguing the area. *Do they really think no one can hear them? Even at a whisper level for them, it's like a megaphone.*

"Word is there's a new player in town," one regular said, his voice slurring. "They're hitting the Twisted Jokers' businesses hard."

Zoe slid a fresh drink toward me.

"Who do they think it is?" asked another patron, leaning in and sending a plume of cigarette smoke up in the air.

"Nobody knows for sure," came the reply, accompanied by a shrug. "But someone's got a death wish if they're messing with the Twisted Jokers."

I clenched my jaw, resisting the urge to ask questions. Who was this new player? This must go into my briefing later.

"Maybe it's an inside job," a third regular chimed in, his words followed by a chorus of murmurs and nods.

"Impossible," snapped Zoe, her eyes flashing with anger. "Our club is a family. We don't betray our own."

"Easy, Zoe," I interjected, voice low and steady. "No one's accusing anyone here."

"Yet," she said, searching for any sign of deceit.

I couldn't afford to lose focus, not with everything at stake. But as I looked into those blue eyes, something within me wavered, threatening to throw me off balance.

"Whatever it is," a fourth patron said, breaking the tension, "I hope they catch the bastard soon. We don't need this kind of trouble around here."

"Agreed," I murmured, forcing myself to look away from Zoe.

Why did she let these things anger her? As far as I could tell, she had never been a true part of the club. Her name was in the system, but only because of her brother. Zoe had never been to jail or suspected of any crime. Yet, she was fiercely loyal to the club. Why?

I must be missing something. The bigger picture here. There must be a reason she stayed around and kept looking out for her brother. Something much bigger than just familial obligation.

6

It was one thing for them to suspect an outsider, but to dare fucking insinuate one of our own being responsible... What the hell was going on? Why was my brother keeping secrets from me? I had no idea there were any issues. He liked to keep me out of the logistics, but when things like that happened right in front of me, it pissed me off. There was clearly something going on and he needed to get to the bottom of it. The club had enough of a bad reputation that we didn't need anymore.

Who the heck did Eli think he was? He had been here all of two days or whatever and already stepping in to try to talk me down. No one would ever keep me from standing up for my family. Most of the members I had known since I was little. They had been to every single one of my birthdays, and even some Thanksgivings. Outsiders were not going to get us all riled up and turning on each other. Not on my watch.

A sudden hush fell over the room, the chatter dying down as if someone flipped an invisible switch. I looked up, gaze immediately drawn to the imposing figure that just entered – Gunner. His dark hair framed his rugged face, and his muscular build filled his leather jacket. Tattoos snaked up his arms, the inked stories of his life in the Twisted Jokers motorcycle club permanently etched into his skin. As he strode further into the bar, the crowd parted before him, each person instinctively giving him the respect he commanded.

"Hey, sis," Gunner greeted me with a tight smile, his voice rough yet warm. "How's it going?"

He should have been here five minutes ago. Although, it wouldn't have been pretty if he witnessed it firsthand. Someone would have ended up with the bare minimum of a broken jaw.

"Nothing I can't handle," I replied with a smirk, flipping my hair over my shoulder. "You get it taken care of? Whatever you were out doing..."

"Club business," he shrugged casually, but his eyes held a hint of tension that I couldn't quite place. "Just thought I'd check in on you while I'm at it."

I knew what he meant when he said club business, and I was just as guilty as him. I was complacent. All my life, I was taught to never question two men in my life: my father and brother. When my father, the former club leader, got killed and Gunner took over, the rule became even more set in stone.

I didn't want to be this person, but it was how I was raised, and it brought me a place to live and protection. After all, even if I were to leave the Twisted Joker's behind, our enemies would always know me as Twisted Joker's property. I wouldn't be safe anywhere. Hell, I'd already been kidnapped four times in my lifetime, and I figured it would happen at least a couple more times. There was something about kidnapping women that these rival gangs loved.

Before I became of age, my mother was the target for years. She never told me that she endured the same brutal attacks, but I knew. Unfortunately, that was how the world operated. The men think of women as property.

"Well, I wanted our friend here to meet someone." His hand fell onto Eli's shoulder. "This is Razor."

I watched as my brother introduced someone I knew as a stranger to his right hand man. Something was off about this. Why did he show up here out of the blue? What were the patrons talking about? Some new guy in town messing with our business?

"It's not like Gunner to take in strangers, but you guys go way back. And after — well we could use someone who we can trust again around here."

I wasn't sure why Razor was kissing this guy's ass all of the sudden, but it had to be because of Gunner. How close exactly were Gunner and Eli? What happened to make him trust him so much already? For someone who told me all of my life, don't trust anyone, he wasn't following the rules.

"So what, he comes in, and you are just welcoming him into the family? Seriously? If you know him so well, huh, why have I never heard of him?" My eyes widened.

From the moment Eli walked into the bar, I knew there was something about him, but until now I never quite knew what it was. Did I met him before? The months after being kidnapped were a blur, lots of partying and drinking, so maybe I was just not putting two and two together?

"Let me go talk to this guy real quick," Gunner said, leaving Eli standing next to me still wondering what the hell was going on.

As Gunner made his way around the room, engaging in brief conversations and sharing gruff laughter with his fellow club members, I noticed the undercurrent of unease that followed him. He was always a man who commanded attention, but tonight there was something different, something darker lingering just beneath the surface.

I tried to shake off my concern as I poured another round of drinks, but Gunner's presence weighed heavily on my mind. Gunner would do anything to protect me, and that thought both comforted and terrified me. After all, there were secrets between them – secrets that threatened to tear apart the fragile balance we'd managed to maintain.

As the night wore on, the bar returned to its usual chaos, the patrons eagerly diving back into their vices. But I couldn't escape the nagging feeling that something was amiss, that danger was lurking just beyond my vision, waiting for the perfect moment to strike. And in this world, danger had a way of finding those who least expected it.

"Hey Zoe," called out a patron, breaking my focus momentarily. I turned back to the counter, expertly mixing a cocktail for the eager customer. My fingers moved deftly, showcasing my skill, but my thoughts lingered on Eli and the unknown danger he might represent.

Gunner's boots thudded heavily against the wooden floor as he approached his sister. The weight of each step mirrored the heaviness in my chest, pulse quickening. Club members shifted aside, parting like the sea before their leader, sensing the charged atmosphere surrounding him.

"Zoe," Gunner said gruffly, his voice barely audible above the music. "We need to talk."

"Sure, what's up?" I replied, forcing a casual tone despite the knot tightening in my stomach.

"Outside." His eyes flicked toward Eli, the unspoken warning clear. As Gunner turned to leave, I hesitated, casting a nervous glance at Eli, who was engrossed in his drink, unaware of the brewing storm.

The door swung shut behind us, cutting off the cacophony of sounds from inside the bar. Under the cold glare of the moon, Gunner's face took on an even more menacing appearance.

"Zoe," he began, his voice strained, "You haven't stopped staring at him since he got here tonight. Am I gonna have to worry about you two?"

"Who, Eli?" I frowned, trying to ignore the budding fear in my heart. "Absolutely fucking not. I wouldn't even consider him a friend."

Okay, so maybe I was lying, but right now there was nothing going on between us and my brother didn't need to know. Instead of focusing on me, why wasn't he worried about this new player in town? My love life shouldn't matter. His priorities were all fucked up.

"Friends can be dangerous," Gunner warned, his eyes darkening with unspoken threats. "Stay away from him, just like I told him to stay away from you."

I swallowed hard, my throat tightening as I struggled to process Gunner's words and my own conflicted emotions. What was it about me that screamed poor little girl. Ever since our dad died, he had been on my case about every man I had ever let into my life. They were either too good for me or I was too good for them.

"Really, Gunner? He's not a threat," I insisted, folding my arms across my chest. "You have been treating him like an ally, so is there something going on that I don't know about?"

"Listen, sis," he said, his voice softening slightly. "I'm just trying to keep you safe. This club is our family, and I can't let anyone hurt us. Promise me you'll stay away from him. You dating within the club is just bad for business. These are my brothers..."

This wasn't about that. I could tell when my brother was lying, and he was omitting. Something was going on with him and Eli. I'm so sick of him thinking he could tell me how to live my fucking life. Not anymore.

7

Seeking solace, I found a hidden nook in the bar, my heart thumping as I struggled to decipher the words I had unintentionally eavesdropped on. The gentle buzz of hushed conversation grabbed my attention, and I slowly moved closer to investigate. Amongst the crowd of Twisted Jokers, two members stood huddled together, their voices drowned by the lively chatter and blaring jukebox.

"...shipment coming in tomorrow night," one of them muttered, glancing around nervously. "Biggest one yet."

"Boss is gonna be pleased," the other replied, smirking. "This is gonna put us on top."

A wave of anger crashed over me as I comprehended just how deeply the club was involved in the trade. It was worse than I'd initially thought. With the need for additional evidence, I battled against my own emotions that were threatening to hinder my judgment. I stepped back, my mind racing with thoughts, desperately trying to plot my next move.

Zoe shouldn't be caught up in this mess, but from what I

gathered, the club was a family affair, even her mother was in it. As parents, they should've wanted better for their daughter, but obviously not. So, she got thrown into the same life they did, and they lost both of their lives because of rivals.

I couldn't let that happen to Zoe. She might be in the club, but it was all she knew. In my experience, the people who had no one else to turn to, were typically the most loyal of them all. To make matters worse, her brother was the leader, and I couldn't imagine her giving him up. Even if it meant she could get away from this life.

This shipment could be exactly what we needed to get some solid evidence to take them down. Maybe I could get Gunner to bring me in on it. Although, he didn't look too pleased when he pulled his sister away. Gripping the edge of the bar, my fingers clenched tightly as I strained to pick up the faint sounds of the hushed conversation between Gunner and Zoe.

"Zoe..." Gunner's voice was low and urgent. "He might be one of mine, but my main loyalty is to you, and I won't let anyone screw you over. We don't need another situation like..."

My Adam's apple bobbed.

"Don't even finish that damn sentence. How could you even bring that up like it was my fault?" Zoe's tone wavered between disbelief and indignation. "You are the one that came in treating him like fucking royalty... and now all of the sudden you are forbidding me from even looking at the guy. Last time I checked, I'm a grown ass woman who doesn't need to ask her brother to get laid."

My heart pounded, each beat a hammer against my ribs. I knew the risks when I went undercover, but there was something between Zoe and I. It was clear how much she wanted a different life than this one. One not full of blood-shed. If I could somehow find a way to get her out of this life, without having her compromise herself, that would be a win.

As I wrestled with my conflicting desires, my grip on the bar tightened, my nails digging into the worn wood. Duty demanded I stay focused on the mission, but everything else urged me to abandon it all for the woman who captured my heart from the first look. The choice was impossible, tearing me apart from the inside out.

What situation were they talking about? Maybe I needed to do a little digging into Zoe.

"Listen, I haven't told anyone but Razor, but he's up to something. The guy hasn't spoken to me since I saw him years ago and he just shows up here, asking around... he's hiding something."

Oh fuck! Gunner was onto me. Or well, hesitant of me. He was definitely not going to let me in on the plans for this shipment. Whatever, all that meant was I needed to get him to trust me again. Like he used to.

"Even if Eli is hiding something, isn't everyone here?" Zoe argued. "How many secrets do we keep from each other, Gunner?"

"Too damn many." His voice cracked, betraying his worry. "But that's not the point. I'm trying to protect you, Zoe. You know what this life has cost us."

The raw emotion in Gunner's voice cut through me like a knife. The pain and loss etched into the man's face, a mirror of his own demons. For a moment, I was no longer an undercover agent, but a man who understood all too well the price of love and loyalty.

Inhaling deeply, I steadied myself, my breath becoming a calming force, as I made silent vow to complete my mission, gather the evidence needed to bring down the Twisted jokers - but I wouldn't let it destroy Zoe. She deserved better than a broken world, and I would do everything in my power to give it to her.

"Fine, Gunner," Zoe conceded, her voice thick. "I'll make you a deal. If you can go two weeks without killing someone, then I'll promise to stay away from him, otherwise I can do as I please..."

A tightness gripped my heart.Did he truly kill that often? Zoe knew about his treacherous ways? All the secrets she must know and be forced to keep. The black circles formed under her eyes now told me a different story. How many nights has she laid awake trying to bury those secrets?

I attempted to remain inconspicuous while quietly observing their conversation. Zoe bit down on her lip.

"I'm serious," Gunner said, his tone grave. "Eli's hiding something, and I don't want you caught in the crossfire."

"Okay, I'll be careful. That's all I can promise."

Gunner nodded, relief flickering across his face before he pulled her into a fierce embrace. "You're all I have left. I can't lose you too."

As they parted ways, a disturbance broke out near the entrance, accompanied by the jarring noise of shattered glass and voices raised in anger. Gunner's head jerked to the side, his features turning grim as he observed the chaos unfolding before him.

I went back to leaning against the worn bar top, knowing that she would eventually go back to serving drinks. *Watch yourself, Jackson.* I let the whiskey burn my throat as I took another sip.

"You must be Eli." Lola slid into the seat next to me, her

hair gleaming in the neon light. "You look like a man with something on his mind."

"Nothing I can't handle," I replied, forcing a tight-lipped smile.

"Good," she said, tipping back her shot glass. "Because things are about to get interesting."

As if on cue, Gunner Morales came back into the bar, commanding attention. Whispers rippled through the crowd, punctuated by the sharp clack of billiard balls as the game continued in the background. The tension in the air thickened.

I drained the last of my whiskey, steeling myself for whatever lay ahead. The stakes were never higher. And as the soft strains of blues faded, I prepared for the storm that was about to break.

8

In the shadowy corner of the room, my heart pounded as Gunner's powerful arm slammed a club member against the cracked, graffiti-covered wall. My eyes narrowed, torn between the fierce loyalty for my brother and the growing unease that twisted my stomach into knots. Gunner wasn't a good guy, I knew that, but he was all I had left.

Gasping for breath, the club member's eyes bulged with terror, every line on his face etching a story of fear. His arms flailed wildly, clawing at Gunner's vice-like grip around his throat. Pain and panic danced across his features like twin shadows, his own loyalty to the Twisted Jokers now a distant memory. The room closed in on itself, trapping everyone within its suffocating confines, and the club member's desperation seeped into my bones.

"Please...Gunner..." the man wheezed. The plea only tightened Gunner's grip around his neck, his face set in stone, betraying no emotion.

"Tell me why I shouldn't crush your windpipe right now," Gunner growled, his voice cold and unforgiving.

My insides churned like a storm-tossed sea. This was not the brother I knew and loved. This was someone else entirely, someone who terrified me. I clenched my teeth, forcing myself to remain silent as the scene played out before me.

"Gun...ner... I'm...loyal," the club member choked out, tears streaming down his pale cheeks.

"Are you?" Gunner snarled, his grip relentless.

I couldn't stand it any longer. My loyalty to my brother and the club warred with my own sense of right and wrong. It was becoming harder and harder for me to reconcile the two. I took a step forward, voice shaking but resolute.

"Enough, Gunner. Let him go."

His face contorted with rage, his dark eyes narrowing as he stared into the club member's fear-filled gaze. "You think you can just betray us and walk away?" he snarled, spittle flying from his lips.

My stomach twisted in knots, the scene unfolding before me like a nightmare I couldn't escape. With trembling hands, I pressed against my throat, my wide eyes mirroring my shock and horror. The brutal force of Gunner's anger was a side of him I never wanted to witness firsthand – and now I couldn't look away.

It reminded me of all the times my fathers anger was displayed. The many nights I spent wondering if my mother would ever walk away from him. Sure, being a leader was stressful, but at some point, everyone had to make a choice. Stand up or lay down.

This was never the life I envisioned for us, but right now, standing here, it was time to stand up.

"Gun...ner," the club member gasped, his face turning an alarming shade of purple. "I didn't... I swear..."

"Save your pathetic excuses motherfucker!" Gunner roared, his grip on the man's neck unyielding. His knuckles turned white, veins bulging beneath his tattooed skin.

Someone had to get through to him. If not, this man was going to die at the hands of my brother.

"Please..." the man choked out, his body beginning to go limp.

The room held its breath, the tension hanging heavy in the air. My heart pounded, my mind racing with thoughts I dared not speak aloud. How did things come to this? Was this really the brother I knew and loved? We had both changed so fucking much over the years. But this? Holy hell!

"Stop, Gunner!" My voice came out sharper than I'd intended, but I couldn't stand idly by any longer. "This isn't you – this isn't who we are!"

His grip on the club member's neck faltered for a moment, and the internal struggle playing out across his features. But then he shook his head, his jaw set in a grim line.

"Sometimes you have to do what's necessary to protect what's yours," he growled, his gaze locking onto mine. "If you can't handle that, then maybe you're in the wrong place."

I flinched at the coldness in his voice, my heart aching with the weight of his words. I looked at my brother, then to the trembling man struggling to breathe, and finally to the Twisted Jokers emblem emblazoned on the walls around them.

"Let him go, Gunner!" My voice cracked like a whip through the air, eyes ablaze with defiance. I took an unyielding step forward, fists clenched at my sides.

His grip loosened slightly, his eyes narrowing as he turned to face me. The anger in his gaze only grew in intensity, his nostrils flaring like a cornered animal. "You dare question my judgment?" he spat, the words leaving his lips like venom.

"I'm questioning your humanity," I retorted, my breaths coming in short, uneven gasps as I struggled to keep my emotions in check. "We're supposed to be a family. We don't treat each other like this."

"Family? You think I don't know what it means to be family?" he roared, slamming the man against the wall once more before finally releasing him. The club member crumpled to the floor, coughing and gasping for breath. "I've done everything for this club – for you!"

"By hurting others? By turning us into monsters?" My voice trembled as I fought back tears, heart racing with a mix of fear and sorrow. "That's not the brother I remember. That's not the club I love."

"Love?" Gunner sneered, stalking towards me with predatory gaze. "If you loved this club, you wouldn't be so fucking weak. You'd understand that loyalty demands sacrifice, little sister – that sometimes blood must be shed to protect our own."

"Is that what you call this?" I gestured towards the injured man, my hands shaking as I forced myself to meet my brother's furious gaze. "You nearly killed him over a fucking rumor! This isn't protection, Gunner. It's madness. You need to cool down and question yourself because last time I checked we don't turn on our own without some sort of evidence."

"Madness is allowing disloyalty to fester within our ranks," he snarled, his face mere inches from mine. "If you can't see that – if you won't stand by me and do what's necessary – then maybe you're the one who's fucking disloyal. Huh, sis?"

Had I been slapped? My heart constricting painfully in my chest. I'd never questioned my loyalty to Gunner or the club before, but now, staring into the eyes of a man I barely recognized, I couldn't help but wonder if I was truly doing the right thing.

"Disloyal?" I choked on the word, the air in the bar grew thicker. "You really think I'd betray you and the club?"

"Your actions speak louder than your words, Zoe," Gunner shot back, his eyes narrowing as he scrutinized me.

"Damn it, Gunner, I was just trying to protect him!" I protested, chest heaving with frustration and desperation. My eyes darted to the bruised and battered club member, still struggling to catch his breath.

Tonight is a fucking nightmare! Why the fuck am I still here?

"By undermining my authority? By questioning my decisions in front of everyone? For fucks sake." Gunner's voice was low and dangerous, each syllable dripping with menace.

"Enough!" I slammed my fist against a table, the sound echoing through the room like a gunshot. The weight of the other club members' gazes left my cheeks flushed, but I didn't care – I couldn't let this go on any longer. "Maybe we all need to take a step back and look at what's happening here," she said. "This club used to be about loyalty and brotherhood, but now... now it feels like we're tearing each other apart. What the fuck is happening? Since when did we let others dictate us?"

"Are you saying I'm destroying the club?" Gunner asked, his voice laced with a deadly calm that sent shivers down my spine.

"No," I replied, shaking my head slowly. "I'm saying that maybe we've lost sight of what truly matters. That we need to find our way back to who we were before all this madness took hold."

"Or maybe," Gunner countered, taking a menacing step forward, "you're just too blind to see that things have changed. The world has changed, little sister – and we must change with it. Grow the fuck up! We aren't kids anymore."

"Is it really worth losing ourselves in the process? Doing shit like this? Almost killing a brother because you have a hothead?" I whispered, heart pounding as I fought to keep my emotions in check.

"Sometimes," Gunner replied, his voice cold and unyielding as he stepped back, "it's the only way."

I swallowed hard, my mind racing as I tried to make sense of it all. How did they come to this? How had we strayed so far from the path that we once walked together – side by side, bound by blood and loyalty?

"Maybe you're right," I conceded. "But I can't help but wonder if there's more at stake here than just our survival. And if maybe, just maybe... we've lost our way."

"Then find your own path, little sister," Gunner sneered, turning away from me. "Just don't be surprised when it leads you straight to fucking hell."

After that, I took myself into the small office at the back of the bar, closing my eyes, trying to control my breathing. How was that my brother? When did he start treating me this fucking way? There was no going back. Gunner was now facing a very dark path and he didn't care who he fucked over or hurt in the process.

I sank onto the worn leather couch, my hands trembling as I replayed the violent confrontation. The images flickered like a broken film reel – distorted and fragmented, yet painfully vivid.

"Hey, you okay?"

"Am I okay?" I repeated bitterly, forcing myself to meet Lola's concerned gaze. "I don't even know anymore. I don't know who I am or what I'm doing here."

"Talk to me," I urged softly, sitting down beside me on the couch. "What's going on?"

I hesitated, feeling the weight of my conflicted loyalties bearing down. How could I put into words the gnawing sense of doubt that took root in my heart?

"Every day, it feels like we're sinking deeper into something darker... something dangerous," I confessed. "And I'm starting to wonder if there's any way out. This isn't the place for me anymore and it's clear that he doesn't want my fucking help."

Lola reached out, placing a comforting hand on my shoulder. "Maybe you need to make a choice, Zoe," she said. "Between your loyalty to your brother and your own moral code."

"Is it really that simple?" I asked. "Gunner's my family. And so is this club. How can I turn my back on them?"

"Sometimes the hardest choices are the ones that define us the most," Lola replied, her eyes filled with understanding. "But you have to ask yourself: what kind of person do you want to be?"

As the words hung in the air, she was right. No more standing idly by while the club spiraled into chaos and violence – not if I wanted to look at myself in the mirror every day. But how could I choose between my loyalty to my brother and my own moral compass? How could I walk away from the only family I'd ever known.

"Maybe," I whispered, feeling as though I were teetering on the edge of a precipice, "it's time for me to forge my own path."

"Maybe it is," she agreed, giving her shoulder a reassuring squeeze. "Just remember, Zoe – whatever you decide, you're not alone. You've got friends who care about you... and who'll stand by your side, no matter what. Twisted Jokers or not, you are my family."

For the first time in an eternity, a tiny flicker of hope ignited within my chest. But even as it burned, I couldn't help but wonder: would it be enough to guide me through the darkness that lay ahead? Or would I still find myself lost, adrift in a sea of secrets and lies, with nothing but my own faltering heart to light the way?

9

What in the actual fuck was wrong with him? I tried to keep my breathing under wraps. Would he really turn his back on his own sister? Just like that? It only cemented what I already knew - he was a bastard. The club itself meant more to Gunner than his own sister, and he would never stop. Maybe he didn't mean to become this person, but being involved in this type of lifestyle, especially as the leader, completely changed his moral compass.

Gunner went after him because of rumors, not even with solid evidence. How could he turn so fast on his own guy? Something was going on, something bigger than just these shipments, and I needed to figure it out. They kept talking about someone new in town. Someone who was after the Twisted Jokers and they obviously didn't mean me, so who was it?

Eli: Do some digging. They are getting antsy and we need to figure out who this new player is before Gunner does.

Tripp would have to do it because something was off and I couldn't just leave Zoe behind. The way the members looked at her when Gunner was basically telling her to go to hell... it was like they couldn't wait. Cause to them, without Gunner protecting her, she would be fair game. These men didn't have any shame. I knew what they were capable of if they got Zoe alone. Awful thoughts popped up in my mind.

Things were escalating to the extreme and it wouldn't be too long until Gunner burned his own club to the ground. He would rather do that than look like an imbecile. Someone was doing things to hurt his club right under his nose, and it would eat at him until he found the person responsible.

I wanted to find Zoe, but not with everyone watching. She went to the backroom and a lady followed her. Whoever she was, maybe she could talk some sense into her. If she had ever been thinking about getting out, now was the time to do it. Her own brother basically gave her permission.

The members were all whispering amongst themselves with Zoe and Gunner out of the room. Gunner couldn't show weakness especially in front of his guys, and now they knew he meant business. If he wasn't going to budge for his own sister, then he wouldn't think twice to hurt or kill any of the members for betrayal either.

I needed to watch my back carefully. After overhearing the conversation between Gunner and his sister, he suspected me of something. He didn't know that I was undercover, but showing up out of the blue after a couple years of being in the dust would raise some questions.

Zoe came out of the backroom, whispered something in the bartender's ear, and walked out of the bar. Where the fuck was she going? I took the last sip of my drink and casually followed after her. She needed to be with someone tonight, not alone. Any of the guys could come after her. No way in hell I was letting that happen. I waited until we were away from ear shot from the bar.

"Wait!" I yelled.

Zoe didn't stop, but kept walking to her car. "You shouldn't be seen with me. Especially right now. Gunner will look for any reason to hurt someone."

"Right now, I'm worried about you, not your brother."

Zoe spun around, looking into my eyes. "Why do you care? You are just another member of my brother's club who wants to live dangerously. I've had my fair share of flings, but trust me when I say, I see exactly what you are doing, and you aren't the first."

Wow! Seriously? How the fuck could she say those things to me? She doesn't need to act like this. Her anger toward her brother was radiating through her and if she needed to use me as a punching bag right now, so be it. One thing though, this chemistry wasn't all in my head. Fuck that!

"Listen, let me take you somewhere to cool off from this. The first place your brother will show up is your place." I stepped a little closer to her. The last thing we needed was someone overhearing us.

Gunner wasn't one to let things go. My ass wouldn't get one lick of sleep tonight without knowing she was safe. There was no way I would let her go home all alone. Everyone knew where she lived.

"Why would I go anywhere with you?" she asked, hand on her hips.

She always had to act like this. Be the tough girl, because of who her family was, but she didn't have to act that way with me. Underneath her tough exterior, there was a girl just begging to get away from all this. If given an opportunity without having to worry about being hurt, she would jump. I knew it. Now, I just had to give her the opportunity.

"Zoe, drop the act. We both know there is some chemistry between us, and we can act like that doesn't exist fine, but I still need you to be safe. What if one of the members comes after you to prove a point? Fuck that, you are coming with me. I don't wanna hear another fucking thing about it."

She scoffed, but didn't argue further. "Fine, but after tonight, we shouldn't even be near each other. My brother clearly thinks there is something going on and no matter what happened in there, he would kill for me. I fucking know it. No one's blood is going to be on my hands. I won't let it."

The poor girl truly believed her brother would defend her, but if push came to shove, the only fucking person he cared about was himself. Now that he was at the top, there was no backing down. He had to keep the members scared of him or it opened him up to a takeover. The motherfucker had no conscience left.

She followed behind me over to my truck. "After you." She slid into the passenger side seat and I took my place next to her. "Don't worry where we are going, they won't find you."

For one night, she needed to be able to let go of the facade. A place where she could let everything that happened today melt away. Gunner would never find her there and this could be the opportunity to possibly get some answers from her.

10

Zoe and I stood in a secluded spot in an abandoned cabin in the middle of the woods, just a few miles outside of town, and provided the perfect refuge for us to be alone. Surrounded by tall pines, our silhouettes stretched like long fingers reaching for the darkening sky.

A cool breeze rustled through the branches above, sending a shiver down my spine as I watched Zoe standing near the edge of the clearing. Her auburn hair danced in the wind.

"Beautiful, isn't it?" Zoe whispered, her breath visible.

"Absolutely stunning," I replied, his eyes fixed on her.

As we stood there, the silence between us grew heavy. I wanted to reach out, to pull her close, but I couldn't shake the fear that gnawed at me. I was torn between my growing feelings for Zoe and the mission that brought me here: infiltrating the Twisted Jokers motorcycle club to find the traitor responsible for my partner's death and taking them down, once and for all. Instead of being back at the bar, hanging with the guys trying to drum up evidence, I was here with her. A part of me knew she had information that could help the investigation.Yet, having her here, this close to me, left me thinking about only one thing.

Zoe turned to face me, her blue eyes searching my face for answers. "What are we doing out here, Eli?"

"Getting away from everything," I replied, swallowing hard. "Those guys want you so bad... and now that your brother publicly announced that you should leave... well they are biting at the bit for their chance. You aren't safe anywhere else tonight."

"Is there really any escape from the danger?" she asked softly. "Especially for us?"

She was right. No matter how far we ran, the danger would always loom in the shadows. It was a part of us now. But I couldn't help but hope that maybe, just maybe, we could find a moment of peace in each other's arms. Eventually I was going to have to come clean with her, but right now she was struggling with deciding which path to go down and I didn't want to be the deciding factor in that decision. She needed to come to terms on her own on what kind of piece of shit her brother was, and just how fast he would turn on her if she got in his way. Tonight proved so much to me, and it might have been the thing to open her eyes. She wanted better for herself and this might just be her opportunity to get the fuck out of dodge.

"Maybe not," I admitted. "But I want to try."

The stakes were higher than ever, but so were my feelings for Zoe. With every moment we spent together, the line between duty and passion blurred further. And as the darkness closed in around us, I needed to make a choice – but what would I choose, and at what cost?

"Being here is like a dream," Zoe confessed. "The view is breathtaking..."

Her eyes locked on mine, full of hope and fear. She reached up, gently tracing the contours of my face, her fingertips lingering on the scar. "Tell me about this," she said.

I hesitated, then sighed. "It's a reminder of the life I left behind. A life where I wasn't always the good guy." I paused, searching for the right words. "I used to be involved with some dangerous people. I had to make a choice, and I chose to walk away from that world. But it came at a price."

"Everyone has their demons," Zoe murmured, her touch tender and understanding.

"But sometimes the past isn't so easy to leave behind."

"Like my brother and the Twisted Jokers," Zoe acknowledged. "I wish things could be different for us, Eli. But the danger... it's always there, isn't it? Now matter where we go – once a Twisted Joker, always a Twisted Joker unless..."

"Would your brother do that to you? You guys seem pretty close?" I admitted, my brow furrowed. Even though I knew the answer. Had she finally realized it yet?

"You have seen what happens when anyone questions him! He freaks out! You know, he wasn't always like this... before my father passed away and he took over... things were different. Gunner wanted to go to college, become a doctor... but my parents were VERY set on him being the next leader."

"So your brother didn't want to?"

"Not then, no. Things changed when my dad was murdered and Gunner needed to take over and find out who killed our father. He didn't believe there was anyone else to lead the group then." A single tear fell from her eye. "I miss that version of my brother. The one that would have never done what he did at the bar."

I wasn't sure if I was going to be able to control my facial expressions, but if she started crying, I would be screwed. If there was one thing I couldn't stand by and watch, it's a woman crying. Especially a beautifully twisted woman like her.

"Sometimes people just get too deep... they forget that the people in the rivals have sisters, mothers, daughters... I try to remember that to keep my morality in check... but most of the guys have completely forgotten that."

The Twisted Jokers left behind a trail of thirty-eight bodies in the last three years. Not all evidence indicated them, but Tripp and I were sure they were the responsible party. The similarities in the murders were too close to other murders that had been left unsolved. Of course, many of them were part of the rival gang, which means it was either the TJ's or just a random act of violence, but the department was trying to take them down for decades, since Gunner and Zoe's dad took over. Now that was a scary dude. Six foot five burley guy, tattoos everywhere, braided beard... if a normal citizen saw him on the street, they would run. See, he had a knack for wanting to try out new ways to kill someone. The things I had seen while reviewing outstanding cases that were connected to the Twisted Joker's... there were a couple times he got sick. Their father was a brutal and dangerous man and now Gunner was the same way. The outburst in the bar against one of his own proved it. If Zoe stayed loyal to him, she would end up buried six feet under.

"What are you thinking about?" I asked.

"What I would've done if you hadn't walked into the bar that night?" she smiled and bit her lower lip. "You know my brother told me and you to stay away from each other... and he will have a coronary if anything happens between us, right?"

"Then let's make every moment count," I urged, stepping closer.

My resolve wavered as I took in the sight of her, the moonlight casting a delicate glow on her upturned face. I couldn't fight it any longer. No one else was around. Her eyes were pools of blue fire, and her lips parted, inviting me closer. The world outside our secluded haven disappeared as the air between us crackled with desire.

11

The intensity of his touch made my body burn, his lips meeting mine in a gentle, lingering kiss, and I chose not to withdraw. My body ached for his touch. Despite being fully aware of the consequences, my desire for him was insatiable. Lola expressed her thoughts that it was only lust, and I viewed this as my chance to challenge her perception. My fingers tangled in his silky hair as our tongues danced a passionate tango. The moment had come to see if the man who had invaded my dreams lived up to the fantasy.

The night collided as if it were a riptide pulling me further and further away from reality. No longer content with the expectations and restrictions of the club, it was a new kind of freedom where I could be whoever I wanted to be.

Being here proved that I needed to take my life back. The longer I went along with my brother's bullshit, the more I would be pulled down the fucking rabbit hole.

His lips parted from mine, and his eyes locked on mine. "You are so beautiful." His finger trailed down my cheek, and my gaze lingered toward the ground. His index finger hooked under my chin, and pulled it up. "Don't you dare do that."

The moonlight illuminated and slid down my skin. I had lived in the shadows for too long, too afraid to venture out. But tonight, being here with Eli, things were changing.

The moment he walked into the bar, my eyes couldn't go far. Everything about him was intriguing. He had lived in my thoughts doing some very dirty things to me. Sex wasn't new to me, fuck I wasn't a virgin, but it meant something to me. I was the girl who had never had a one night stand. However, standing next to him right now, maybe that would all change.

He was a man with well-defined muscles that left my mind wondering how much fun a night with him could be. When I felt his eyes locked on my body, butterflies took over. What the fuck was wrong with me?

"We shouldn't do this," I said, my hand on his chest. "We both know what would happen if the others were to find out."

"I don't give a fuck about your brother."

The energy radiating off of him was intoxicating. His lips were back on mine, and my whole body was begging for his touch. *Please! Just fucking touch me!* We inched toward the cabin, not wanting to tear our lips apart, and then we were inside as Eli shut the front door and slammed his back against it. The atmosphere was electric.

Our eyes met, the intensity in Eli's gaze drawing me in. My knees were weak as he moved closer, coming to rest his hands on my hips. His heat radiated through the fabric. This man was fucking unbelievable.

Eli's lips brushed against mine, his kiss gentle but demanding. I gasped, my body coming alive with desire as

Eli's tongue explored my mouth. I moaned softly as his hands moved up my body, caressing every inch of my skin.

My hands moved up to Eli's shoulders, pulling him closer as our kiss deepened. Eli moaned into my mouth as our tongues tangled. I wanted him more than anything, and Eli wanted me just as much.

Fuck everything! No more making excuses! Tonight is all about what I want and right now I fucking want Eli.

Eli's hands moved lower, slipping beneath the fabric. He pulled me even closer, his mouth exploring my neck and shoulders. I trembled, my body alive with pleasure. Eli's touch was intoxicating, and I never wanted it to end. It had been a long time since someone's hands had the pleasure of touching me and sometimes I forget just how amazing giving into the intoxicating desire was.

His hands moved down my body, cupping my ass and pressing me against him. "I just can't stay away from you!" When a growl erupted from his throat, I knew right then, I was in trouble.

I gasped as Eli's lips moved down my body, exploring every inch of my skin. His tongue caressed my stomach, and I moaned softly as his hands moved between my legs.

"Do you want me to stop?" he asked, looking dead in my eyes.

"Don't you fucking dare."

His hands slipped between the soft material of my underwear and my skin.

"Holy hell..." he licked his lips and then crutched his bottom lip with his teeth. Eli hooked my left leg around his waist and held it there, then easily slid a finger inside me. My head threw back. Was he teasing me? His grip on my thigh was rough, but fuck!

His lips came right next to my ear and whispered, "I want you to come for me."

My knees went weak at his words, but when he slipped a second girl in and started rocking my hips in sync with his fingers, I thought I was going to fucking lose it. This man was a god and within two minutes I was screaming him fucking name at the top of my lungs. Good thing we were in the middle of nowhere. My chest heaved and his eyes were on me.

"You look even more beautiful when you come."

He picked me up by my ass, legs wrapped around his waist, and took me into the bedroom. At this point, all I wanted was to feel him inside of me.

Eli sat me down on the edge of the bed. He stepped between my legs, his hands exploring my body as his mouth moved back to mine. I moaned, my body burning with desire as the kiss deepened.

I've had plenty of sexual encounters, but none like that. Men didn't usually worry about my orgasm, and the fact that he put me first right out of the gate, this night was going to be fun.

He took off his jacket, letting it hit the floor, before reaching for the hem of his t-shirt and dragging it up his body. My eyes followed up his torso, trying not to come right there. He was a masterpiece, but like all of us, we had scars to bear.

He stood in front of me, and I undid his zipper and then pulled his pants and boxers down. It was time to return the favor. He was hard and bigger than anyone else I had ever been with, but I liked being challenged. My hand went around him, and he groaned the moment it did, which only made my lips surrounding him more fun. His hand never touched the back of my head, instead letting me control the pace.

"Fuck, Zoe. Where have you been all my life?" He said in a low, husky voice.

He was getting harder and harder, but when he was close, he pulled himself out of my mouth. "No. I want to come while inside you," he said, a determined look on his face. He grabbed his wallet out of his pants and ripped the package open with his teeth, sliding it onto his hard cock. "Are you ready for me?" He asked, his voice a mix of yearning and anticipation.

I pulled him closer, wrapping her legs around him and arching her back. "Yes," she breathed, her voice low and inviting.

With that, Eli entered me. He moved slowly at first, teasing me as his pelvis brushed against mine.

He entered me slowly, taking his time to let me feel every inch of him. His hips moved in a steady rhythm, brushing sweetly against mine. His hands were everywhere, exploring my body as we moved in unison. The intensity built until I was about to burst with pleasure and then he pushed into me harder and faster, the sensation over-whelming.

I gasped as Eli pushed me closer and closer to the edge of ecstasy. His muscles tensed as he thrust into me over and over again, sending waves of pleasure coursing through my body. His hands moved up my sides, his touch awakening every nerve ending in me with every stroke. I felt my orgasm building within me, the intensity mounting until I couldn't take it any longer and I let out a loud cry as I came undone in his arms.

Eli followed soon after, his body shuddering as he

released himself inside of me. We stayed there for a while, both of us breathing heavily and trying to catch our breath. Finally, Eli rolled off of me and pulled me into his arms.

"That was incredible," he whispered, pressing a soft kiss to my forehead.

I nestled closer into him, feeling completely content. This wasn't where I saw the night going, but no regrets. Sometimes I needed to do things for myself without worrying about others.

Tonight was about me!

12

As I embraced Zoe, my mind raced with a whirlwind of thoughts. The warmth of her body sent shivers down my spine, and my hands tightened around her waist.

"Zoe," I whispered between kisses, the words barely escaping my throat. "We need to talk."

Her eyes fluttered open, confusion clouding her gaze before it sharpened into determination. She pulled away from me slightly. "What is it? What's wrong?"

"Nothing's wrong," I reassured her, but my voice wavered. Images of my late partner, flashed through my mind—memories of laughter and friendship now tainted by the blood that stained my conscience. I couldn't afford to lose focus on the mission, not when so much was at stake. Yet, every moment spent with Zoe threatened to break down the carefully constructed walls I built around my heart, making it harder for me to stay focused.

"You have to understand... I'm afraid that being with me would only put you in more danger."

She studied me for a moment, her eyes searching my

face for any sign of deceit. "I know the risks, Eli. But what we have here—this connection—I can't just walk away from it. Not without giving it a chance. Screw my brother! I'm not willing to walk away from the first man that has made me feel this way."

"Even if it means putting yourself in harm's way?" I asked, my voice strained.

"Especially then," she replied. "I've spent my whole life put in danger. My dad wasn't exactly the father of the year... I've been kidnapped and hurt more times than I can count... but I can tell that you would put me BEFORE the club and that's exactly what I've been looking for..."

"Zoe, I..." I hesitated; my heart heavy with the weight of the decision before me. How do I keep her out of this mission? Things were complicated now. I had sex with her and now I had to take down her family's gang and possibly her if she doesn't cooperate? What the hell did I get myself into?

Her thumb traced circles on the back of my hand. "But what we can do is face whatever comes our way together."

"No matter what happens, I'd never let your brother, or any man hurt you. Over my dead fucking body... and I mean that literally!"

Would Gunner hurt his own sister? After his demonstration in front of everyone else, he might. He was so immersed in this world that he might be willing to hurt his own sister if she got in the way of his almighty club.

My resolve crumbled under the fierce determination in her eyes. Maybe, just maybe, there was a way to balance the dangerous world of the mission with the all-consuming protectiveness I felt for Zoe.

The sound of approaching engines broke through the

quiet serenity, startling us apart. My heart raced, and I instinctively moved to shield Zoe from whatever danger might be lurking.

"Get behind me," I commanded, my eyes scanning the surrounding area outside the window.

"Wait, it's... it's Gunner!" Zoe exclaimed, recognizing the familiar roar of her brother's motorcycle. "But why is he here? How did he find us?"

We struggled to get dressed. My mind raced, conjuring up countless scenarios that could explain Gunner's unexpected arrival. But one thing was clear: our secret was out, and there would be no turning back now.

"I need you to listen to me," I said urgently, my voice barely audible above the approaching engines. "No matter what happens, just stay behind me." I took her face in my hands, pressing our foreheads together as I locked eyes with her and then sealed it with a desperate kiss.

As the roar of the engines became deafening, I braced myself for the confrontation that was about to unfold. Razor's menacing figure emerged from the growing darkness.

"Thought you could hide from us, did you?" a cold, mocking voice rang out, sending chills down our spines. Razor's tall, lean frame silhouetted by the faint glow of the moon.

Zoe trembled in my arms, and I squeezed her hand in reassurance, silently willing her to stay strong. Facing Razor would be dangerous – the man's ruthlessness was legendary within the club, and his loyalty to its interests unwavering. But I came too far and risked too much to back down now.

"Razor," I greeted, refusing to let the other man see the fear that coiled like a serpent in the pit of my stomach. "What brings you here?"

"Club business," Razor sneered, prowling closer with the predatory grace of a panther stalking its prey. His gray eyes were cold and calculating, promising violence if provoked. "But it looks like I've stumbled upon something far more... interesting."

"Stay away from her," I warned, voice low and danger-ous. I was no match for Razor in a fight – the man had years of experience and cunning on his side – but I would die before I let anyone hurt Zoe.

"Or what?" he taunted, a cruel smile twisting his lips. "You can't protect her from the club's wrath."

I gritted my teeth, hands clenched into fists as I fought to control my anger. Razor was right – in the hierarchy of the Twisted Jokers, I was little more than a pawn. But that didn't mean I would surrender without a fight.

"Leave us alone," I spat through clenched teeth. "This has nothing to do with the club."

"Everything she does reflects on the club," Razor coun-tered, his voice dripping with menace. "And if I find out you've been jeopardizing our mission to take down the traitor in our ranks for some lovesick foolery, I will personally see to it that you pay the price."

The threat hung heavy in the air, a suffocating cloud of danger and uncertainty that threatened to choke the life out of us.

"We know something fishy is going on with you. You waltz back and Gunner might have to blind at first to see what was going on, but he isn't now. How fucking stupid are you? His sister? I'll be surprised if you are alive tomorrow."

Zoe took a step forward. "You're not touching him."

Razor's cold, calculating gaze flickered to her. "Stay out of this. This is club business."

It only took a couple of minutes before another engine was coming down the road, and then Gunner appeared. This was going to be a challenging night, but I must find a way to get out of this. The mission was too important.

How did they find us here? The only way they could know about this place was if they were tracking me or Zoe.

"Eli's done nothing wrong. He's been loyal to the club."

"By sleeping with you?" Razor sneered. "That's not loyalty. That's a weakness. He's not the only one that would love to have a piece of you. We all would, but we would NEVER betray our leader."

My stomach twisted. Hearing that only confirmed what I already suspected. If Zoe was left unattended, she would get hurt. Gunner had no idea what he was doing, putting his own sister in direct danger for the sake of the club. She needed to be very careful.

"Love isn't a weakness," she countered.

"Zoe, don't—" I began, but she silenced me with a glance, holding my intense brown eyes for a heartbeat longer than necessary, silently reassuring me that she would fight tooth and nail.

"Let him prove himself," she urged. "Give him a chance to show that he's still committed to the club."

Zoe was sticking up for me and I should be thankful, but without her knowing the whole story of my being here, she was just digging a hole.

"Enough!" Gunner barked, the fury boiling within him. "This isn't up for debate. Eli's fate has been decided." He turned his icy gaze back to me, who stood rigid.

"I won't let you tear us apart just because of some twisted sense of loyalty."

"Your loyalty should be to the club first, sister," he stepped closer. "We're your family, not him."

Was he seriously coming at her with club loyalty? Any one of the members would go after Zoe if Gunner took his eyes off her for a second. Doesn't this mean he had no fucking loyalty for her?

"Blood doesn't make a family." Zoe's voice trembled.

"So this guy comes along and you are willing to throw your own brother away? Wow, really didn't think you were the selling out type, sis?"

Gunner was trying to keep a straight face, but I could sense his heartbreak. His own sister was turning against him. Good girl! Maybe she was finally catching on to what a sadistic monster he was.

"Remember this, brother: if you take him from me, you'll lose me too."

Gunner started to walk away and Razor followed, but Lola came closer. She rode with Razor, obviously not knowing what was going on. Even within the club, this woman had Zoe's back.

"Damn," she muttered under her breath, shaking her head as she studied me. "You sure know how to stir up trouble."

"Trouble has a way of finding me," I replied. I glanced toward Zoe, who stood by the window, her body tense as she stared blankly into the night. Her vulnerability tugged at my heart, but I knew I had to stay focused on the task at hand.

"Gunner isn't one to back down easily," Lola warned. "He'll be watching you like a hawk, waiting for you to slip up."

I nodded, clenching my fists at my sides. "I understand. And I'll do whatever it takes to prove my loyalty to the club."

"Let's hope so," Lola replied. "Because if you don't, there won't be anything any of us can do to save you. Not even Zoe."

After she gave Zoe a hug, she went on her way, leaving me to take in the gravity of the situation. It was no longer just about taking down the Twisted Jokers or avenging my partner's death; it was about protecting Zoe.

She finally turned to face me, her blue eyes shimmering with unshed tears. "What have we done?" she whispered.

Maybe bringing her here was a mistake, but I couldn't let her go home alone and face the wrath that was surely to follow by the members. Neither of us knew we were being tracked. The dread set in. Gunner would come up with something horrible to have me prove my loyalty. I didn't want to go through that again. The things I had to do undercover last time still haunted me.

"My brother isn't going to leave this alone. You need to be careful."

As we stood there, our fingers intertwined and our hearts aching with the weight of our choices, the future loomed before them like a dark cloud, full of unknown dangers and consequences. The only question now was whether we would be able to survive the storm.

13

Tripp sat hunched over a cluttered desk, his salt-and-pepper hair glinting under the solitary desk lamp. Things yesterday didn't go according to plan, and my position might be compromised, but I wasn't giving up hope for justice.

"What's going on?" I asked, my eyes searching for answers. When he called me an hour ago, it sounded important and he demanded my presence as soon as possible.

"Sit down, Eli," Tripp said, gesturing to the chair across from him. "We've got a problem."

"What kind of problem?" My muscles tensed, focus unwavering.

"Sources tell us there's a shipment of illegal weapons coming into the city in two days." Tripp leaned forward, his hands clasped together. "We need to intercept it before it reaches the Twisted Jokers."

My heart raced, pounding against my chest like a drum, while adrenaline surged through my veins, fueling my every move. The world around me became a blur as I felt my senses heighten, my breathing becoming a symphony in my ears. What the hell were we going to do? We couldn't let this shipment reach them. It would mean more casualties. The gravity of the situation pressed down on me like a vise, demanding immediate action. I clenched my fists, nails digging into the soft flesh of my palms. "Where's the shipment coming in? Do we know how they're transporting it?" My mind raced, scanning through possible scenarios and strategies.

"Dock 17. But we don't have any details on how it's being moved yet." Tripp's voice was grim, revealing the frustration of working with limited information. I knew the drill. Tips weren't already trustworthy, but with the gravity of the situation, we had to take the informant on their word.

"Alright." I stood up, jaw set. "I'll go to the docks, try to gather some intel. The more we know, the better our chances of stopping this."

"Be careful." Tripp's eyes held a mixture of concern. "I know how important this is to you."

I had a duty to protect those I cared about, and I would do whatever it took to bring down the Twisted Jokers. I was so fucking sick of seeing the people in this city die from the hands of that menace. As I left the room, the weight of the task ahead settled on my shoulders, but it did little to diminish my determination.

Failure was not an option.

The sound of my own heartbeat echoed in my ears as I strode purposefully through the hallway, each step bringing me closer to the woman who held the key to stopping the shipment. At this point, it was time to come clean to Zoe. Tell her everything. She was close enough to the club that she might be able to get information that could help us. I knew that this would put a strain on what happened between us, but right now, justice had to come before our relationship. This case was years in the making, and I couldn't let my feelings for her override the need for justice.

Departing the office, I headed straight for her place, ignoring the cacophony of ringing phones and clicking keyboards. The whole way trying to go over in my head how to break the news. How would she react to me being an agent? My sole purpose was to bring down her brother and his club. She had seen first hand how her brother was going down a sick and twisted spiral, and it might just be what she needed to come to our side. Yet, her loyalty would be questioned and that would infuriate anyone.

As I approached her house, my chest tightened, the air thick with anticipation. The sight of her front door sent a shiver down my spine, its weathered paint whispering stories of the past. The distant sound of chirping birds filled the air, their cheerful melody contrasting with the heavy silence within me. A faint scent of blooming flowers wafted through the breeze, mixing with the nervous sweat on my brow. This could completely derail our investigation if she chose not to cooperate. I wouldn't be able to stay undercover either.

My knuckles rapped against the worn wooden door. "Zoe, we need to talk. Let me in."

The door creaked open, revealing a sliver of her piercing blue eyes framed by a cascade of auburn hair. She hesitated for a moment before stepping aside, allowing me entry into her sanctuary. She had no idea what was about to happen, and my gut twisted.

"Alright, but make it quick," she said, her voice strained.

I stepped inside, the room filled with the intoxicating blend of her floral perfume. My gaze fell upon the numerous photographs adorning the walls; images of happier times, when the weight of her brother's criminal empire hadn't yet crushed her spirit.

"I just found out there's a shipment of illegal weapons coming into the city in two days. I need your help to stop it," I said urgently, my eyes locked onto hers, searching for any hint of reaction. She wasn't grasping yet.

"What the hell are you talking about? You are supposed to be proving yourself, not making things worse." She crossed her arms across her chest. "Someone is coming after us... them. You heard them in the bar." Her eyes widened, and she looked away quickly, guilt etched into every line of her face. My heart clenched at the sight of her anguish, but I pushed forward, knowing what had to be done.

"Zoe, you have the power to help me bring them down and put an end to the violence they're spreading," I pleaded, his voice softening.

There it was. The truth would set me free.

She bit her lip, her hands wringing together as the weight of my words settled upon her. I could see the internal struggle playing out behind her eyes, and I knew that this was her chance to break free from the chains that bound her for so long.

"So, you aren't just another member? You are trying to take my brother down? You've been using me this whole time!"

Fuck! She couldn't be more wrong. Yes, she did have information that could help us, but she wasn't some conquest. I developed real feelings for Zoe. We had much more in common than she even comprehended, and yet I wish I didn't have to ask her to do this. Turn on her own brother.

"Are you fucking kidding me?" I walked over to her and took hold of her chin, raising her eyes to mine. "I would never use you for information like that. You are the most complicated, stubborn, and wonderful woman I have ever..."

"Ever what, Eli?"

"From the first moment I saw you... something told me that you weren't as bad as the assholes in this club. You were different. Even with your rough exterior, as soon as I start to see you break down the layers, I started falling for you."

Her eyes flicked to mine for a split second. "Don't hand me that fucking bullshit. You knew he was my brother from the moment you stepped into that bar."

"I'm not saying I didn't."

Her hands went up in the air. "Now, after sleeping with me, you want me to just give you information that would put the people I care about away? You are out of your fucking mind. Gunner was right to warn me about you. He knew something wasn't right and instead I went against him."

Did she really think that her brother gave two fucks about her? She was just property to him. He would throw her under the bus if it meant saving his own ass. "Your brother is a fucking murderer. And we aren't talking just a couple of people, Zoe. He has over forty people's blood on his hands, not to mention, the countless innocent lives that will be taken if those weapons get into his hands."

This was a long shot. My heart ached for her, but she had a choice to make and that would determine our future. There was no way I could be with someone willingly fucked up enough to stand beside someone like Gunner. Everyone had their own shit to deal with in life, but Zoe was way better than this. She just doesn't give herself enough credit. Once she got away from that asshole, she would understand that her life could be a thousand percent better.

"How do you expect me to just turn on my family? The people who have been there for me my entire life. Even they have children, wives, and husbands. You are asking me to help send them to prison."

I took her hand. "As long as the others cooperate, they might get a deal, but your brother and Razor won't get any leeway. Do you have any idea how many bodies have been found that are traced directly back to Gunner and his right hand man? How many unsolved murders there are in this city?"

"Too many to count." Her eyes were stuck on the floor. She couldn't even look at me.

"Exactly! Let's stop this. Please. I can't do this without you," I implored, my heart aching with the knowledge of the danger I was asking her to face. "I know that you are better than this. Better than this club. You grew up in it, and the sense of loyalty you feel to your people, I get it, but they are doing terrible things... things that you have the option to stop. Think about what you want for yourself for a minute... because if you say no to this, and he kills people, your conscience will never let it go."

Zoe's eyes met mine once more, a fierce determination flickering within our depths as she took a deep, steadying breath. I watched as she fought with herself over what choice to make. She had to know that until Gunner was stopped, he would continue to hurt people. He claimed to be doing these things for the good of the club, but that wasn't the case. She wasn't stupid.

"Maybe this is the only way to get him to stop. The road he is going down... it's ugly. If someone doesn't stop him, he'll become worse than my dad."

There you go! You are starting to understand.

I pushed a stray hair behind her hair. "A shipment of weapons..." I looked deep into her eyes. "He is planning something big. We have to stop him before... more people die."

She hesitated and took a seat on the couch. "I want to help you, but I'm scared. If the club finds out I'm working against them... I don't know if I can survive their wrath. You've seen what they do to traitors."

Without insider intel, we would never find the shipment in time. The deaths caused by them would be on my hands. I couldn't live with that. "I understand your fear. But focus on all the innocent lives that could be affected if we don't stop this shipment. You have the power to make a real difference here. Don't let your brother turn you into a killer."

She sat on the couch, head in her hands, sobbing. It took everything in me not to bring her into my arms. My knowledge of the Twisted Jokers proved that unless she was willing to help, more lives were at stake, and no matter what loyalty she felt to her brother, Zoe wasn't a criminal. There was no way she could look the other way knowing that she would be helping them get away with this murder spree.

"You know, about a year ago, I thought about getting away from all of this, or attempting to again, but my brother was on a warpath and if anyone knows how he reacts, it's me. I guess a part of me thought that if I stuck around, maybe he would eventually grow a conscience. But after seeing what happened in that bar, how quick his fuse goes off, I'll do it."

As we sat there, hands intertwined, the weight of our decision hung heavy in the air. There was no turning back now, and the road ahead would be fraught with danger, betrayal, and heartache. We were both ready to face the darkness head-on, ready to fight for the greater good and protect those we loved.

14

There was still so much he didn't know about me. I should just keep my mouth shut, but then omitting the truth was just as bad. He obviously trusted me. The man wasn't stupid. Now that I knew he was working against the club, there was no reason for him to lie.

For years, I of the clubs to sweep me off my feet and take me somewhere e to sweep me off my feet and take me somewhere else. Now, here he was, and I couldn't believe it. The situation was far different from what I had expected, but my prayer was answered. I should be happy to find out that he wasn't indeed one of the bad guys my brother turned, but I'm not. Was it worse that he was going against my family? So had I. One of these days, I was going to get far away from here, and this gave me the opportunity to do it even sooner. There would be repercussions though.

I pulled my knees up to my chest, feeling the fabric of my worn jeans against my skin. Resting my head on the soft cushion of the sofa, I couldn't help but question my actions. What the hell was I doing? This went against everything my family had ingrained in me. Memories from my childhood flooded my mind - the echoing voices of my parents, their words teaching me to protect our own at any cost. But now, as I sat here alone, I couldn't deny the truth. My father, flawed as he was, had never been the best man. The isolation at school, the lack of friends, all because of who my parents were. In that moment, my thoughts turned to Gunner. We were never meant to find ourselves in this position. We had shared such grand aspirations, but when our father was brutally taken from us, our dreams seemed to dissipate like smoke. The weight of uncertainty pressed against my chest, making it hard to breathe. I couldn't help but wonder what our lives would have been like if we had managed to escape before they ended our father's life. Maybe, just maybe, Gunner wouldn't have felt the relentless pull to take over the club.

This was all just so fucked up. I didn't know how we got so far down this rabbit hole. We were better than this. Going places! And yet here I was, making the biggest decision of my life. Turn on my brother or countless innocent lives taken by protecting him.

Fuck! If I had never met Eli that night, then this wouldn't be happening. I was covering for the other bartender. Oh, how different this situation would be if I hadn't fallen for him first thing. And a part of me still wondered if he did seek me out to follow orders, at first, and then he started falling for me. It made sense. After all, I was his sister, and Eli was good looking. Maybe his superiors figured his charm would work on me, and I would just give him up. Yet, there was something brewing between us, something bigger than just his mission, and I had to remind myself of that.

That night at the cabin, he didn't have to take me. He could have let me go home and left things be, but he sought me out. The passion when he touched me wasn't fake. That I knew for sure. But somehow, I was always going to wonder until we took them down and it was over.

Thoughts raced through my mind like a relentless barrage. Memories of countless instances when I yearned to escape, yet held back. I could still hear my brother's evasive response, claiming it was "club business" whenever I dared to inquire further. Deep down, I acknowledged his culpability for the lives lost, yet I remained. Wasn't that a reflection of my own guilt? An undeniable accomplice in his crimes?

All those times I could have said more, tried to stop him, but didn't. I knew my place within the club wasn't much, most women weren't taken seriously, but at first my brother listened to me. Before he went off the deep end and let this world cloud his judgment.

Fuck, how am I going to do this? Act like everything is fine around my brother when I'm secretly working behind his back to put him in prison?

Could I truly betray my own flesh and blood? I shake my head, feeling the weight of the decision pressing down on me. My eyelids remain shut, shutting out the world as I contemplated this impossible situation. My brother, once vibrant and full of life, has strayed onto a treacherous path. The darkness that engulfed him threatening to consume him entirely. If he continued down this road, he would meet a grim fate. Conflicting emotions surged within me as I grappled with a selfish desire to see him locked away, rather than succumbing to an untimely demise.

If he was in prison, then that means he might also gain

some protection, especially if many members of the club were picked up on charges. But I knew from first-hand experience what happens when one of us goes to prison. My mind settled back on Tommy from five years ago. He was the guy that took a wrap for something that he didn't do to keep my brother out of prison, and he didn't even last a week before he was murdered while in custody. This could very well happen to my brother, but at the same time I have to take into consideration everybody else's lives.

The flash of small children playing in a park succumbed me. I couldn't let him do this anymore. I knew the awful things that my brother and the club did to the people and to the community. They would not stop. Their selfishness took many innocent lives, and this was my chance to make right.

As much as I didn't want to turn on my brother and the people that had been there for me for most of my life, it would do the world good for them to be put behind bars. They couldn't wreak havoc from there. My father was probably turning over in his grave right now, but he would have done anything to save his own skin. He might have been all for protecting the club, but if given the opportunity to save himself from going to prison, he would take it. As much as I loved him, he did countless horrible things and the world was better off without him in it.

Eli came over, his footsteps muffled by the plush carpet, and settled down beside me on the worn-out couch. The comforting scent of his cologne filled the air as he gently placed his warm hand on my trembling back, offering solace. However, in this moment of despair, his touch felt distant and inconsequential. The weight of my own thoughts consumed me, drowning out the faint hum of the television in the background. I had to convince myself that choosing this path was my only option, even if it meant risking my life.

If the Twisted Jokers found out I was turning on them, they wouldn't hesitate to kill me. Even though I want to believe that my brother would do nothing to hurt me, he has shown me he puts his club before his own blood. Time and time again. He doesn't listen to reason, and he is not someone who has remorse.

He didn't say anything, just sat there and offered me some comfort. He had to know what he asked of me was detrimental. It was going to fuck me up regardless, but he wanted to give me time to come to terms with my decision.

"This is a fucking nightmare. Why couldn't I have just left years ago... I wouldn't be in this fucking position!"

All I can think about is the countless members murdered at the hand of my brother, whether he did it himself or had another member do it for him. So many good men who refused to do the things that he wanted. Who the fuck does that? He was becoming more and more like my father, and that scared the living shit out of me. Because at some point, he was going to suffer the same fate as our father. And he might think that's a noble death, but was it?

Eli's hand rests on my knee. "I know this is a lot to take in and I'm so sorry to put you in this position, but you are better than your brother. You are better than everyone else in that club and this is our chance to make it right for all the things that they have done wrong."

"That doesn't make it any easier. I never saw myself being the person who sent my brother to prison. Even after all the awful things that he's done... he has become the devil. He is putting his own needs above everybody else. Including the club. And he doesn't give a fuck who goes down. As long as he can still reign over the club."

Eli jumped back, probably surprised from the pure hatred spewing from me right now. I was pissed. Gunner put me in this position. He didn't have to be like our father. Gunner had every opportunity to walk away when he died, instead he picked up the jacket and assumed the role that he talked shit about all our lives.

"Once we take your brother and razor down. I don't think anybody is going to come after you. There are a lot of members that I think know what they are doing is wrong, but when you're in a club like this, it's hard to turn your back on them. It's hard to see the difference between right and wrong when you have been doing heinous acts for so long at the hands of somebody else."

Everything coming out of his mouth made sense. I shouldn't even be worrying about the consequences of doing this, because it was the right thing to do. If my life did end, at least it would be for doing something good for a change.

Eli took me into his arms, and tears just started rolling. It was still terrifying and to think that he was going after them too. He was someone who stood up for what he believed in and I could take notes from him.

"How are you still alive? My brother is usually so good at sniffing out cops, and yet here you are."

"I did some horrible things for him to earn his trust... and i'm not proud of them, but it was effective. Without his trust, I couldn't have gotten the information I did."

Eli sacrificed to gain information on the club and that took balls. He risked everything to see them off the streets and that made me fall in love with him even more.

"I think it's best you come to my office and we do an official interview with you. That way if your name comes up in any statements from the club after I arrest them that might implicate you, we can say you were a cooperating witness."

I nodded and went into my room to grab a sweatshirt. "Whatever we need to do to take him down.

A single tear fell as I walked out of the door.

15

The low rumble of the truck's engine reverberated through the quiet drive to the office, creating a constant hum in the air. Zoe was having a hard time grappling with the situation, but she understood it was the right course of action.

Her delicate hand lightly pressed against the cool, smooth surface of the window, her fingertips leaving faint smudges on the glass. With a distant gaze, she stared out into the vast expanse of nothingness, lost in her thoughts. The silence in the room was only broken by the faint sound of distant traffic, a reminder of the world outside.

As I watched her, a heavy sense of guilt washed over me. I couldn't help but wonder if she was angry with me. And honestly, I couldn't blame her. The request I had made of her was undeniably terrible, a burden no one should have to bear. But I held onto the hope that once we had them in custody, she would have the freedom to leave and become whoever she desired. A fresh start in a new state, a chance to rebuild her life.

Yet, deep down, I knew my desires were selfish. I yearned for her to choose a destination where we could give our connection a chance. But there was no guarantee that she would want that. After everything was said and done, it would be all too easy for her to place the blame solely on me, to leave me behind without a second thought.

We pulled into the parking lot, and she sat straight up. Her shoulders appeared tense.

"You alright?" I asked as I came to a halt in a parking space.

"You aren't lying to me and just tricking me to come in and arrest me, right?"

Wow! Did she really think I would do that? "If I was going to arrest you, I would have done it at your house."

Her eyes locked on mine. To be fair, I just dropped a bomb on her so it might take her a minute to fully trust me. "Seriously, come on. Tripp will be waiting to do your interview and then we can start coming up with our plan."

As soon as I stepped out of the car, a gentle breeze brushed against my skin. I stood there for a moment, the faint sound of birds chirping in the distance filling the air. I resisted the urge to rush her, knowing that she needed the space to take her own time.

Zoe followed behind me almost like she wanted to leave enough room in case she had to duck out. As we approached the front doors, she took a deep breath before she stepped inside. I put my hand on the small of her back and guided her back to my office where Tripp was waiting.

"You must be Zoe." He reached out his hand, but she didn't budge. "Eli said you are willing to help us gain intel on the Twisted Jokers. I commend you for coming forward. We are gonna spare countless lives because of you."

She wasn't the type to trust easily and now she was in a building full of agents. This was going to take a minute for her to relax.

"Why don't I take her to grab something to drink and we'll meet you in Room 2."

Was she having second thoughts? Her whole demeanor seemed different now.

"I can't believe I'm doing this. My brother has people everywhere. What if someone here is working for him? I'll be dead tonight just for being here."

"If he did, then he would know about me already. Plus, I'm not leaving your side now. Your brother knows about us so there's no reason for you to be staying alone." A sprite clinked down the vending machine and I handed it to her. "You can have the harder stuff later."

Once she got into the room, she tensed up again, which was to be expected. I needed to cover all of our bases though because once they found out she helped us they could try to fabricate stories to get her wrapped up in charges, but if we had the DA agree to give her immunity in exchange for her cooperation and intel then anything they said wouldn't matter.

"We are going to record this interview." Tripp said before turning on the camera. "Please state your name and that you give your consent for this to be recorded."

"My name is Zoe Morales and I agree to being recorded."

I stood behind Tripp, leaned up against the wall. She didn't want to be left alone with him.

"Do you have any knowledge of a shipment of weapons coming in?"

"Nothing more than what Eli told me."

Tripp went on to ask a million questions over the next two hours. My back was killing me by the time he turned off the camera and let her know she was free to go.

"Don't worry, this was to make sure you were protected in all this. I told you I was looking out for you."

She leaned into me. "I'll just be happy when all this is over."

She was going to be working with me closely from now on, and I needed to be sure she could protect herself.

"We are taking you to a gun range to practice. You will need to carry a weapon and we need to make sure you know how to handle it and shoot if needed."

Her eyes squinted. "I have practiced before, but its been years. My father taught us very young and my brother took me a couple years ago."

We went straight to the range, and she was right. Her shooting wasn't perfect, but she knew how to hold the gun and judge the pushback. At first, I wasn't sure if this was the right thing to do, but bringing her here proved she needed to know she was capable of protecting herself. God forbid something were to happen when I wasn't around. Now, I had the upmost certainty, she was safe.

She set the gun down, took the earplugs and eye glasses off, and the worker came behind and took it. "I'd say I did pretty well considering."

"I wouldn't want to be at the other end of the gun you were holding..." I kissed her forehead. "What do you say we go back to the house and have some dinner? We will need to start going through everything tomorrow and this might be the last night we have before things go haywire."

Once we figured out more about where the drop was being made, things would move fast, and tonight I just wanted to spend time with Zoe. Our relationship was not conventional by any means, but she still meant a lot to me, and after all this was over, she might decide not to pursue this relationship further. At least for right now, I wanted to spend as much time with her as I could.

16

Eli and I huddled over the makeshift table, maps and blueprints spread out before us. The sound of rain pattered against the windows, creating a soothing backdrop. Eli's eyes darted across the table.

"Alright, here's what we know," Eli began, his voice low and steady. "The shipment will arrive at the docks. We need to intercept it before it reaches its destination." He pointed to a spot on the map, tracing a route with his finger. "This is where you come in. I need you to get us access to the docks without raising suspicion."

I bit my lip, heart pounding as I processed the magnitude of my role in this operation. But as my eyes locked onto Eli's determined gaze, I couldn't back down now. "I can do that," I replied. "I'll make sure we slip past security unnoticed."

"Good," Eli said, nodding. "Once we're in, we'll split up. I'll take point and locate the shipment while you keep an eye out for any unexpected surprises."

My fingers danced over the assortment of gadgets and weapons spread across the battered wooden table, each item meticulously chosen to ensure the mission's success. My pulse thrummed with urgency as I selected a sleek handgun, ensuring it was loaded before sliding it into my holster. This wasn't the first time I carried a gun, but lucky for me, I never had to fire one. Target practice was about as far as I ever got.

"Are you sure about this?" I asked, my voice tinged with doubt. I gripped an unopened box of ammunition as if it were a lifeline, knuckles whitening beneath the strain.

"Absolutely," Eli replied, his gaze never leaving the task at hand. "We've been over every detail, every contingency. We're ready."

I nodded, jaw set as I joined Eli in assembling our arsenal. My hands, though trembling slightly, moved with practiced ease as I filled magazines and secured weapons in holsters and pockets. The cool metal against my skin served as a chilling reminder of the stakes we faced.

"Tell me again when we'll make our move," I said, seeking reassurance in Eli's unwavering confidence.

"Midnight," he answered, eyes narrowing as he studied a map. "That's when they change the guards at the gate. We've observed them long enough to know that's our best chance to slip in undetected."

"Right." I swallowed hard, my throat dry. "And we'll be out before they even know what hit them."

"Exactly." Eli reached for my hand, giving it a reassuring squeeze. "Trust me, Zoe. We can do this."

Silently, we turned our attention to gathering the necessary equipment. Eli meticulously inspected each weapon.

"Hey," I called from across the room, voice tinged with uncertainty. "Do you think... Do you think we have a chance of stopping them?" Eli paused. The odds were stacked against us, but I couldn't afford doubt – not when lives were at stake.

"We have to try," he replied. "We're their best shot at stopping this nightmare."

Eli and I immersed themselves in the intricate dance of preparation. We reviewed the club's routines and patterns once more, searching for any overlooked detail that might prove pivotal. But the plan remained solid, our meticulous observations paying off.

"Are you ready?" Eli asked as he locked eyes with me. The gravity of our mission weighed heavily on us both, but we came too far to turn back now.

"Let's do it," I replied, steeling myself for the challenge ahead. I knew the risks, the consequences of failure – but I also knew that love and loyalty were worth fighting for, no matter the cost.

As we packed the last of the gear – a sleek assortment of surveillance equipment and communication devices – The weight of the task was bearing down on me.

"Promise me something," I whispered as we finished packing. My eyes shimmered with unshed tears, my vulnerability shining through despite my best efforts to keep it hidden. "Promise me that no matter what happens, you and I will figure out whatever this is..."

"I promise," he murmured, sealing his vow with a gentle brush of his fingers against my cheek.

Even though we needed to focus on this shipment right now, in the back of my head, all I could think about was my future. If this didn't go according to plan, my brother would have me killed. He couldn't take the chance of letting the guys know he was soft, and killing his sister for betraying them would be a way for him to cement his loyalty to his club. What had I gotten myself into?

Together, we stood on the precipice of danger, hearts pounding in tandem as we prepared to face the unknown. And as the rain continued to fall outside, washing away the remnants of our fears, Eli and I steeled ourselves for the challenges ahead, ready to fight for the greater good and protect the lives that hung in the balance.

Night fell, where Eli and I crouched in wait. The air was thick, punctuated by the shallow breaths as we focused on the task at hand. We both knew the stakes were high – if we failed to stop the shipment of illegal weapons, countless innocent lives would be at risk.

"Are you sure about this?" he asked, his intense brown eyes boring into mine. "There's still time to back out if you're having second thoughts."

Fuck, if he only knew! But I had to be strong. No matter how scared I was right now, this was the right thing. "It's not that." I sighed, tucking a strand of hair behind my ear. "I just... I'm struggling with my loyalties. You know how much I care about Gunner, and I don't want to hurt him. But I also can't deny what's happening between us, Eli."

Eli stepped closer, his hand gently resting on my shoulder. "I understand. But we both know what the Twisted Jokers are doing is wrong, and your brother is caught right in the middle of it. We need to intercept the shipment for the sake of justice, for the sake of everyone involved."

"Even if it means betraying my own brother?" I whispered, pain etched in my voice.

"Sometimes we have to make difficult choices for the greater good." Eli's voice was soft but firm. "I'll be there with you every step of the way, Zoe. We'll face the consequences together."

For a brief moment, I allowed myself to be enveloped by the warmth of Eli's gaze and the strength of his touch. The fierce determination that once been my shield now wavered, replaced by a vulnerability I'd never allowed myself to show anyone else.

"Alright," I said, taking a deep breath. "Let's talk about the plan."

Eli nodded, and we walked side by side toward the warehouse, our footsteps echoing in the empty space. As we discussed the details of our operation, there was a growing sense of dread in the pit of my stomach. We were putting ourselves in immense danger by going up against the Twisted Jokers, and there was no guarantee we'd come out unscathed. But with Eli at my side, I found a small measure of solace.

Eli cupped my face in his hands, his thumb brushing away a stray tear. "We're in this together, and we'll come out the other side stronger than ever. For us, for Gunner, and for everyone caught up in this twisted web."

"Remember, stay in contact through the earpiece, and stick to the plan," Eli whispered, his brown eyes meeting mine, seeking reassurance in our depths. I nodded, my fingers trembling ever so slightly as I adjusted my grip on the compact firearm in my hand.

"Got it," I murmured, forcing a brave smile that belied the fear churning inside me. "Let's do this."

The moon cast a silvery glow over the warehouse as Eli and I crept through the shadows, our footsteps muffled by the damp earth beneath us. The distant hum of motorcycles echoed in the night air, a reminder of the danger that loomed ever closer.

"Over there," Eli whispered, pointing to a rusted metal door on the side of the building. "That's where they'll unload the shipment."

I nodded, my piercing blue eyes scanning the area with practiced precision. I noted the narrow alleyways that snaked between the crumbling buildings, the graffiti-streaked walls standing sentinel over our secrets. This place was a haven for those who thrived in darkness, and I knew its hidden pathways well.

"Let's map our escape routes first," I suggested, my voice hushed yet steady. "We'll need quick access to multiple options if things go south."

Eli agreed, and together we moved like ghosts through the shadows, marking each potential passage with a subtle chalk mark. As we worked, I couldn't help but marvel at the ease with which Eli navigated this unfamiliar terrain – a testament to his own survival instincts, honed during his years in the military.

"Three exits should be enough," Eli murmured as we returned to their starting point. "Now we just need to confirm the arrival time and any extra security measures."

I took a deep breath, steeling myself for what came next. I despised using my ties to the Twisted Jokers for personal gain, but the stakes were too high to let sentiment cloud my judgment. With a flick of my wrist, I pulled out my phone and dialed a familiar number, waiting for the click that signaled a connection.

"Hey, it's me," I said, voice tinged with reluctance. "I need some information about tonight's shipment. Anything you can tell me would be helpful."

The voice on the other end hesitated, clearly weighing the risks of betrayal. But after a tense moment, we relented, offering up a time and a whispered warning about increased security patrols. I thanked them, gratitude mingling with a pang of guilt as I ended the call.

"Nine o'clock. And there'll be extra guards on duty. We'll have to be careful."

Dark clouds rolled ominously across the sky, casting shadows on the cracked concrete as Eli and I huddled together. The air hung heavy, our breaths mingling in the chill that crept through the cracks in the walls. We came here to finalize their plan – a last chance to seal our fates before the storm broke.

"Alright," Eli began, his voice low and steady. "We know when and where the shipment will arrive, and we've mapped out our escape routes. It's time to go over the details one last time."

I nodded, eyes meeting his in a silent promise of unwavering support. "We can't leave anything to chance. Every step must be calculated, every movement precise."

Eli traced a finger along the tattered map spread out before us, outlining the path we would take to intercept the weapons. "I'll take care of the guards on the perimeter while you slip inside. Once you've secured the shipment, let me know. I'll draw their attention away from you, giving you enough time to make your escape."

"Are you sure you can handle them alone?" I asked, concern furrowing my brow. My hands trembled ever so slightly, betraying the fear I fought to keep hidden beneath my fierce exterior.

"Trust me," Eli reassured me, the intensity of his gaze never wavering. "You focus on getting those weapons out of their hands, and I'll make sure they don't lay a finger on you."

"Once I'm clear, I'll head for the rendezvous point," I said.

The rain turned the rough gravel and dirt beneath our feet into a treacherous muck, each step a precarious dance between stealth and stability. My heart pounded like an erratic metronome, keeping time with the staccato rhythm of the raindrops as they pelted against the brim of my hood. I glanced sideways at Eli, his face half-hidden by shadow, but I could see the steady focus within his brown eyes.

"Stay close," he murmured, his voice barely audible above the rain. I nodded, my fingers curling around the cool metal of the pistol – a comforting anchor amidst the swirling uncertainty that threatened to engulf her.

As we approached the location, my breath hitched, the weight of our actions pressing down on me like a shroud. From our vantage point behind a stack of rusted shipping containers, we surveyed the scene before us: the low-slung warehouse, its walls scarred by graffiti, stood like a sentinel amidst the chaos. Raucous laughter spilled from the club members gathered near the entrance.

My gaze lingered on the familiar faces of my brother's men, heart twisting. "Eli," I whispered. "They're here."

"Get ready," he replied, his hand finding mine for a fleeting moment, our fingers entwined like strands of fate. And then we slipped apart, each assuming our role in the carefully choreographed dance we'd planned.

As the rumble of an approaching truck signaled the arrival of the shipment, my pulse quickened, the blood singing in my ears like a battle cry. I knew the risks, the potential consequences, but I also knew that Eli and I were united by a common goal: to bring down the Twisted Jokers and forge a new path for our future.

The truck rolled to a stop, its headlights casting an eerie glow on the rain-slicked pavement. With a nod from Eli, I stepped out from behind the shipping container, heart thundering against my ribs as I approached the group of club members gathered around the truck.

Eli waited for the perfect moment to strike, his heart pounding a fierce rhythm against his ribcage as he watched them. Finally seizing his chance, he crept forward and incapacitated the man with a swift, precise blow, dragging him into the shadows before he could raise the alarm.

"We need to move – now."

"Right behind you," I replied.

The clock continued to tick down, each second bringing them nearer to either triumph or catastrophe.

Would we be able to pull this off?

17

I tightly held onto the fragile promise I had made to Zoe - that we would emerge from this night triumphant, unscathed by the dangers that lay ahead. A lump formed in my throat as the towering shipment came into view. The warehouse was filled with countless wooden crates, stacked one upon another, each containing the potential for catastrophe and demise.

"We're in position."

"Copy that," she replied.

With trembling fingers, I cautiously made my way towards the closest crate. The lid resisted as I pried it open, my heart pounding in my chest. As the lid creaked open, a sight greeted my eyes - rows upon rows of sleek, black rifles neatly nestled against one another. The faint light reflected off their cold metal surfaces, creating an eerie gleam. A wave of nausea overcame me, as the weight of their purpose settled heavily on my shoulders. "Found them," I uttered.

"The explosives are ready - two minutes and counting – meet me at the rendezvous point." she said.

We dashed through the dimly lit warehouse, the sound of our hurried footsteps reverberating off the cold, metal walls, creating a rhythmic cacophony akin to a frantic drumbeat. Each step we took sent tremors through the floor, adding to the sense of urgency that pulsed through our veins.

"Almost there," she panted, her eyes locked onto mine as if to draw strength from my unwavering gaze. "Just a little further."

"Stay focused," I urged her, the words a command and a plea in equal measure. "We can't afford any mistakes now."

As we reached the rendezvous point, I marveled at the strange partnership we forged – born from necessity and blooming into something far more potent than either could have anticipated. My feelings for Zoe were a tangled web of conflicting emotions: admiration, desire, and above all, the need to protect her from harm.

"Three... two... one!"

The earth trembled violently, causing a deafening roar that reverberated through the air. In that fleeting moment, it felt as though the very fabric of reality was unraveling, sending shivers down the spine.

"Did we do it?" Zoe gasped, her eyes wide with a mix of hope and terror. "Is it over?"

"Only time will tell," I murmured, gaze never leaving the inferno that consumed our enemies' plans. "But tonight, we made a difference."

As the flames danced, casting eerie shadows across our faces, our journey was far from over. And yet, as I looked into Zoe's eyes – a stormy sea of blue that held the promise of redemption – I couldn't help but feel a flicker of hope amidst the darkness.

As the adrenaline began to wane, fatigue set in, making

each step feel like an insurmountable challenge. "We can catch our breath and figure out what to do next."

"God, what a mess," Zoe whispered, sinking down beside me.

As we huddled in our makeshift sanctuary, a cold breeze whispered through the shattered windows. She wrapped her arms around herself, trying to ward off the ghosts that haunted her.

"Zoe," I began, hesitant. "You did what you had to do. You couldn't have let those shipments go on."

She looked up at me, eyes shadowed with doubt. "I know, but... Gunner's my brother, Eli. And the club – it's all I've ever known. How can I turn my back on them? On him?"

"Your loyalty is admirable," I replied, pausing in my restless stride. "But sometimes, loyalty can be misplaced. Look at what they were doing – endangering innocent lives for profit. Is that really something you want to be a part of?"

Zoe bit her lip, staring down at her trembling hands. "No, it's not. But betraying my own family... I never thought I would be capable of that."

"Choosing the right path isn't always easy," I said, kneeling down in front of her. "But you're strong, Zoe. Stronger than anyone I've ever met. If anyone can walk this road, it's you."

Her breath hitched, and she blinked back tears. "Do you really believe that?"

"More than anything." I reached out, my hand warm and solid. "You're not alone in this. I'm here, and I'll stand by you every step of the way."

My lips dropped to hers for just a moment.

"Remember," I continued, brushing away some tears. "The club doesn't define who you are. You do."

Zoe nodded. "You're right. I can't let my past dictate my future. It's time to break free, and forge a new path – no matter how hard it may be."

"Then we'll do it together," I promised, my voice strong and steady in the face of uncertainty.

"But first, I've got to find us a place to go for a couple of days." I pulled out my phone. "Hey, I need a favor."

"Jaxon?" Chris' voice held a note of surprise. "It's been what, two years?"

"Remember that cabin of yours in the woods? Is it still available?" I asked, my voice steady despite the emotions churning within me.

"Of course, man. You're welcome to use it anytime. Planning a little getaway?" Chris asked, his tone teasing.

"Something like that." I hesitated before adding, "But it needs to be discreet."

"Say no more," Chris replied, understanding the gravity of the situation. "I'll have the place ready for you. Just text me when you're on your way."

"Thanks, Chris. I owe you one." I stared at the phone for a moment, considering the risks involved in taking Zoe to the cabin.

Where else could we go?

18

As we drove to the cabin, I stole glances at Zoe. The moonlight danced on her face. With each passing mile, her confident demeanor seemed to fade, replaced by a subtle curiosity that sparkled in her eyes.

I wondered if, somehow, she could sense the depth of my feelings for her. Truly understand the intensity that consumed my heart.

We ventured onto the path that wound through the dense woods. The towering pine trees whispered secrets to each other, their branches swaying in a gentle breeze.

After parking the car, the scent of pine mingled with the fragrance of damp earth, enveloping us in a cocoon. It added a touch of intrigue to the air, heightening the sense of mystery that surrounded our destination.

As we walked along the path, the crunch under our feet echoed in the quiet night. There was truly something magical about being in the woods. The Twisted Jokers couldn't find us here. We were safe.

The soft glow of fireflies danced in the air, illuminating the darkness. "Another night in the woods with you?"

The distant hoot of an owl echoed through the trees, adding a haunting melody to the ambiance. "You didn't complain last time?" I smiled, thinking back to our first night together.

The cabin stood before us. It was a place of solitude, a sanctuary where we could escape the chaos of the world and embrace the unknown.

"Wow, Eli, this is... amazing," she breathed, her eyes sparkling. "How did you find this place?"

"Let's just say I know some people," I replied, a hint of a smile tugging at the corners of my mouth as I unlocked the door.

Inside, the warm and snug cabin embraced us. Guiding her with gentle steps, I brought her to the window, where a breathtaking sight unfolded before us. The tranquil lake below sparkled and danced in the moonlight.

"Tomorrow, we can go hiking, try some fishing, even cook together," I suggested, watching her reaction closely.

"Really?" Zoe's face lit up at the prospect. "That sounds like so much fun!"

"Good," I said, feeling a warmth spread through my chest. "I thought it'd be nice for us to get away from everything."

When was the last time she was able to do something for herself? She always put on a brave face and did what her brother told her, but she had a chance at a different life now. One that didn't revolve around crime. Once the Twisted Jokers were put out of commission, she would be free to do whatever she wanted. Be whoever she wanted.

"Let's just get some rest tonight and then we can explore around tomorrow."

I could barely keep my eyes open. I hadn't been sleeping much since Jason's death. Plus, with being back inside the Twisted Jokers, I must be alert at all times in case I was found out. They would come when I least expected it.

The first light of dawn kissed the treetops, casting long shadows across the dew-covered grass. The air was crisp and cold. I stood on the porch of the cabin, a steaming cup of coffee cradled in my hands, watching the world awaken.

"Morning," Zoe murmured, stepping out onto the porch beside me, her breath visible in the chilly air. She wrapped her arms around herself for warmth, but there was no denying the radiant glow emanated from her skin—happiness suited her well.

"Morning," I replied with a soft smile, taking in the sight of her disheveled hair and sleep-filled eyes. "It's beautiful out here, isn't it?"

"Almost as beautiful as the man standing next to me," she teased, a playful grin tugging at her lips.

I chuckled, feeling warmth spread through my chest at her words. But as I looked out at the forest, the weight of the mission ahead settled heavily on my shoulders. The Twisted Jokers were still out there, plotting our next move, and I couldn't afford to let my guard down—not when Zoe's life was at stake.

"Zoe," I began, voice serious, "I need you to promise me something."

"Anything," she replied without hesitation, her blue eyes searching mine for answers.

"Promise me you'll stay vigilant. This... us... we can't let it distract us from what needs to be done."

She hesitated for a moment before nodding resolutely. "I promise. I know how important this mission is. I won't let you down."

"Good," I said with a sigh of relief, my hand reaching out to rest reassuringly on her arm. There was an urgent need to protect her, to keep her safe from the dangers that lurked in the shadows. But I was also aware that she needed to be strong and capable in her own right, especially if we were going to face the challenges ahead together.

"Let's enjoy this moment while we can," she suggested, wrapping her fingers around mine, her voice tinged with both hope and sadness. "The world out there can wait just a little longer."

As the sun continued to rise, bathing us in its warm embrace, our stormy future awaited us. The road ahead was treacherous, filled with unknown dangers and threats that would test our newfound love at every turn. But as I stood there, side by side with Zoe, I knew one thing for certain: whatever obstacles lay in our path, we would face them together.

"We are going back tomorrow, like nothing ever happened."

"Everything will be fine...."

And suddenly, the future—no matter how uncertain—didn't seem quite so daunting.

After breakfast, we spent most of it exploring the woods, laughing and sharing stories from our pasts. I was captivated by Zoe's resilience and courage. We hiked along winding trails, our laughter echoing through the trees as we teased each other.

"Did you ever think you'd end up here, with me?" Zoe asked.

"Life takes mysterious turns," I admitted. "But somehow, fate has a way of bringing people together when they need each other the most."

I stood at the edge of the lake, watching the sun dip. The sky blazed with hues of orange and pink. The truth: I was falling for her, hard. It wasn't just her beauty or her strength, but the way she challenged me, made me question my own beliefs. She was a storm, a force of nature I couldn't control, and it terrified me.

As if sensing my turmoil, Zoe turned to face me, her expression softening. "I've never felt this way about anyone before."

I closed the distance between us, my hands coming to rest on her waist. I could feel her heart racing beneath the thin fabric of her shirt as I leaned down to capture her lips in a tender kiss.

"I promise you, Zoe," I whispered against her mouth, "once this is over, we'll find a way to make it work. We'll face whatever challenges come our way together."

"Promise?" she asked, her voice wavering with uncertainty.

"Promise," I confirmed, sealing my vow with another soft kiss.

As we stood there, wrapped in each other's arms, The path ahead would be treacherous. Juggling my duty and my growing affection for Zoe would test me at every turn. But as the sun dipped below the horizon, surrendering to the darkness, I also knew I wouldn't trade this moment for anything in the world.

19

Things were getting complicated, but how could they be anything less? My life had been nothing but pure chaos since I came out of the womb, and being in this cabin, sitting next to him, it just seems... perfect. When was the other shoe going to drop?

After being stuck in the endless loop of the chaos with the club, I thought for sure I would never find someone who truly thought of me as an equal. Most men around me think of women as property. Hell, my parents raised me to always do everything to make the men in my life happy. Not for one second have I ever felt like I needed to dumb myself down for the likes of Eli.

This might not last long-term, things happen, but knowing that real men were out there, away from the club, was enough for me. After all was said and done, I was going to start over somewhere else.

"I wouldn't mind living out in the woods away from everyone after this." I snuggled up to him. "It's so peaceful."

With everything going on while I was younger, we didn't

really get to take vacations. There was always something that prevented us. Honestly, we weren't the most normal family unit, and that probably had a lot to do with it. My mother was under his spell.

"Well, my friend will probably let us rent this out whenever we want. He doesn't use it too often. So anytime, just tell me."

"Wish we could just stay here forever..." he said, running his fingers through my hair as his heart thuds against my ear. "If we could get away with it, I would. Yet, we both know that going back is important."

"We can come back another time. The only thing I care about right now is you."

Our relationship went from one to hundred in a matter of weeks, and honestly he was the perfect man for me. Sure, we had hit some bumpy roads, but even then he was protecting me.

He nudged me off of him, and he went to the kitchen.

I looked over the back of the couch, watching him wander around. "So, what is your vision of the perfect life?" Such a corny question.

"Honestly, a wife that I'm madly in love with, a couple kids, maybe a dog." He came back and handed me a cup of hot cocoa, and sat down next to me. "Once we get through this, we can figure out what our perfect life is together."

Once the Twisted Jokers were out of commission, Eli and I could finally take our relationship seriously. Right now, there was too much focus on the mission and even though we spent time together, we were always having to watch our backs. He proved to me that I deserved happiness, and one day I would be able to bask in it.

"You know, before you came into my life, I honestly

never thought I'd find someone. Betrayal has been such a big component in my life with others, and yet you have never betrayed me that way."

"Listen, I've already told you that no matter what happens, you will always have a piece of my heart. When all this is over, if you decide you want to start a new life without me, I won't hold it against you. You have suffered for many years, and the only thing I want for you is happiness after this."

How could he think that I would ever want to leave him? There weren't many good guys left. "The only man I want is you, Eli."

I took his cup and mine and set them down on the coffee table. "Let's just focus on having the perfect night."

He leaned back into the couch, giving me a little more room to straddle him. His cologne made my panties wet, but the way he looked at me had the same effect. "Are you sure? I mean..."

I put my index finger over his mouth and then took off my sweater. "Holy hell. If I knew you weren't wearing a bra all day..."

"You what?" I whispered into his ear, standing up to take off my jeans. "I'm also not wearing any underwear." His eyes watched as my jeans slid down my legs and reached the floor.

"Fuck!"

I leaned over and undid his belt and then unbuttoned his jeans. "Tonight, let's focus on us. As many times as we need to."

Eli sucked in a breath as I got on my knees and put him inside my mouth. He was already hard, me being completely naked and all, but I bob my head, taking him all the way.

The way his fists closed around the back of the couch, and his head flew back, it was all because of me.

"You keep going like that... I'm gonna!"

I stopped and crawled up him, put one foot on the back of the couch, positioning myself just above his mouth. "Your turn... and I don't want you to stop until I come."

There was no hesitation on his part, and let me just say, Eli knew exactly what to do with his tongue. That man was a fucking god! It took all of three minutes tops for me to beg him to stop before I passed out.

He laid me back on the pillow on the couch, his eyes longing to search mine. His lips took mine as he slid on a condom and slowly pushed himself inside me. The initial shock caused me to gasp, but then it was like heaven. He moved with precision and purpose, but not hot and heavy. His hands roamed across my entire body, and I felt worshiped.

"I don't want to be with anyone else. Ever. This is what I want. Everyday for the rest of my life."

One last push into me and we came together, my teeth nibbling on his ear set him over the edge.

Neither of us knew what would happen in the coming days and taking a little bit of time to connect meant the world. Hell, we could both be dead by the end of the week, but knowing that I was loved by a good man was the perfect way to go out.

"Let's just lay here and enjoy our last night."

I wouldn't want anything more...

20

My heart pounded, each beat echoing in my ears, as Zoe and I crouched behind a stack of weathered crates, our eyes fixed on the Twisted Jokers' gathering. The dim, flickering glow of a solitary light bulb cast eerie shadows, revealing the hardened expression on Gunner's, Razor's and the other club members' faces.

"Alright, let's go over the plan one more time," Gunner said. "I don't want any screw-ups."

Zoe's hand gripped my forearm with a vice-like strength, her nails almost piercing my skin. The sensation of her tight grasp sent a jolt of pain up my arm. Despite all of the distractions, we remained steadfast in our shared mission to dismantle the very source of our anguish. "Can you hear what they're saying?" Zoe whispered, her breath warm against my ear.

"Bits and pieces," I replied, pressing my ear closer to the gaps between the crates. "Something about a shipment coming in tomorrow night. We need to find out more."

"Let's split up," Zoe suggested hesitantly, her eyes darting between me and the unfolding meeting. "I can get closer to Gunner without raising suspicion. You focus on Razor and the others."

I frowned, reluctant to separate from her. The risks involved in the mission were enough to make my stomach churn, but the thought of leaving Zoe to face them alone was even worse. Despite that, I couldn't deny the logic in her plan. We needed information, and we needed it fast. The longer we tiptoed around working together, the better chance we had to be found out by Gunner and the others.

"Alright," I agreed. "But be careful. If they suspect anything—"

"Trust me, I've been playing this game for years," she interrupted, trying to reassure me.

I nodded, watching as Zoe slipped away from our hiding spot.

As I listened to Razor discussing their plans with the other members, I thought about the consequences of failure. If we couldn't find a way to dismantle the Twisted Jokers from within, more innocent lives would be destroyed, and we might never uncover the truth about what happened to my former partner, Jason.

The weight of responsibility bore down, but backing down wasn't an option. I must trust in our partnership, in our ability to work together and outwit our enemies. We came too far to give up now.

Zoe trusted me to keep her safe and take down the Twisted Jokers. Deep down, what would happen if she was found to be a traitor? She might think her brother might spare her, but I knew better. That man would not. He would most likely use her as a prime example that no one was an exception.

I listened on the earpiece for anything awry.

"Razor's getting reckless," Zoe whispered into my earpiece, her voice a lifeline in the darkness. "He's planning something big, but I can't make out the details."

"Stay close, but not too close," I warned, my breath hitching as I caught sight of Razor's menacing silhouette stalking past stacks of wooden crates. "We need to be careful."

"Always, partner." Her response was laced with warmth, a contrast to the chilly atmosphere that surrounded us. Over time, our partnership evolved from one of necessity to genuine trust, but the growing feelings between us remained unspoken, a quiet undercurrent that pulsed beneath the surface.

"Razor's heading your way," I said, eyes tracking the dangerous man as I wove through the maze of crates and barrels. "Let's try to find out more about this plan."

"Got it," Zoe murmured.

As she moved closer to her target, I admired her stealth and determination. It was that same resilience that drew me to her in the first place, and now it bound us together, strengthening their bond with each passing day.

"Zoe, I found something," I whispered urgently, his attention diverted by a stack of papers I'd discovered tucked away in a corner on top of a crate. "Blueprints for some kind of facility. Looks like they're planning a raid."

"Can you get a photo?" Zoe asked.

"Already on it," I assured her, snapping pictures with my phone as quickly and discreetly as possible.

"Good. I've got Razor talking to someone about the plan. I'll record their conversation."

I could hear the faint rustling of fabric as she adjusted

her position, and I held his breath, waiting for any sign that we'd been discovered. But the voices continued uninterrupted, and I let out a silent sigh of relief.

"Got it," Zoe whispered triumphantly, moments later. "Let's get out of here and regroup."

"Agreed," I replied, carefully tucking the blueprints into my jacket before making my way back toward our rendezvous point.

As we steadily faded into the blackness, our hearts pounded. The crisp night air caressed our cheeks, carrying with it the faint scent of the distant water. Our eyes strained to adjust to the darkness, searching for any sign of danger ahead. The sound of rustling leaves and distant voices echoed through the stillness. Yet admit the uncertainty, there was an unspoken bond between us, a silent understanding that we were in this together. There was solace in the fact we were a united front, hand in hand."You are starting to like sneaking around, aren't you?" I asked.

She smiled. "It's thrilling, actually. Although I feel like I've been sneaking around my whole life. As much as I don't want to be lumped in with the club... that's how people have always seen me."

I caressed her cheek and then kissed her. "After this, you could be whoever you want. Change your name, move away from here... you will finally get your fresh start away from this place."

Besides finding out who was responsible for Jason's death and taking them down, she was the other reason I must see this through. Zoe was brought up in a world of death and corruption and it was what she ever knew. Once she got outside of all this, she would blossom.

Zoe and I huddled over the stolen blueprints in a motel room.

"Alright," I began, rubbing the stubble on his chin. "These blueprints show multiple entrances to the facility. We need to figure out which one would give us the element of surprise."

Zoe's eyes scanned the drawings with unwavering focus. "There's a service entrance here," she pointed to a small door discreetly placed at the back of the complex. "It should be less guarded."

"Good catch," I praised, appreciating her keen attention to detail. I could count on her to spot things he might miss.

"Thanks." She gave me a small, proud smile before adding, "But we need to be prepared for anything. They won't hesitate to kill us if they find out what we're up to."

My heart clenched at the reminder of the stakes. As much as I wanted to protect her, she was right. We both knew the risks involved, and this mission was far from a guarantee. "We gotta make sure they don't see us coming."

"Exactly," Zoe agreed, leaning closer to me as they strategized. The warmth radiating from her body comforted me, making me acutely aware of how much I'd come to rely on her presence. "We should split up and approach from different angles. That way, if one of us gets caught, the other can still carry out the mission."

"Sounds like a solid plan. Get in and secure the documents and get it." I acknowledged, though the thought of us separated made my stomach churn. "But we need an escape route too. If things go south, we can't afford to be trapped."

"Right," she murmured, biting her lip as she traced a possible path through the complex. "I see a way out through this side door. If we can make it there, we'll have a better chance of getting away undetected."

"Perfect." My eyes flicked between the blueprints and Zoe, admiring her resourcefulness. "Your knowledge of their operations has been invaluable. I don't know what I'd do without you on this mission."

"Absolutely," Zoe nodded, her eyes locked on mine. For a moment, we lingered in the intensity of our connection, before she gently cleared her throat. "Let's finalize our plan, then get some rest. We'll need all our strength for tomorrow."

"Agreed," I said, my heart pounding. As we continued to pore over the details, I wondered what the future held for them and whether we'd come out victorious or pay the ultimate price for our daring endeavor.

21

Eli and I cautiously approached the warehouse, our footsteps muffled by the overgrown grass. The distant laughter of unseen figures and the rumbling engines reverberated through the air, a chilling symphony of menace. Our eyes locked in a silent, apprehensive exchange, our chests tightened. My brother kept his paper trail hidden. At first, I wasn't sure if I should even tell Eli, but the longer we were working together against the club, the more dangerous things got. Every day our lives were more and more in danger. We both wanted the same thing.

"Ready?" Eli whispered, adjusting his kevlar vest beneath his jacket.

"Let's do this," I replied, my eyes flickering with determination that belied the fear lurking just beneath the surface.

With bated breath, we inched forward. Moonlight casted eerie shadows, guiding us towards our target. The cold metal of the fence sent a shiver down my spine as we effortlessly hoisted ourselves over its imposing height.

Navigating our way through the intricate labyrinth of

towering shipping containers, a sharp metallic thud pierced the stillness, sending vibrations echoing through the night. Time seemed to freeze as both of us held our breath, our hearts pounding. Silence lingered for a moment, then another, yet no alarm shattered the tranquility. A wave of relief washed over us, and we exchanged a glance filled with gratitude, urging ourselves to continue our journey.

I nodded, eyes searching for any signs of activity. "We get in, find what we need, and get out."

Progress was slow but steady, navigating with precision. The stakes were higher than ever, and the weight of responsibility threatened to crush us both. But together, we found strength and resolve, pushing through the paralyzing fear.

"Over there," I whispered, pointing to a dimly lit trailer near the center. "That's where Gunner keeps his records. If we can get our hands on them, we'll have enough evidence to bring the Twisted Jokers down for good."

"Stay close," Eli urged, his eyes scanning the area for threats. As we inched closer, a group of club members emerged from the shadows, laughter slicing through the tense silence.

"Go!" Eli hissed, shoving me behind a stack of crates. We crouched low, backs pressed against the cold metal surface as the gang members passed by, mere feet away. I held my breath, body trembling with adrenaline and fear. I could feel Eli's hand on my arm, steadying me, providing comfort in the midst of chaos.

"Stay here," he whispered. "I'll handle this."

"Be careful," I replied, my heart lodged in my throat as I watched Eli slip away into the darkness.

As he moved, I knew the risks involved in splitting up, but we must get the documents. If we left without them, it only added more time on our clock before we were made. We could only sneak around for so long before her brother caught on.

The club members' laughter echoed off the walls as Eli crept closer, my eyes darting back to make sure he was okay as I made my own way to my destination.

He pressed the button on the remote start, causing the car engine to roar to life, its rumbling sound echoing. The noise drew the attention of the members, diverting their focus away from me as I stealthily approached the trailer. Adrenaline surged through my veins, causing my hands to tremble uncontrollably as I delicately manipulated the lock, feeling the cool metal beneath my fingertips. Inside the trailer, the air was heavy with the scent of old paper and musty documents. The dim light filtering through the windows illuminated the stack of papers. With a sense of urgency, I sifted through the piles, the crisp texture of the papers grazing my fingertips. My eyes darted across the words, scanning each page in search of the crucial evidence we needed.

"Hurry, they won't be gone for long!"

The strain of the mission threatened to tear us apart, but it was a risk we willingly took – for justice, for redemption, and for each other. All we needed was some concrete evidence that tied the club to the deaths in the city. Gunner kept meticulous records. My dad did the same. He liked to call them trophies. Like father, like son. Proud of the people that had been taken out by their power.

I moved on to the other desk, and stopped when I saw sheets stapled together. This was exactly what we needed. Yes! There was nothing Gunner could do to get out of this one. Paper evidence was crucial to making a concrete case against him and Razor, and as long as we made it out of here tonight, they were going down.

As my fingers closed around the damning documents, a sense of triumph washed over me. The partnership was put to the test, pushed to its limits in the face of overwhelming danger. Yet together, we proved that nothing was insurmountable. There was a drive sitting on top of the documents so I grabbed that too. Who knows what was on it, but maybe it would only solidify the case more.

"Got it!" I cried, bursting from the trailer. "Let's get out of here!"

With the evidence secured, we raced through the compound, adrenaline fueling the escape. As we leaped over the fence, hearts pounding, we passed a crucial milestone in the mission. But the path ahead was fraught with peril, and we would need to rely on each other now more than ever. This wasn't over until Gunner was in handcuffs being shipped off to prison. We still had a bit to go, but what we found tonight would make a huge difference.

"Zoe, look at this," Eli called out, his voice tinged with urgency as he held up a worn documents and a tape.

No clue what was on the tape, but the documents proved the shady business dealing her brother and Twisted Jokers were doing and I even found a list of names that have been crossed off.

"Is this a victim list?"

I watched as Eli's face grimaced when he noticed Jason's name marked out. "We are going to put a stop to this. No more names are being added to that list."

I wished I could take away his pain. Hell, everyday in my life was painful. When was the last time I woke up happy? Basically never until Eli came along.

"There are so many names... I bet they match up with the deaths you guys are investigating. One more thing to use in court against them, right?"

Eli kissed me. "You did an amazing job. We are so close to this being over and starting anew."

As we got to the car, my heart was racing. My brother was responsible for some many deaths and I just stood by and let it happen. I could have put a stop to this years ago, and yet I was complacent.

Maybe this would be enough to take him down and I could finally get a fresh start.

22

I leaned against the worn brick wall of the bar. The weight of my choices were bearing down. As an undercover Special Agent, I infiltrated the notorious motorcycle club with one purpose in mind – justice for my partner. However, I hadn't anticipated falling in love with the captivating sister of the club's leader.

"Hey, you okay?" Zoe's warm voice pulled me from my thoughts. Her hair fell in waves down her back, and her eyes held a hint of concern as she studied my face. The sound of the jukebox playing classic rock faded into the background as I focused on the woman standing before me.

"I'm fine," I replied, forcing a smile. But Zoe knew me better than that. Over the past few weeks, we grew closer than I ever thought possible. She was like an anchor in the stormy sea of deception that surrounded me.

"You're not fooling me," Zoe said, stepping closer. "I know something's been bothering you lately."

I sighed, running a hand through my hair. How could I

possibly reveal the truth about my mission without risking everything? Yet, keeping the truth from Zoe was like a betrayal in itself.

"You know I care about you. More than I ever thought I could," I confessed, my eyes meeting hers. "But there's something I need to figure out."

The worry lines around her eyes deepened, but her expression remained resolute. "We've been through a lot together. We've faced danger, secrets, and even my brother's disapproval. Whatever it is, we can handle it."

"Your brother..." I hesitated, struggling with my conflicting emotions. "Gunner. He's always looking out for you, trying to protect you. But sometimes I wonder if there are things he's keeping from both you."

"Like what?" Zoe asked.

"Something... something that could change everything," I admitted.

"Alright," Zoe replied softly, reaching up to gently touch my cheek. "But don't shut me out."

I nodded, knowing she was right. Together, we already weathered countless storms – our shared history and the strength of our bond undeniable. But now, as I grappled with the implications of my investigation and my love for Zoe, I was more lost than ever before.

"Promise me you'll be careful," she whispered.

"Always," I promised, pressing a tender kiss to her forehead.

As Zoe walked away, my thoughts returned to the mission at hand. Justice for my partner was within reach, but so was the potential cost of losing the woman I loved. With each passing day, the line between duty and desire grew increasingly blurred, leaving me to question whether it was possible to have both.

Whatever was on the tape found in Gunner's office, he had it hidden. It was important to him which meant whatever was on it most likely implicated him. Honestly, I wanted to spare Zoe watching her brother murder someone on tape so this needed to be watched by only me first.

Once back at the office, I shut my door and plugged in the adapter to play the tape on my laptop. My heart raced as I stared at the grainy surveillance footage. Was I ready to watch this? It could be anything.The timestamp on the video confirmed it: this was the night Jason was murdered.

"Dammit," I muttered, eyes scanning the video for any sign of the killer. I couldn't allow myself to be distracted by thoughts of Zoe, not now. I hit play and prepared myself. The images flickered, and there, caught in the dim light of the streetlamp, was a figure I knew all too well. My stomach twisted into a knot as I recognized her – Zoe, the woman who held my heart captive, standing just steps away from the crime scene.

"Zoe," I whispered, her name barely escaping my lips before I slammed the laptop shut, the sound echoing through the empty room. I clenched his fists at my sides, my knuckles turning white as a wave of nausea washed over me. How could she have been there? What did this mean? She killed Jason?

The room started to spin. I had been sleeping with the enemy this whole time. A part of me didn't want to believe it. Not my Zoe. Surely there was an explanation.

"Hey, Eli," came a voice from the door, startling him out of my thoughts. It was Tripp carrying a steaming cup of coffee.

"'Tripp," I croaked, struggling to maintain my composure. "What are you doing here?"

"Thought you could use a pick-me-up," he said, setting the coffee down on the desk. "You've been working late a lot lately."

"Thanks." I replied, attempting a weak smile. But my mind was racing, trying to reconcile the image of Zoe in the video with the loving, fiercely loyal woman I'd come to know.

"Everything okay?" Tripp asked, his brow furrowing.

"Actually, no." My voice trembled slightly. "I just found something... disturbing. I don't know what to do."

I hesitated to talk to Tripp further because he would have to turn the information over to the whole team and that would implicate Zoe. Was I seriously considering hiding this evidence?

"Disturbing how?" he inquired, leaning against the desk.

"Zoe was there," I blurted out, unable to contain my emotions any longer. "The night Jason was killed. She was there."

"Are you sure?" Tripp's eyes widened. "Maybe it's a mistake."

"I wish it were," I whispered, shaking my head, pressing play. He watched from the beginning. The look of utter sorrow in his eyes, knowing how I felt about her. "It's her."

"First, we need to find out why she was there," he suggested gently. "There could be an explanation."

"Maybe," I conceded, but the doubt gnawed at me like a relentless beast. The truth slipped through my fingers, leaving behind only questions and heartache.

"Talk to her," he urged. "You owe it to both of you to get some answers."

I would confront Zoe, as much as the thought terrified

me. I couldn't allow Jason's murder to remain unsolved, even if it meant risking everything I held dear.

Tripp left the room and I tried to work up the courage to go over to her place. The last few weeks had been less depressing with her around, and then to see her on that tape... I didn't know what to believe anymore.

I grabbed my keys off my desk and rush over to her house. No good could come from pushing this off, and I needed answers. She obviously knew more about Jason's death. Why else would she be there?

The car screeched outside and I stood before her door, heart thundering, raising my hand to knock.

"Zoe," I whispered against the cool night air, still unsure of what I would say when she opened the door.

"Hey, you." Her voice startled me. "You look like you've seen a ghost."

"We need to talk," I said, my voice strained with the weight of the revelation that threatened to shatter our world.

"Alright," she replied cautiously, stepping closer. "What's going on?"

I looked into her piercing blue eyes, searching for any trace of deceit or guilt. "I found out something today." My words caught in my throat, the heavy truth struggling to be released. "About Jason's murder."

"What did you find?" Zoe asked, her eyes widening.

"There is footage of you, Zoe," I finally managed. "The night he was killed."

"Wh-what?" She stumbled back, her face paling. "Eli, I...I don't know what you're talking about."

"Please," I pleaded, desperate. "I just need the truth. Did you kill him?"

"Of course not," she insisted, her voice wavering.

"Then how do you explain this?" I demanded, holding up a grainy photograph that clearly showed Zoe at the scene of the crime. "Then why are you standing over his fucking body? How do you explain this?"

"Where did you get that?" Zoe asked, her voice trembling with fear.

"Zoe, please," I begged, my heart aching as I grappled with the conflicting emotions swirling within me. "If there's something you're not telling me, now is the time to come clean."

"Alright," she whispered, tears pooling in her eyes. "Yes, I was there, but I didn't have anything to do with it, Eli. I swear."

"Then why were you there? And why didn't you tell me?" Betrayal and hurt seeping into my tone.

"Because I was scared!" She cried, her voice cracking. "My brother called and asked me to meet him there. I didn't know what to do. How the fuck was I supposed to know he'd be dead?"

"Zoe..." I trailed off, my thoughts racing. I desperately wanted to believe her, to wrap her in my arms and assure her that everything would be alright, but the gnawing doubt refused to relent.

"Please," she pleaded, reaching for my hand. "You know me. You know I could never hurt anyone, especially not Jason."

I stared at our entwined fingers, the warmth of her touch unable to penetrate the cold dread that settled over me. I loved her, but was that enough to make me turn a blind eye to the possibility of her involvement in my partner's death?

"I need time to process," I said quietly, pulling away from her embrace. "I don't know what to believe anymore. You could have told me this in the beginning, but you chose not to."

As much as I cared about her, my heart and my brain were fighting each other. My brain focused on Jason's murder and my heart focused on keeping Zoe.

What the fuck am I going to do?

23

I paced back and forth in my apartment, footsteps muffled by the worn carpet. The icy tendrils of doubt snaked around my chest, constricting my breaths into shallow gasps. I could feel the perspiration on my brow as I clenched and unclenched my fists, fighting the turmoil within me.

"Dammit!" I spat out, kicking the leg of a nearby chair. The sound echoed through the space, momentarily breaking the oppressive silence that settled over me like a thick fog.

"Stop freaking out. She could be just an innocent bystander." Tripp said.

"I don't know what to do," I confessed, my throat tight. "I never thought I'd be in this position."

"Come on, let's sit down and talk it through," he suggested, gesturing toward the small kitchen table. They sat down opposite each other.

"Zoe... She was there when Jason was killed," I choked out, clenching my jaw as the words left a bitter taste in my mouth. "How can I trust her after that? But at the same time, I can't imagine my life without her."

"Look, Eli, I've seen you two together. You care about each other, deeply," Tripp said, his voice soft yet firm. "But you need to remember why you got into this line of work in the first place: justice. If you let your feelings for Zoe cloud your judgment, you're jeopardizing not only yourself but also the mission."

My heart ached as the truth of my words sank in. The thought of losing Zoe was like a knife twisting in my gut. "But if I pursue this... if I find out she's involved..." He couldn't bring himself to finish the sentence.

"Then you'll have to make the hardest decision of your life," Tripp said solemnly.

The worst part of all this was that the person who helped me succeed this mission could have been lying to me the entire time. Hell, she could be very well working against me and just putting on a facade. Did I let my feelings for her cloud his judgment? The footage doesn't lie and she even tried to disregard it when I first showed her. Zoe could just be making up things now. Trying to cover her tracks. How the hell was I going to go forward?

"Zoe," I whispered, my voice thick. "How could you be part of this?" The image of her standing beside my partner's lifeless body haunted me, chipping away at the foundation.

A tap came on the door, and Zoe entered. Tripp got the hint it was time to leave.

"Zoe," I murmured, shifting my gaze to meet hers, my heart skipping a beat. "What brings you here?"

"Can we talk?" she asked, fidgeting with the hem of her shirt. "I have something important to tell you."

"Of course," I replied.

"Look, Eli... I've been keeping something from you," she

hesitated, her gaze flickering between me and the ground beneath her feet. "And I can't hold it in any longer."

"This has to do with Jason, doesn't it?"

"God, this is so hard," she choked out, taking a deep breath before continuing. "I... I was involved in the murder of your partner, Jason."

I froze, my blood running cold. The air thickened around us, the once serene setting now suffocating me. My mind raced to process what she confessed, the words echoing through my skull like an ominous chant.

"Wh-what do you mean, 'involved'?" I stammered, my voice strained. A thousand scenarios darted through my mind, each more horrifying than the last.

"Please, let me explain," she pleaded, tears threatening to spill down her cheeks. "I didn't want any of this to happen, Eli."

"Explain? How do you explain that?" I demanded, my knuckles turning white as I gripped the edge of the couch. The hurt in my eyes was palpable – a mix of betrayal and disbelief. In that moment, the woman I came to know and care for vanished before my very eyes.

"Jason's death... it wasn't supposed to go down like that," Zoe whispered, her voice breaking. "My brother called me and told me that he needed backup at that location. He must have known I would call Jason..."

"Why would he want to kill Jason? He was his right hand man... What the hell happened?"

"I didn't find out until afterward, but they figured out he was working as an informant. They wanted to send a message, but knew that I would never play a role in the death of anyone." Zoe's cheeks became wet as she used her forearm to dry them. "I didn't pull the trigger, but I played a part in setting it up without even knowing. And I'm so, so sorry, Eli."

I struggled to find words that could convey the storm of emotions raging inside me. The pain of losing Jason was unbearable, but this new revelation threatened to shatter me entirely.

The world held its breath as I stood up in front of Zoe. The distance I put between us was more than just physical – it was the manifestation of a rift that suddenly appeared in our relationship, threatening to swallow us whole.

"Zoe," I said, "why didn't you tell me sooner?"

"I wanted to, Eli, I swear," she murmured, her fingers twisting nervously in the hem of her shirt. "But I was scared you'd leave me if you found out."

"What makes you think I won't?" I shot back, my eyes searching hers for any hint of deception. A part of me wanted desperately to believe that there was a way past this, but the thought of Jason's lifeless body haunted me, casting a dark shadow over my hope.

"Because I've seen the kind of man you are," Zoe replied, her voice trembling. "You're dedicated, loyal, and you fight for what you believe in. But most importantly, Eli, you know what it's like to be trapped in a world you never asked for." She paused, swallowing hard, as though the words were a bitter pill to take. "I'm not asking for your forgiveness, Eli. I don't even know if I deserve it. But I am asking you to understand why I kept this secret for so long."

As she spoke, my mind raced, torn between the woman I'd grown to care for and the ghost of my partner, whose death now weighed heavily on both our shoulders. I studied Zoe's face, etched with fear and vulnerability, and even beneath her bold exterior lay a woman who was fighting her own demons all along.

"Understanding won't bring Jason back," I said quietly, chest tightening with the effort to hold back my own tears. But as much as it pained him to admit, anger and vengeance wouldn't bring me back either.

"Maybe not," Zoe agreed, her gaze never leaving his. "But maybe, just maybe, it can help us find a way forward. Together."

"Zoe," I said, voice strained, "how can I trust you again? You kept something this big from me. How am I supposed to believe anything else you've ever told me?"

She lifted her gaze to meet mine. "Eli, please," she implored. "I know I messed up, but I was so scared. Scared of losing you. Scared of facing my past alone."

In that moment, Zoe's fierce facade crumbled, leaving only her raw vulnerability exposed. As I watched her struggle, I found myself battling an internal war – torn between my duty to seek justice for Jason and my growing feelings for the woman who came to mean so much to me.

"I want to understand, I really do," I admitted, stopping my pacing to face her fully. "But every time I look at you, all I see is Jason, and the life that was stolen from him."

I took a deep breath, trying to steady the whirlwind of emotions threatening to consume me. "I need time to process all of this," I continued. "I need to figure out if I can move past it – if we can move past it."

"Please," Zoe pleaded. "Don't give up on us. On me. We're both flawed, we've both made mistakes. But we're stronger together, aren't we?"

My heart ached as I considered her words, the truth in us resonating deep within me. Neither of us were perfect, but we found solace and strength in one another amidst the chaos of our lives.

"I don't know if I can ever truly forgive you for this... you just threw my trust away because you were scared!"

"Take time. Remember the kind of person I am. You know I would never intentionally play a role in someone's murder." she whispered. "I'll be here, waiting for you. And when you're ready, maybe we can find a way to work through this – together."

As she reached out a tentative hand towards me, I hesitated for a moment before allowing my fingers to intertwine with hers, our grip a fragile promise of hope amidst the storm.

Zoe brushed away a tear that escaped the corner of her eye, its salty trail glistening on her flushed cheek. I clenched his fists at my sides, the muscles in my forearms contracting with tension as I struggled to process the weight of her confession.

"Zoe," he began, his voice low and measured, "do you understand the gravity of what you've just told me? Your involvement in this... it puts both of us in danger."

Her eyes brimmed with fresh tears, but she refused to let them fall. "I understand that more than anyone. It's been tearing me apart for months."

My jaw clenched as I fought to control my emotions, my mind racing as I considered the potential consequences of her actions. If word got out about her involvement, we could both become targets – not only from the Twisted Jokers, but also from those within law enforcement who might view her as an accomplice.

"Every day I live with the guilt of what happened," Zoe continued, her voice trembling. "I can never undo my past mistakes, but I want to make things right. I want to help bring justice to those who have been hurt by the Twisted Jokers... and to protect you from any harm."

"Protect me?" My laugh was humorless, a bitter sound that cut through the heavy silence. "How can you protect me when I can't even trust you?"

"Trust isn't something that can be won back overnight," she admitted. "But I'm willing to do whatever it takes to prove myself to you. Because you mean more to me than anything else in this world."

My heart ached at her words, my love for Zoe warring with the betrayal. I could see the sincerity in her eyes, the desperation etched across her face as she pleaded for a chance to make things right.

Something had to give. Why would Gunner use his own sister to get Jason down there? Why not just call him himself? Something was off about this. Something more was going on.

"This still doesn't explain why he had footage of you at the crime scene and why would he keep it?"

Zoe crossed her arms over her chest. "He was trying to keep me in line."

Gunner. What a fucking piece of shit. He framed his own sister. His plan wasn't hard to figure out with the clues. Gunner was going to wait until the investigation was focused on him and he could anonymously send in the tape of his sister next to Jason's body. The police would have never thought twice, but would have just been glad to have some solid evidence of who Jason was with when he died. What a sadistic son a bitch.

"This proves it, Zoe. Your brother isn't looking out for

you. He'll throw you to the wolves just as much as the next guy."

I looked into Zoe's eyes knowing that this revelation was going to fuck her up. The only family she left was going to sell her out to save himself.

Zoe was, in fact, an innocent bystander and my gut churned. Was I being used?

"I can't help but love you."

"Love?" Zoe's voice trembled, and she looked away. "How can you love someone like me?"

"Because I see the real you," I insisted, reaching out to gently cup her face in my hands. "I see a woman who is strong, fierce, and unapologetic. A woman who has been through so much and still manages to keep going. A woman who held on to her loyalty for her brother even after being torn down too many times to count."

"Loving me only puts you in more danger."

"I'll do whatever it takes to protect you. Gunner won't get away with this and even though we might not be able to prove that he killed Jason... there is plenty of other evidence to lock him up."

As we stood there, I let my guard down further. I shared with her my hopes for a future where we could both live without fear, find solace in each other's arms, and build a life together. The vulnerability in my words brought a new level of intimacy between them.

"Sometimes, I feel like I'm drowning in guilt and regret," she confessed. "But our time together, the laughter we've shared and the love that has grown between us, I feel hope. With you by my side, Eli, I believe I can find redemption."

Her words struck a chord, and I knew just how much courage it took for her to express these thoughts. I brought her hand to my lips, kissing it gently, and said, "We'll face our pasts together, Zoe. Whatever comes our way, we'll conquer it as a team."

"We can overcome what happened to Jason - it wasn't your fault. He would want me to be happy. If he knew what happened and what led to your involvement - he wouldn't be angry with you, but with Gunner for putting you in that position."

"Honestly, I always had a feeling Jason wasn't one of us... but I hoped my brother would never figure it out."

"When I lost Jason, I didn't just lose a partner—I lost a piece of myself. I've spent so long trying to find justice for him, to bring down the Twisted Jokers and make them pay for what they did." As he spoke, his voice grew stronger. "But now, it's not just about Jason. It's about us, too. About making sure we have the chance at the life we deserve, free from the shadows of our past."

We couldn't move on until the Twisted Jokers were disbanded for good.

"The team is back at the office going through all of the paperwork we found. We don't want to rush this case, because we will only get one shot."

"Then I say we get back to it."

24

Everything was laid out in the open. I betrayed Eli. How could I tell him that I was there the night his partner was killed? Honestly, I never thought he would find out and didn't want him to hate me for it. And now, my own brother might have used that to frame me for the murder? What the fuck? My loyalties had been in the wrong place and I'd never trust Gunner again. He deserved what was coming to him tenfold.

"You need to go about your business like normal. We don't want them to suspect anything."

I just needed to bide my time until they were arrested. Only a couple more shifts at the bar, and then off to a new life. But where would I go? When I was younger, I wanted to go to Florida, so maybe I'll travel a little bit.

As we were coming to the end of our mission, it felt like more weight on my shoulders. There was always the possibility something could go wrong and being back at the bar, surrounded by the people that I was actively betraying, felt like a brick. What if they figured it out? My brother had been keeping a closer eye on me than normal, but I didn't think he suspected anything. Honestly, he would never think I would do this to him and that meant that I was lucky in that aspect. I needed to keep him in the dark about all of this and not cause any reason for him to investigate further. He knew about Eli and I, but he was forthcoming about not trusting him. Even though he was completely right, he didn't need to know that.

Eli kissed me and I jumped out of his truck to go inside the bar for my shift. "See you later?"

He smiled. "I'll be back in a couple of hours."

I waited until he pulled out of the parking lot before taking a deep breath and going inside. It was time to turn on the supportive member bullshit for at least one more night. After that, Gunner would be in a jail cell and I'd be on my way to somewhere else.

I opened the door and stepped inside, the smoke instantly hitting me.

"Hey! Was wondering if you were going to show up tonight?" the bartender asked. "I was supposed to be off an hour ago."

"Sorry, I got my days mixed up." I walked around the bar and started prepping. "Hopefully we will have a good crowd tonight. The tips have been crap this week." Honestly, I was just trying to keep the conversation going when I saw my brother in the corner with his eyes locked on me. Something was off. When he started to walk my way, my stomach turned.

"So, where have you been? You start fucking Eli and all of the sudden this place is less than? Don't forget where you come from, sis."

I bit my lip and took a towel to clean the outside of the

glasses. "Maybe you should stop worrying so much about me and Eli and start worrying about all the crap going on around you. Find the person bringing your shit down yet?"

His eyes narrowed. "Damn... you got a man and now you think you can just start talking to me like that? Treat me with respect! I'm the fucking leader. Anyone here will do exactly as I say."

Was he seriously threatening me? Every guilty bone in my body suddenly felt relaxed. This motherfucker deserved to spend the rest of his miserable life in prison. This was no longer my brother, he was the Devil.

"Razor and I got some business to take care of tomorrow, so we will have another conversation when I get back. Don't think this is over." Gunner said, walking away from the bar and out the door.

I waited a couple seconds before making an excuse to go to the bathroom and call Eli to let him know they were on the move. We had documents and evidence, but getting more wouldn't hurt to cement the case and nail it shut. There could be no chance of them getting away this time.

The next few hours were cringey. I was on edge and things were escalating. Gunner was on a rampage and something big was coming. We needed to take him down now!

Me: Tell your guys to work faster. I have a bad feeling.

Eli: Is there something you want to elaborate on?

Me: The guys are whispering about some big ambush tomorrow.

Gunner was definitely overcompensating for his lack of leadership in the last few weeks. Things were going to shit and he knew it. It was just like him to do something to stir the pot. If he wasn't arrested before this went further, more lives would be lost.

Eli: They are almost done. Once we get the go ahead for an official arrest. I'll call you.

The bar was packed and the guys seemed to be drinking more heavily than usual. My brother didn't exactly clue me in on his plans, but I could read him like a book most times. They were pregaming. Celebrating before the actual victory of whatever was to come. I didn't like it all.

Instead of focusing on what they were saying, I did my job and kept serving drinks, biding my time until I heard from Eli. I understood they wanted a concrete case against my brother, but did they really want to chance more people dying because we waited another day?

The door opened and in walked Eli. He had a smile on his face, chalking it up with some of the members before he came over and gave me a kiss in front of them. He got close and whispered, "It's time."

Finally! My eyes went wide and he took my hand leading me out to his truck. The other bartender shouted at me, but I ignored her. This was the end. If this went smoothly, I would never have to step foot back into that hell-hole ever again.

25

My heart pounded as we huddled together in the dark alley, the icy wind biting at our exposed skin. The time had finally come to take these fuckers down. The papers that Zoe secured from his trailer gave us a paper trial of shipments, hits, and money laundering. It was the nail in his fucking coffin and I couldn't wait to be the one to cuff him.

"It's almost over, babe." I glanced over at Zoe. We were about to infiltrate the warehouse once more, this time to apprehend the criminals that caused us both so much pain with a team in tow. We didn't want to leave anything to chance, so Tripp called in an entire team in case things got out of hand apprehending Gunner and Razor. In this situations, suicide by cop was common, but we couldn't let either of them get off that easy. They needed to pay for what they've done and suffer. No taking the easy way out.

"Ready?" I whispered, studying the sharp angles of her face, illuminated by the sliver of moonlight sneaking through the clouds.

"Let's do this," she replied.

We crept forward, shadows among shadows, until we reached the entrance to the warehouse. I took a deep breath, my hand tightening around the grip of my gun. Zoe mirrored my movement, her own weapon clenched in her slender fingers. Our eyes met for a moment. We were bound not only by our shared desire for justice but by the love that blossomed between us.

"Once we're inside, I'll take the east wing, and you take the west," I instructed, my voice low and urgent. "Stick to the plan. We'll meet up in the central office, where Gunner and Razor should be."

Zoe nodded, her lips pressed into a thin line. "Be careful."

"You too," I replied, the words heavy with unspoken emotion.

With a final nod, we pushed open the heavy metal door and slipped inside. Two teams separated to finally take down the Jokers once and for all. The dimly lit interior was eerily quiet, as we moved stealthily through the corridors. Our targets weren't expecting us, and we needed to take them by surprise. Our footsteps echoed softly off the walls, punctuating the silence like a ticking clock, counting down the moments until confrontation.

All of my years undercover played into this moment. Jason gave his life for this justice to be served and we would finally be able to end the reign of the Twisted Jokers over the city.

As I approached the east wing, my pulse quickened, adrenaline coursing through my veins like liquid fire. The thought of finally bringing Gunner and Razor to justice fueled me, driving me forward. Suddenly, a door creaked open up ahead, and I pressed myself against the cold concrete wall. My breath caught in my throat as I watched two shadowy figures emerge, our voices low and menacing. It was Gunner and Razor. The team paused behind me, waiting on their orders.

"Stick to the plan," I reminded myself, my heart hammering against my ribs. I waited for them to pass before slipping into the central office, where I found Zoe waiting, her weapon trained on the door.

"Ready?" she asked, her eyes searching for reassurance.

"Ready," I replied, voice steady despite the turmoil raging.

We stood shoulder to shoulder, poised to confront the monsters.

My grip tightened on my weapon, the cold metal pressing into my palm – a reassuring reminder of the justice we sought. Zoe nodded.

"Let's do this," she whispered before kicking the door open with a force that belied her slender frame.

"Freeze!" I shouted, adrenaline pumping through my veins as I aimed my gun at Gunner, who whirled around to face us, their faces twisted in surprise and rage.

His eyes landed on Zoe and then a smirk emerged. "Little sister," Gunner spat, his voice dripping with venom. "You really thought you could take us down?"

"Drop your weapons!" Zoe retorted, her voice unwavering despite the pounding of her heart. "It's over."

My mind raced, my senses heightened by the danger that lurked in every corner of the warehouse. There was a lingering scent of motor oil and sweat, and the distant echo of footsteps as the other teams stormed the building. There was nowhere for them to escape. By now, the building was surrounded by police vehicles.

Gunner barely moved. "Nothing my sister told you will hold up in court. My father taught me well. Apparently, I can't say the same for you."

Zoe held her gun adamantly. "You just wait brother... you might think you are the king here in this place, but once you are behind bars, all your enemies will have a chance with you."

"Traitors!" Razor snarled, lunging toward us with a feral growl. A shot rang out – I wasn't sure if it was mine or Zoe's – and Razor crumpled to the floor, pain etched across his face. "You fucking bitch! You shot me!"

"Enough!" Gunner roared, his eyes blazing with fury. "You think you've won, but the Twisted Jokers will never be defeated! Someone else will just take over. Don't you know that you will never be able to show your face in this town again?"

I looked at Zoe and she looked taken back. He wasn't going to get into her head right now.

"There's nowhere for you to go, asshole. Your reign of terror is over," I said. "You'll both pay for what you've done."

He attempted to flee but Tripp cold cocked him as soon as he got to the door. "You aren't going anywhere." He began to read him his rights as I cuffed him. Tripp walked him past the team.

"Are you okay?" I asked, pulling her into my chest. "He's a horrible human being, but he's still your brother. It's okay to be conflicted."

She shook her head and looked up at me. "My brother was a menace to everyone around him. He deserves whatever comes from this."

Zoe and I walked out of the building, hand in hand, my

chest puffed out feeling good about finally being able to bring this case to an end. Years in the making.

"Nice work," Tripp said. "You two brought these monsters to justice."

"Justice?" Gunner sneered, glaring at his sister one last time before being led away. "We'll see about that."

26

A shiver crawled down my spine, but I pushed it away, focusing instead on the dismantling of the Twisted Jokers operation. As police officers seized illegal weapons and arrested club associates, we made a difference – that our determination put an end to years of fear and suffering.

"It's over," I whispered. "We're free."

The weight of my words settled like a comforting blanket, chasing away the lingering chill of fear and uncertainty. Eli reached for my hand, drawing me closer to him until our fingers intertwined. "Yes, we can finally move forward."

As we stood there, hand in hand, the remnants of our tumultuous past crumbling around us, it was as if the world itself was reborn. Gone were the shadows that haunted our every waking moment, replaced by a sense of hope and possibility that surged through our veins like liquid fire.

"Everything that held us back is gone," he murmured, his eyes never leaving mine. "No more secrets, no more lies. Just you and me."

A slow smile spread across my face, eyes shining with

unshed tears of happiness. "I never thought I would see the day when I could trust someone again," she confessed, her voice thick with emotion. "But you proved me wrong."

As we started to walk away from the chaos, hand in hand, our journey was far from over. But whatever challenges lay ahead, we would face them together.

He wrapped an arm around my shoulder, drawing me close. I leaned into him. Our bodies melding together, strong and unbreakable, like the bond we forged.

"Zoe," he murmured softly, heart pounding with newfound love and respect for the woman who stood beside him. "I know we've been through so much, and I just want you to know... you can finally be yourself."

The wait was over for this day to finally come. A day when we could be together without anything else lingering over our heads. Now that Gunner and Razor were in custody, we could both breathe and regroup.

Once inside his truck, it was like all of the stress melted away. There was no longer any pressure on my shoulders. I didn't have to go back to work at the bar... what the heck was I going to do?

"So what do you say we celebrate?"

"Sounds perfect," I replied.

The past few weeks had been one thing after another, lots of ups and downs, but Eli was someone I couldn't let slip away.

"When do we get to start this new life of ours though?" I laughed and took his right hand into mine from the steering wheel.

"After the arraignment. Once we know they are in jail with no bond pending trial, I'll take you anywhere you wanna go."

Everything seemed more crisp now. I could enjoy my time with him without having to worry about the consequences at my brother's hand. He couldn't touch me anymore. And Gunner would find out soon enough that he wouldn't be a badass in prison.

Karma is a bitch.

We stopped at a mom and pop restaurant, just wanting to eat and enjoy ourselves after the worrying this mission had brought us. The weight had been lifted and I could breathe.

"Here's to us," he raised his glass, eyes never leaving mine. "To justice, and to new beginnings."

"New beginnings." I clinked her glass against his. We each took a sip of the rich red wine, feeling its warmth spread through us, chasing away the lingering chill of our harrowing journey.

As we savored the flavors of our meal, I was lighter, more carefree now that the shadow of the Twisted Jokers no longer loomed over us.

"Zoe," he began, setting down his fork and reaching for my hand across the table. "I can't tell you how proud I am of what we've accomplished together. I know it wasn't easy, but we did it – we brought those monsters to justice."

I nodded, my fingers tightening around his. "We did." Her gaze softened, and she added, "But we didn't do it alone. We had each other, and we have Detective Tripp to thank for his support. It was a team effort."

"True," he conceded. "But it was your help that kept us going, even when things seemed impossible. You're an incredible woman."

A blush crept up my cheeks at his words, and I ducked my head slightly. "You were my rock throughout this whole ordeal. I couldn't have faced it all without you."

Our eyes met, and I lost myself in the depths of his gaze, feeling a swell of love and gratitude for the man who fought so bravely by my side.

"Promise me something," he said softly. "Promise me that we'll never forget what we've learned from this experience – the importance of trust and standing up for what's right, no matter the cost."

I squeezed his hand, expression resolute. "We'll carry those lessons with us, always."

"Always," he echoed, sealing our vow with a warm, lingering kiss.

"Can you believe it's finally over?" I asked, voice filled with wonder. "We really did it."

He nodded, a smile tugging at the corners of his lips. "We did. And now, we have the chance to build something new – something better."

Our gazes met, electric and full of promise. We stood on the precipice of a new beginning, the weight of our past struggles a distant memory.

"I want us to move forward together, no matter what comes our way. Let's dream big and chase those dreams with everything we've got."

"Yes, I don't even know where to begin. I've been dreaming about this day since I was like seven."

At this point in my life, I would need some time to get adjusted to the new way of living. No more living in a crappy apartment, working at that bar, or even living in this town. For the time in my life, I had choices.

"Where do you see us five years from now?" he asked, eager to know my thoughts and desires.

I hesitated for a moment, as if gathering my courage, and then replied, "In five years, I see us happy, healthy, and making a difference in the world. Maybe working together to help others who've been through similar situations. And... maybe even starting a family?"

"Starting a family..." he repeated.

I imagined tiny versions of him running around, our laughter echoing through our home. The image filled me with warmth and happiness.

"Would you like that, too?" I asked cautiously, searching his face for any hint of hesitation.

"More than anything," he assured me, pulling me closer and planting a tender kiss on my forehead. "Together, we can create a life that we can both be proud of, but I'll have to stop going undercover. I will never put you or our future kids in jeopardy.."

"Sounds perfect," I murmured, resting my head on his chest.

"Here's to our future," he whispered into my ear, feeling a renewed sense of purpose. "May it be bright, beautiful, and filled with love."

27

This was the start of something bigger and now that the mission was over, Zoe and I, we were going to have to figure out what our next steps were. After years of being undercover, and finally taking down the Twisted Jokers, the career aspect wasn't appealing to me anymore. All I wanted to do was enjoy life, and my time left spent on this earth. The biggest thing for me in terms of our relationship was that I wanted Zoe to be happy. And I would go to the ends of the Earth to make sure that happened. She wanted to get away from the city, the same city, that caused all of the trauma in her life. And I couldn't blame her, but this meant starting over somewhere else away from where my career was. At first I was hesitant, but if I didn't walk away now, when would I? Zoe should not have to worry about me coming home from work every day and being undercover was very dangerous. I would never want to leave her behind in this world especially now. She had shown me what I have been missing my entire life. One day I hope to have a family with her and to share the joys that life can bring. In order to do that, sacrifices had to be made. I could still work with the FBI, just in a different capacity and not undercover.

"Hey babe, do you know what you want for dinner tonight?" Zoe asked, walking into the living room.

"Honestly I thought we could just order in. There are a lot of things that we need to talk about because I put in my notice at work."

Her face went ghost white "Wait, are you fucking kidding me? I mean I know you talked about it, but I never actually thought that you would leave the FBI, didn't you want to move up the ranks?"

"Babe, if there's one thing that I have learned from all this... it's that my career doesn't have to come first. My priority is us right now. You have the ability to go wherever you want, be whoever you want now, and that means going along with whatever you decide."

She came over and sat beside me on the couch. "So, you are serious? No more undercover work?"

"The reason I wanted the job was to put bad guys away and I can walk away knowing that I successfully took down one of the biggest threats to the city."

There was so much more to life than working, trying to climb up the ranks, always reaching for the bigger and better office or job position. We could travel around the world and not be tied down to a job here. Honestly, it was a decision long overdue.

She snuggled up to me, and some tears were shed. One thing I loved was how supportive she was even if I decided to stay on here. Yet, this woman went against her own brother to do the right thing and the least I could do was make it worth her while.

Her whole life she had followed orders. First, from her

father, and then from her brother. I wanted to watch her flourish and blossom. She could do things on her terms.

"You know I love you right?" Zoe asked.

"Always," I replied, giving her a peck on the lips.

Life can be messy and complicated, but sometimes the best things came out of those situations. Without that case, I never would have met Zoe, and wouldn't be as happy as I was right now. There was a reason I was asked to be on this case, and fate wanted us to be together.

Right now we just needed to figure out what our next steps were because I couldn't wait to start sharing our lives together far away from here.

When I brought up where she might want to go, she clammed up. The world country was her oyster and it was like a kid in a candy store. "Do you want to go somewhere warm or cold? West or East coast?"

I grabbed my tablet off the coffee table, and went to my bookmarks. Last night after she fell asleep in my arms, I took the liberty of looking at some listings all around the United States to see which ones piqued her interest. She scrolled through and stopped at the second to last listing in Lake Placid, New York.

"This one is perfect."

It was only about six hours away, but far enough. Personally, I had always wanted to live in a smaller community by a lake. She already knew my love for the woods and cabins. This could be a wonderful start to our new life.

"So, this one is only for lease right now, but it does say that after two years, we could talk to the owner about purchasing it. It seems they want to make sure it will be in good hands." I said, reading the listing a little bit further.

"When can we leave?" The excitement was bursting

from her and it was amazing to see. Such a different atmosphere. There was no need for us to watch our backs anymore. Most of the members were in jail on charges, and those that weren't, turned on the others and took a plea.

"I'll reach out and see what they can accommodate."

There were so many things to figure out, but all in due time. I wanted to surprise Zoe though. She had been in such high spirits, and she needed a little pick me up.

A knock sounded.

"Are you expecting someone?" she asked, almost jumping off the couch.

"Yes, it's okay."

She sat back down and the stress in her face whisked away when I opened the door.

"Oh my god! You're here!"

Lola rushed in and enveloped Zoe with a hug. "I told you that once you got out, you wouldn't be alone."

"I was going to call you, but with everything going on - I didn't want to put you in the middle..."

She swats at her. "You did what you had to do and now we can both breathe a little. Start our new lives, free and clear. Right?"

I leave them to talk things out because I had a new mission.

"Yes, I am calling about your listing in Lake Placid."

———

Zoe

Lola had been my best friend for some time and always had the best intentions. She was the only one that truly never judged me for my association with the club. Now, she was here in Eli's house, and this meant that she was in the free and clear.

"So, I'm sure they took you in for questioning. What did you tell them?" I asked.

"The truth. My association with the club was second-hand and I never had any ties to anything against the law."

Lola dated one of the members, unofficially, on and off for years, but she never got her hands dirty. She wasn't that type of person. If anyone was completely innocent, it was her. "Well, i'm so glad you didn't get caught up in all this nonsense. So what are you going to do now?"

"I'm moving out to Georgia. My brother lives out there and he offered to let me stay with him until I get my own place. It's time to mend the relationships I destroyed."

Lola had a fucked up past, like me, but I was so proud of her for trying to make amends. Once upon a time, she was close to her brother, but in the end, she pushed him away.

"Enough about me, what's going on with you and lover boy? I was so surprised to find out you helped him take Gunner down. Good for you!"

"He was in it for the right reasons and I can't fault him for that. No matter what, I was more than just the mission. We are trying to figure things out right now, but we are happy."

A tear fell from Lola's eye. "Finally getting what you deserve."

We hugged and cried for the next several minutes.

"I'd love to stay longer but my flight leaves in a couple of hours and I need to get to the airport. Don't be a stranger."

I hugged her even tighter before following her to the front door. "Call me once you get there and settled."

She nodded and walked down to her car.

"So, everything okay?" Eli asked. "Why were you guys crying?"

"You wouldn't understand. It's a girl thing."

Things might not be perfect yet, but I knew in my gut that it wouldn't be long before we would be living somewhere else and starting a new life.

Happy and carefree.

A smile took over his face. "Well I have good news."

I stepped closer to him. "What? Tell me!"

"They said that we can move in next week if we want and they are open to us buying the house after two years. So, are you ready to start over?"

I jumped up and down. "I'll start packing."

28

"Can you believe we're really doing this?"

I glanced at her before returning my focus to the road. "I can," I said, my voice steady. "After everything we've been through, we deserve a chance to start over."

Zoe sighed and ran her fingers through her long, auburn hair. "I just hope we can leave our past behind us for good."

As we pulled into the driveway of our new home, a modest brick cottage surrounded by a white picket fence. There were so many things on my mind. My time as an undercover Special Agent put us both in dangerous situations, and the loss of my partner, Jason Stevens, still haunted me. But I was determined to make things work with Zoe, despite the challenges we'd faced.

We stepped out of the truck, stretching our legs after the long drive. The scent of freshly cut grass and blossoming flowers filled the air.

"Being all the way out here... no one will even know me. What's left of the Twisted Jokers would never find me."

I wanted to take a moment to really take this in. It was a

new beginning to our relationship. One without the strains of our past haunting us. We could be ourselves here, whatever version of that we wanted to be.

The moving truck pulled in behind my truck and it was finally sinking in. Zoe chose me. Even after everything. Lake Placid might not be our forever home, but it was a great starting point and I'd travel anywhere to be next to her.

"Let's start with the boxes marked 'kitchen,' okay?" I suggested. With Gunner and Razor both going to prison for a very long time and awaiting trials, all I could do was move on and start a new life.

"Sounds like a plan," Zoe agreed, her smile hesitant but genuine.

As we carried box after box into our new home, we encountered unexpected issues. The front door jammed, forcing me to spend precious time fixing it while Zoe sorted through our belongings. Later, we discovered that some of the pipes under the sink were leaking, and made a trip to the local hardware store for supplies.

"This place has more quirks than we thought," Zoe remarked, her hands on her hips as she surveyed the mess in the kitchen.

I wiped the sweat from my brow with the back of my hand. "We'll figure it out, together. Just like everything else."

As we continued unpacking, an old photo of Jason and I fell out of one of the boxes. We both stared at it, the reality of our past creeping in once more. I believed Zoe. She didn't have anything to do with what happened that night, but I still wanted justice for my friend.

"Hey," Zoe said, placing her hand on my arm. "We can't change the past, but we can control our future. Let's focus on that."

I nodded, swallowing the lump in my throat. "You're right." I looked around at our new environment, the cozy house filled with potential. "This is our chance to build something new, something better."

"Exactly," Zoe agreed, her fierce gaze meeting mine.

As we worked through the night, organizing our belongings and making the house feel like a home, we faced each challenge head-on, determined to start fresh and support one another. It wouldn't be easy, but we were committed to overcoming the obstacles that lay ahead and forging a stronger bond in the process. And as the first light of dawn broke over our new town, Zoe and I shared a sense of hope and optimism for the life we would build together.

I leaned against the railing of our new porch, taking in the serenity of the small town we now called home. Zoe stepped out to join me, wrapping her arms around my waist and resting her head on my shoulder.

"Beautiful, isn't it?" she murmured, her breath warm against my neck.

"Very much so," I agreed.

As we stood there, drinking in the sight, our thoughts turned inward, reflecting on our past experiences. The weight of our choices hung heavy in the stillness between us.

"Remember when we first met?" Zoe asked, breaking the silence. "I never thought we'd be here—starting over in a new town. Building a life together."

"I know," I admitted, a soft smile playing on my lips. "But I'm grateful for the journey that brought us here. We've grown so much since then."

Over the days that followed, I was mindful of Zoe, encouraging her to share her insights. I wanted to know what was going on in her head. There was no discussion about what she wanted to do once we were settled. What kind of work did she want to do? Did she want to go back to school? This was her chance to do anything without worrying about anyone else.

"So, have you given any thought to what you want to do for work?" I asked.

She leaned in closer. "Actually, the recreation center downtown is looking for a front desk person. Measly hours and pay, but it would be nice to be able to help kids. Maybe spot some of the signs that they are heading down the wrong road."

I was astonished. "That sounds perfect for you. Money doesn't matter. The house is paid for and you can do whatever you want. I just want you to enjoy whatever you do."

Zoe and I supported each other's goal wholeheartedly. Within three months, she was promoted to being an in-house counselor to help with troubled youth and I continued my search for proof that Gunner was responsible for Jason's death. We stood beside one another through setbacks and victories.

As the weeks turned into months, Zoe and I became pillars of our community, admired for our resilience and dedication to making a difference. Our love for each other blossomed like the flowers in our front yard, nurtured by the foundations of open communication, compromise, and unwavering support.

"Partners," we would remind each other, our voices filled with warmth and conviction. And as we faced the challenges life threw our way, hand in hand, we were stronger together than we ever could be apart.

About the Author

Ashley Zakrzewski is known for her captivating storytelling, sultry plots, and dynamic protagonists. Hailing from Arkansas, her affinity for the written word began early on, and she has been relentlessly chasing after her dreams ever since. She also writes under the Pen Name Kaci Bell for clean romance.

Her favorite thing is to hear from readers - so if you loved a book, hit the contact button and shoot her an email to make her day!

If you would like to sign up for her newsletter to hear the latest news and get an email when she releases something new, then you can sign up for that here: https://view.flodesk.-com/pages/638f846544fd43768982b30a

Go follow her on TikTok where she goes live often to talk to her fans and shop her exclusive signed shop: https://www.tiktok.com/@authorashleyz